The Angel Criminal

Shane Kavanaugh

· Chicago ·

The Angel Criminal

Shane Kavanaugh

Published by
Centaur Books
an imprint of **Joshua Tree Publishing**
• **Chicago** •
CentaurBooks.com

Cover Image Design: Shane Kavanaugh

Disclaimer:
This is a work of fiction. Names, characters, places, and incidents are the product of the author's imagination or have been used fictitiously. Any resemblance to actual persons, living or dead, events, locales or organizations is entirely coincidental.
.

Printed in the United States of America

Dedication

For Shadow and Chance

Rest in Peace, Sweet Boys

Table of Contents

Prologue:
The Last Bit of Happiness

In a nation filled with destruction and agony, a mother and her child walked through Camby Zoo, although the child's excitement did not let him walk slowly. He practically skipped around, his eyes sparkling as he watched the giraffes eat leaves from someone's hand.

"Mom, Mom, can we do that? *Please!*" The child pleaded, tugging on his mom's cargo shorts. The mother patted his head with a soft smile.

"Of course we can. Whatever you'd like."

The child erupted with joy, sprinting over to the line. Today was his favorite day: his birthday. It was the one day of the year he and his mother could do anything he wanted. The mother scooped her child up into her arms, helping him feed the giraffe a large leaf. The boy cringed as the giraffe licked the food off his palm.

"Eww, that's gross!" he giggled.

The mother laughed as well. The two were enjoying their time together. As she strolled behind her son, the mother's phone buzzed in her purse. She swiftly rustled through the bag. The number ringing was whom she expected: Samuel.

"Hi honey! Is everything alright?" The mother questioned anxiously. She let her son gain some ground between them, slowing down and watching him approach the zebra exhibit.

"You two need to get home now. You are not safe there," Samuel muttered. The mother glanced around. She could sense something was off. "Gem, don't draw any attention to yourself. Just walk Kyle out. David is watching from a distance. You will make it out safely, you just need to leave now." Gem hung up the phone and took a deep breath.

"Kyle, sweetie, it's time to go!" Kyle gave an exasperated sigh as he trudged over to his mother. "I'm sorry we have to leave so soon." The two walked back the way they came with no problems. This confused Gem. The way Samuel's tone sounded on the phone, she expected to be ambushed and be lucky to make it out of the zoo alive.

The ride home was very quiet. Kyle was pouting in the back seat, upset his birthday was cut so short. Gem peered at him through the rearview mirror. Before she could muster up any comforting words, a loud explosion shook her bones. Far in the distance behind them, the zoo had been bombed. Kyle turned around and knelt on his seat, watching as Gem sped faster, weaving through cars on the busy road. They finally made it home where Samuel was standing in the front window. Gem picked Kyle up out of the back seat and ran into the house. She was hyperventilating as she put her child down.

"Kyle, go to your room," Samuel demanded, placing his hands on Gem's shoulders.

"First you ruin my birthday trip, now you're sending me to my room? This is so unfair!" Kyle retorted, squeezing his hands into fists. Samuel glared down at him and clenched his jaw.

"Now."

Kyle angrily obliged, stomping up the stairs and slamming his door.

Samuel's stern facial expression melted as he hugged his wife, walking her away from the large window. "I'm so sorry baby."

"Wh–What was that? Who set that explosion off?" Gem questioned between her deep breaths. Samuel looked at his phone and saw David was calling him. Instead of answering, he placed the phone back in his pocket and kissed Gem on the cheek before hugging her again.

"I'm not sure yet, I'm having a few of my people look into it." Gem nodded, digging her face into his shoulder.

"I'm scared, Samuel. I'm scared of what they'll do to me . . . what they'll do to our son."

Samuel took a deep breath. He continued rubbing her back as he nodded. He pulled off the hug and looked her in her scared, tear-filled eyes.

"This can't keep happening. You can't keep getting caught up in these situations because of that child and me."

Samuel clenched his jaw as tears formed in the bridges of his eyelids. A pit grew in his stomach as he said, "I won't let you be hurt by this anymore."

Chapter 1

The Fateful Day

The world is a twisted, dark, cold place, but some have an easier time surviving in it than others. I, Kyle Straiter, know this all too well. Ever since humans developed superhuman abilities, the world has evolved into an everlasting battlefield, split between heroes and villains. Everyone in this world has the ability to evolve a part of their body based on their surroundings—or, very rarely, genetics—and this evolution has been known as strengths. It is what makes us strong. People are only able to unleash and use one strength; for if they used more than one, their bodies would use so much energy that they would begin eating away at themselves to keep up. One man in particular attempted to develop and use more than one strength, and his story was the most known . . . for now.

The man's hero name was HotSauce. He was the top hero in society for many years. He gave the people hope, saved civilians with his lava strength, and overall fit the definition of a "hero." However, all men have imperfections. HotSauce wanted to be stronger, to save more people, so he trained toward unleashing a new, second strength. He spent his days at bodies of water trying to control the water, completely abandoning his heroic deeds. One day, his efforts were rewarded with a second strength: the ability to control water. With this, HotSauce thought he could finally defeat the monster on top of the underworld.

In this battle of the century—the devil versus the saint—HotSauce's body failed him. He was massacred by the villains' corrupt mob boss, **Tyrant.**

Tyrant ruled the criminal society for as long as HotSauce was a hero and used his strength, Devour, to keep it that way. Devour gave Tyrant the ability to eradicate any person's strength at the taste of their blood. Combining this with his inhuman athletic abilities, he was an unstoppable force.

Stories said Tyrant had no family connection, was abandoned at birth, and had lived in the shadows all of his life; this was untrue. They said he had no wife, no children . . . a complete fabrication. Tyrant had a wife, Gem Straiter, and he murdered her in front of his only son, Kyle Straiter.

Tyrant was a bloodthirsty bastard who acted only on his desire for power. Like his societal name, he wished to rule the world in fearful tyranny. Tyrant attempted countless times to force me into villainy, to train me hard so I could continue his actions, but I refused. I could never fall to the depths of villainy, not after all the trauma he'd put me through—abuse, neglect, ridicule . . . every horrible act in the book. Because of my constant refusal, Tyrant one day took matters into his own hands. He murdered my mother, then abandoned me. That day, I vowed to kill him, no matter what it took.

That's exactly what I will do.

The story of my abandonment was something out of a nightmare.

Tyrant barged into the house, as usual, and broke the door off the hinge. This sudden action scared my mother and me, making us jump out of our seats on the couch. He stood in the doorway for a few moments, clenching his fists and gritting his teeth, before taking a step forward.

"Kyle, it's time. You must come with me to my base of operation, now," Tyrant demanded as he stomped over to me. He grabbed my forearm, dragging me towards the doorway. Tears dripped down my cheeks and, although full of fear, I took a stand. I stomped my foot, halting our movement, then ripped my arm from his grasp.

"No, I won't!" I shouted. "I don't care about my stupid future in crime or whatever, I want to be a hero! Why won't you just listen to me?" Tyrant's eyes didn't show disgust, but instead a sorrowful rage.

"You are seven years old; you will do as your father tells you!" he erupted as he slightly pushed me. He glanced over at Mom, who was standing with her hands by her chest. After she nodded Tyrant crouched in front of me. "Kyle, this is what's best for the family. You must come with me, please."

"I don't want to be a villain! I don't want to hurt people like you; I want to help them! Why do I always have to do what's best for the family? What about me?" I retorted with a shaky voice.

Tyrant's calmness was quickly fading, and then and there, I saw true hatred for the first time.

"Dammit Kyle, *you live under my roof, so you'll do as I say!* You can't become a hero; you have nobody here to support you!" Tyrant erupted as he stood.

"That's not true. I have Mom! She'll always help me! I'll get super strong, go to the best hero school, be the most perfect student anyone has ever seen, then become a real hero, and take you down!" I exclaimed. I could feel my cheeks and ears burn due to my building rage. Tyrant looked up at Mom again, but this time his eyes looked distraught. His jaw shook. Mom walked over to him.

"I do appreciate a goal and planned future. I really do, but there's just one problem with that," Tyrant vaguely stated as he stared at Mom.

I was confused, and looked down at my fingers, counting off the steps.

I'll train super hard, get good grades, study a lot, help Mom with work to get enough money to go to the best hero school, then become a top hero . . . What could be the problem?

"Honey, please just forget all of this. We can let our son grow up happily, live a better childhood, and have better opportunities than you ever did. Isn't that what you want?" Mom asked as she grabbed Tyrant's hand and caressed it softly. He clenched his jaw and looked at the floor, not responding. "You know you don't have to do this. Please, don't do this," Mom pleaded with a cracking voice. Tears welled in her eyes, then fell down her cheeks.

Tyrant was now crying as well, and he squeezed her hand harder. With the crack of a broken finger, he swiftly drew his pocketknife, a ten-inch switchblade, and stabbed Mom through her chest. She didn't cry out or anything, but instead looked at Tyrant with the most remorseful, heartbroken expression imaginable.

"I love you," she quietly whispered before falling to her knees and coughing.

"M–Mom?" I whimpered as my hands dropped to my side. Blood droplets were staining Tyrant's grey shirt. Mom fell on her side, motionless.

"How could you? Y–You just killed her; *you killed my mom!*" I screamed as I ran toward him. I began punching and grabbing at Tyrant's clothes. He lifted his right foot up, then kicked me in the stomach. I stumbled back and fell hard onto my butt. Tyrant whipped his knife into the ground as he swiveled to face me.

"*This is the world, Kyle! This is what happens when you act out of line! People die, your loved ones die, everyone's life ends at some point!*" he erupted ferociously. "Happiness is a filthy lie, and you'll learn as you grow up: anything you do, anything any of us do, *will always end in someone getting hurt!*"

"So what? I don't care if it hurts someone if they're a monster like you! *Heroes take down people like you and bring happiness to everyone and justice to the people who deserve it!*" I screamed with tears pouring down my cheeks. Tyrant looked as if he was about to explode with exasperation.

He roared, "*Shut up, Kyle, shut the fuck up! I hate you. I hate you with every ounce of my being!* You've done nothing but hurt this family! Your selfish attitude is going to get you killed!"

Even though I hated Tyrant for all he'd done to me, those words broke my heart. Hearing my father curse me out and tell me how much he hates me was just as painful as seeing my dying mother on the floor. Tyrant marched toward the front door, then stopped before walking out.

"Make me a promise, Kyle. For once, just listen to me; be the best there ever was. Ace all your finals, get into the top school, and be the best prospect in history. Once you're ready . . . come kill me."

I stared at my mom, then looked up at him with cold, unforgiving eyes.

"I–I promise. I'll be the one to kill you."

Tyrant didn't smile but instead wore a frown. He walked out the door and left my life for the rest of my childhood years. I swiftly scrambled over to Mom and held her head as I stuttered, "M–Mom, you're gonna b–be okay. You can't die, it's not possible!"

"Kyle, listen to me." She softly grabbed my arm with her left hand, then reached over, ignoring the pain, and caressed my face with her right thumb.

My lip quivered, but I didn't wail. "You're going to do great things. I can tell. You're a gift to this world, never forget that. You'll always be the light of my life—this family was my light."

"M–Mom, please don't leave me! I don't wanna be alone, *please!*" I pleaded. I couldn't contain it anymore; I placed my face on her chest and cried loudly. She continued crying as well, looking up at the ceiling. She gave the world one last smile.

"I love you more than anything." With that, she took her last breath. I lifted my head, staring at her blank face in disbelief. A pool of blood was spreading from under her, soaking my pants. Unexplainably, while in my arms, her body began shattering into beautiful shards that looked like stained glass. They shimmered in the light, creating a rainbow on the ground as they floated into the air.

"No, Mom, *please don't leave me! I don't want to be alone! I'll be better, I won't be selfish, I'll be a villain, just please stay! Mom!* **Mom!**" No matter how loud I cried, the shards continued floating into the sky, then through the ceiling. Just like that, she was gone.

I don't know why she disappeared like that, vanished into the sky, but what's done was done. I trembled on the ground, then punched and broke the wooden floor. I glared up at the door, seething with murderous eyes and exhaled sharply.

"Tyrant, *I'm going to fucking kill you.*"

That day was the fuel I needed for the rest of my life. That day was the kick start to the joy, rage, pain, and suffering of my life that led to the end.

Chapter 2

Not as Planned

The mailman knocked on my door and dropped some mail on the welcome mat. Usually I don't receive any, so it was surprising to actually hear the noise of a paper packet. The house was dark and messy. After getting up off the couch, I had to maneuver past trash and broken furniture to reach the front door. I opened it and stared at a large packet with a fancy, cursive E.H. I raised an eyebrow, then picked up the papers, and took them inside.

What the hell is this?

"Greetings heroes of the future," I read, scratching my head. "Seeing all the students who are shut down financially by private hero schools in the area breaks my heart, so I've decided a change needs to be made. My name is Simon Lane, and I will be opening a new school named Eccentric High. It is a public school, no tuition required; however, there will still be the usual entrance exams, both written and physical."

My eyes lit up, and I held the packet in the air.

No way, there's no way.

"I can go to hero school!"

I laughed giddily and continued reading the introductory letter. The important details I noted were that the entrance exams were next Wednesday, the school year would start three weeks from today, and all students were required to live in a dorm system on campus to ensure their safety or some crap. My excitement was unmatched. I immediately called a certain hero to help me train.

The week and two days went by fast, too fast. I guess what they say is true: time flies when you're having fun. I wore an ordinary blue tank top and five-inch inseam white shorts. My shoes were originally white but are now an eggshell white from dirt. I tied around my head the last gift my mother had given me: a faded black ninja headband. I opened the front door and stood tall. Today was the start of a rocky road toward a successful hero career.

The walk wasn't very long, just ten minutes. For some reason, my palms were sweaty. I felt sick to my stomach. I was actually nervous for the first time in years. I shook it off and continued on. The school was massive, covering three blocks worth of land. My eyes sparkled with amazement, then I felt a bump from behind. I stepped forward, looked behind me, and saw a boy and girl standing with each other while facing me. I gave the boy (who obviously was the one to hit me) a side eye, before he apologized in an innocent tone.

"Sorry, I wasn't paying attention!" He rubbed the back of his head and smiled nervously, but through my scowl, I could see him shaking. I assumed he was just anxious like me, so I forgave him.

"Yeah, whatever, it's fine." We stood in silence for a few minutes. I couldn't tell whether they were waiting for me to introduce myself or something, so I started walking away. They were both surprised and glanced over at each other, then back at me.

"Wait, are you a freshman?" the girl yelled. I nodded and stopped, then she explained, "Oh, we are too! We came from Edith!" Edith was a very popular private school in the area. The student population was around two times the number my unpopular public school had.

"Oh, that's a pretty expensive school." Apparently to them it wasn't. I could tell by the expressions they gave me. "Well, I'm from Trinity Plus, it's a mile or two away." They both immediately cringed.

"So, you're a part of that famous odd-squad grade?" I raised an eyebrow, then realized what he meant and quickly denied.

"Oh hell no, that was the grade below ours. We were the grade with the ninth-ranked student in the country, Cade Stale. I think he's going to B.E.G.

(pronounced beg) or something." B.E.G., also known as Bade's Exceptionally Gifted, was the top hero school in the country.

There was a large line forming, so I walked over to get in it. Sadly, they followed and talked my ear off the entire time we waited. We reached the front, and there were five teachers sitting at a long, foldable table. I stood in front of a very muscular man with a large sword at his side; I couldn't help but gulp.

"Your name and strength?" he questioned.

I took a deep breath. After remembering the long consideration I'd given it during the past week, I let out my breath and smiled confidently.

"Kyle Straiter, my strengths are Enhanced Strength and Fire Conjuration."

The teachers stopped, and the students signing up stared at me. The man with the sword crossed his arms, giving me a glare of disbelief.

"Are you pulling my leg, kid? You're telling me you have two strengths when nobody has ever, in all of history, survived with two?"

I nodded and didn't back down with fear. I knew if I wanted to be a great hero like I promised, I would need to reveal from the start what makes me so special. From a young age, I constantly developed new strengths. Ever since the age of five, I randomly gained a new strength every so often, then it abruptly stopped after the age of ten. In total, I ended with ten strengths, two a year. However, even though it was technically telling a lie, I could not tell them how many I have altogether. For now, having two that work well together and give me the opportunity to be the strongest front-line attacker ever was good enough for me.

"Cross my heart and hope to die, sir, I have two strengths."

He whispered to the woman next to him, then wrote down my name and strengths and called for the next student. I walked over to the building and leaned on the wall, waiting for the exams to start. The girl and boy didn't follow me this time but instead started talking with a big group that gathered a few yards in front of me. I closed my eyes, but after a minute, everyone went silent. There were whispers all around, so I opened my eyes to see what was going on. A boy was marching up through the line and stood in front of the sign-up table.

"I don't believe it; you're here to attend our school?" the teacher with the sword asked, standing up and looking down at the boy.

His hair was spiked in the front in a middle part with one crooked bang sticking out the center. One half was earthy brown while the other was sky blue. In the middle where it parted, the two colors faded. He was wearing a long-sleeved shirt, a pair of plain black shorts, and thick boots instead of regular gym shoes. I closed my eyes again, but after another minute, I heard footsteps approach and stop a few feet away.

"So, you're the multi-strength kid I've been hearing about?" the boy asked after sticking his hands in his pockets. I moved off the wall and wore an antagonizing leer.

"What of it? Who are you anyway?" I interrogated. The tension between us was already thick, and people started gathering around, expecting either an argument or fight. We stared at each other for a few moments, then he broke the silence.

"Surprised you haven't heard. I'm ranked the top of our grade level nationally. Didn't think I'd need to introduce myself to anyone, but the name's Tonuko Kuntai (Tuh-new-ko Kuun-tie)." He held out his hand for a handshake, but I didn't give him one.

Instead, I responded, "I mean, those dumb rankings don't matter until hero school anyway. Number one or number one thousand, doesn't matter to me." The teachers were calling us over, so as I passed him, I smirked, "Either way, I'll kick your ass ten out of ten times."

He gritted his teeth while following the rest of the group. There were around fifty first years, but only thirty-two would make it in. We were split into five groups of ten, then led to the classrooms where the written exam would be held. In my group, to nobody's shock, was Tonuko Kuntai. Clearly, they would have us battle, which was perfectly fine with me. After we were seated, the woman who led us stood behind the podium and smiled brightly.

"In front of each of you is the one hundred question written exam. You will have one hour to complete it. Good luck!" She was very cheerful and wore what I estimated to be a gallon of makeup.

I opened the exam, grabbed the provided pencil, and got to work. The test was actually very easy; so easy, in fact, that I finished it first, in ten minutes. After flipping the last page, I thought, *Wow, I guess that school actually taught me something.*

I was confident enough I didn't make any mistakes that I didn't bother checking my answers. After I turned my test in, there were whispers all around the room, but the teacher shushed them. She graded my test because there was so much time left, and I rested my head on my desk. Finally, after what felt like an eternity, the hour was over. One girl had turned her test in just five minutes after me; she had long, brown hair in a ponytail and bangs. Tonuko finished at the halfway point, and a few others followed soon after him. At this point, I was very unimpressed with the supposed "top of our grade level" kid.

"Very well done. I'm impressed everyone finished on time. That was the government's test that every school in the nation uses, including Bade's Exceptionally Gifted! Good luck to you on your physical exam, and I hope to see every single one of you in my homeroom class, freshman honors!"

Oh, so this is the freshman honors' teacher. I would have definitely thought that big guy with the sword would be the honors' teacher. Is this teacher really stronger than him?

She clapped cheerfully as we walked out, and over the speaker a man announced, "All students please report to the Dome for your physical strength test battles. Each of you will be assigned a partner to duel with when you walk in. Please stay in a single file line to give the instructor an easier time. Thank you for your cooperation."

We walked in an orderly fashion, following the other groups that were led by the sword man. One at a time, a man with bulging muscles and longer hair—half of it in a short ponytail—assigned each student their duel partner. He held a clipboard with a list of all the battles that would occur. Tonuko was in line in front of me, and when he walked up to the teacher, the teacher grinned.

"Tonuko Kuntai, you'll be facing your buddy behind you, Kyle Straiter. Good luck boys, I'm very intrigued on how this battle will turn out."

We were seated on a balcony that had a view of the entire stage. After reluctantly sitting down next to Tonuko and the short girl from earlier (whose name I had already forgotten), I took a deep breath.

"Tsch, already scared Straiter? Don't worry, I'll end you quickly, then I'll never have to see your smug face again." I looked at him like he was crazy and snorted.

I retorted, "I'll knock you out in ten seconds flat. That's not a threat, it's a promise."

He was shocked at my statement, then looked forward, irked. The first fight was between a boy named Donte, who was short and had spiky, light blue hair, and a boy named James, a plain looking boy with longer black hair. When the battle started, Donte dashed around the stage at lightning speed, overwhelming James. Donte took out James' legs from under him, then punched him as he was landing. James launched outside of the stage, giving Donte the win.

Few battles really caught my eye, whether it be because I was confident of my own abilities, or because I just thought less of all the wannabes around me.

None of these kids have a goal, want it as much as I do. They're all looking to be just heroes, not real heroes. I'm looking at the big picture, I'm carrying somebody's will with me. I'm better than all of these posers.

Finally, my time was up. The last battle of the day was between Tonuko Kuntai and me, Kyle Straiter. He took the stairs down to the main floor while I decided to be a little flashy and jump from the balcony. I landed, sputtering a flame wheel around my feet. I marched proudly to my side of the stage; on the other hand, Tonuko stood nonchalantly on his side. I cracked my fingers while letting little flames ignite in my pupils. The teacher announced for the battle to commence, so I wasted no time.

Ten seconds flat, that's all the time I need.

I leapt at him and used flames as boosters on the soles of my feet. Tonuko stomped his foot on the ground, bending the cement and creating a dozen spikes in front of me to block my path. I jumped off a few of them, then charged directly at him.

Five . . . Four . . . Three . . .

He created a massive wall, but I wound up a punch and smashed my fist through the wall. It shattered upon impact, and through the falling rocks, I wound up again and punched at him. He threw up his forearms to block, but

I was too strong and hit him out of the stage just as I counted the last second in my head. He skidded across the white line painted onto the cement—signifying the stage boundaries—then fell onto his butt. I stood in the spot he used to be in and held my smoking fist in front of me. My knuckles were split and bleeding, and behind me, the spikes Tonuko had created crumpled down back into the ground.

"Did that random kid just beat *the* Tonuko Kuntai untouched?" a girl in the stands asked as people stared in awe. I glanced down at my hand as I walked toward the stairs. Tonuko held his left forearm, the one that took the blunt of the hit. The bone was shattered. The nurse who had attended the event to heal injuries knelt by his side and used her powers to heal Tonuko's arm. She was, surprisingly enough, the most famous healer in the country: Nurse Amy Blavins.

Amy Blavins, Strength: Recovery—she can heal any wound no matter the permanent damage but cannot heal common sickness or disease. She uses her own natural healing factor to heal her patients, so over-healing can rapidly drain her energy.

"Well done all who came to join my school. As you may have guessed, I am the principal of Eccentric High: Simon Lane. Being forced to not take all of you in truly hurts me, but I was very impressed with the display of strength I just witnessed. Letters of acceptance shall be mailed one week from today, and school starts the Monday after that. I am ecstatic to be able to meet all the promising students who will attend the first-ever freshman class at Eccentric High."

The kids applauded the principal with the ponytail, not sure why, but they did. I walked out first, hoping to avoid any conversation. Apparently, it was my lucky day because nobody stopped me, so I was able to walk home immediately.

Unsurprisingly, a week from that day, there was a knock on my door. I answered and a letter with a cursive E.H sat on the welcome mat.

Chapter 3

Brand New Life

The letter stated, "Kyle Straiter, you are hereby accepted into the pristine hero academy of Eccentric High. Words cannot describe how overjoyed we are to be able to teach such an anomaly. Not only did you manage to beat the national top student of your grade level in only a few seconds—in addition to destroying a two-yard-thick wall with a single punch—but you also received a perfect score on your entrance exam. Coming directly from your principal, I cannot wait to see you on our campus."

I dropped the letter and smiled brightly. I looked back at my disgustingly messy living room, then my eyes were drawn to the only untouched spot in the house: the spot where my mother perished.

"So, I punched through a two-yard-thick wall, eh?" I looked down at my scabbed knuckles and smirked, "Figured as much. Combining fire power with enhanced muscles will break some thick-ass walls." I clenched my fist, and my smile turned to a stern stare at the spotless area.

I promised Tyrant and Mom that I'd be the top of my class. No matter what it takes, I'll be the strongest, the smartest, and the best in the nation. The Hero Olympics is the ranking event, right? When it comes around in December, I intend to win with flying colors.

The Sunday night before the start of school I packed any clean clothes I had, even some I'd bought that day. I went to sleep early that night to try and calm my nerves. I wasn't nervous about being the center of attention or Tonuko maybe getting accepted, but more so nervous about the expectations set upon me. Even though I felt like I wanted to throw up, I was still extremely happy. I would finally be able to go to hero school and fight bad guys like all the famous heroes do. I guess I let my guard down, one of my many mistakes . . .

Tyrant's Facility, an Abandoned Factory in the Middle of a Field:

"What a pleasant surprise, you've impressed me yet again. Killing the eighth-strongest hero, not an easy feat, but you've accomplished it flawlessly! I'd assume you put in most of the work, Kaci?" Tyrant asked, a smile stretched across his face.

Kaci had white hair with one long spike of a bang going down the right side of his face, and he wore a seemingly expensive watch.

"Actually, sir Tyrant, the new guy took care of it all by himself. All I had to do was sit back and enjoy the show."

The new guy Kaci was referring to was a man with red skin. His hair was in a heap of curls that accentuated his twisted horns, and he wore a black and gray trench coat that covered his sheathed sword. He licked his lips, then devilishly, near psychotically, smiled.

"That's true, I did it single handedly. Did it with ease, in fact. If that's what the heroes are made of, taking them down one by one will be nothing more than child's play." Tyrant clapped his hands joyfully, standing from his handmade throne, built from animal bones.

"Why don't you go scout my boy's new school? I trust you with all my heart BloodShot, and as of now, you are the leader of my posse. Not only have you recruited someone else with an unreal strength, but you have yet to lose a battle. Go out there and give little ol' Kyle a warning shot."

BloodShot's grin stayed, and his eyes scrunched.

"I will happily do so!" He walked off seemingly looking for someone, then Tyrant sat back down and sighed. He crossed one leg over the other and rested his head on the back of his chair.

The Next Day: Monday, August 19th:

I slowly opened my eyes and blinked a couple times. I sat up in my bed, yawned, then checked my phone for the time: 7:50 a.m. My eyes widened. I swung my head back and groaned.

I swore, "Shit, I'm gonna' be late!" I rushed to the bathroom, brushed my teeth while showering, then dressed, grabbed my phone and wallet, and ran out of the house with my suitcase. After all that, it was 8:20 a.m., just ten minutes before the introduction day started. I noticed that the boy who ran into me during the entrance exam was across the street, also running. As much as I wanted to laugh at him, I was in the same boat. We both arrived with minutes to spare, but we were still the last ones. I didn't recognize a single kid to be from Trinity Plus, whether I should have or not. I was panting with my hands on my knees, and the other kid who ran was right next to me.

"Man, I guess we both slept in late, huh?" he chuckled through his deep breaths. I shrugged and saw he reached in front of me for a handout. "My name's Alex, nice to meet you again, Kyle."

I stood up straight after catching my breath, looked down at his hand, then walked away.

"Oh, no you don't! We're all classmates, and that means you have to get to know us!" the short girl from the entrance exam shouted as she grabbed my arm. Dumbfounded, I looked down at her as she forced me to shake Alex's hand.

"Now my turn, I'm Cindy!" She shook my hand, then she and Alex talked about classes.

What just happened? Get to know them? Why the hell should I care at all about them? Just because we're classmates doesn't mean we have to be best buds; it just means in the field of battle you're an ally I don't have to fight.

"I figured you'd have made it in, you cocky son of a bitch," Tonuko muttered walking up to me and crossing his arms. We stood facing each other for a couple of seconds, then a very peppy girl whistled, grabbing everyone's attention.

"Welcome all you freshies! My name is Hazel Sparks! I'm a junior here in the honors' class, and I'll be giving you your dorm assignments. Each floor will have twelve people, but the top will have eight. They're sectioned off into hallways of six or four, so whoever is in those will be your floormates for any future training groups!"

Tonuko and I ignored her, then I smirked.

"I didn't think they'd take somebody who got babied like you did. I mean, ten seconds flat, I predicted that perfectly, didn't I?" I taunted, causing him to tense his fist and clench his jaw.

"My ass you predicted that perfectly. I wasn't even trying; I didn't want to waste so much energy on someone who I thought was at the level of a preschooler. I can admit I underestimated you, but you better believe that won't ever fucking happen again."

My smirk turned to a frown, and I balled my fist. It looked like we were about to start fighting, so the junior walked up and stood between us.

"Woah, take it easy guys. I've heard of both of you, and you're both insanely strong for first years. Shouldn't you be happy to have such powerful allies? You're classmates; you're on the same team!" Hazel explained.

"I came to this random ass new school to be the strongest one here! I'm the number one, I'm the national favorite. Now, this random kid thinks he can strut right in and boast about being the strongest?" Tonuko snapped. He pushed the junior away with one arm, but then she reached out and out of her arms, two massive, muscular, pitch-black, translucent arms grabbed our torsos and trapped our arms in the process.

Hazel Sparks, Strength: Phantasm—using the illusion of a demon, she can increase all parts of her body with a set of shadow parts. The parts she can increase include: all limbs and their strength and all senses. She can even gain new abilities such as night vision and the ability to stretch out new limbs up to fifty feet.

"The hell? Let me go! He's the one being a sore loser. I was just standing here!" I argued while squirming around, then she dropped us on our butts.

Hazel commanded, "Get along, and I don't ever wanna hear that kind of talk again. I don't care what your rank is nationally, don't ever patronize your classmates!" She turned to me and pointed, "And you, don't egg him on by being cocky! You won one fight, big whoop! The real training hasn't even started yet, so don't go pissing yourself with confidence!" She took a deep breath, then smiled again and shouted, "Alright, everyone, let's get on into the dorm!"

Tonuko and I sat on the ground while everyone else left. After a couple more seconds, he stood first and followed the group. I looked down at the grass, my face full of fury.

Who the hell does she think she is? Pissing myself with confidence; I have all the right to be confident! I'm probably stronger than her! Whatever, if they want me to prove myself, I'll happily oblige.

On the first floor of rooms, Hazel scanned the piece of paper in her hands. "Camilla, Donte, Claire, Steven, Jessica, and Jaxon, you'll all be on the left side. On the right are Rake, James, Bryce, Ana, Rebecca, and Anya!" Hazel read off. The twelve students headed for their rooms, then the rest of us walked up to the next floor. Hazel announced, "Oh boy, on the left we have Cindy, Khloe, Iris, Alex, Kyle, and Tonuko! On the right . . ." She continued naming people, but I blocked out her voice and went straight for my room.

I put my hand on the doorknob and heard Tonuko groan, "Why the hell do I have to be on a floor with him? Can't somebody change up the arrangements or something?"

In response, I chirped, "Do you think I wanna be on a floor with you, Moody Earth, and the clumsy ass kid over there?" I was referring to Alex. "Just shut up and deal with it!"

"Moody Earth, who the hell are you calling moody? I swear one win, and you already think you own the place!" Tonuko yelled. I snorted and gave him a mocking grin.

"Maybe I do." He squeezed the handle on his suitcase. Our floormates clearly did not want to deal with our bickering.

"Would you two just shut up already? God, you're like a couple of little kids! If you're both so high and mighty, act like it!" Khloe seethed walking past Tonuko. She was the girl who finished the test shortly after me.

Iris added quietly, "Yeah, we can all get along if we try!" She was so innocent, if I so much as raised my voice at her, she'd probably break.

I rolled my eyes and shook my head, then entered my room. It was dark, but with the flick of a switch, the room was actually decently sized. It had a desk, full-sized bed, bathroom, and wardrobe. After unpacking, I took a nap for a few hours. Today was just move in day, so the name "Introduction Day" was pretty misleading. Tomorrow started the first school day, and I had no idea what kind of weird friendship crap we'd do. When I awoke, I decided to take a walk around campus to see what it was like.

When I opened the front door, I could see the path that connected us to everything. I followed it and walked up to a forest-looking park. It had a little river with a waterfall coming out of an artificial rock, fish in the pond, and a ton of trees. I stood on top of the bridge that connected two sides of the park and smiled while looking down at the beautiful coy fish. It seemed like nothing could go wrong, but everything did when I heard someone running up to me. I turned my head, then threw my arm up to block the sword a red man just swung at me. After the blade dug into my skin, he smiled.

"Little Kyle Straiter, son of Tyrant. I'm so glad to finally meet you! The big man up top said I could give you a warning, so I'm here to do just that!"

I jumped back and ripped my arm out of his sword in the process, then tensed my fist. No matter how angry I was at Tyrant, I couldn't help but shake with fear. The man's aura was disturbing. With the tree shadows blocking out most of the sunlight, he looked like a demon. "Look at that, you're shaking like a frightened child! If I didn't know any better, I'd think you were one!"

"I—I'm gonna take you down!" I stuttered, but we both knew it was just an empty threat. He took a step forward, I took one back, then he darted faster than I ever could have predicted. With one swoop, his sword was through my stomach and out my back. Blood soaked the grass we stood on, and after he tore his blade out of my body, he licked the blood off of it. I feared for my life thinking that his strength had something to do with the taste of blood like Tyrant's; however, nothing happened. I coughed a few times into my hands, soaking my fingers with spit mixed with blood, then a pain worse than I'd ever felt struck.

"There it is, the most beautiful form of murder. I'm sure Tyrant won't mind if you die, not like you were gonna' join us willingly anyway!" The wound in my stomach ripped more; it was expanding. My flesh tore apart slowly, and the gash in my arm did the same.

This is it, I'm gonna die already? I made a promise to Mom, I can't go out yet! I just—can't! Her death will be in vain, it'll be all my fault. Tyrant killing her was because of me, now I can't even man up and accomplish what she asked of me. How pathetic am I?

My savior came in an instant. The principal swooped in and stabbed at BloodShot a few times, but he dodged each one.

After thinking for a moment while avoiding the principal's weapon, BloodShot verbalized his decision, "Not worth it to risk death here. Good luck, little ol' Kyle!"

Before passing out, I noticed that the principal was using a massive nail as a sword. After he dropped it, it shrunk back to its regular size. I blacked out. Once BloodShot evaded the teachers and was a certain distance away, the wound expansion stopped.

BloodShot, Strength: Inflation—when he cuts someone, he can forcibly make the wound slowly expand after two minutes of the first injury. The expansion only continues if he is in a twenty-four-foot radius, but the pain rates as one of the top ten in the world.

I was rushed to the nurse's office, and Nurse Blavins, after half an hour, healed me to perfection. Supposedly, BloodShot's strength had caused damage that was meticulous and time consuming to heal, as well as energy consuming. She had to sleep for the rest of the day, while I woke up a few hours later.

Some students entered a few minutes after I awoke. I recognized Alex and Cindy, but there was one I hadn't talked with yet.

"Oh Kyle, this is Rake! He's in the honors' class, and Alex and I have known him since we were little!" Rake nodded with a smirk.

He commented, "Wish I could've met you when you weren't in a hospital bed, but y'know, gotta' take it as it comes." I couldn't help but chuckle, then looked down at the sheets. There were a few red stains, and my left arm was wrapped with bandages.

"I feel so bad, I wish we could've helped!" Cindy whined as she looked out the window at the attack site. There were guards and a man with a white jacket inspecting the area.

Alex nodded in agreement, but Rake thought otherwise. "It's best we didn't, honestly."

Cindy and Alex were stunned he'd say something like that, but I understood where he was coming from. "Just think about it: is it better to have one student injured and the teacher's help, or countless casualties and no one able to call for backup?"

"Yeah, he's got a point. I do feel horrible though, you've got to be in a lot of pain. I'm sure your parents are devastated to hear about this," Alex sighed.

I shrugged, then looked over at Nurse Blavins.

My parents . . .

"No, I'm really fine. Since Nurse Blavins was able to heal me so perfectly, I'm sure I'll be able to go to class tomorrow for the first day."

Principal Lane walked in the room and clasped his hands.

He happily stated, "I talked with Nurse Blavins before she went to sleep, and you are able to return to the dorm at any time. Your injuries are all healed, but you will be sore for a few days."

The three were happy for me, then Principal Lane asked, "Would you three excuse us for just a few minutes? There's something I need to speak with Kyle about." They waved and left, then Principal Lane pulled up a chair next to my bed. "Kyle, we need to have a talk about your strengths and connections."

"What about them? I have two strengths, sure, but what kind of connections do you mean?" He crossed his arms and leaned back in the chair.

"You don't need to put on an act for me Kyle. Gem Straiter died eight years ago at the hands of her husband, Samuel Straiter, also known as Tyrant."

I clenched my jaw, thinking the worst.

What are these heroes going to do with me? I want to be one, too. I'm not like Tyrant. Don't take me down just because you're superstitious.

"Listen, I'm not here to do you any harm. Others might, but I want you to grow past your . . . well your past. I know your family doesn't define you, but it does influence you. A strong hate for Tyrant, that's what drives you, isn't it?"

"Yes," I responded, "I'll do whatever it takes to end him. He's taken everything from me: a normal life, a normal family, my mom. Even if it kills me, I'll kill him first."

Principal Lane nodded, then exhaled deeply in disappointment.

"Who on the staff knows about my family?" I asked.

"Just the vice principal, the leader of our security, and myself. We felt it wouldn't be right to spread this information about you to the rest of the staff without your approval."

I thought for a moment, then gave him my answer.

"I'd prefer the teachers don't know. I want as few people as possible to know I'm the son of the top villain before I've done any major heroic deeds."

He rubbed his chin, understanding my reasons.

"I'm assuming since you know about Tyrant, then you know how I have more than two strengths."

"No, I didn't know that actually. Just how many do you have, and how were you able to develop more than one when the strongest hero ever couldn't handle two?"

"For your first question, I have ten total strengths developed over a five-year span. As for the second, I can't answer that because I'm not sure how I was able to develop so many."

Principal Lane was dumbfounded and counted out ten on his fingers.

"That is absolutely ludicrous. Ten strengths, *ten*? I am extremely overjoyed that you chose to attend our school, and I hope eventually you will be able to use all ten of those gifts publicly." He sat in thought for another second, then stood and said, "Well, I'll let you go now. I'm sure you want some rest in a comfortable bed, not one of these hospital cots."

He left, and shortly after, I did as well. I quickly headed to my room to avoid any confrontation and slept immediately. I didn't even realize I hadn't eaten in more than a day.

The next morning, I woke up an hour and a half before school started and went for a run around campus. I avoided the park this time and navigated around it instead. After my run, I showered, then finally ate something. It was noted in the acceptance letter that for now we would have no school or training uniforms, so we were allowed to wear any clothes we wanted. I wore a white t-shirt and black shorts but kept my ninja headband in my pocket for when training started. For breakfast, I ate an apple and some yogurt the school provided. I walked to class ten minutes early. To my surprise, Tonuko was already there. We were told to stand and wait in the front of classroom so the teacher could give assigned seats when everyone arrived.

Tonuko crossed his arms and looked away, then muttered, "I heard what happened. I'm–glad you're not hurt too severely." I looked at him and laughed. "I'm only saying that cause I want you to be full power when we fight again! Don't get the wrong idea!"

"I'm glad I'm not hurt too." Once the rest of our class arrived, the teacher stood and smiled.

"Welcome freshman honors' class! I'll be your teacher for the year. I'm Ms. Palkun! Let's get started by getting everyone seated!" She picked up a piece of paper and took the glasses off the top of her head. She put them on correctly, then read names for the front row from left to right. "Alex, Anya, Jaxon, and Steven! Next row: Donte, Jessica, Tonuko, and Camilla! After that, Rake, Khloe, Cindy, and Kyle. Finally, the fourth row, Zayden, Iris, Cora, and Scarlett!"

We took our seats, then the girl in front of me looked back with her head upside down. Her bright blonde hair, very similar to mine, hung low.

"You're Kyle Straiter," she bluntly stated, still staring directly into my eyes. I awkwardly smiled and nodded.

"Yeah, I am."

She lifted her head and looked forward, leaving me utterly confused.

The teacher leaned on her podium in the front of the classroom and stared at all of us. She exclaimed, "Now for the fun part! I want each person to stand and introduce themselves, then describe their strength!"

The class got all giddy, but I put my chin in my hand and looked out the window. The campus was bare now, unlike earlier when I was walking to school. I had a direct view of the park, and near the area where some trees were cut down because of the incident, I could see a red patch of grass. I tensed up, then heard the first person introducing themself.

"Hey everyone, I'm Alex Galeger! First off, I can't wait to spend the next four years with you all! Anyway, my strength is Angel!"

Clearly, he was the pretty boy of the class, since all the girls were already fawning over him. He was tall, not very muscular, but defined, tan, and his hair was parted down the middle. The ends of his bangs shaped his face, and the rest of his hair was a ruffled mess.

Alex Galeger, Strength: Angel—he can conjure a bright light from any body part that is hot to the touch, hot enough to cause blemishes when in contact depending on how much light is produced. He can also control the brightness of the light, ranging from blinding like the sun to a dim lightbulb. Along with this light, he has angelic wings that perch on his outer back (special clothes are made for individuals with wings).

We clapped, then Ms. Palkun stated, "Very interesting Alex, interesting indeed." Her presence was bizarre, neither evil nor good, but obsessive. She looked at the next girl, who then stood.

"My name's Anya Lokel, and don't you forget it! My strength is Mechanics, pretty awesome right?" Out of the corner of my eye I could see Tonuko snort, so I assumed they already knew each other. Her skin had a slightly gray tint, and she had long, straight black hair.

Anya Lokel, Strength: Mechanics—using any material present, she can create any kind of machinery or armory immediately or at most within five minutes, depending on the item she creates. The machines are powered by her sweat, which contains a small dose of oil, and at will, or after thirty minutes at most, the creations crumple back into the basic material.

We clapped again, not me specifically, but the class did. The teacher didn't comment this time. Instead, she checked her watch and looked at the next person.

"Uh, I'm Jaxon Call." He clearly had a perm, a new perm in fact, and one of his eyes were purely red. He was skinny but stood tall. "My strength is Sargent."

Jaxon Call, Strength: Sargent—using a gas that seeps out of his mouth or nose, he can control anybody who breathes in the smoke. He controls who is affected by the smoke, and the spell can be broken by immense pain or loud noises, or it can fade. The smoke dissipates after one minute, and the effect dispels after five. Both can be increased with training, and Jaxon can control up to twenty-five people.

I swear I've heard of that strength before . . .

Ms. Palkun complimented, "That's pretty unique, don't think I've heard of that strength. Anyway, you're up Steven!"

Steven stood and stuck his hands in his pockets.

"Yo,' I'm Steven Mallnen, the Cyborg! If you didn't know me yet, trust me, you will after our first fight!"

He was pretty muscular, but on the shorter side. I rolled my eyes.

Bold claim coming from someone who defines themselves as a hunk of metal.

Steven Mallnen, Strength: Cyborg—he can transform any body part into robotic at will, but only two body parts at a time (can be increased with training). The feeling of a robotic part for him is that of ice being pressed against your skin, and his robotic limbs can get rusty or lock up.

The teacher stayed quiet again, but we were finally in the second row. Up first was the blonde girl in front of me. She stood and said plainly, "I'm Camilla Xavier, and my strength is Wind Control!"

Camilla Xavier, Strength: Wind Control—as it sounds, she can control any wind or oxygen by the sway of her hands. When used correctly and trained, Wind Control can nullify natural tornadoes and hurricanes.

It seemed we were taking longer than Ms. Palkun thought we would because she wasted no time and moved on to the next person.

Tonuko stood and boldly stated, "You all know me, I'm Tonuko Kuntai. My strength is Ground Control."

Tonuko Kuntai, Strength: Ground Control—he can bend and manipulate any surface in any way, but only from the ground. He cannot manipulate walls or ceilings, and he does not create new material; he only stretches the objects he manipulates.

When he sat down, the next girl immediately shot up. She had curly, short brown hair, and a sunflower was perched at the front right side of her head.

"Hello everyone, I'm Jessica Alter! My strength is growth, and my beauties can take down anyone!" Out of the tip of her hand, a rose grew rapidly, then she tossed it up at Alex. He caught it, and she blushed happily.

Jessica Alter, Strength: Growth—she can grow plants on any surface and amplify the amount of water in the air to make them grow instantly. As well as this, she can control her plants by a mind link with each one and command them to do nearly anything.

She sat down gracefully, then the next boy stood. I recognized him from the day of the entrance exams, mostly because of how easily he wiped out his opponent.

"Hey all, I'm Donte Gavinson. As you all saw during the entrance exam, my strength is Enhanced Speed!"

His pinkie nails, I could see, were painted sky blue.

Donte Gavinson, Strength: Enhanced Speed—as it sounds, he can move at inhumane speeds. Not only do his legs move faster, even though he has shorter strides, all his movements are increased when he activates his strength. Like many strengths in society, activating his requires an extreme tense of his body, then when it feels like his body pops, the strength is activated.

When he finished and sat back down, I sighed out of relief to myself.

Finally, two rows done; just two more and we're finished with this boring introduction crap. Man, I'm starving too. I wonder what kind of food they serve on campus.

It was my turn, so I stood and put my hands on my hips.

"You should all know me, I'm Kyle Straiter, the kid that beat Tonuko. My two strengths are Fire Control and Enhanced Strength."

People still seemed surprised to hear I had two strengths, but I took no notice of it. It was flattering, quite frankly.

Kyle Straiter, Strength Three: Fire Control—not only can he control any fire in his vision, but he also can conjure fire from any part of his body. Having fire on his body for too

long will cause burns, and he can control the temperatures of his flames.

Kyle Straiter, Strength Four: Enhanced Strength—on command, his muscle mass will rapidly increase. Depending on how much of an increase is pushed for, his muscles may physically grow.

"Gosh, two strengths that work so well together. It's so amazing, I must say, Kyle Straiter," Ms. Palkun gawked.

I awkwardly smiled then sat back down. I looked out the window again as the next girl went.

"Hey, I'm Khloe Basken and my strength is Intelligence."

Khloe Basken, Strength: Intelligence—her I.Q. is increased to three times its natural state (100). This specific type of I.Q. strength gives her a better strategic awareness, and she uses this to her advantage by calculating her foe's and her own attacks.

We moved on to the next girl, Cindy, who was obviously eager to go.

"Hey everyone, I'm Cindy Theon! My strength is Agility Enhancement!" Her hair was somewhat short, but her two ponytails hung low at the back of her head. Her eyes were big, and she had had a smile since I first saw her. For some reason, my cheeks felt hot.

Cindy Theon, Strength: Agility Enhancement—when holding her two specialized shotguns, she can increase her speed and agile ability ten times her normal rate. This effect has no backlash and can last for an entire day.

"Wow, that's pretty cool," I said, not realizing I spoke out loud.

She blushed and smiled at me, and I blushed too, but not because I was happy, more so embarrassed. I saw a couple of people around the room giggle, even the stern Khloe. I rolled my eyes, then the next person saved me by going.

"Yo, I'm Rake Clause; kind of a weird name, I know. Anyway, my strength is Snake as I'm sure you could tell."

It was pretty obvious—his hair looked like it had the texture of scales, but when he ran his hand through his long bangs, it looked soft and normal. Also, his pupils were not circles but instead small, thin lines.

Rake Clause, Strength: Snake—he can remove his fingers like fastening tape and turn them into snakes almost instantaneously. The snakes are venomous, but the venom is fed through his blood so he can control the potency. As well as this, these special snakes can burrow through any surface and grow wings within one minute of detachment.

"Bro, that's so badass!" Steven shouted in awe.

Rake grinned and sat down, then the girl behind me stood. She leaned over her desk and blew on the back of my neck. A shiver went down my spine, so I turned around. She had big, red lips, scarlet hair, and she stood boldly.

She smirked, "Hey boys, my name's Scarlett Yalvo, and my strength is Potent Perfume." She was staring directly in my eyes as she said that, and honestly, it was very intimidating. I didn't cower though, but instead stared right back, causing her to blush.

Scarlett Yalvo, Strength: Potent Perfume—she can change her body's smell to control people in certain ways. Examples are to change people's emotions about others or herself, cause people to obey her or others, and decrease the power of others' strengths. Depending on the effect and how much a person inhales, the effect can last up to three days.

"Strange, but pretty interesting!" Ms. Palkun complimented.

The next girl took a moment to stand. She had long purple hair and looked as if she hadn't slept in a few days. Quite honestly, she looked pretty dirty and smelly.

"I'm Cora Wavice," she sounded like she could fall asleep at any second, "and my strength is uh . . . oh yeah, Boost."

How the hell can you forget your own strength?

Cora Wavice, Strength: Boost—she can dramatically increase anybody's senses or strengths at will just by the touch of her finger. For example, this can dangerously

increase someone's hearing, give someone a bloodhound type of smell, or even increase a person's strength so dramatically that they would be on the same level as the number-one hero or villain. Obviously, accomplishing such a large feat requires years of training.

She sat back down and rested her head in her arms. I even noticed that her eyes blink one at a time. The next person stood, but she was shaking a lot.

"I–I'm Iris Blavins, and m–m–my strength is recovery!" It seemed like she was trying to yell those last words, but her yell was about as loud as someone's regular talking.

"Eh, what did you say? Speak up!" Steven complained giving her the stink eye.

Ms. Palkun threw a piece of chalk at his head, then she looked back at Iris. Iris, like her mother, had long, wavy white hair, and her eyes were a pink color, almost fuchsia.

Iris Blavins, Strength: Recovery—because she inherited her mother's one-of-a-kind healing strength, she can heal any physical damage to one's body. This healing is renowned as the top heal strength in the country at the very least, and Nurse Blavins is the top healing hero in the country.

Finally, we're at the last one. This better have all been worth it.

"Hey guys, I'm Zayden Attack! As you can tell, my strength is Shark!" As he said, it was painfully obvious. He had sharp teeth, dark gray skin, and small gills on his cheeks. A dorsal fin sat on the back of his head as well.

Zayden Attack, Strength: Shark—half shark, half human, he can swim through the ground as if it's water and through small slits at the bottom of his palms, he can create and shoot shark teeth.

"Amazing, you are all just so amazing! Now, the moment you've all been waiting for, training! Let's have a little fun with it, shall we?" Ms. Palkun gushed.

I lit up and smiled, but some others were more nervous. Most notably, Iris.

Chapter 4

First Training Tournament

We blindly followed Ms. Palkun to the Dome, which sat next to the school. It looked as magnificent as ever and smelled like a freshly cleaned car. The stage was fixed up from after Tonuko's and my short fight, and it seemed slightly bigger as well.

"Welcome to the place where we will host our training tournament! Principal Lane decided we should start a new tradition, so this is it—the Freshman Battle. Pretty cool, huh?"

Tonuko rolled his eyes and crossed his arms.

"We'll be having a tournament with preset standings, and whoever wins will be seated at the top of your class! To win, you must get both of your opponent's feet out of the stage lines, knock them out, or immobilize them! This doubles as experience with real, unpredictable fighting and a ranking system!"

"So, we're gonna' be the entertainment for your little show? Fantastic," Cora sharply remarked while rolling her eyes. Ms. Palkun was saddened by our lack of enthusiasm, but I cheered her up. I flexed my arm and smirked.

"Sounds like there are some cowards here who are scared to face me. Don't worry, I won't beat you too badly!"

This lit a fire under everyone, and the entire mood changed.

"How do we know who we're facing?" Alex asked.

The teacher muffled her chuckle, then pointed to the giant screen perched at the top of the back wall. It turned on, showing the bracket:

Kyle (1)	Cindy (8)	Steven (5)	Camilla (4)	Rake (6)	Alex (3)	Jaxon (7)	Tonuko (2)
Khloe (16)	Cora (9)	Scarlett (12)	Donte (13)	Zayden (11)	Jessica (14)	Anya (10)	Iris (15)

"How the hell am I a five seed? I should easily be top three!" Steven yelled at the teacher.

Donte was just as shocked, as was I.

Surprising that they put him at thirteenth even though he won just as fast as I did. Makes you wonder how weak that other kid really was.

"Khloe, how are you sixteenth? No offense Iris, but your strength is just support, so it seems like you'd be ranked last considering we were ranked on the physical exam," Scarlett asked standing with the two. Iris smiled.

"Don't worry, none taken!" Khloe twirled her ponytail in her fingers, then dropped it.

"Probably because during her fight Iris continuously healed herself to keep fighting. Smart strategy, but unreliable and reckless. However, it made her last way longer than I did."

Cindy hopped up to me, and that's when I noticed Alex standing next to me.

"Kyle, if we both win, we get to face each other! Don't you dare lose, I really wanna' battle with you!" Cindy exclaimed.

I blushed and rubbed the back of my head.

"Would you lovebirds quit it already? Kyle and Khloe, get on that stage! The rest of you come up to the viewing deck with me!"

Alex nudged my arm and giggled, but I slapped him away, then walked up to the stage. Khloe stood on the other side with her arms crossed. Ms. Palkun began the match, and I decided to let Khloe get the first hit in considering how unfair the battle was. While I tied my headband on my head, she thought for a moment, then grinned.

"Are you gonna go all out in this tournament to try and impress Cindy or something?"

I felt my cheeks get hot again, and before I could respond, Khloe used the opportunity of my distraction to try and get a blindsided kick in. I caught her foot before it made contact, then shoved it back at her. She fell over, so I knelt on her stomach and let some flames dance in my palm.

"Easy fight, easy win," I boasted looking down at her.

She kneed hard into my thigh, giving me a cramp. I stood back up gripping my thigh, but she stayed on the ground and kicked my feet out. As soon as I landed, she flipped up onto her feet, ran over, then sat on my stomach. She grabbed both my hands and stuck them together, then smiled.

"Look at that, I just upset the top dog that was gonna' kick everyone's asses. Oh well, easy fight, easy win!" I sighed and forcefully pulled my hands apart.

"I was gonna go easy on you, but–" I kneed the back of her thigh, then while she was distracted, slid my feet between her legs and kicked her stomach as hard I could without enhanced strength. She flew off me and skidded on the ground after landing. I stood, ran over, and jumped into the air. Fire swirled around my feet, and I swung them around in the air before landing over her head.

My feet grazed the sides of her head, then she stuttered, "I–I tap out!"

My fire burned out, and I walked away.

"Great first fight kids! Now, Cindy versus Cora, get down there!"

They walked past me as I walked up the stairs along with Khloe. Alex called me over, and I saw the open seat next to him. I sighed as I sat down.

He complimented me, "Nice win, man, you really made her think she won, then just kicked into a whole new gear!"

I shrugged while looking down at the arena.

Cindy held out her hand for Cora, who shook it.

"Good luck, Cora!"

Cora nodded, then the match began. Cindy immediately drew her guns and fired off a round each at Cora.

Cora tapped her legs and muttered, "Boost." She dodged all six of the bullets (each of Cindy's guns shoot three bullets at once), then tackled Cindy. They wrestled on the ground for a moment, but Cora was stronger and eventually pinned Cindy down. She cupped her hands on Cindy's ears, saying "Boost."

"That's not good. Cindy's gonna pop an eardrum with her ears boosted," Alex analyzed while running his hand through his hair.

I agreed and sat up in my chair. The room was silent, but Cora leaned in next to Cindy's ear, then screamed as loud as she could. Cindy cried out and headbutted Cora. As she reached for her head, Cindy swung a gun and hit Cora in the side, knocking her off. Cindy jumped up, then ran to the opposite side of the stage.

"Look," Rake nudged my arm, "her ears are bleeding."

I squinted and saw he was correct. A small blood trail dripped out of her right ear, and it was safe to assume that since her left ear was the one Cora's mouth was next to, it was bleeding as well.

Cora practically hugged herself and stated again, "Boost."

Cindy blinked a few times, then her face softened. She shook her head, then spun the guns around in her hands a few times. Cora's arms grew bigger as she ran at Cindy. She punched at her, but as soon as her shoulder slightly moved, Cindy leapt into the air, flipped backward, and kicked Cora down. Cora turned to get up but was met with two shotguns in her face.

"I tap out," she sighed after putting her hands up.

"Good game, that was close!" Cindy smiled; she put her guns away and reached out her hand to help Cora up. Cora took it with a sigh, then the two walked toward the stairs.

"Great fight you two, very entertaining indeed! Now, it's eh . . . oh right, Scarlett and Steven! Scarlett, do me a favor and show this boy why he wasn't ranked top three!"

"I thought you were supposed to be unbiased!" Steven shouted as he walked past.

The teacher shrugged with a grin.

"I am, for everyone except you! Now, you two can begin once you're both ready!"

Steven cracked his fingers, and Scarlett stood with her hand on her hip, the same seductive smile she'd had earlier stretched across her face. A pink smoke crept out of her body, then flew back in. Steven took a deep breath, then he tensed his arms. The noise similar to metal bending came from his arms, and they faded to a gray. Wires snapped out (his veins), and he punched his fists together. He charged in, but Scarlett put one finger up, letting the pink smoke shoot out and cloud Steven's face. He punched at her a few times, but she dodged each one.

"Sorry little boy, but this is game over."

Steven's face turned purple, and although he tried hard to resist, he was forced to gasp for air. He inhaled almost all of the pink smoke, then fell over. "Do me a favor and leave the stage. I'll do anything you want if you do!" She put her finger on her lip and gave him the puppy-eye look.

Steven hopped onto his feet, before running off of the stage.

"Does that mean you'll love me forever?" he screamed while gawking at her.

She gagged, and the effect wore off a few seconds later.

Steven blinked and was visibly confused. "How the hell did I lose?" He stomped past Scarlett toward the stairs while thinking, *Dammit, if only I could turn my organs robotic. That would be so useful.* Scarlett's name was moved up in the bracket, and Steven's was crossed out. She happily skipped back to her seat, then Donte and Camilla were told to take the field.

Donte stretched out his legs and hamstrings, then Camilla smirked.

"Donte, don't worry, you'll be just fine!"

He raised an eyebrow, but his confusion was answered by her saying, "I'll end this real quick!"

Donte grumbled to himself as the fight began; he started out like he did against James. However, this was clearly a mistake. His constant motion created powerful gusts of wind that would knock anyone to the ground, except Camilla. She swayed her hands, and the winds wrapped around her arms. After a second, the winds shot out in a spiral and intercepted Donte's path. He was blown off his feet into the air, then crash landed and skidded across the building. He hit his head on the wall and took a few seconds to get up.

"What a quick match! Well done, Camilla, very nice! Donte, you should try to do this useful thing called using your brain!" Ms. Palkun mocked while clapping.

Donte was blushing, clearly embarrassed as he walked toward the stairs. Camilla's name moved up on the large screen, then it was time for the next battle: Rake and Zayden.

Rake stood from behind me and took a deep breath. He was clearly very nervous.

"Ay," I said, "You have a clear advantage over him man. All you gotta' do is realize it."

Rake's eyes showed confusion, but he smiled at me and nodded. He made his way down to the arena along with Zayden. The two shook hands and took their places. Ms. Palkun announced for them to begin.

Zayden immediately leapt straight up and dove into the ground. The noise of his ground swimming sounded like a jackhammer, but he left no tunnel. Suddenly, he popped out of the ground behind Rake and kicked his back, then flipped backward, and dove right back into the ground.

Rake stumbled forward, then pulled off his pinky. In Rake's hand, it grew longer and skinnier and grew a head. A green snake formed, and it crawled out of his hand, burrowing into the ground. Rake focused on his mind link with the snake, but Zayden released an onslaught of unpredictable attacks from all over.

"Dammit," Rake huffed while hunched over and resting on his knees. "Clear advantage? What fucking advantage do I have against someone who can hide in the ground?"

Zayden's barrage of blows stopped, then he jumped from the ground across the stage from Rake. He wiggled off the snake that had bit onto his finger before diving right back down.

"That's it. That's what Kyle meant!"

Rake scurried over to his pinky snake and put it back on his hand, then ripped off all five fingers from his left hand. He squeezed them in his right hand, creating a ball that had a similar texture to clay. Rake dropped the ball, and when it touched the ground, it stretched on its own. After a few seconds and a few punches from Zayden, the ball became a seven-foot-long, very thick snake. I couldn't believe my eyes.

How could a strength cause just a few fingers to transform into such a large animal?

Rake continued taking blow after blow, until Zayden didn't come up. The arena was silent, and the students around me were watching intently. I rolled my eyes with my arms crossed, then took a deep breath, and stretched my arms above my head.

"Why are you so invested? It's obvious, Rake won," I stated with a mocking tone.

Tonuko glanced at me and grumbled something to himself.

Like I said, Rake won. Out of the ground came Rake's large snake, which was gripping Zayden in its mouth. However, to my surprise, Zayden wasn't upset or angry but was instead laughing and smiling.

"Man, I thought I had you! This thing was just too big to maneuver around, and damn, it's fast!" Zayden exclaimed. He hung from the snake's mouth in front of Rake, and his head was upside–down.

"I'm lucky I figured out your weakness, or I would have collapsed! You hit pretty damn hard man!" The snake dropped Zayden, then he stood and shook Rake's hand.

People around me clapped. Why? I have no clue.

The next battle was Alex and Jessica. They took their positions, but the battle ended as quickly as it began. When the teacher yelled for the fight to start, an extremely bright light blinded us all. After a few seconds, the light dissipated, revealing Alex standing over Jessica. She was breathing heavily, and there were burnt flower petals all around her.

"What just happened?" Rake asked me.

I shrugged, genuinely confused.

Did Alex's light produce heat?

"Your power is beautiful! You had so much control too! It's a shame it wasn't enough though," Alex smiled while reaching a hand to Jessica. She hesitated, then blushed, and took his hand while slightly smiling. He helped her up just as her name was crossed off on the screen, and his moved up in the bracket.

Anya and Jaxon were up, and as they made their way to the stage, I snorted.

"What's so funny, Straiter?" Tonuko asked with his arms crossed.

"Nothing really. It's just that this will be another fast battle. That Anya girl doesn't stand a chance considering all that guy needs to do is breathe out some of that mind-controlling smoke crap," I stated. I put my feet up on the railing in front of us and closed my eyes, but apparently my statement annoyed Tonuko.

"No, Anya has a plan. She wouldn't go out that easily. Stop acting like you always know what's going to happen."

I was confused and slightly angry by his sudden insult, but instead of arguing, I rolled my eyes and watched the fight.

After it commenced, Jaxon breathed out his smoke, which, contrary to his green style, was pink. It moved swiftly and swarmed Anya's head. She quickly crouched and created something so fast none of us could see just what it was. Anya stuck her hands into the ground, and when she pulled them out, concrete in the shape of boxing gloves came with them.

"You can't hold your breath forever!" Jaxon mocked while backing up and standing defensively.

However, Anya didn't let his words get to her but instead charged head on. He dodged her first punch, then Anya pulled her right hand back—the one she swung at him—and hit Jaxon in the side of the head with the back of her glove. He stumbled a couple feet, then Anya took a powerful step and punched him in the stomach. Jaxon coughed as he flew backwards and landed outside of the stage. He skidded on his butt, hitting the wall underneath the balcony after a couple seconds. The smoke disappeared, revealing Anya's small secret to winning.

"With these nose plugs, it was so much easier to not breathe that stuff in!" Anya informed everyone after taking out a rock from each of her nostrils. Jaxon swore as his name was crossed out and trudged back to his seat.

The final battle of the first round was very one-sided, Tonuko versus Iris. They both made their way to the stage, but before the teacher could yell for the fight to commence, Iris revealed her thoughts.

"Wait, I forfeit!" Iris shouted with her soft voice, shocking some of the students.

"Iris, this is your chance to show off what you can do!" Scarlett yelled, standing from her seat.

Iris rubbed her arm and looked down. She had a surge of confidence and proudly stated, "I have shown what I can do! I've been healing everyone who got injured! That's my purpose, to heal the people who can fight! Trying to fight with Tonuko wouldn't help me or him!"

I, for one, thought her little testimony was painfully obvious. Of course, someone with a strength to heal shouldn't battle to show off her skills; that would be ridiculous.

"Works for me. I honestly would have felt bad fighting someone who isn't training to be a fighter," Tonuko admitted with a sigh. He stuck his hands in his pockets and walked with her back up the stairs.

"This first round has been absolutely amazing! You are all performing as I expected, excellent work! We will take a ten-minute break before beginning round two, then you'll perform the semi-finals and finale in front of the whole school tomorrow!"

Students began standing up and stretching out their legs, then communicating amongst themselves. I continued resting in my chair with my feet on the railing, but I opened my eyes to look to my right. I saw Tonuko, Alex, Anya, and Cindy all talking and laughing.

I strongly considered getting up and joining them, but it was as if someone was telling me not to. I felt as if I could hear a voice commanding me to stay seated.

You have a job to do, you are more important than these people. Do not stoop to their level and start socializing for fun.

But what if I want to have fun?

There is no time for fun. While you're out having fun, Tyrant is destroying another family.

He can't be killing more people at every moment. He has to have some kind of a heart.

Tyrant isn't like everyone else. He has his toys that can kill at every moment. You aren't strong enough to stop them, so you aren't strong enough to care for others.

So, I kept myself distanced for the ten minutes. Instead of meeting new people and connecting with students who had similar goals as me, I focused on beating Cindy in the next match. I would have to be nimble and unpredictable to avoid her bullets and keep up with her athleticism.

After a few more minutes, Cindy and I were told to take the stage. I stretched in one corner and mentally prepared myself for another victory. I was so focused I didn't see Cindy walk up to me and reach out her hand.

"Good luck, Kyle! Let's both do our best!"

I couldn't help but slightly snort as I shook her hand. I could tell she was confused, so I decided to tell her what I found so amusing.

"I mean, I don't think I'll be needing any luck. Thanks though."

Her smile faded to a slightly angry frown. She nodded, then walked back to her corner.

Ms. Palkun announced for the match to begin, so Cindy drew her guns, and I stood ready to dodge any bullets coming my way. Cindy shot a few rounds at me, but her aim was a little off and I was able to dodge them without a scratch. I charged in and tried to land a few punches, but she was inhumanely nimble and bent her body in ways I didn't know a person could. After my last punch, she jumped up and kicked off my head as she leapt across the stage.

"Wow, that's pretty embarrassing," Zayden chuckled. He was sitting next to Steven and Donte; Scarlett and Jessica were sitting behind them. Steven joined in on the laughing, but Donte scratched his head.

"How is Kyle going to win when Cindy's specialty is dodging up-close attacks? Kyle doesn't seem smart enough to figure out a way to beat her," Donte thought aloud. Instead of other's joining him in thought, they laughed at him.

"No offense, but you probably shouldn't be the one to call someone else dumb. You literally lost because you created wind for your opponent when her power is manipulating wind!" Scarlett mocked. Donte grumbled to himself and turned to face the stage.

I continued avoiding bullets, but I found myself getting very tired. I was quite surprised; my endurance usually exceeded my peers. I didn't realize it at first, but this downfall in energy cost me greatly. Cindy reloaded her guns and fired off a couple more rounds, and I was able to dodge only half of the bullets. Three bullets embedded themselves into my left arm, two into my left thigh, and one hit the back of my neck. I fell onto my right knee and felt extreme pain throughout the left side of my body. Clearly Cindy didn't think that many of her bullets would land, so she stopped fighting and looked shocked.

Like hell I'm gonna' lose to a nobody like this girl! I gotta' focus, I can't let any more bullets connect or I'm done. How can I stop a bullet when I'm this tired and weak?

Cindy seemed to be getting worried about my injuries, so she wanted to end the battle quickly. She decided to try and immobilize me swiftly by out-speeding me. She ran around me in a circle for a few seconds, then lunged at my back. While panting, I surprised everyone by flinging a quick punch with my injured left arm. I focused all of my super strength into that arm, causing her to fly out of the stage and crash through the wall. She laid on debris and grass outside; since Cindy was outside of the stage, I won.

Iris began healing me first, but I waved her off.

"Go help Cindy, I'm fine for now."

Iris was too scared to argue, so she ran over to Cindy and began healing her wounds. I was officially in the semi-finals, and after we were all patched up, Ms. Palkun repaired the wall. She picked up one of the scraps of wood on the ground, then tossed it toward the hole in the wall. The piece expanded and after mere seconds, the hole was repaired as if the wall had never been touched in the first place.

Diana Palkun, Strength: Build—using a piece of anything broken, she can rebuild the entire structure or parts of it. For example, if she has a scrap of a car, she can recreate the car the scrap is from.

The next battle was Camilla against Scarlett, but the one-sided fight was almost laughable. Scarlett's strength relied on her opponents breathing in her scents, but Camilla could wipe away all the scents with her strength; The battle ended quickly with a Camilla win.

Now, it was the fight I was most interested in: Rake against Alex. They were both on a whole other level of combat compared to most of the class. I would say they were on the same level as Tonuko, but obviously nowhere near me. My first thought toward Rake and Alex after seeing their fights was how great of assets they could be.

When the match began, Alex did the same move as before. He created a blinding light, causing us spectators to not be able to see the fight.

"Man, I hate watching this kid fight. I can't see anything!" Tonuko complained.

"Yeah, but I guess it is what makes him strong! If we can't see anything from up here, imagine how bright it is down by Rake!" Zayden noted. For Tonuko being ranked number one nationally, he was pretty dumb.

Rake threw four of his finger snakes out at the direction Alex used to be in, but he couldn't seem to navigate his opponent even with the snakes. Suddenly, Rake felt a burning sensation on the knuckles where the four finger snakes use to be, and the light faded. Alex was standing a few feet behind him and all four snakes found their way toward a body part of his.

"Wow, I was not expecting that! Great job!" Alex complimented. Even though he was being slightly detained, and didn't know how much venom each snake contained, he still had a wide smile. I could not understand why.

"So, does that mean I win?" Rake asked with a slight grin.

Alex shook his head, then both his arms lit up. This time, the light wasn't nearly as bright. However, two snakes let go of his arms, then the other two let go from his waist. When the snakes returned to Rake's hands and morphed back into fingers, they were burned horribly. Alex let out his wings, then flew full speed at Rake. In response, Rake bent back, then swiftly threw up both hands and touched Alex's stomach. All his fingers fell off and the newly formed ten snakes latched onto Alex's gut. His wings stopped flapping, and he fell to the ground, skidding near the stage line but never crossing it. "Now, I definitely won!"

Why is he so quick to jump to conclusions? Use your head a little more, Rake.

"Relax man, you didn't win! Gosh, you have no faith in me, do you?" Alex's stomach glowed brightly, and all the snakes were burned off. He scurried to his feet and charged at Rake before the snakes could crawl back. Rake blocked a slew of punches and kicks, but once Alex began using his light as a power increase, it was over for Rake.

Alex punched with his right, and as soon as Rake reached to block, Alex swung his body and kicked Rake in the side of the head. Rake stumbled to his left, then Alex led with a fist into Rake's stomach. He soared off the stage, landed on his side, and skidded a few feet.

"Now I won!"

"Damn, I really thought I had you!" Rake sighed while still sitting on the ground.

Alex walked over and helped him up.

Anya and Tonuko headed down to the stage, but they shocked me when they hugged each other before the match began.

"Let's both do our best, alright? I don't want you to hold back just because it's me," Anya stated while looking Tonuko directly in the eyes.

He smiled and nodded, then the two took their places, and the match began. Behind me, all I could hear was Khloe and Camilla discussing strategies on how Anya could win.

"Well, Tonuko is going to be constantly bending the arena, so that should give Anya the advantage because her strength uses rock, right?" Camilla asked Khloe.

Khloe nodded, then responded, "Anya should gain an advantage that way, but Tonuko is smart enough to know that. He won't give her enough time to create anything big. Since they know each other, they know how the other fights."

Please, would you two just shut up?

For some reason, I bit my tongue and didn't ask that out loud.

"Hey Kyle, I was wondering; Why do you and Tonuko hate each other so much? You're always bickering back and forth," Khloe asked with genuine curiosity.

I snorted before responding, "It should be pretty obvious: we have very similar personalities. We're both cocky and think we're the best. Obviously, two individuals like that would butt heads." Khloe and Camilla nodded, satisfied with the answer. The two of them distracting me caused me to miss most of the fight, but I did catch the ending.

Tonuko created a barrage of sharp spikes and attacked Anya with them. Previously, she had created stone boots with a sweat-powered spring that let her perform a super-jump. She leapt into the air and landed directly above Tonuko. He swung his arm, bending the ground below him to create a barrier. Anya landed on the barrier, then flipped off it. She continued jumping back and took a large piece of each spike as she passed. Anya lifted a large clump of rock and wore a large, eerie smirk.

"I've been working on something since summer started! You can be my first test subject, Tonu!"

The clump of rock had a hole down the center that began glowing. Tonuko readied his finishing move as well, and when the gun shot out a large spike, the ground underneath Anya flowed like a wave, then launched her backward. The spike–bullet pierced through Tonuko's shoulder, and there was so much wind pressure that he was thrown back. They were both barreling for the out-of-bounds lines, but Tonuko managed to brush his foot against the ground and create a massive spike above him. He grabbed onto it, saving himself from touching out of bounds, but Anya was unfortunate and landed a mere couple feet outside of the stage.

"Wow, that was pretty close," Rake stated while cracking his back. I nodded, surprised that Anya gave Tonuko such a run for his money. Tonuko let go of the spike and fell onto the ground. His shoulder was gushing blood, but besides that the two were relatively unharmed.

After Iris healed Tonuko's shoulder, the first day of the training tournament was officially over. It was a good thing that it ended, too, because clearly Iris was on her last leg for her strength today.

"Alrighty students, that was a blast to watch! You're all so . . . talented! I cannot wait to see the semi-finals and finale tomorrow, and neither can the rest of the school! You four will perform in front of all the other classes, as well as the teaching staff!"

It seemed Alex was feeling the pressure, but Cindy comforted him. Alex honestly shouldn't have had anything to fear, it wasn't like anyone could see his battles anyway.

"Also, before you leave, I should let you know that we will be going on a little field trip this weekend! A permission slip has been sent home to your parents, and the permission slip will allow you to go on all trips that take you away from school!"

Shit, so I have to go to my house to get that thing tonight? Man, I'm already tired . . .

We were dismissed, and all the honors' class students wanted to have a little get-to-know each other party on the main floor of the dorm. I thought it would be absolutely useless, so I went straight upstairs to my room. I took a long nap, and after three hours, I awoke to see the sun was gone. I checked my phone and saw it was 8:00 p.m. My plan was to pray to my mom, then sneak out to grab the permission form.

"Hey, mom, it's been 2,369 days since you died. I really miss you. It's been kind of a weird first day if I'm being honest. The students here are so sensitive and emotional . . . it's confusing. I don't understand why they make efforts to talk to each other and make new friends; friends are just a burden. They make you feel like you really have to protect them. If they get hurt, you'd feel so much more pain than if it was some random civilian. I don't know, I'm just really confused. I wish I could ask for your advice . . . but I can't . . ."

"Hey, what's he saying?" Camilla asked Tonuko, whose ear was pressed to the small crack in my door.

"I can't tell!" he responded in a whisper–yell.

Tonuko, Cindy, and Camilla attempted to look into my room and listen to what I was saying.

Chapter 5

Smarter

I could feel the eyes watching my back while I prayed, so upon completion I stood and closed the door. Through the small crack, I couldn't see who was spying on me, and quite honestly, I didn't care who it was. Since this dumb teacher mailed my permission slip to my house, I had to escape campus to go retrieve and sign it. Obviously, neither of my parents would be happily waiting at home to sign a form for their son. I opened my window and jumped out.

A few minutes earlier, Alex saw two girls and one boy peering through my door: Cindy, Camilla, and, surprisingly, Tonuko.

"Hey, what are you guys doing?" Alex asked in a slight whisper. Whatever it was they were doing, he could tell they were snooping and didn't want to get caught.

"We're trying to see what this kid is doing instead of having fun downstairs with everyone else," Tonuko explained while looking through the crack in the doorway.

In the room, they could see me kneeling before my bed with my back turned to them. Alex sat beside Camilla and looked up at the popcorn ceiling, not necessarily interested in spying on me, but more so just wanting to spend time with the group.

"Tonuko, I have to ask: why do you and Kyle hate each other so much even though you barely know each other? Is it really just because you want to know who's stronger or something?" Camilla asked with genuine curiosity.

Tonuko thought for a moment, then concluded, "Well, I don't hate him. I just can't stand his little mystery boy act." Tonuko stopped peering through the door and sat against the wall next to Cindy. "For someone to have two strengths, that's unheard of; now he beats me easily even though I'm the number one ranked prospect in our grade level? It's all just fishy to me. I don't know. I wouldn't be as against him if it wasn't for the fact that he's that strong and unranked as well as unheard of."

"It is a little weird. Makes you wonder if he's hiding something more," Cindy added with an uneasy expression lingering on her face. After the words left her mouth, I shut the door and left the building. The four were shocked at the door suddenly closing and sat for another minute before building up the courage to open the door.

"Where the hell did he go?" Tonuko shouted after entering the room.

Camilla pointed to the window, making the answer obvious. In the distance, they could see me run through the front gate and leave the campus.

After jumping out the window, I scaled down the wall and leapt around ten feet from the ground, causing my ankles to sting quite a bit upon landing. I ignored the pain and began running as fast as I could without any strengths. If I did get caught leaving, it would be better to get caught at just that rather than also at using a strength unknown to others. I ran through the front gate unnoticed, not sure if that was a good or bad thing.

This school's security is pretty weak. Especially considering that BloodShot guy was able to sneak right in on the first day.

I crossed the street and made my way to my house. Unfortunately, nothing went smoothly for me. Lagging a block behind were my four classmates who had been watching me in my room. If I hadn't known any better, I'd think they were obsessed with me. I managed to lose them two blocks before reaching my house, hopped the fence to my backyard, and entered through the back door. I never locked the doors to my house when I left. What point was there to doing it? There was nothing to steal anyway.

Sure enough, slipped under the door was the permission form. I grabbed it, brought it to the counter, and signed it with my mom's signature, which I had forged so many times I had practically perfected it. I folded up the piece of paper and stuck it in my pocket, then looked around the dark room. I stared at the clean space where my mother died, took a deep breath, then walked out. Suddenly, I heard a voice behind me, one I had heard many times.

"Happiness is a filthy lie."

There stood Tyrant, with crossed arms and a large smile. On the ground in front of him was my mother in the spot where she perished. She sat up, then her neck cracked as she turned her head to me faster than I could blink. She whispered something, but I couldn't hear it. Water formed in my eyes.

"*YOU FAILED ME!*" Mom screamed. The screech was extremely loud and barely comprehensible; I stumbled back and tripped over some garbage. After falling, I looked up and didn't see the two anymore. My hands shook, and a shiver crawled up my spine, so I left the house through the backway.

Should I go find the four just to make sure they get back safe? Who knows who or what is creeping around out here.

I walked down the block and passed by one of the many large alleyways around town. The city of Camby was relatively large and divided into two areas: suburbs and city. The city part was smaller than the suburbs but had large skyscrapers and a dozen hero businesses. Since Camby did not have anything of importance, it was not generally a target for criminals. However, with the new addition of a hero school, a strong worry plagued the townspeople that villains would migrate here for easy crime considering the few heroes in the area.

In the large suburbs of Camby, there were ten alleyways that stretched for miles. An old friend and I would use this alley near my house, called Cat Alley, to travel to each other's houses. However, he moved to a different city four years ago because his parent's hero business was going bankrupt due to the lack of crime in the area. They moved to Parane, the next city over, and I haven't heard from them since. My memory is hazy, but I think my friend's name was . . . Daniel? All I can remember about him was his long, brown hair and that he was never seen without a big smile.

As I passed the alley, I saw my four classmates looking around, confused. Camilla squinted as she looked through the alley, then saw me. She waved and shouted, "Guys, I found him! He's right over here!"

I walked toward them with my hands and the form in my pockets. A trashcan near me shook. I assumed it was a cat—strays were all over—but the shaking became much more aggressive. My classmates stopped walking as well, but not for the same reason. From where they were standing, they could see a man standing behind me. Only his silhouette was visible because of the shadows and streetlights, so all they could see were his magenta eyes, top hat, and long jacket.

"Kyle, watch out!" Tonuko warned after taking another step forward.

The man leapt at me and reached out his hand, but I quickly reacted by ducking. As soon as I could see the attacker's fingers, I reached up, grabbed his wrist and forearm, then threw him on his back. The attacker grunted when hitting the ground, then let out a small, sharp whistle. Out of the trashcan burst a large, muscular arm that appeared to be made of shadows.

What the fuck is that thing?

The beast that emerged from the trashcan was extremely muscular, but its body parts were misshaped. Its arms were much longer than its body and its legs bent inward at the knee joint. The creature's head was very small, and the only facial feature was two, small magenta dots for eyes. I stared up at the creature, wide-eyed, watching as it swung a punch down at me. Tonuko ran up and slightly pushed me as he swiped his arm up. He bent a part of the concrete and wrapped it above us. The creature continued punching the concrete structure, starting to crack it.

"Everyone, we need to get out of here! If we can make our way over to a main street, there might be police force or pro-heroes around to take care of this guy!" Tonuko commanded.

However, I wasn't one to back down from a fight. I was too scared last time and nearly let myself get killed by BloodShot. This time, it would be different.

"Hell no! I'm gonna kick this rando's ass!" I argued.

My fists engulfed in flames and more fire spiraled around my feet. I used the flames as boosters to launch myself into the air, then I released an explosion of burning fire onto the creature. Tonuko frowned watching me fight but was more distressed to see my attack had no effect. The creature was unfazed. It launched a counterattack by punching my side. I tried to block the punch with my forearm but was instead thrown into the wall to my left. I fell off the wall and landed flat on the ground. My entire body ached, and my head was pounding.

The creature moved to step on Tonuko and his weakened shield, but Camilla created sharp wind blades that pierced the creature's translucent skin. With the small amount of wind created, it surprised us to see the creature fall over and vanish. The attacker stood while chuckling and ran back to the end of the alley. He held his hands up and out of the shadows rose two more of his creatures.

"You children should leave now! I only want him!" The man pointed at me, and after a few seconds, I pushed myself to stand.

"Who are you to make demands?" Cindy argued while reaching for her guns. The man laughed hysterically, wiping a tear from his eye before answering.

"You heroes-in-training are always amusing. Who am I? Why, I am one of the majesty's loyal followers, one of his Care-Givers! I am Bobby Mamien, the crawler in the dark!"

Bobby Mamien, Strength: Illusion—he can reincarnate dead animals or transform his own shadow into ghost-like creatures that can't be hurt by most physical attacks. They have extreme strength yet are very fragile and can be easily damaged if even slightly hit.

I recognized the name; he'd been a Care-Giver for as long as I had known them. Tyrant talked a lot about him to my mom.

"You heard the man: get back to school! I'll take care of this runt!" I smirked boldly and marched past Tonuko. Out of the corner of my eye I saw his dumbfounded expression, so I decided I needed a little more force in my words if I wanted them to listen. "Do I need to repeat myself? *Get the hell out of here!* I'll take care of this!"

I stomped on the ground, sending a large crack toward Bobby. Flames danced on my hands up to my forearms and my feet up to my calves., then I charged in. I dodged the two creatures' attacks and wound up ready to punch Bobby. He ducked under my fist, swiped my feet from under me, then the creature on his left stomped down at me. I formed a square of flames above me and let the fire roar out at the creature. I could tell the heat was affecting it, but not enough.

So, I need hotter flames, huh? Fine by me!

I focused on the temperature of the flames, which started turning blue. The extreme heat of the fire caused the creature to dissipate into thin air. I hopped to my feet and stood ready to attack again. Bobby was shocked to see his creature get erased by my fire but tried to hide his doubts. I charged head on toward him, maneuvered my body to the left to avoid the remaining creature, and threw myself at Bobby's side. He turned to defend but was outpowered by my enhanced strength. After I swung a hefty punch, he soared into the wall behind him. I gave him no time to think by charging into the wall, ready to give a finishing blow. Bobby dodged the attack while breathing heavily and holding his ribs.

"Damn, he's good," Camilla complimented, watching in awe.

Alex tried to take charge by saying, "We really should get out of here! This is way too advanced for us!"

Tonuko agreed and backed up to the group, but none of them could bring themselves to stop me. Was it fear holding them back, or did they want to keep watching me fight without restrictions?

To attack both Bobby and his creature, I decided to make myself like a bomb filled with flames. Through my bright smile, an orange light glowed brighter. I ran at Bobby, and when the creature jumped in to defend its master, fire poured out of every hole in my body. Tonuko bent the ground up to create a large wall to defend himself and his friends, but the pure wind pressure from the large attack nearly swept them all off their feet. Even though Bobby was down and nearly unconscious, I still wanted to fight. I stomped toward him with a large grin smeared across my face. I could see the burns all over Bobby's body and could tell he was in great pain. However, something inside me wanted to inflict more pain on him. After taking a few more steps, I felt someone grab my arm.

"Kyle, stop! He's already too hurt to fight any more. We should just call the police and get to a safe place in case Bobby has backup!" Alex yelled while trying to hold me back. I pushed him off, causing him to trip and fall backwards.

"I'm not done yet," I stated sinisterly. The four continued trying to stop me from getting closer to Bobby, but I pushed them out of the way and stomped forward. When someone strongly grabbed my arm and stopped me, I turned to look and saw the four faces. Alex was desperate, Tonuko was angry, and Cindy and Camilla were terrified. I stopped walking and stood dumbfounded.

N—No, no why are you looking at me like that? I'm saving you; I'm taking the bad guy down . . . so why . . . why are you giving me that look like I'm a violent villain?

I let Tonuko drag me down the alley away from Bobby and saw a blue and purple portal form near the Care-Giver. BloodShot stepped out of the portal, threw Bobby over his shoulder, and smiled at me before walking back into it.

Why is he here again? Don't come near me . . . please . . .

A police car drove by, stopping and reversing when the officers saw the fires in the alley. We were scolded for reckless behavior and taken back to campus in the cop car. One of the officers told Principal Lane to punish us all; however, I spoke up and admitted I did all the fighting. I told Principal Lane and the officer that the other students wanted to leave and get help, but I wanted to fight back. My punishment was having to clean the Dome's seats tomorrow morning before our ranking tournament as well as being prohibited from leaving campus alone for a month. The police escorted us to our dorm rooms before leaving.

After the adrenaline rush, I couldn't sleep—I was haunting my own nightmares. In my first-ever battle against a villain when I actually fought back, I went overboard. Tonuko, the top kid in our grade, watched as I mercilessly beat down a man who had already fallen. He wanted to run away and find help.

Is that what I should have done? I beat the bad guy, right? Isn't that how these fights should end? Good beats evil and saves the day! It's not like any of us are gonna die fighting, we're too young. People this young don't just die, that's not how it works. Maybe I am right, and everyone else is just too scared . . .

The next day, I woke up an hour earlier than usual so I had time to clean the Dome's seats. It didn't take very long, mostly because the principal had me just wipe them down and even stopped me halfway through so I could go to class. I was the last person to my seat. The teacher was impatiently waiting for me.

"Took you long enough Kyle Straiter," Ms. Palkun seethed while everyone watched me get settled. Ms. Palkun rolled her eyes, then looked at the papers on her podium. "Today is the second and last day of the training tournament. All other classes are gonna be watching you four, and our class rankings will be announced on the big screen after the final battle. That's about it for today."

The students began talking with kids around them about the fights happening today, but I just leaned back in my chair and stared out the window. I felt Scarlett tap my head, so I glanced back at her.

"So, do you think you're gonna win it all?" Scarlett asked while leaning on her right hand.

Without hesitation I responded, "Yeah, I'm going to one hundred percent win it all. No doubt about it." I heard Tonuko grumble in his seat, so I smirked and asked, "What, got something to say Moody Earth?"

"I'll see you in the finals," he retorted quickly.

Tonuko's confidence shocked me; it shocked me so much, in fact, that I didn't respond and just nodded. I heard a couple people's snickers; my cheeks and ears felt hot: embarrassment. I hated the feeling of embarrassment. It made me feel inferior to others, even though I know I'm not.

Ms. Palkun took us to the Dome, which was filled with students and staff. Four benches were against the left side wall underneath the seating balcony, and at each bench was a person holding a headband. Tonuko, Camilla, Alex, and I walked over to the benches. One of the four walked up to each of us. Hazel handed me the black headband, which had a bold, white "four" in the center.

"What's this even for?" I asked while looking at the thick headwear.

"I picked you in a bracket to win it all, so I get to give you this headband that signifies you are an elite of your grade.

They really made brackets about us?

The highest-ranked boy is known as the king and the girl is known as the queen, but the number-one spot is saved for the class representative!"

Hazel informed me as we sat at my bench. I scratched my head while looking at the headband, confused about a few things.

"What does a class representative do, and what's the point of having a king and queen for every grade?" I asked.

"Well, a class representative is more so just a title. You don't have any extra work or anything, but you will be known publicly as the top student in your class. This means that students all over the nation will know your name more than any other student at E.H. in your class. That's basically the same point of the king and queen, and there's one for every grade to allow the top guy and girl of each grade to have their own spotlight."

I nodded.

We were interrupted by a man announcing over the speakers, "Hello ladies and gentlemen! I am your very own Eccentric High Guard Captain, Fox-Tails. Welcome to our most exciting event: the freshman final four!" The crowd roared with excitement. When I looked over at Alex, who was sitting on the bench to my left, he looked nervous and paler than usual.

Fox-Tails is the tenth-ranked hero; what is he doing here at E.H.? Why would such a strong hero care to protect a public school like this?

"Today we have quite the battles for you! First, the strong Kyle Straiter will face off against the careful Camilla Xavier; then the quick-witted Alex Galeger will face off against the one, the only, Tonuko Kuntai!"

Why does Tonuko get to be the "one and only?" I beat him already, he's not even that strong . . .

"Alrighty folks, let's get this show on the road!" Fox-Tails was very cheerful, and he quite honestly had a good announcer voice.

"Kyle and Camilla, go ahead and take the stage! The fight will begin in two minutes on the dot!"

I stood and looked back at Hazel, who gave me a reassuring nod. I don't know why, but her nod gave me more confidence. I smiled, then turned and walked to the stage while putting on the headband. Camilla stood staring at me, then held out her hand.

"Good luck, Kyle. Let's both do our best!" She gave me a smile, but my smile faded as I looked at her hand.

"Good luck? I don't need any. This shit's a warmup for the finale," I stated before turning to walk to the other side of the stage. While walking, I stretched my right arm over my head.

The audience apparently didn't like my statement because a wave of ridicule and anger swept my ears. I rolled my eyes and continued stretching. On the big screen, Camilla's first day picture and my first day picture appeared along with a thirty-second countdown. I took a deep breath to collect my thoughts, then wound up both my hands, and slapped my cheeks hard. I heard some gasps from the audience but ignored them as I was finally mentally prepared to battle.

"Let's go, Kyle! Stay focused on the prize!" Rake yelled while smiling big. Anya, who was sitting next to him, looked over with a confused expression.

"What's got you on the Kyle Straiter train all of a sudden?" Rake continued looking down on the stage with sparkles in his eyes.

"Kyle helped me with my first fight and actually got me the win! I don't think I've ever had a friend like him before!" Rake looked at Anya. "It's kinda cool to know you're friends with someone so advanced and a clear future top hero, don't you think?"

Anya was utterly shocked by Rake's enthusiasm for me.

"But what about Tonuko? You've been friends with him for years; don't you feel the same around him?" Anya asked, sadness lingering in her voice.

Before Rake could respond, Steven spoke up from behind them.

"Honestly, Tonuko and Kyle seem so different. Sure, Tonuko is super strong, but Kyle just gives off a whole other vibe. I mean, he beat Tonuko in ten damn seconds! I watched it in person and still can't believe that happened!" Steven exclaimed.

The final ten seconds began counting down on the big screen, and when it hit five, Fox-Tails joined in the countdown.

"Yeah," a boy who sat at the edge of the advanced class stated, "Kyle is pretty damn awesome."

When the clock hit zero, the boy's deep blue hair sparkled from the light of the flames that burst from my arms.

Chapter 6

My Place

On the roof of the Dome, a figure lingered in the window. She had long, strawberry blonde hair styled into pigtails, and a constant, closed-mouth smile. She peered into the arena, then squealed when the timer began.

"I can't wait to watch Kyle fight! He's so dreamy, and so strong!" She sighed happily, then sat down with her legs crossed. "I'm so happy Tyrant let me come to watch these fights!"

After the Timer Struck Zero:

I waited a moment before striking, trying to lure Camilla into using her winds. The flames on my arms danced and roared, encouraging her to attack. I could tell from her personality the first couple days that she was easily provoked. She swayed her hands, and that's when I struck.

I ran at Camilla and threw two fireballs that landed just outside her hands' reach. The flames combined with the winds Camilla was manifesting, causing them to rapidly increase in power and throw her off balance. I slid in front of her and punched her right in the stomach. As she was soaring backward, I used flames to increase my speed tremendously and swiftly soared behind her, landing another punch on her back.

She was launched around twenty feet in the air; as she was landing, I announced, "You've had an easy path here Camilla, but it ends now. Don't feel bad. It's not fair you had to face me. Life isn't fair though."

Winds exploded on the ground and blew in every direction. I stomped my foot, sticking it into the ground so I wouldn't be swept off my feet.

"Come on, Camilla, prove that cocky bastard wrong! He's all bark and no bite, trust me! He's just trying to get into your head!" yelled the guy who sat on Camilla's bench, trying to encourage her. The guy's hair was very long and black with white lines that strongly resembled a spider's web. His bright green eyes contrasted his earth-brown skin, and his dark, baggy clothes looked dirty and rugged. I looked to my right and saw Hazel smirk as she glanced at the man.

"Don't listen to Devin, just focus on the fight! You've got her weakened, so don't fuck up; finish the job! You got this, Kyle, I believe in you!"

I nodded and slightly smiled again. For some reason unknown to me, Hazel's words of encouragement always put some kind of smile on my face that was hard to conceal. I turned back to Camilla, who had successfully formed two tornadoes while my head was turned. I tried to take a step back, but I apparently grounded my foot deeper than I thought. My foot was stuck in the ground, and as hard as I pulled, it wouldn't budge. I slightly panicked as I heard Fox-Tails over the intercom.

"It appears the tides have turned for Camilla! Kyle's foot is trapped in the ground, and he has two powerful tornadoes heading straight toward him! Can you feel that wind pressure folks? It's nauseating!"

I continued my attempt to pull my foot out, and only successfully did it when it was too late. One of the tornadoes sucked me up, then threw me into the sky. They dissipated, then Camilla soared toward me and landed a punch on my face. My body was turned in the air. I hit the top of the glass dome face first. The glass sizzled, and I was enraged. I pulled my feet under me and pushed hard to send myself flying toward the ground. With my feet under me again, I flipped in the air and landed upright on the ground. My landing caused a rumble throughout campus. A divot formed in the concrete beneath me.

You're gonna regret that big time, Camilla. I thought this would be just a simple warmup match . . .

I stomped toward Camilla, my fists bawled, and my eyes locked on hers. I rushed toward her, and she slowly backed up while raising her arms.

She threw a blade of wind at me, but I ducked underneath and then swiftly punched her hard on the cheek. She fell to her right, then I kicked her stomach, sending her sliding a few feet and leaving behind a small trail of blood from her mouth.

"What a powerful hit from Kyle! It appears blood has been drawn, meaning this fight is getting interesting!" Fox-Tails shouted into his mic after standing up from his seat. I heard countless people booing and screaming at me.

I ignored the ridicule and stepped toward Camilla. However, when I saw her eyes closed and how peaceful she looked . . . I stopped dead in my tracks. Her face reminded me of my mother's after being stabbed. I looked down at my hands, seeing her blood splattered on them. I slightly trembled, then a large gust of wind sent me flying into the air. Almost instantly, another gust of wind threw me to the ground. The impact sent cracks across the floor of the Dome, then a black hand made of sharp winds picked me up again.

"Oh, wow, what an amazing creature created by Camilla! That thing is as tall as the entire building!" Fox-Tails' smile faded slowly as he looked down at Camilla, who hadn't moved since my punch. "Wait a second, Camilla is unconscious on the ground. If that's true, then who's creation is this?"

The wind titan lifted me to its head, then slammed me into the ground again. I gasped for air when it lifted me yet another time but was quickly thrown into the ground once more. My right arm shattered, and blood was pouring from my head.

"Students, stay in your seats! The staff will handle the attack! Please remain calm!" Fox-Tails commanded.

I faintly heard screams from the crowd and looked at my frantic class before being slammed into the ground yet again.

"Quick, Devin, we gotta save the kid!" Hazel screamed after jumping from her seat.

Devin crossed his arms in front of his chest as he was running, then threw spider webs at the creature's feet. It tried to take a step forward but fell and dropped me in the process. As I was falling through the air, Hazel reached out with her demon arms and caught me. The creature vanished after it fell. I breathed heavily as Nurse Blavins and Iris ran to my aid.

On the Roof:

"How could you attack him like that Stafer? Tyrant specifically told us we aren't allowed to attack!" the girl who was watching the fight yelled at the man standing next to her. He continued peering into the arena, then turned around and yawned.

"Sorry little girl, but I was bored as hell. I wanted to see that kid in action—he intrigued me. Sadly, he couldn't handle my strength though," Stafer commented.

Stafer Candreon, Strength: Amplify—he can copy any person's strength and amplify it to an extreme using a dark power. If one of the people he copies is weak, he can combine a strength he has copied before to create one attack, such as the monster of Bobby's illusion and Camilla's wind.

"Don't you mean the girl's strength? You're just a phony whose entire being relies on the strengths of others," the girl retorted before crossing her arms.

He looked back at the girl with cold, ruby eyes.

"Don't insult me Laci, unless you wanna end up like Kyle. I'd suggest you keep your mouth shut with that weak ass mace of yours."

Laci pouted, then threw her hand in front of her and flung a mace at Stafer. The mace appeared out of nothingness, and it flew straight toward Stafer's face. He caught it with his bare hand. One of the spikes pierced directly through his palm. Stafer stared at his palm and watched as the wound healed itself. The mace fell to the ground, then sizzled and faded.

"How dare you attack one of your fellow Care-Givers? You can trust me that BloodShot will hear about this."

"Go ahead and tattle to that asshole, you lapdog!" Laci hissed as Stafer turned and walked away.

He made his way to the side of the building, then jumped off. In the air, a swirling black and yellow portal formed, then sucked in on itself after he passed through.

"I hate him!" Laci turned back to the glass dome and saw the event was cleaned up.

Back in the Arena:

I sat on my bench feeling very sore. The Blavins' healing can heal wounds but not cure the damn soreness. Yet, I was still very grateful for . . . both of them. Hazel put her arm around me, sighing.

"Well, that was a scare. Thankfully, whoever attacked you is gone now it seems."

I felt safe in her arm, and sighed as well, then smiled.

"You're lucky to have a friend (and a friend's mom) with such good healing powers, Kyle; otherwise, I don't know if you would have survived!"

I looked at the floor and squeezed the end of my shorts.

"Phew, that was quite a scare! However, the show must go on! Tonuko Kuntai and Alex Galeger, take the stage. Know security is searching campus for the attacker, and you two are completely safe!"

My eyes were watery, but I wasn't sure why. Hazel noticed my lack of response, but I spoke before she could ask anything.

"Do you really think that people think of me as a friend?" There was a painful silence, so I knew the answer.

What am I thinking? Why would anyone be my friend? Hell, I barely even know what a friend really is.

"Seriously? Of course there are people who think of you as a friend! I mean, I'd say we're becoming friends!" Hazel yelled after taking her arm off me and turning to face me.

I looked at her, then back at the ground. Even if I tried to hide it, my smile was growing.

There're people who think of me as a friend . . . I can't believe it. Even though I'm cocky, even though I'm an asshole about my goals, there are still people who . . . care . . . about me.

The screen counted down the final three seconds, then Alex and Tonuko's battle began. Tonuko immediately stomped his foot, changing the entire layout of the stage. There were random hills, spikes, tunnels, and objects.

"Why did he do that? What's his strategy?" I asked.

"Well, now he knows the terrain he just made, and Alex doesn't. It gives him an advantage by knowing all the nooks and crannies of the stage."

I nodded and stared at Alex, who was analyzing his surroundings. "Either way, I think Alex can outsmart Tonuko. He's pretty bright, both literally and figuratively."

"Yeah, he does seem to be pretty smart, and his strength is amazing," I added.

"Well, not necessarily. For raw fighting skills, sure, but in missions where heroes need to be stealthy or hidden, it is actually a hindrance. In any dark situation—like nighttime or in a dark building—Alex can be seen fighting from a mile away."

My eyes widened, and I glanced at my hands. I squeezed them into fists, then looked at Hazel.

"I never thought of it like that. It's the same with my fire. I can be seen fighting almost anywhere in a dark situation." Hazel nodded and crossed her arms while leaning on the wall behind us. My eyes sparkled with amazement, then I complimented, "Woah, you're so smart Hazel!"

"Thank you, but don't count yourself out in dark situations. You also have that enhanced strength, which is a powerful and versatile strength on its own. Once you learn how to control and use your strengths here, you will be able to use your strengths in separate instances."

I smiled and looked up at the sky through the glass dome.

"I can't wait to be able to control my strengths more. I'll be able to handle myself and save those around me. I'll be able to fight better than I could against BloodShot, and Bobby in the alley, and now this wind user–"

"Boy, these villains are really coming after you, huh?"

I swiftly looked away and nodded, clenching my jaw.

Shit, thanks for making it obvious you're after me Tyrant; you jerk.

"It must be because of my two strengths. Not trying to sound cocky but having two strengths that work this well together sure makes me a threat to villains like Tyrant, right?" I bluffed.

"Yeah, you know that is true. Let's discuss this more after the tournament; it seems like this battle is getting really intense!"

She was definitely right, because when I looked up, I saw Alex flying at Tonuko, who had a large chunk of the ground stretched with him while he was about twenty feet in the air. The cement on his torso also stretched onto his fists, creating concrete gloves. Alex used his wings combined with the power of his light to beam at Tonuko at speeds I don't think I would be able to react to. However, Tonuko swung a quick punch at the same time as Alex. They punched each other (Alex hit Tonuko's face and Tonuko hit Alex's hip), then both flew in opposite directions. The cement around Tonuko's arms and torso shattered, and one of Alex's wings dangled and was broken. Alex used his other wing to glide back to the ground a few feet away from Tonuko, who had stood and was breathing heavily.

"Damn, you're strong Alex," Tonuko panted.

"Yeah, but this earth manipulation makes it so hard to get a solid hit on you. No offense, but it's pretty annoying," Alex said with a weak smile.

They both chuckled, then Tonuko reached out a fist.

"Let the best man win," Tonuko stated, offering a fist bump. Alex fist bumped him and nodded with an even bigger smile than before, then Tonuko stepped back and took a deep breath. Alex did the same, exploding into a mess of light. The light still helped increase Alex's speed, even with its weakened power, and he was able to speed around, then punch Tonuko in the back of the head before Tonuko could react. He stumbled forward, then Alex swiped Tonuko's feet out from underneath him and let him hit the ground hard.

"Th–That's it, I win," Alex gasped as he struggled to stay standing. The ground beneath Alex wrapped around him from the feet up, eventually reaching his neck. Alex was clearly in pain as the cement's grasp grew tighter, so he shouted weakly, "Y–You win, you win!"

Tonuko stayed on the ground, but I could see his grin as he stuttered, "Don't c–count your chickens before they h–h–hatch." The ground let go of Alex, causing him to fall face first at Tonuko's feet.

"Wow, what a fight! These two are very skilled. Well done boys! But now, the moment we've all been hoping for! The rematch of the century: Kyle Straiter versus Tonuko Kuntai. We will be taking a thirty-minute hiatus before returning for the finale!" Fox-Tails announced. He put the mic down and hit the mute button, then took a swig of water. His happy expression faded to a stern stare as he looked over at Principal Lane, who was seated next to him.

"Well, what do we do about that attack? This is the second on-campus one on Kyle in just the first three days of school, and the third in total."

"We must increase security around campus and look for any weak points in and around the walls. As well as this, we must contact the Seven Influential about perhaps a teleporter within the Care-Givers. I'm unsure, but I have a feeling that they aren't just waltzing in over our wall. Instead, these criminals are being placed in specific locations where Kyle is," Principal Lane answered while looking toward Hazel and me.

Hazel went to talk with Devin, so I took a breather and sat on my bench. When I looked at the sky, I saw a man looking down at me. He had sky blue eyes and blonde hair that glistened in the light. We made eye contact, then I snapped and ran out of the arena before anyone could stop me.

What the fuck are you doing here, you bastard?

A Few Minutes Prior:

Tyrant stepped out of a portal extremely similar to the one Stafer jumped into. He ran his hands through his hair, then looked over at Laci. Tyrant wore a magenta dress shirt with a solid red tie, and sleek black dress pants along with black dress shoes. He fixed his tie, then spoke.

"Laci, what's this I hear about Stafer attacking Kyle, and you attacking Stafer?" Tyrant asked while staring intimidatingly into her eyes.

She gulped, then explained, "W–Well, Stafer came out of nowhere and a–attacked Kyle. I was so mad that he d–disobeyed you, so I threw my mace at him to scare him off."

Tyrant slowly walked over to her, then raised his hand.

Laci flinched and exclaimed, "I only did it because I don't like when people disrespect you! Stafer and BloodShot don't give you the respect you deserve!"

Tyrant lowered his hand and put it on her head. She looked up and saw his comforting smile.

"Laci, you don't need to be afraid of me. Thank you for protecting my rules but don't resort to violence on your own allies. They are both new, both need time to grow and learn to trust us and themselves. Never forget, with great power comes even greater responsibility."

Laci relaxed and smiled, then Tyrant peered into the arena. He and I made eye contact, and he smiled as I ran toward the doors of the Dome.

"Looks like we're going to have a little visitor."

I made my way up the ladder to the roof, then jumped from the last step, and stood ready to attack. Never in my life had I been so close to killing someone.

"Wh–Why are you here? Get the hell away from this campus!" I screeched before igniting my hands.

Tyrant put his hands up, clearly not wanting to fight.

"Don't try and pussy out on me now! You abandoned me seven years ago, and now you show up and just look at me from a distance?" My voice croaked as I shouted, "You ruined my life, took everything I loved away from me!"

"Kyle, listen to me: If you draw too much attention to us up here, then someone is going to find us and hear you talking like you know me," Tyrant stated after taking a step closer.

I backed up and trembled more violently.

"You took *everything* from me! I don't care who knows, *I just want to kill you!* If you're gone, then nobody else will have to suffer like I have my entire life! If you're gone, then I fulfill my destiny! If–"

"If I'm gone, then *what will that make you?* What will you do after I'm gone, what's your plan for the rest of your life?" Tyrant cut me off.

I stood wide eyed; my lip quivered. "You're so focused on me all the time, how about you focus on yourself for once? Look down there!" Tyrant pointed behind him before continuing, "There are people down there who are going to be with you every step of the way for the next four years! Why can't you open your eyes and stop obsessing about something that happened seven years ago?"

"I don't care how long ago it happened; I think about it every fucking day! You don't get to tell me what to do, nobody does! Only my parents can, and tell me, Tyrant, were you really a parent to me?"

Tyrant clenched his jaw and gave me the same dirty, intimidating, furious look he'd given me all my life.

"You ruined my life, dammit! For once, leave me the hell alone!"

"I ruined your life? Are you serious? Ever since you were born, you've ruined mine! You are the reason the only thing on this planet I loved is gone!" Tyrant erupted while stomping his foot at me.

I took a step back.

"Wh–What do you mean? You killed my mom. You took away the only person who loved me! What right do you have to say I ruined your life?"

Tyrant's fists were shaking with rage; he pointed at me after letting out a huff.

"The only reason Gem is dead is *you!* If *you* weren't born, I wouldn't have had to kill her! If *you* weren't born, I wouldn't have had my family blackmailed by my own people! If *you* weren't born, my wife would still be alive, and everything would be normal! But no, since *you just had to be here, she's fucking dead, and you're the only one to blame! Kyle, your stubbornness killed your mother!*"

My lip quivered and my head spun.

"N–No, you're lying. You're a villain, you killed her. How could it be my fault? I was innocent, the victim!" I responded, on the verge of tears. Water brimmed in my eyes before a tear dripped from each one.

"You were so rebellious; you just wouldn't listen to me. God, you made me so angry, I didn't know what to do! Pressure was building, rumors were spreading: my son was going to be a hero, he wouldn't join the Care-Givers! I don't know, nor care, about how heroes would treat that, but criminals threatened me, my wife, my home, my family! And no, that does not include *you.* I couldn't care less about what they did to you! I hoped they would kill you so Gem wouldn't have to stress anymore!"

He's lying, he has to be. I couldn't have killed my mom. So why . . . why does he look so certain?

"Kyle, the criminals were going to kill her. They would ransack the house, burn it to the ground, and trap her inside. I couldn't let that happen! They would find her; there were eyes watching my every move, so I did the only thing I could to give her a peaceful death. Now look at you, I'd hoped you would have just killed yourself by now," Tyrant explained.

I stepped back, shaking my head and crying.

*Stop, please stop. It's not my fault, it's not my fault, **it's not my fault.** It's your fault, it's your fault, **it's your fault.** I hate you, I hate you, **I hate you!***

With one more step, I fell off the roof. Tyrant didn't bother helping me, he just turned and yelled, "I'll be watching! Don't disappoint me like you disappoint everyone else!"

While falling through the air, I hoped I would hit the ground and not wake up. However, I was caught by Fox-Tails. We landed and slid a few feet. He looked up at the roof while placing me down. I stuttered, at a complete loss for words. Fox-Tails sighed.

"I know Kyle, I heard some of it. Don't listen to him. He's manipulative and pure evil. If you let what he said go to heart, then he's already won."

I nodded, then took a deep breath and calmed myself. After a moment, I walked past Fox-Tails.

"Are you okay?"

"Yeah," I stated, "I'll be fine. Right now, I just need to win this fight."

I marched through the doors of the Dome and made my way to my bench, then sat down. Hazel walked over and sat next to me.

"What was that all about? Are you alright?"

"I'm fine!" I snapped while looking at the ground. Hazel clearly didn't believe me but nodded and put her arm around me. I felt goosebumps form and moved away from her reach. This worried her more, but before she could say anything, Fox-Tails cleared his throat while on the mic.

"Well folks, the break is over! Time to reveal some little fun facts about our contestants!" Everyone looked over at the screen that flashed Tonuko's grade-school picture. He looked much younger; his hair was shorter and straight, and he was much skinnier. The picture moved to the top-left corner of the screen, then a list of information appeared:

<u>Name: Tonuko Kuntai</u>
Age: 14
Parents: Danielle Kuntai (Vice Principal of Eccentric High) and
　　　　David Kuntai (Pro-Hero: Savior)
Strength: Ground Manipulation
Age of Control: Seven years old
Elementary School: County Elementary

"Tonuko gained control over his strength at the young age of seven and was named the top prospect of the incoming freshman class! He comes from the great school of County Elementary, and his parents are our very own vice principal and the famous hero Savior!" Fox-Tails informed the crowd. Everyone cheered, shouted, and whistled. All seemed to be rooting for him.

Tonuko's information faded, then an old picture of me popped up on the screen. I had hair a little longer than my current style and two black eyes along with missing teeth and a few band aids plastered on my face. In the background, a man who could be seen only up to the stomach was wearing a black tux and holding my shoulders.

<u>Name: Kyle Straiter</u>
Age: 14
Parents: N/A
Strength: Fire Control and Enhanced Strength
Age of Control: N/A
Elementary School: Trinity Plus Elementary School

The crowd's cheering was gone at this point and confused whispers could be heard all over.

"Uh, well, Kyle Straiter is a generational talent with two strengths and . . . he came from Trinity Plus. That is . . . all the information we have on him," Fox-Tails stated nervously.

The crowd turned angry and started yelling; they were confused and scared of me.

"Well, I don't know about you folks, but I love a battle between the popular boy and mysterious boy! Let's get this party started!" Fox-Tails screamed, trying to change the mood.

The crowd almost instantly cheered again, and I took a sigh with relief. I stood and looked over at Tonuko. He gave me a smirk, then walked toward the stage. I did the same.

"Hey, Kyle, let the best man win," Tonuko said while holding his hand out to me.

I looked at his hand, then shook it.

"Let the best man win, Tonuko."

He looked surprised that I actually shook his hand. We then went to our corners. Fox-Tails announced for the fight to begin, and the boy with blue hair jumped out of his seat.

"Come on Kyle, you got this bud!" the boy shouted happily.

"Just who are you? You keep talking as if you know him," Khloe asked snarkily. The boy with blue hair didn't need to introduce himself because Jaxon had him covered.

"That's Daniel Onso. He, Kyle, and I went to the same elementary school. I don't expect Kyle to remember us though. Kyle and I grew apart last summer, and Daniel moved cities a few years ago," Jaxon explained while leaning back in his chair.

Daniel nodded but didn't take his eyes off the stage.

Tonuko changed the entire scenery of the stage again, bending the ground to make weird hills, spikes, twists, walls, and holes. I analyzed the area I was in, then saw a ripple in the ground to my right. I leapt into the air, effectively dodging a wave in the ground Tonuko had created. Fire burst out of my feet, allowing me to keep levitating. Tonuko growled, then smacked his hands on the ground. Spikes flew at me, but I dodged each one, then I charged in at rapid speeds. Tonuko swiftly threw up his hands and created a wall late enough to stop me before I could charge a strong enough punch to break it. I flipped back, landing a dozen feet away from where he stood.

I was really hoping to knock him out in one hit again. Oh well, now I know most of his tricks. He changes the environment to gain an advantage, uses spikes and waves to attack, and walls to defend.

"What great defense by Tonuko! We know Kyle was able to beat Tonuko swiftly before, so let's see what Tonuko can cook up this time!"

Tonuko became angry at the statement and ran toward me. He created a few spikes to distract me, then dodged my punch and dragged his hand on the ground before swinging at me. When he dragged his hand, he created a concrete glove and socked my right cheek, sending me flying to my left. I skidded a few feet and hit a wall hard. Tonuko didn't stop the onslaught; a pillar flew through the air before hitting me on my stomach and chest. I coughed blood, then wound up and punched down on the pillar, causing it to shatter.

"This won't end like last time Kyle. I'm prepared this time! I know how you fight; my senses are much more on edge now, ready for you to blindly attack whenever!"

I slowly stood; my chest hurt with every movement. Tonuko punched me in the face, then kicked my side. I hunched over as he stated, "You're too cocky for your own good, and if you become a hero, it's gonna lead to someone getting killed."

I briskly grabbed his head, then smashed it into the ground. The ground cracked, and bits of rubble flew everywhere. I panted heavily while looking down at him. My face was full of rage.

"Just shut up already," I seethed before throwing him into the air.

His body spun around, then I jumped and crashed into him, leading with my shoulder. He flew into the Dome's glass, and I followed up with a kick, pushing both of us through the glass. We landed on the roof of the arena, and there, a dozen feet away from us, stood Tyrant and Laci.

Chapter 7

Building Trust

Tyrant laughed while looking at the two of us. "Oh my, it looks like you brought me a new toy, Kyle! Thank you so much!" Tonuko was shocked and looked over at me. I stood to the side of him but stepped to block Tyrant's view of Tonuko. I moved my left hand back toward Tonuko and my right hand in front of me toward Tyrant and Laci.

"S–Stay back Tyrant. Leave us alone, don't hurt us." It took all my might to not tear up thinking about our earlier interaction, and it felt like something was stuck in my throat. Tyrant cackled as he took a step forward, but I didn't back down.

"You can do whatever you want to me but leave Tonuko out of this."

Tonuko was shocked to hear this and couldn't form any words. He just stared wide-eyed at the back of my head, then glanced at Tyrant. Tyrant's smile was gone. He instead looked at me bitterly.

"Look at that, Kyle Straiter acting all noble. The same kid who everyone hates, who is violent and disobedient, is acting like a hero again. You aren't a hero Kyle, you're a violent criminal waiting to conform. Once you do, *you're mine.*"

Tyrant ran toward me, and though full of fear, I punched at him. He dodged my fist, then pushed me aside. I fell and hit the ground hard. I looked up and saw Tyrant staring eye-to-eye with Tonuko.

"You are a nuisance. Maybe I should just take your strength now so you don't get stronger for the future."

I can't let him hurt Tonuko. Tyrant is my responsibility; I won't let him hurt anyone else!

I tackled Tyrant, then stood and pushed Tonuko through the Dome's glass.

"Laci, attack him!" Tyrant commanded while pointing at me.

Laci threw out her hand and let her mace fly at me. I looked Tonuko dead in the eyes while a couple of tears dripped down my cheeks, then Laci's mace hit my back, and I fell face first through the window. Tonuko was shocked, and Hazel's arm caught him. Hazel missed me though, and I fell to the ground. A loud crash was heard throughout campus, and the ground rumbled.

Before I hit the ground, two black tentacles shot out of my chest and absorbed the blow. When I had landed, I was relatively unscathed from the fall, but there were multiple holes in my back from Laci's mace. I breathed heavily, stunned from what just happened.

"Kyle!" Tonuko screeched after being put down. He ran over to me, but I looked up at him and put a finger over my lips.

"Don't tell anyone about what happened up there. I'll explain it all later, I promise."

Tonuko stuttered, then closed his mouth and nodded. Hazel and the guy who was at Tonuko's bench ran to make sure we were okay. Once they deemed us fine, we continued the fight. Fox-Tails told everyone we had been fighting on the roof and fallen. Thankfully, Tyrant's name was not mentioned.

Tonuko and I seemed off our game. We were both making simple mistakes: missing attacks, letting our guards down, and moving slower than usual.

"What's up with them?" Rake asked with a yawn. He leaned back in his seat and rested his hands behind his head.

"They must have said something to each other while on the roof that either pissed them off or confused them. Also, I'm sure Kyle isn't feeling great after that big fall," Khloe analyzed. She was much more focused on the battle than her peers.

"You're way too smart Khloe, it's kinda scary. You're so perceptive," Scarlett stated. She acted like a shiver crawled up her spine. Khloe giggled and sat up straight.

"I mean, it's just how my strength is. Hey, looks like those two might finally be waking up a little," Khloe excitedly informed Scarlett as she pointed at the stage.

I avoided three pillars that Tonuko sent after me, then ran at him. He sent a pillar at my head from the ground next to him, but I slid under to dodge it, hopped back up, and socked him in the face. He soared back but managed to maneuver his body in the air so his feet were up and his head was near the ground; then he dragged his fingers on the ground and swiftly threw his hand behind him. A piece of the ground curved up and caught him before he fell out of the stage boundaries. Usually, he would jump off the bent ground and gather himself; this is what I expected. Instead, he threw himself at me using a pillar to boost his speed, and we collided heads before falling to the ground. I laid on my back for one-too-many seconds. Tonuko used the ground to throw me into the air, then created two huge fists that soared at either side of my body. He used his own fists to control the concrete hands and punched the right side of my body. I soared into the other hand's palm, then it threw me back into the air. My vision was hazy, and I felt very weak. Tonuko wound up his fists over his head, intertwined his fingers, then swung as hard as he could. The concrete hands punched me extremely hard, and I went flying down and crashed into the ground. The entire campus rumbled. The two concrete hands crumpled on top of me.

"Oh my folks, that might just be it! Tonuko unleashed a beautiful attack that must've left Kyle feeling sore! I'm calling it now; this fight is ova'!" Fox-Tails screamed in the mic while standing up excitedly.

Tonuko panted and stood with a hunch, trying not to fall over.

"Come on Kyle, you have to get up! Don't lose!" Daniel erupted his feet.

Some of the students around him were shocked by the random scream, and Steven laughed.

"Sorry fanboy, but I think that's it! Kyle is done!" Steven contained his laughter and looked over at Daniel. Daniel was staring back with cold eyes and a sharp smile."

"Nah, you don't know Kyle like I do. He's not done until he wins," Daniel stated boldly.

Steven choked for a retort, then rolled his eyes and looked back at the stage.

The rock pile moved slightly, then it exploded in a fiery mess. Tonuko was swept off his feet and exploded rubble bits rained down on the stage and crowd. I weakly stood in the crater made by my fall; my head was gushing blood, my jaw and left arm were broken, and my right eye was swollen shut. Tonuko looked at me wide-eyed and tried to stand.

Stay down, asshole.

Out of my right foot, a wisp of flames shot at Tonuko and covered his legs. He fell over again and wrapped concrete tightly around his legs. When the concrete fell off, his skin was horribly burned, and he had bleeding blisters all over his legs. While Tonuko was down and in agony, I went in for my finishing blow.

This is it, time to finally end this. Everyone here will know I'm not to be messed with . . . everyone.

Flames erupted out of my right hand, and I slowly raised it above my head. The flames roared above me and grew bigger while forming into a blade-figure. I took a step forward, then swung my hand down toward Tonuko. The blade of fire landed directly on him. The bottom of the stage was covered in flames, then, when the flames touched the ground, there was a massive explosion between us. I was thrown off my feet but used fire as a booster again and stabilized myself in the air. Tonuko, however, flew out of the stage boundaries and hit the wall behind him, then slid to the ground. Since he was outside of the stage, I won.

"What. A. *COMEBACK!* ***KYLE WINS IT ALL!***" Fox-Tails screamed while jumping up and down like a kid.

There was a mix of cheers and boos all around. I fell onto my back and looked up at the glass Dome. I didn't see anyone looking into the building anymore, but I still pointed to the sky, tensing my other fist.

I know you saw me Tyrant, you saw how much I've grown. Be afraid, this is me, this is Kyle Straiter. I will kill you; I will avenge Mom. I didn't kill her, you did. I'll take down the villain society you built step by step. Just you wait.

Hazel ran onto the stage and knelt beside me. She put her hand behind my head and looked down at me, snapping in front of my eyes.

"You alright Kyle? You have some pretty serious injuries," Hazel asked before waving over Mrs. Blavins.

"Of course I–I'm fine, I won!"

Iris was healing Tonuko, and Mrs. Blavins began healing me.

Principal Lane announced on the mic, "Will all freshman honors' students please make their way to the stage. The rankings will be listed on the screen in one minute."

My classmates walked down the stairs, and after I was healed enough, I stood and walked over to Tonuko. He looked up at me with a stern, but defeated, expression. I could tell he was expecting me to insult him.

If I want to be a hero, and not be like Tyrant, then I have to start acting like one. Everyone else did this, so maybe I should too.

"Good fight," I said while reaching out my hand. Tonuko snickered and shook his head, then took my hand and stood.

"Yeah, yeah, good fight," he responded. His legs were shaky, causing him to fall over again. Alex grabbed Tonuko's other arm. We helped him stay upright while the rankings appeared one by one.

In order from last to first, our class rankings were as follows:

Donte Gavinson, Jessica Alter, Jaxon Call, Zayden Attack, Iris Blavins, Cora Wavice, Steven Mallnen, Khloe Basken, Scarlett Yalvo, Anya Lokel, Cindy Theon, Rake Clause, Camilla Xavier, Alex Galeger, Tonuko Kuntai, Kyle Straiter.

"No way I dropped five places! This is so dumb!" Steven complained with his arms crossed.

Khloe snickered and shrugged.

"Maybe just be a little smarter and you would have moved up majorly like me!" Steven growled and turned away from her.

Donte looked down, clearly pretty upset with his ranking. He looked at his hands, bawling his fists.

"I'll just have to work harder and be smarter. I won't make a dumb mistake like I did against Camilla ever again!"

He looked up and smiled, then Rake threw his arm around Donte.

"You got this man! Just start using your speed in ways you haven't, and you'll get crazy stronger!"

Rake smiled at Donte, then looked up at his name.

"I gotta say, fifth place is pretty nice, but I can be better!"

I did it, I actually fucking did it. I did it for you Mom, I fulfilled one of my promises. I'm number one.

"We are very happy with this freshman class. You all are amazing and have so much potential! I cannot wait to see you grow over the next four years! As your principal, I will protect you, guide you, and be someone you can look up to and go to if you have any concerns! Good luck with your training and work hard!"

Principal Lane's speech was motivating. I kinda wished he'd said something motivating before we fought, but y'know, it was still a nice gesture.

The classes were dismissed, and we were sent to our dorms to recover and prepare for our tomorrow, when our first day of real training would begin.

While I laid in my bed, I heard a knock at my door. I stood and looked through the peep-hole; Tonuko was standing in front of my door with his arms crossed. I opened the door, and asked, "What do you want?" He looked me dead in the eyes, it was pretty intense.

"So, you said you would tell me later about Tyrant. What the hell was that on the roof?"

I felt a pit grow in my stomach, but I didn't let my nervousness and fear show.

Instead, I explained, "It may sound cocky, but since I have two strengths, I'm pretty valuable to both heroes and villains. That being said, Tyrant has been out to get me since he discovered me. He acts like I'm just a destined criminal. I'm not, I'm a hero. I didn't want you to get involved, so I pushed you back into the arena, away from the villains."

Tonuko nodded while I told the fake story, then sighed.

"Alright, that makes sense. I'm gonna go out on a limb and say you don't want people knowing you have a vague connection with Tyrant, so I'll keep it on the D.L."

I smiled slightly and nodded.

Wow, he's actually being pretty understanding about this. What if I told him the truth, would he act the same? No, of course not. If anyone finds out that Tyrant and I are blood related, not just a villain who wants me in his posse, then I'd be arrested and probably put to death.

"Let's tear down Tyrant's society. We're both really strong, we're both destined to be highly ranked heroes. Let's be the ones to finally defeat him," Tonuko suggested while holding out his fist.

I looked at his fist and felt slightly offended.

"I appreciate the offer, but I won't be needing to team up with you to do it. I'll kill Tyrant, that's what I'm meant to do." Tonuko raised an eyebrow as he put his fist down. "Tyrant will die at my hands; I promise you that. That's all I'm training to do." I turned around and walked back into my room. I tried to close the door, but Tonuko stopped it from fully closing.

"We're literally wanting to do the same thing. I've watched Tyrant terrorize heroes for years, and it pisses me off so much. I hate that man; I hate everything related to him. I'm not saying you need my help. I'm just saying let's both work hard to beat him. You get it?"

I took a deep breath, then stated, "You must have not heard me; *I* am going to *kill* Tyrant. It's *my* destiny, it's all *I'm here for.*"

Tonuko felt uneasy with that last sentence. Before he could say anything, I pushed him back and closed my door while looking down at him.

Tonuko won't take this from me, no one will. I'll be the one to kill Tyrant, I have to. If I can't do that, then why the hell was I even born?

I laid on my bed and closed my eyes.

Mom, people are weird. They keep trying to make relationships with me, but what's the point? Why get close to people when I'll just lose them eventually? No, I'm gonna train myself, get stronger, and live out what I'm meant to do. That's all life is, living up to expectations. People are going to have very high expectations of me now, and I'll live out them all.

I fell asleep within minutes and was terrorized with nightmares about Tyrant.

For the next few days, my schedule was the same. I went to class and had two separate training sessions for two hours each, slept between sessions, and maybe ate something; then trained more on my own and went to sleep. I barely talked to my classmates, but they were all beginning to bond with each other. I felt like an outcast, but I didn't care.

I'm not here to make friends, I'm here to kill Tyrant. The less people I know along the dangerous path, the less I'll have to hold me back.

On Friday, we packed our bags and waited for Ms. Palkun and the advanced teacher to get us so we could leave for Veena. The school bought two buses for us, each with barely enough seats to fit both classes when we were doubled up in the seats. Ms. Palkun told us two juniors and two sophomores would be joining us, so we'd have extra supervision since Veena wasn't a very safe city.

Veena was the wrestling capital of the nation and about a four-hour drive from E.H. Wrestling was the most popular sport in the world because people love watching others fight with their strengths in a controlled environment. We would go to the most nationally renowned fighting tournament where the famous new fighter, Foul Odor, would take on Catastrophe, an older and stronger fighter. While I waited on the couch in the dorm, a boy with blue hair sat next to me. When I looked over, my eyes widened.

There's no fucking way.

"Hey Kyle, long time no see!" Daniel exclaimed with a big smile. I stared at him with a heavy feeling in my stomach, and I let out a small gasp.

"D–Daniel, you're here? But you left me four years ago, why are you back?"

Daniel and I dapped each other and smiled, then pulled in and hugged.

"Sorry we moved away, but I'm back! We still live in Parane, but since this is a public hero school, my parents sent me here! Isn't that great? We can be best buds again!"

I chuckled and looked at his blue hair.

"So, what the hell is this about? You dyed your hair blue?"

Daniel nodded and his smile faded. He looked over at the other kids who were downstairs to his right.

"You remember my sister, Abby, right?" I nodded, now a little worried. "She was flown out across the country to track the Care-Giver's Strategist because he was making suspicious moves involving drugs. That was four years ago, and she hasn't been heard from since. We were sent her sunglasses from her hero costume two years ago and were told she had passed in battle. I dyed my hair the same color as hers so she could be with me every step of the way of my hero journey!"

I could tell Daniel was still sore about it, but he wasn't going to be all sappy and would keep pushing forward. I respected that but didn't understand how he could do it.

"Let's go students, we gotta' get on the road! Everyone pick a seat buddy, or whatever, and give your bags to Excalibur at the buses!" Ms. Palkun demanded after opening our dormitory door. Daniel and I agreed to be seat partners so we could catch up on the bus ride. After handing our bags to Excalibur, we made our way onto one of the buses and sat in the second to last seat on the right. I sat in the window seat and looked out at campus.

After everyone was on a bus, Ms. Palkun climbed aboard the one I was in, and Excalibur took a seat in the other bus. Tonuko and Anya were in the seat across from Daniel and me, and Alex and Rake sat in front of us. Behind us was Hazel and a sophomore girl I had never seen before. She knelt on her seat and looked down at me, then held out a hand.

"Hey hotshot, I'm Kate! I'm Queen of the sophomores and the top of the sophomore honors' class! Nice to meet ya'!"

I looked at her hand and shook it, then she pulled me up and put me in a headlock.

"I'll keep you in check during this trip! Don't need you having any freakouts or anything like that! Let's all just have a nice, villain-free trip!"

I pushed her off me and rolled my eyes, then sulked in my seat. It would be a long, long four-hour drive.

Once we arrived at the hotel, we unloaded and grabbed our bags. My eyes sparkled as I looked at the deluxe hotel. I heard Excalibur inform some students, "This is the same hotel where all the pro-wrestlers will be staying.

You should all be thanking Kyle Straiter and Tonuko Kuntai for getting us this amazing hotel. The owner is very ecstatic to meet the two of them!"

Tonuko walked up next to me while sighing.

"Welcome to the fame, Kyle. This is gonna happen a lot," he stated. When I didn't respond, he looked over at me, confused. "Kyle?"

"What did you say? Sorry, I was just in such a trance looking at this massive hotel. It's so much nicer than my house!" I exclaimed.

"Really, this is way nicer than your house?" Hazel asked, walking up to Tonuko and me with Kate, Devin, and a sophomore boy.

The sophomore boy leaned on Tonuko and ruffled his hair. I was shocked at his height; he had to be around six-foot-eight. Tonuko and I were pretty similar in height, around six-foot-two.

"Get off me Jon!" Tonuko grumbled, pushing Jon's arm. Jon chuckled, then walked past me with Kate into the hotel. I entered as well with Tonuko, and a familiar-looking man walked up to us. He was no older than twenty and had slicked-back auburn hair and short, wide silicon tubes sticking out of his arms.

"There they are, Tonuko Kuntai and Kyle Straiter! It's a pleasure to meet you two!"

I recognized the man now—it was Foul Odor. I shook his hand and smiled. Tonuko did the same.

"Follow me, the big man wants to meet you!"

We followed Foul Odor to an office in the back of the hotel. When the three of us entered, there was a very large man sitting in a big chair. He had long, golden locks and wore a tight button-down shirt.

"Ah, Tonuko Kuntai and Kyle Straiter, nice to meet you. I am Mr. Clarence, I run the show. You two are very strong."

We both nodded and stood tall. Compliments were pretty damn nice.

"Now, have fun and enjoy the tournament. Be careful wandering around town though, there have been a lot of kidnappings lately."

Kidnappings? I had heard about teenagers and young adults going missing around the area. I've wondered who's in charge of it though . . .

"We'll be sure to watch out, thank you for the warning," Tonuko said with a smile. We said goodbye to Mr. Clarence, then walked out with Foul Odor.

"Yeah, it's pretty dangerous around here right now. I'm kind of surprised your class was allowed to come here. The kidnappings have gotten way worse over the past month, and I've heard it's got something to do with Tyrant." A pit grew in my stomach. "Oh well, I'm sure you will all be fine. Just don't go out too late, alright?" Foul Odor held out his fist, offering a fist bump. I gave him one, then he walked away.

"That can't be good. An increase in the number of kidnappings in the area, but no one is in a rush to solve the problem? Really?" Tonuko thought aloud while looking around the hotel lobby.

It was vast and very open. You could see all the doors to the hotel rooms if you stood in the middle of the lobby. There was a water fountain, and the elevator walls were made of glass. Tonuko looked at me for an opinion, but I just shrugged at him.

"Oh come on, you can't tell me you're not curious about solving this kidnapping problem."

I walked toward a couch and waved for him to follow. We sat down and my leg started bouncing.

"I didn't wanna show it around the director since he's such a professional, but holy shit I wanna solve this so badly!" Tonuko smirked and crossed his arms. "We can act like real heroes and stop the kidnappers! What do you say?"

I held a hand out to him. He shook my hand while smiling with a closed mouth. He let go of my hand and flipped one of his bangs out of his face, then sighed.

"I completely agree with you, but we're gonna need to get some backup. As confident as I am in myself, the two of us are amateurs, and this is a major scandal. There's no way we could beat the kidnapper, or kidnappers, by ourselves."

I rolled my eyes and scoffed, "Oh come on, of course we could. You back me up with defense, and I charge in and beat them down, piece of cake!"

Tonuko tensed his fist. He stood and grabbed his backpack.

"Use your brain a little, Kyle This isn't training; these villains would want to kill us if we tried to fight them. I'll talk with the juniors and sophomores then get back to you." Tonuko walked toward one of the three elevators and started talking to Alex, who was waiting for the elevator as well.

I shook my head, pissed off with Tonuko.

Whatever, I could beat those villains all by myself if I wanted to. I thought you were confident like me, what the hell is this backing out bullshit? I'll find and beat down those kidnappers, especially if they have a connection with Tyrant . . .

I entered an elevator a few minutes later with Daniel, and he sighed loudly after we took off.

"Man, my parents have been assholes lately. They were so disappointed in me when I was put in advanced instead of honors. Like, c'mon, give me a break!" he complained.

I rolled my eyes, a little annoyed with him.

"Relax Daniel, they're just setting goals and expectations for you. If there was no one to set those goals or expectations, then no one would get anything done."

He looked through the glass and muttered, "But they set goals not even you can reach. They're assholes."

I clenched my fist and closed my eyes, absolutely furious.

"At least you have parents! Don't complain when you can go home to a loving family!" I screamed at him.

"I get it Kyle, I really do. I feel horrible about what happened with your family, but that doesn't invalidate my problems! Not everything is about you!" Daniel erupted, shocking me.

The elevator door opened.

Before walking away, I stated, "Don't take your parents for granted, and do not tell me about my past problems. You left, the fuck would you know?"

Daniel was sweating bullets, and I could somewhat tell he didn't exactly mean what he was shouting. However, what was said was said.

Daniel is selfish now too. What the hell is wrong with people? I should've never been friends with him in the first place if he's gonna act like that.

When I entered my room, I laid on my bed and fell asleep within minutes. I needed a nap and wouldn't get much sleep for a while after tonight . . .

Chapter 8

Involvement

Around 8:00 p.m., there was a knock at my door. I answered after a couple of minutes and was met with Tonuko, Hazel, Kate, Jon, Devin, Alex, Camilla, and Anya.

"Come on Kyle, let's get a bite to eat. There's a nice restaurant down the block," Hazel suggested. I looked back at the dark hotel room.

"I guess I'll stop having *so* much fun to hang out with you guys," I retorted with a grin.

Hazel giggled, and we left for the restaurant.

The place was a classic inn with booths and round tables, along with a long table in the middle of the room. We sat in a booth and asked a waitress if we could pull up an extra table to seat us all together. After she agreed, we settled in and ordered drinks.

"Well," Hazel started with a sigh, "we all know what we need to discuss here. The fighting tournament starts tomorrow, so we need to have a plan on how we're going to approach tracking down the kidnapper."

A couple of people nodded, but I just sat back in my seat and took a deep breath.

Lame, why do we need to come up with a strategy?

"Let's just sneak away while the fighting is going on since everyone will be distracted, then start our search from there. It shouldn't be too hard to track down the kidnappers with the strengths we have," I suggested before yawning.

To my surprise, the group agreed.

"Yeah, if we leave while the fight is getting intense, no one will really be paying attention to us. Even if we do get in trouble after, when we have the kidnapper captured, they won't be too mad at us," Jon agreed with a smile.

I'd never seen this sophomore around school, surprisingly, but I liked him already. He had a bleached buzz cut, but he'd worn a bandana over his head most of the time I'd seen him. He also had ear piercings.

"Since when did you think so logically Jon?" Tonuko snickered in his corner.

Jon grinned and held up his hand, allowing electricity to aggressively flow through his fingers.

"I can kick your ass Tonuko, so don't be makin' too many jokes over there!" Jon laughed.

We all agreed on the plan and decided we'd leave at the climax of the first fight. It would be the biggest and would give us the opportunity to be gone the longest. If we didn't find the kidnappers before we got caught, we would get in serious trouble.

"This is gonna be pretty dangerous; can we even pull this off? How are we gonna find kidnappers?" Alex asked, clearly nervous.

Devin rolled his eyes while taking a sip of ice-cold water in a fake-glass cup.

"You first years are something else. Jon's strength allows him to sense reverberations in the ground, so if they have some kind of an underground lair, we'll be able to find out where it is. Combined with my acid webs and Kyle Straiter's super strength, we'll be able to find their base in no time."

Alex, Anya, and Camilla still seemed a little on edge so Devin assured them, "If things get bad, we can tell Foul Odor or Catastrophe. Foul loves Kyle and Tonuko, and Hazel and I had a nice talk with Catastrophe about the kidnappings. They trust us, and Catastrophe said to put our trust in them. Now, who's in?"

Within the minute, everyone agreed with the plan and cleared their doubts.

After we ate and refined our plan, we came up with a way to find a lead. Since we were heroes-in-training, and all have some form of fighting skills, we would send out Tonuko, Hazel, and me during the night to see if we could find anything suspicious.

"It's always good to have a lead," Jon said.

As we were walking back into the hotel, I was stopped by a duo. One of them had spikey, black hair, a black sweatshirt, and red shorts; the other guy had long blonde hair with immaculate flow, and he wore a flat-brim hat, a black and white windbreaker, and gray short-shorts.

"Ay, you're Kyle, right?" the spikey-haired one asked.

I nodded, so he put out a hand and smirked, "I'm Hunter, and we're pretty similar if I do say so myself!"

"Oh yeah, how so? The top kid of the honors' class is similar to some random advanced kid?"

Hunter was clearly a bit frustrated, and he crossed his arms.

"Hot shot of honors, hot shot of advanced, we're pretty similar in the sense that we're the best of our classes by a long shot!"

I couldn't help but chuckle and stood tall with my chest puffed out.

"The key to being able to call yourself a hotshot is having skill to back up your claim. I can already tell, you clearly don't. Maybe fix your style first before going around boasting about yourself. What the hell is your strength anyway?"

I heard a few snickers from behind me, most notably Kate.

"Mine? Oh, just a little thing called Cancel. It's pretty similar to my Queen sister Kate over there!" Hunter boasted.

Hunter Sanders, Strength: Cancel—he can create spheres of magic cancellers out of his body and nullify almost any strength or attack. These spheres cannot be thrown and take a lot of stamina to use.

"Oh wow, *so* cool. You're really the best of your class with a defensive strength like that? You kinda sound like a sidekick to me," I stated in a monotone voice, expressing the sarcasm in the first statement.

"Why yes, I am! This is Zach, the third best of our class! How about the three of us become a little trio, then we can be the strongest group this school will ever see?" Hunter suggested while holding up his right fist and flexing his arm.

I tried to contain myself, but I burst out with laughter, embarrassing Hunter.

"Really, are you being serious? Why would I associate with advanced kids when every single honors student is stronger than you? Come on man, think a little!"

Jon walked up beside me and leaned on my shoulder, chuckling as well.

"Yeah, he makes a good point Hunter. Valiant effort though, and great confidence!" Jon complimented.

Hunter's cheeks and ears were bright red, so Zach decided to speak up.

"No disrespect, but if that's true, then why do you hang out with Daniel?" I thought for a moment, then shrugged.

"I've known him for a long time, and he helped me a lot when I was younger. It doesn't really have anything to do with strength." Zach nodded, then held out his hand.

"Well, uh, I'm Zach, as he said. Pleasure to meet you, Kyle." I shook his hand with a smile.

"Maybe you should do the talking for your duo. You're much more approachable than little anger issues over there." Zach chuckled while looking back at Hunter, who was even more flustered now. We walked away from them and agreed to meet down here at midnight.

I went straight to my room and sat on my bed while clicking through the channels on the T.V. I saw a news report about the kidnappings and saw the picture of who was supposedly behind the crimes. There was a weirdly built thing, and a tall, average-looking man. The thing had very long arms, inhumanely long in fact, a very short and stocky torso, skinny legs, and no hair. The man had a bandana mask covering his mouth, a cloth tied around his right bicep, and wore a plain t-shirt with baggy pants. I noted their appearances, then continued to scroll through the channels.

Midnight came faster than I expected, and at 12:02 a.m., I made my way down to the lobby. Everyone was waiting impatiently for me.

"Finally! Do you have any sense of urgency Kyle Straiter?" Camilla yelled angrily.

I rolled my eyes and walked up to Jon, Hazel, Tonuko, and Kate.

"Alright you three, make your way outside and keep us updated through call. Hazel has two wireless earbuds connected to her phone, so Tonuko and Hazel will wear them while we're on a call. You ready?" Kate asked looking directly at me. I nodded with a smirk, then Devin put his hand on my shoulder from behind.

"Kyle Straiter, I don't like you, but I'm trusting you."

Why doesn't he like me? I feel like I've never talked to him before.

"I won't let you down, Devin," I responded.

The three of us went outside and waved to the others. We started walking in the same direction as the restaurant we had eaten at earlier. The city was quiet and peaceful, there were barely any sounds. We made our way down a few blocks, then passed a dark, massive alleyway. Since Camby had so many alleys, I was used to them, but this one was weirdly bigger. Hazel stopped before the alley, then put her hand in front of my chest.

"Stay back, I'll look to see if there's anything suspicious." I rolled my eyes and moved her arm away from me.

"Thanks, but I don't need your precautions. If they attack me, I'll beat them." I walked out in front of the alley and put my hands up. "Well, if you're in there, come and get me!"

"Kyle, what in the actual fuck are you doing? Get the hell back here!" Tonuko exclaimed angrily.

"Oh yeah, and what are you gonna do about it?" I retorted while turning to the two of them. Hazel was looking down the alley, then her face turned to fear, and she swiftly looked back to warn me. However, she saw I was looking to my right with just my eyes into the alley.

"Come and make me move why don't you?"

A rock flew out of the alley, but I reacted quickly and caught it, then chucked it back at the man who threw it at me. He narrowly dodged it. The rock crashed into a dumpster and exploded into rubble.

"You shouldn't be out here kids, it's dangerous. There are . . . kidnappers on the loose," the man sinisterly stated in a deep voice. I could see the outline of the thing behind him creep up slowly, then two stretched arms shot out at me. The fingers looked like claws, and as they stuck into the ground, the thing's body flew at me.

"Kyle Straiter, it really is you! I'm the Creature, it's my pleasure!" the Creature creepily exclaimed while sitting on my stomach. I swung a punch at its face, but the Creature's legs stretched, and it jumped high into the air. "I can't take you yet, that would be boring!"

"Dammit Hazel, tell Kyle to get out of there! We know what they look like, and Jon knows their reverberations! Get the fuck out of there!" Devin screamed into the phone.

"I know, I know dammit!" Hazel shouted back while stretching her demon arms. The arms were absolutely massive and muscular; her right hand grabbed the Creature. I crouched, then went to jump at the Creature, but the ground beneath me bent in a curve above my head, causing me to hit my head hard and fall back to the ground.

"What the fuck are you doing Tonuko? I had a clear shot on him!" I angrily yelled while turning all my focus to Tonuko. I stomped toward him with my fists tensed.

He argued, "We aren't here to fight right now, we're here to get data and go! Think a little, Straiter!"

I sped up my walking, then punched him in the cheek. He fell over and the earpiece fell out of his ear, then the other man walked over and stomped on it, breaking it.

"Oh no, you won't be getting any information back to your posse. We knew you would come searching for us Kyle Straiter. It's in your blood to be near villains."

Tonuko was confused by the statement, but too frustrated and flustered to even think about what it could mean. I punched at the man, but he tackled me by my waist and slammed me into the ground. The ground took me in and wrapped around my body.

What the fuck, what is his strength? It's so similar to Tonuko's, right?

Tonuko tried to hit the man's blindside, but when the man had his hand on the rocks and me, more rocks crashed onto his hand and created a boxing glove. He socked Tonuko square on the nose, then looked back at the Creature. The Creature's arm stretched through Hazel's demon arm and pierced her hand; it followed through and dug its claw into her shoulder. She grimaced with pain. The Creature's arm was striped black and white, and when it pierced Hazel's shoulder, the white part turned purple. It looked like something was pumping into Hazel's body, then she passed out. My eyes widened and I broke out of the rock around my body. Hazel's demon arm disappeared, then the creature wrapped its arm around her body like a rope and, while its legs were still stretched, walked back into the alley. Its strides were so long that it traveled a block in a second. The man looked down at the two of us, spat at us, and ran away. Tonuko was shaking, but he stumbled to his feet and grabbed my shirt.

"Come on, we have to go before they come back for us!" Tonuko commanded.

I knew he was right and didn't argue this time. I knew I fucked up. We ran back to the hotel, panicked and panting when we arrived. Tonuko was consoled by Anya, Jon, and Alex. On the contrary, Devin stomped up to me and punched me on the cheek. I fell over and looked at his face. It was filled with pure rage.

"What the fuck is the matter with you? While in the middle of a fight with strong villains, you go over and punch Tonuko? Are you fucking kidding me? Were you trying to get Hazel kidnapped? Did you purposefully sabotage the mission?" Devin screamed while looking down at me.

"N–No, I–"

"Just shut up, I don't want to hear your excuses!" Devin looked at the rest of the group and commanded, "We will continue with the original plan regardless of what happened. Now, instead of just capturing the villains, we have to save Hazel as well! Also, the teachers are going to be asking where she is. I'll cover for her. Got it?"

Everyone said yes then went to bed.

Before Devin and I left, I yelled to him, "I promise I'll get her back and take down the kidnappers!"

Devin stopped when I shouted, then shook his head, and entered the elevator. I went up to my room shortly after and sat up awake in my bed.

"Were you trying to get Hazel kidnapped; did you purposefully sabotage the mission?"

No, I wasn't, I swear. They're wrong about me. I just made a mistake. I'll get Hazel back; I'll save everyone and take down those kidnappers. **They're as good as dead.**

In the morning, both classes met up, and we headed over to the arena, which was about a mile walk. Like Devin said he would, he covered for Hazel. Actually, Ms. Palkun didn't ask any questions about her disappearance, but Excalibur did. We arrived in the arena, which was breathtaking. The stage was in the center and above it pipes spelled out "CHAMPIONS," the name of the arena. We sat in our front row seats, and the seven of us waited anxiously. Our school was introduced as special guests, then Mr. Clarence introduced the first two fighters.

"FIRST OFF, WE HAVE THE BEST UPCOMING FIGHTER IN THE NATION: FOULLL ODOR! IN THE OTHER CORNER STANDS THE MAN, THE MYTH, THE LEGEND WHO'S BEEN ON TOP FOR THE PAST YEAR! GIVE IT UP FOR CATASTROPHE!" Catastrophe was a very muscular man who had a shiny bald head, wore a cape with no shirt, and had skin-tight pants yet no socks or shoes. The bell rang, starting the fight.

A purple mist seeped out of Foul Odor's tubes, filling the bottom of the stage. Catastrophe activated his Earthquake strength, causing Foul to stumble.

Jeremy Hunderaks/Catastrophe, Strength: Rumble—he can create strong earthquakes in specific spots that reduce a person's ability to focus. They can span up to a mile radius. It takes a lot of muscle and focus to create these, so he must keep a powerful body and serene mind.

From the crowd across the stage from us, a man with a cloth mask stood and clapped loudly, then a couple of crows made entirely of shadows swarmed Catastrophe's head.

"Marvelous, just marvelous!" the guy who had been sitting next to the masked man applauded. "You heroes are just so amazing to watch up close!"

The man stood, and as he did so, a large hawk made of shadows formed out of the ground. He hopped onto it, then flew into the air above the arena. The other man ate his mask, revealing an eerie sight. His mouth was very wide, he had no lips, sharp teeth, and a long, pointy tongue. His hair was brown, messy, and long, drooping in his bloodshot eyes. He wore camouflage jacket and pants, along with big, black boots. The other man in the air wore a black trench coat over a grey collared shirt, a fedora, and black pants.

"Kane," Foul Odor grumbled.

"Nobody moves, or else my good buddy David over here will shoot the place up!"

David jumped onto the stage holding two automatic rifles he had hacked up seconds earlier. There were a few screams from the crowd at first, but everyone was silent now. Catastrophe snapped out of his daze and activated his strength on Kane, causing him to fall off his hawk.

I stood, glancing to my left toward the others who were supposed to leave, and looked for confirmation. Devin nodded, so while commotion and worry were happening around us, I led the group and ran out of the main stage room into the short hallway. I panicked and ran into the boy's bathroom and the others followed. David didn't try to stop us; instead, he let out a snarly chuckle and turned back to Foul Odor.

"Kyle, what are we doing in here? We need to hurry!" Tonuko shouted at me before running his hands through his hair and looking out the bathroom door at the main stage. Alex washed his hands, then walked over to use the hand dryer. Tonuko and I continued arguing, then a weird warping noise filled the room and Alex was gone. Kate was staring at the hand dryer and gulped.

"Alex just got sucked into that thing . . . It must be some kind of teleportation device built to kidnap people," Kate stated while walking toward the hand dryer.

Tonuko and I followed. A plethora of gunfire came from the main stage area, then Devin inhaled deeply and took charge.

"We said we're doing this, so we're going to follow through! Camilla and I will stay back and help against the Care-Givers. You all go save Alex and Hazel!" Devin's confident, straightforward attitude gave us a little bit of courage, but Kate still had her rational doubts.

"Devin, these are freshies you left me with! Jon didn't follow us so we can't track the reverberations of the kidnappers! You're expecting me to watch over all of them and make sure every one of them doesn't do something stupid that will get them killed?"

Devin turned back to face us and walked toward Kate and me. He looked me in the eyes before grabbing the collar of my shirt.

"Kyle has a big promise to uphold Kate. He's stronger than you, faster than you, and has a higher battlefield awareness than you; you are not alone. Tonuko is smarter than you, and Anya will keep Tonuko in check so he doesn't get killed. All I'm asking for you to do is make sure Kyle doesn't go berserk, or make sure he knows his limits. The other two will help you, I trust them."

I was angered by his last statement and pushed him off of me.

"So, you don't trust me; you don't think I can do this?" I glared at Devin, and he scowled right back at me.

"No, I don't think you can beat criminals with powers unknown to you by yourself! Wow, isn't that a fucking shocker! Listen to Kate and don't get yourself, or anyone else, killed!" I didn't argue. I decided my fists would show him that he couldn't order me around.

Devin looked at Kate and nodded, then ran to the bathroom door, and tapped Camilla as he ran by. The two left, leaving Kate, Tonuko, Anya, and me in the room. I stood in front of the hand dryer, cracked my knuckles, then took my headband out of my pocket, and tied it on my head. Tonuko put his hand on my shoulder to stop me, but my skin was extremely hot, and it slightly burned his hand. I reached my hand toward the heat fan; it felt as though my body was stretched and suddenly, I was in a tunnel barreling into the darkness. I hit the ground and rubbed my back. Tonuko fell on me, Kate followed, and Anya was last. We stood and I saw a wooden beam on the wall, so I threw some fire at it. The torch lit up a portion of the corridor we were in.

"Everyone stay close; we don't know who or what is down here," Kate commanded while standing in front of the three of us. In the distance, a bright white light glowed, then vanished from the bottom up, signifying Alex went down something.

"Alex!" I shouted, pushing past Kate and running.

"Kyle, what the hell are you doing?" Tonuko yelled, taking a step.

Before any of them or I could react, a man covered in rough, cream—white scales ran out from the darkness, lowered his shoulder, and rammed me into the dirt wall to my left. The ceiling rumbled, causing dirt and dust to rain onto the ground. Along with the man, a teenage boy and young girl walked toward us. The man who had hit me smirked, then his mouth and nose grew into a long dinosaur snout and his fingers grew longer and sharper. Bones in his body cracked and creaked; eventually his knees were bent in the opposite direction and his arms were twice as long as before. Sharp spikes stuck out from his spinal cord, forcing him to stand in a slightly hunched position.

"Looks like I get a go at the almighty son, huh?" The man snickered as he raised his right arm. He swiped down and clawed my right arm, which I had used to block his attack. A pillar of dirt flew toward the lizard man and knocked him off me. Kate ran over and grabbed my arm, dragging me back toward the group.

"The name's Spike, Kyle Straiter. You will be mine; I'll be the one to take you back to him."

"Kyle, who is he talking about?" Anya yelled at me while I was still sitting on the ground.

"I—I don't know! This is some psychotic kidnapper; he's probably just talking out of his ass!"

Spike slowly walked toward us, letting his sharp claws drag on the ground.

"You know exactly who I'm talking about. Once I bring you back to my bosses, they'll take you to where you belong . . . the base of—"

Without thinking, I activated another strength and sped at lightning speed at Spike. I landed a punch square on his snout, then, as he was soaring backward toward the other two criminals, I blasted flames at them. The little girl hopped out in front of the two guys, then stretched and expanded into a massive blob with a normal-sized head and small limbs. The fire was absorbed by her body, then she shrunk back down to her usual size.

"Did you know that rubber absorbs fire! So cool, right?" the little girl informed me while wearing a large smile.

I was sweating but my fear was detained by the raging fury that grew every time I thought about Tyrant.

"Kyle, watch out!" Kate screamed as Spike charged in and swiped at the left side of my body.

I was too angry and lost in thought to notice, so Kate quickly stepped in and formed two cancellation orbs. Spike's claws clashed with the orbs, creating a loud static noise, which ejected the force Spike had used back onto his arm, causing him to spin around in a circle. I snapped out of my daze, jumped up, and kicked Spike in the head. He flew into the wall on the left side of the hallway, then a huge pile of dirt fell on top of him. I stepped backward toward Tonuko and Anya, but Spike leapt out of the dirt pile and on top of me. Anya ran to my side while dragging her fingers on the ground. She formed the same gloves she had during the training tournament and punched Spike in the side of the head. He tumbled into the teenage boy who had yet to make a move.

"Dammit Pete, are you going to do something? I'm getting quadruple teamed out here!" Spike shouted furiously.

Pete nodded, popping a neon blue piece of gum in his mouth. After chewing for a couple seconds, he blew a large bubble that began floating toward us. The bubble split into multiple tiny bubbles. Anya reached out her finger and touched one of the blue bubbles. It popped and covered her glove in a sticky acid that melted the dirt around her hand. Anya let the dirt glove fall off, then she nervously backed up to Tonuko's side, who created a large wall that absorbed the rest of the bubbles.

Spike's nose was broken and bloody, and one of his claws had ripped off in my skin. I hopped to my feet and took charge of myself. I cracked my shoulder and tensed my entire body. After tensing hard enough, an audible click echoed throughout the hallway, and a bright yellow layer of mist seeped off my body. With a quick step, I launched myself into Spike. We hit at such high speeds that I bounced off his body. However, I used this bounce to grab his arm, twist around in the air, and throw him into the ground. The entire tunnel rumbled, but I ignored the danger signs and punched down on Spike's stomach. He coughed and his eyes widened, then I kicked him into the wall in front of me. Another large mound of dirt fell onto his body, but this time Spike didn't get back up.

Kyle Straiter, Strength Five: Energy Conversion—he can convert any energy in his cells into a speed boost that is represented by the layer of mist that covers his body. Of course, using this strength takes a massive amount of stamina and can have deadly side effects since it is taking energy from necessary processes in Kyle's body.

"Wow, you're so amazing Kyle Straiter!" The little girl yelled with a sparkle in her eyes.

I turned around and blasted fire at the girl, so she stretched out again and absorbed the flames. What I didn't know was that Anya and Tonuko were charging up a special attack. Anya had a suit of hardened dirt, a near rock material, and Tonuko used a hand he formed from the ground to wind up and throw Anya at the rubber girl. Anya led with her hands flat, palms pressed against each other. When she hit the girl's stomach, it stretched far, then Anya's body ripped through the girl. Blood splattered on my face, and Pete's eyes grew very wide as the hole in the little girl's body hissed and spat out a sprinkler of blood. Her body was thrown all over because of the wind pressure escaping her inflated body, then she hit the ground hard and lay unconscious. Her blood was everywhere.

"N–No, no Katrina, it can't end like this. We were gonna escape with the heroes and be free!" Pete screamed after dropping to his knees and looking at Katrina's dead body. Anya tumbled a couple feet, then lifted her head up and looked back at the girl she just killed.

"I–I just . . . killed someone . . ." Anya stated quietly while staring with a horrified expression at the dead body.

Kate rushed over and knelt at Pete's side.

"Is this your sister?" she asked. Pete nodded with tears streaming down his face

He explained, "W–We were just normal students, like you guys. We dreamt of being heroes, getting in the action and beating up bad guys, saving the day, y'know? One day though, we were kidnapped before we made it to the bus stop . . . by those monsters. I was beaten and nearly killed every day for a month before the Creature finally gave us an ultimatum: join their side or be put down in the most painful way we could think of. I was ready to die right there, finally have it all end, but Katrina spoke up and saved my life . . . Now . . . "

Pete swiftly looked up, causing tears to fly off his face, and he looked over at Anya.

"You're a hero, right?" Pete screeched as he got up and ran at Anya with his hands out and full of gum. "Then how could you fucking murder a little girl? She was only seven years old, *you monster!*"

Before Pete could reach the shocked Anya, I led with a knee to the side of his head and hit him into the wall. This crash was much larger than any of Spike's and was the limit to what the tunnel could handle. The ceiling began collapsing behind us.

"We gotta get the hell out of here! Come on!" Tonuko commanded. We all ran down the tunnel, but I used my energy strength to speed ahead of them.

"That asshole was hiding another strength, are you serious? Just what else is he hiding . . . who was that Spike guy gonna' bring him to?" Anya shouted frantically with fury lingering in her voice.

"All that matters is he's on our side. I don't know what secrets he's keeping, but if all these criminals want to bring him down with them, we have to stop them," Kate stated trying to hide her frustration and panic.

The three continued sprinting after me but saw I had stopped at the edge of light. Above me was a bright blue sky with many clouds, but below me was a dark pit. I looked back and saw the tunnel continue to collapse behind the three, who were running as fast as they could, but it wasn't fast enough. I rolled my eyes, then activated my energy strength and sprinted back toward them. I pushed them forward, sending everyone stumbling toward the edge. Tonuko extended the ground, catching Anya and Kate, then looked back at me. I was holding up a large rock that fell from the ceiling, but the ground beneath me cracked. Suddenly, the ground crumbled, sending me downward into the unknown.

"Kyle!" Tonuko shouted, but before he could make a move to save me the tunnel collapsed the rest of the way. The platform Tonuko had made cracked—the floor was now gone because the tunnel was filled in. Tonuko placed his hand on the wall and looked down at the darkness beneath the three. He focused hard, his bangs dripped sweat, and he panted heavily.

"That idiot Kyle is gonna get us killed now! He should have known you can only bend the ground! All he's done is create more problems for us!" Anya complained while frantically looking around for a way to save the others and herself.

Tonuko clenched his fist, then turned and erupted, "That 'idiot' Kyle just saved our asses back there and now he might be dead because of it! We don't know how far that drop was! It could have been all the way down to wherever the hell the ground is!"

Anya was surprised by Tonuko's sudden explosion of anger but stood her ground as usual.

"We don't know that he saved us! We were outrunning the dirt; we didn't need his help! He just created another problem for us to solve because he was trying to be the big, amazing hero!" Anya shouted at Tonuko while walking closer and pointing her finger at the newly formed dirt wall.

"*We just killed someone! Kyle didn't create that problem for us!*" As Tonuko shouted, his voice croaked and the ground they were standing on continued cracking. "That little girl is *dead* and the guy probably is as well because *we* left him in the collapsing tunnel to save ourselves! *That's not what heroes do!* Kyle ran into death and saved us, *now he's gone!* Don't you understand Anya? *We've done nothing, we're doing nothing, and we're going to die just like Kyle, like Hazel, like Alex, and like **the child we just killed!***" With the last words, the ground shattered, and the three were sent falling into the abyss.

Back in the Arena:

Excalibur stood from his seat and demanded of the classes, "Stay in your seats! This is a real villain battle; I don't want any of you making a dumb decision and getting hurt!"

Excalibur grabbed his large sword from behind his seat and jumped onto the stage. He swung at David, but a shadow hyena leapt and took the hit. Excalibur was surrounded by a group of hyenas. Suddenly, multiple blades of wind exploded around him and took out all of the animals. Excalibur looked back and saw Camilla and Devin standing at the top of the arena stairs.

"Don't worry Excalibur, we'll back you up!" Devin exclaimed while running down the stairs.

Excalibur shook his head, then Camilla floated into the air and created a mini tornado between Kane and David.

While they were distracted, Camilla announced, "Everyone evacuate the building! We'll distract the Care-Givers while you leave!"

Civilians poured out of the exit, and every time David shot at them, his bullets were absorbed by the tornado. He seethed to himself, then coughed, and threw up a large sniper.

David Blake/Care-Giver Weaponsmith, Strength: Weaponry— using antimatter found in his stomach acid, he can form any weapon and throw it up through his widened mouth. His teeth are reinforced to not be affected by the stomach acid, his esophagus is hardened as to not get punctured by any sharp items, and his tongue is razor sharp and long to guide the weapons out of his mouth. If David creates too many weapons over a few hours, he will start to vomit blood and become very ill.

David aimed quickly and shot a heavy-duty bullet that avoided the tornado and pierced Camilla's stomach. She fell out of the air but was, luckily, caught by Devin. David eerily giggled and on pure instinct ducked. Foul Odor's fist flew over his head, then David shot one of his assault rifles straight up and wounded Foul's left arm. Following Devin's command, Iris ran to Camilla's aid, then Daniel stood from his seat, ready to fight.

On the stage, David aimed his rifle at Foul Odor, causing a distraction that allowed a group of hounds to pounce on Foul Odor's back. He tried to wrestle the beasts off but only succeeded when he managed to release his strength-weakening gas.

Keith Stratop/Foul Odor, Strength: Stench—he can release many different odors from the silicon tubes coming out of his arms that correlate to different defects for the opponent. He has learned four different smells so far, as he is a very

young fighter, only twenty years old. He can emit a purple stench that temporarily blinds people, a green stench that makes it difficult for people to breath, a blue stench that causes people to lose their sense of touch and taste, and a yellow stench, which causes others' strengths to weaken to half of what they were.

Kane covered his mouth after breathing in some of the foul-smelling gas, then he was rammed from the side by an unknown force. Daniel fell over and hit the ground hard, revealing his position. Kane jumped to his feet, then kicked Daniel in the chest, sending him flying into the stands. Kane formed a large boar at his feet, letting it charge at Daniel.

"What a nuisance," Kane sighed.

Kane Ine/Care-Giver Animal Creator, Strength: Life Form— he can create any animal from his shadow, and depending on how big his shadow is, the bigger his beasts will be. If it is nighttime, he has no limit to the size except for what his body can handle (that currently is forty feet). He hears the thoughts of whatever animals he creates, so creating too many will tire him out and make him go crazy.

The boar leapt at Daniel, who was no longer invisible, but a red laser wall formed from the ground and caught the beast, causing it to sizzle and disintegrate.

"Don't worry Daniel, I gotcha'," Zach calmly stated while walking up to Daniel. He reached a hand to Daniel, who thanked him and used his hand to stand.

Zach Taling, Strength: Laser—he can create extremely powerful lasers that burn anyone or anything that comes within six inches of contact. He can shoot them by making a gun formation with his fingers or he can create walls of laser at will.

Foul dodged a few bullets nimbly, then released more of his yellow toxin out of his right arm and some of his blue stench from his left arm. More dogs tackled him and ripped the flesh on his arms. Suddenly, Steven collided with one of the hounds, lowering his bionic shoulder, and made it crash into an empty part of the stands before vanishing. After that, Donte bolted in quickly and broke through the other dog's exterior, causing it to disappear.

"Get away boys! This is too dangerous! Where the hell is Diana to keep you safe?" Excalibur erupted while stepping between Donte and Kane.

Kane smirked, then shrugged.

"Oh, you mean Diana Palkun? Silly heroes, that's the Diana Palkun of the Care-Givers, better known as Lady Patch!"

Excalibur's eyes widened and he stared in awe at Kane.

"Are you serious, this entire time a Care-Giver has been this close to our students? What if she kills any straggler students who will trust her as their teacher? *Dammit!*"

He charged in at Kane and swung his massive metal sword. The sword's blade burst into flames, but Kane flipped into the air and jumped down on the blade, causing it to get stuck in the ground. The blade's form changed to water, and Excalibur was able to easily rip it out of the ground. As he swung it again, the blade hardened back into metal and sliced a cut across Kane's upper chest, narrowly missing his neck.

David aimed his assault rifle at Excalibur, but an invisible Daniel knocked it out of his hand, then Zayden burst out of the ground, uppercutting David. David led with his elbow into Zayden's head, and proclaimed, "Stupid kids these days, you think you have a chance. No, none of you do, except Kyle Straiter. However, he'll be dead by night!" He began cackling but while lost in psychotic laughter, he ate a knuckle sandwich from Rake.

Cindy shot a few bullets; one of them managed to burrow itself into David's forehead right above his nose. Blood dripped down his face, over his lips. He licked the blood all the way up his nose and smiled horrifically.

"Thanks for the snack, little girl," David stated in a low, scratchy voice.

Rake ignored the creepiness of this Care-Giver and threw five of his fingers at David. A snake molded while in the air and latched on to David's head.

"Venom, 500 milliliters," Rake smirked. "If you move, that snake will seep every last drop of venom right into your bloodline, stopping your heart. The choice is yours, you fuckin' freak."

David began gagging and gargling.

"You asked for it!" yelled Rake.

David opened his mouth with a smile and sitting on his tongue was a grenade. He used one of his teeth to pull the pin, then the grenade fell out of his mouth and onto the stage. It exploded, causing people to be swept off their feet and throwing off the entire battle. Rake collided into Zach as they crashed into a couple of seats.

While on the ground, Zach looked up and saw a wolf pounce on Steven. He created a laser box around the two, then swiftly threw up a wall when the wolf tried to bite Steven. The wolf backed up and whimpered. The box around the wolf shrank instantly, killing it. A couple of crows tried swarming the three boys, but Steven took out two and Zach shot down three more.

"Damn, you're pretty good for the advanced class!" Steven smiled while holding a robotic thumbs up to Zach.

Zach smiled back with a snicker.

"Thanks, you're not too bad yourself."

Hunter ran to Zach's aid, calling for Iris. Iris, though out of breath, ran over and began healing Zach. Zach winked at her when she looked up at him, causing her to blush and look right back down at her hands. While Iris was healing, dozens of shadow snakes burst out of the ground and crept at the group. Zach shot countless lasers at them, but they were too nimble and little for him to hit. However, an advanced girl stomped on the ground a couple of feet away from them. Her stomp created a wave of air pressure that killed all the snakes.

"Thanks Rose," Hunter said before high-fiving her. The girl grinned and looked over at the injured Daniel.

"Ugh, I hope he's okay! He charged in blindly!" Rose complained.

Rose Valington, Strength: Stomp—when she stomps her foot on the ground, she can create powerful waves of energy that shoot in all directions. She can only stomp to activate them, and how hard she stomps computes the power of the waves.

"Iris, go help Foul Odor! If he goes down, we're screwed!" Scarlett yelled while hiding in the stands.

Iris gulped, then slowly made her way over to the knocked-out Foul. She began healing him while crouching in hiding next to the stage. After a few seconds, Foul opened his eyes and jumped up. He ran to Kane and swung a kick, but Kane ducked and swung his fist, punching Foul's airborne leg and throwing him back. Foul flipped over in the air and landed on his hands, then pushed hard and jumped back onto his feet. After dodging a few crows, Catastrophe grabbed Kane's head and smashed it into the ground, but a leopard jumped out of Kane's chest and tackled Catastrophe. However, Catastrophe had enough time to activate his strength on Kane again.

"Catastrophe . . . and your pathetic strength . . . you will never be anything in this damn hellhole of a world!" Kane erupted.

He created dozens upon dozens of crows that swarmed the few actual heroes on the stage, then threw a knife he had picked up from David at Catastrophe. It stabbed through Catastrophe's stomach, causing him to fall over. A giant acid spiderweb fell on top of Kane, burning his skin. David was thrown into the air by an electric explosion. Jon collided into him at high speeds, sending him crashing between the stage and the spectator seats. Foul managed to fight off the crows around him and stomped onto Kane's back, who coughed up blood and wheezed for air.

"You're through Kane. Stand down," Foul Odor stated while releasing his purple stench.

Kane tensed his fist and clenched his jaw so hard his face turned red.

He screeched, "David, *kaboom!*" David's eyes turned from bloodshot red to all black, and he marched toward the stage with a giant smile.

"Boom, boom, boom," David chanted.

He opened his mouth, and countless grenades poured onto the ground, all ready to be detonated. David hacked up a large bomb, and when he threw it up, blood fell from his mouth onto the wires, detonating it.

"Boom, boom, boom!"

Everyone nearby began running away, but there were still some students knocked out and others severely injured. There was too much commotion for anyone to escape, then every explosive blew up. The explosion sent a quake for miles, and the entire arena was damaged. It was so damaged, in fact, that the ceiling cracked and started crumbling.

David grabbed Kane and hid under the stage while Kane created giant manta rays to cover them from the falling debris.

Within a couple seconds, the entire ceiling fell.

Chapter 9

Real Combat

Tonuko's stomach dropped when the ground broke, and the sound of the wind as the three fell was deafening. Suddenly, a bright light swooped in and grabbed the three, then they hit the wall hard. Tonuko looked up and was met with Alex's bloody face.

"Alex, you're alive?" Kate screamed with relief.

Alex smiled, pushed off the wall, let go of the three, and fell to the ground. He was breathing heavily and one of his wings was bent a weird way. The bright sky contrasted the dark environment around them, and a faint light grew in the distance. Tonuko heard a click, then torches all around the box they were in lit up. The concrete walls were pale black; the floor was still a rough dirt and gravel mix. Across the large room in front of the four was a grand, golden throne. In the throne sat the horrifying creature who stole Hazel, and next to it was his accomplice.

Anya's eyes welled as she stared at the man, who in return was equally shocked at seeing her.

"D–Dad?" Anya whimpered before standing. Anya's dad took a step forward, then the Creature's arm stretched out and stopped him.

"Don't even think about it, Lokel. That's not your daughter anymore, remember? You're a part of my lovely family now, not that braindead hero's!"

Lokel took a deep breath and nodded. As he sighed, his facial expression swiftly changed from distraught to stern. The Creature's stomach grumbled, so it reached its hand toward the group. Alex grabbed Tonuko's arm and pulled him out of the way. The Creature reached into an inground pool behind the four and pulled out a large, live cod fish. Its arm was quickly sucked back toward its body and returned to its normal length. The Creature then opened its large jaws, revealing sharp, red-stained teeth. It ripped off the fish's head and gulped it down before continuing with the rest of the body.

"Ah, much better!"

"That was fucking disgusting . . . what am I even looking at?" Tonuko stuttered with a shaky voice.

Alex held his shoulder, then revealed bite marks.

"I don't know what that thing is, but don't let him near you. We need to escape quickly; it moves fast and is unpredictable with those rubber limbs," Alex informed the group as he breathed deeply.

The white stripes on the Creature's arms faded to a rich magenta, then it stood and cracked its fingers. The Creature's arms stuck into the ground, and it launched itself at terrifying speeds toward the group. Tonuko stomped his foot on the ground, bending the dirt in front of the group upward and creating a thick wall between the soaring Creature and the group. In an instant, the Creature maneuvered above the wall, stuck both hands into the ground on either side of Tonuko, and threw itself into him. Tonuko crashed into the ground along with the Creature. While Tonuko was down, the Creature injected him with a purple liquid through the claws on its hands.

"Tonuko!" Anya shouted while crafting her gauntlets again. To her and Kate's surprise, a bright light shone and the two were swept off their feet before the Creature stabbed them.

"Look at that Lokel, my poison worked! In no time, these four will be my little puppets!" Alex's already purple eyes glowed brighter and Tonuko's yellow eyes faded to a bright magenta. Lokel stood stiff and sweated while looking at his daughter. He didn't fight or argue, just quietly stayed in his place.

After the students fully converted to the kidnappers' side because of the poison, I burst a hole through the wall behind the fish tank and stood in the opening with Hazel.

Directly After Kyle's Fall:

I hit the ground hard and groaned in agony. My back was broken, and my head was pounding. After around a minute, my body swelled with a deep, rich darkness. I couldn't see for a moment, then my pain went away. I was scared but happy to feel no pain after falling such a distance. My eyes adjusted to the pitch-black room, and I could see vague silhouettes moving on the walls around me. My stomach dropped, then I heard a familiar voice call out.

"Please, whoever's there! Let us free!"

Wait a minute, is that–?

"Hazel?" I shouted while frantically looking around. "Is that you?"

I heard chains rattling, as well as moans and groans—ranging from children to adults—crying out for help. I ran around blindly, then heard her voice directly to my right. I ran to her and broke the chains that attached her to the wall. Hazel fell and breathed deeply through her wheezes.

"Holy shit, what did they do to you?" I asked.

"Y–You don't wanna know. For now, we need to get out of here and alert authorities that all the kidnapped people have been found."

I hesitated, then stated, "No, we have to save Alex first. The kidnappers got him too; he was taken by one of their traps."

We heard the loud commotion of the Creature fighting Tonuko, and then a massive explosion went off miles above us.

"Alright, but let's hurry. That explosion can't be good."

"Yeah, it must be the Care-Givers. David and Kane attacked the arena before we left," I explained while looking upward, though I couldn't see anything because it was so dark.

Hazel took another minute to gain the energy to stand, then we walked toward where we heard the commotion. I wound back my fist and punched through the wall.

Through the hole, I saw my classmates sitting around while the Creature laughed at them.

Confused, I shouted, "What the hell are you doing? Come on, Tonuko, stay focused!"

To my surprise, a bright beam of light zoomed at my face, and Alex tackled me to the ground.

"Alex, what are you–?"

Alex punched at my face, but I caught his hand and rolled over on top of him, restraining him. "Snap out of it!"

"Kyle, something is up with them! Their eyes all changed color!" Hazel informed me while backing up to Alex and me. I peeked behind me and saw the other three slowly approaching, then looked back at Alex and quickly thought.

I need to get whatever is controlling them out of their system. It must be about the same thing the Creature used to make Hazel pass out, so some kind of liquid. Maybe, if I use Infection, I can suck the juice out of their bloodstream and allow them to regain consciousness!

My fingertips lost all color, and small, extremely thin white tubes seeped out of my fingernails and crept toward Alex. My eyes also lost all color as I stared at the struggling Alex. I could see faint purple cells swirling around his bloodstream.

Kyle Straiter, Strength Six: Infection—this strength can create tubes out of Kyle's fingernails that act as syringes to take out any bacterial cells found in a person's bloodstream. This strength also allows Kyle to see any system of the body and any infectious cells. This strength has been used by doctors in this society to see infectious diseases such as cancer cells.

When the tubes were mere inches from Alex's heart, we were both thrown into the air by a dirt pillar, then I was punched in the back by Anya, who had built more rock gloves. I wheezed and was sent flying into the ceiling, which was much closer than I anticipated. My head spun as I fell, but Hazel caught me and knocked Tonuko and Kate off their feet.

Hazel and I backed away from the group, then Hazel whispered, "I don't know what that strength was, but if it's gonna stop them from being controlled, then use it."

I looked at Hazel and nodded.

"Can you promise you won't tell anyone about my other strengths? This stays between us, right?" I asked earnestly.

Hazel nodded while taking a deep breath; this meant I would be able to fight unrestrained. I smirked as I cracked my knuckles, then crouched and put my hands on the ground. My Infection tubes stuck into the ground, then four replicas of me rose from the dirt on my left; they were all connected to Infection tubes.

The clones charged at the mind-controlled four and dodged their attacks. I ran in directly behind them and tackled Kate. She struggled on the ground, but I was able to easily overpower her and stick an Infection tube in her chest. The tube sucked out all of the poison in her blood system, allowing her real consciousness to reawaken. Kate blinked a few times, then looked around in a dazed state.

I smiled at her and said, "Morning sunshine!"

Right after those words left my mouth, Tonuko tackled me off of her. We rolled a few feet and before I stopped I morphed a clone out from underneath him that grabbed and wrapped itself around his body.

I've got him now. With Tonuko and Kate back on my side, I'll be able to get Alex and Anya out of that state in no time. Thank the Lord nobody is dead.

One of my clones managed to restrain and convert Anya. To my surprise Tonuko destroyed the grasp of my other clone before his transformation could be completed. The ground suddenly burst into a giant square underneath me, sending me flying across the room. I crashed into the far wall and slid down, then saw to my right a very malnourished boy, who looked no older than the rubber girl from earlier. I was determined to save these kids; I could only imagine what they'd been through. Considering how the Pete guy I'd encountered reacted when talking about leaving and being free, I assumed these kidnapped people would be used as henchmen for the two bosses. I stood but was struggling to stay upright, and the world was slowly spinning around me.

I've gotta convert Tonuko and Alex quickly. I don't know how much longer I can stay conscious, but I still have to beat the kidnappers and the Care-Givers too. Oh man, it's gonna be a long day.

White tubes crawled out of all my fingers on both hands, then I charged at Tonuko. Alex tried to ram me out of the way, but Anya punched him with a dirt glove, sending him crashing backward. To my surprise, Anya shouted, "Come on, Kyle, save him!"

I ran at Tonuko, ducked under the pillars he sent toward my face, then grabbed him and body slammed him into the ground. He swung a punch at me, but I grabbed his fist and bashed my forehead into his. Tonuko was stunned, allowing me to finish the conversion. Tonuko blinked a couple times, then groaned and held his head.

"Fuck, you didn't have to headbutt me so damn hard!" he complained but grinned immediately after. I chuckled, then stood and held out a hand to him.

He took it and stood, then I stated, "As soon as I convert Alex, we can go and beat those kidnappers! Let's do this . . . together." I held out a fist to him as I smirked.

He smiled with his eyes closed and gave me a fist bump, but then we heard, "Guys, *watch out!*" Hazel screeched while throwing her demon arm at us.

I turned my head and was met with Alex's hand covered in light as it stabbed through my body. He punctured next to my stomach and pushed his hand out the other side. I coughed blood and hunched over after he ripped his hand out of me.

"Alex, you bastard!" Tonuko yelled while punching Alex in the face. Alex stumbled back, then lunged at Tonuko. Tonuko and Alex fell, then Alex stood over him and held out his hand with the intention of blasting Tonuko with a laser of light. Before he could, I swiftly tackled him. We rolled on the ground, then I threw him into the wall next to me—the one that separated us from the kidnappers.

"Tonuko, trap him!" I shouted. Tonuko moved quickly and wrapped dirt mixed with rocks from the ground around Alex, successfully trapping him. Since he couldn't move, I was able to convert Alex from his mind-controlled state. At this point, Alex's head gushed blood, one of his wings was broken, and his right arm was soaked with my blood. He panted as he glanced around, then he looked at me with complete shock as Tonuko freed him.

"Kyle, I'm so sorry," he whimpered while walking toward me. He hugged me and I returned it while wheezing.

"D–Don't worry about it, Alex. It wasn't your f–fault," I stuttered. I looked back at everyone else. "You all should get back to the arena and–" Before I could finish, we heard a monstrous explosion that caused dirt to rain down from the ceiling. "Get back to the arena and provide backup there. I'll take care of these guys."

"Kyle, are you mad? We're not leaving you alone to take on two villains when you're that injured. We should get you to the surface safely and inform any heroes or police around the area that we found the kidnappers' base," Kate argued.

I stood my ground.

"By the time the Care-Givers are defeated, these kidnappers will be long gone. It's now or never. I'll be fine, a little cut won't be the end of me." I turned to walk toward the hole in the wall to meet the kidnappers, but Tonuko interjected.

"How about we send Alex to the surface, since he can fly, and the rest of us will fight down here? We know the kidnappers' powers so we can adjust accordingly. We don't need to defeat the kidnappers, just stall long enough for backup to arrive," he suggested.

Although I really wanted to beat down the kidnappers myself, I agreed along with everyone else. We ran out into the main room where the kidnappers sat.

The Creature clapped and giggled. "Well done, Kyle Straiter, very well done! You are so interesting; I can't wait to take you!" the Creature snarled.

Hazel told Alex to go, so he charged up and flew into the sky as fast as he could.

"Oh no you don't!" The Creature roared while sending its arms flying into the wall. It sling-shotted itself at Alex, but I used flames to jump high and fast into the sky. I intercepted the Creature and crashed into it. We were both falling toward the ground, but I managed to get another kick in before Hazel caught me. The Creature soared into its throne and broke clean through it.

"Nice one Kyle!" Kate cheered while I was being lowered.

The Creature shot up from the rubble while facing away from us, then turned and looked straight at me.

"Lokel, I want you to get Kyle! I'll provide backup by taking out the others!"

Lokel and Anya's gazes met, then Lokel closed his eyes and nodded.

"Yes, sir."

Lokel put his hands on the ground and formed two swords. He held them by his waist as rock boots formed around his feet. The boots had springs in the back sole that allowed him to produce super-jumps without a jump-enhancing strength. They also helped him run faster than usual.

Lokel charged at me and tossed one of his swords. Confused, I grabbed it out of the air, then our blades collided. The rock was strong and surprisingly sharp.

"I used metal alloys from the ground to form sharpened rock swords," Lokel explained while locking eyes with me. My stomach was hurting badly from Alex's stab, but I ignored the pain and smirked at Lokel.

"Interesting, also an interesting strategy to give your foe a weapon. Respectable, but risky," I expressed aloud. Lokel smirked back at me, but I stopped his smile by asking, "So tell me, why would you leave your family for this kind of a life?"

"What the fuck would you know about family?" Lokel angrily erupted while pushing his sword into mine.

I stumbled back, then he spun around and swung his sword at my head. I deflected with my sword in my right hand and spun it around a few times while backing up. To my left, Tonuko was holding off the Creature.

"Everyone, just hold them off until backup arrives!" Tonuko demanded.

I rolled my eyes and leapt in for another attack. Lokel and I clashed swords a few times, then I landed a cut. I sliced a gash across Lokel's cheek. It wasn't deep, but it was enough to anger him. Lokel threw his sword at me, and it exploded mid-air into countless pebbles. I held my arms up to cover my eyes from the barrage of rocks, then I was tackled off my feet. It wasn't a regular tackle though; Lokel used his boost-shoes to send us flying across the room. I landed on my back, then Lokel flipped me over, knelt on my back, and grabbed the back of my head. He pushed my head straight into the pool of fish. I opened my eyes and saw the fish swim away. I tried to get up, but I couldn't. Lokel was creating a thick barrier of rocks from his shoes, making it impossible for me to move from my position.

Fuck, I can't hold my breath for very long. If I stay like this, I'll drown.

I struggled and splashed around, but Lokel didn't budge. He gripped my head tighter and pushed his kneecap into my stab wound. I screamed underwater, then breathed and swallowed a mouthful of water. I began coughing, and my lungs were burning.

"We have to get him off Kyle!" Hazel yelled while reaching for Lokel with her demon hand.

The Creature swung around the wall Tonuko had created and threw itself at Hazel. Its legs stretched and wrapped around Hazel's neck, then it flipped and threw her into the sky. Hazel was already weak from her earlier kidnapping and spinning around while soaring through the air caused her to black out. Anya used her own boost-shoes to catch Hazel, and she watched as her dad drowned me. I began feeling very heavy, and my peripheral vision faded.

I feel . . . so weak. Please, someone save me.

At the Fallen Arena:

A laser wall held up a majority of the debris. Zach was breathing heavily down on one knee while his hands held up the laser wall. His arm muscles were bulging, and he was sweating bullets.

"C–C'mon guys, get out of here! I can't–hold on to this for much longer!" Zach gasped through his wheezes.

Steven used his robot legs to run in and out of the fallen building, grabbing as many students as he could. A few others joined him, but only about ten students were brought out before the laser wall vanished and all the debris fell on the remaining students and civilians.

"*Zach, no!*" Hunter screamed while running toward the debris. He started throwing small pieces of the ceiling behind him, then saw a leg and pulled on it. Hunter dragged Daniel's unconscious body out from under a large pipe. He dropped the leg and put his hands over his mouth. Police sirens grew louder behind him, and ten police cars along with ten S.W.A.T. cars pulled up to the scene. A couple heroes jumped out of the vehicles along with dozens of police officers.

"We'll get the civilians from the rubble; you get to safety!" a hero commanded to Hunter.

Hunter nodded and ran to a group of students. After the safe students were grouped, Alex soared into the sky from the pit next to the crashed building. He floated in the air like an angel, but then he tumbled down and crashed into the ground—he couldn't control his flying because of his broken wing.

"W–We have to send help down there. Kyle, Tonuko, Anya, Kate, and Hazel are fighting the kidnappers! They need help, Kyle might die!" Alex screamed as he slowly stood.

A hero looked over, shocked.

"Y–You students found the kidnappers? Are all the kidnapped people down there too?"

Alex nodded, then the hero looked back at the police cars. Out from one of the cars stepped Principal Lane and Vice Principal Kuntai.

Mrs. Kuntai looked at Alex, then stated, "We will not be sending any more of our students down in that hole. However, I want Daryll's unit to go and fetch our students who are already there!" Daryll was the head chief of the Veena police force. He had very long blonde hair and held an automatic rifle in his hands. Daryll nodded, then looked over at his unit of five police officers.

"Let's retrieve those students immediately. As of now, we will not be going for the kidnappers. Do you understand me?" His voice was deep and scratchy, as well as intimidating. The members of his unit nodded, then ran over to the pit. Daryll peered over the edge, sighed through his nose, and looked back at one man in his squad. The man was already setting up a rope system so they could safely get down the hole.

"Damn Kyle Straiter is down there. That boy has been nothing but trouble since the day his daddy ran away," Daryll seethed to himself. "I'll get you up here, Kyle, and get you fixed."

Meanwhile, other police officers set up a line of riot shields between them and the Care-Givers. A police officer shouted, "Expand!" then the shields grew to twenty times their original size. Kane regained his sense of sight, something he lost from Foul Odor, and David scooped up a pistol he had previously spat out. David aimed the pistol at Zach, who was crawling out of the rubble, and shot a round at him. Zach saw David shoot and retaliated with his own laser at the bullet. The laser sliced the bullet in half, impressing David.

Heroes stood in front of the riot shields now, ready to attack the Care-Givers. Kane smirked and cracked his neck. When the crack was audible, two giant hounds formed out of Kane's large shadow. The hounds pounced at the heroes and managed to take out two of the seven. The heroes in this city were known for being from the bottom of the barrel, so two Care-Givers would clearly be too much for them to handle on their own.

Lucky for them, Danielle Kuntai was there. Roots made of dirt crawled out from the cracks in the cement and wrapped around both hounds' legs. The roots seeped up the hounds, causing them to whimper. When the roots were all over the hounds' bodies, they squeezed, killing them.

"Ugh, those things were seriously grossing me out," Danielle cringed while taking out her ponytail.

Danielle Kuntai, Strength: Root—she can bend dirt into cylinder shapes, hence the roots, and manipulate them in any way she can think or move with her hands. The roots can only be made of dirt, can dig through any material, and can seep through any hole no matter the size.

"Mrs. Kuntai, please let us go down in the pit to help our friends!" Cindy pleaded. Seeing Alex so injured worried her about the state of the rest of us. Mrs. Kuntai shook her head, but her eyes watered.

"Trust me Cindy, I'm just as worried as you are. I don't even want to imagine what could be happening to my baby boy . . . but I will not allow heroes-in-training to be sent into a life-threatening situation." She looked over at Jon and Devin, who were both inching toward the pit. "That goes for you two as well! Nobody is entering that pit except Daryll's squadron!"

"You're such a bummer!" Jon groaned while trudging away from the pit. He leapt into the air above the police officers and unleashed an electric attack on Kane and David. Bolts of lightning shot out at the two Care-Givers and created a mini explosion on impact. David was thrown into the sky, but he landed on a newly created hawk that was gliding through the air.

David grinned devilishly, then gagged out another assault rifle. He unloaded on the cops on the ground while screaming, "Thanks for the help kid, now I have a clear shot on these coppers!" Devin calculated swiftly, then intercepted the hawk with a small acid web. The hawk vaporized, sending David falling to the ground. David reacted swiftly while still in the air and coughed up another grenade. He chucked the grenade, pulling the pin as he let go, and it fell into the center of the group of cops. It exploded, sending chunks of men and women flying everywhere.

"Students, you should get out of here. Go back to the hotel, this is a horrific fight. I don't want you seeing this!" Principal Lane ordered while stepping in front of the small group of uninjured students.

"Principal Lane, we can help the heroes! We know enough to fight these Care-Givers! Who knows, maybe we can take them down!" Camilla exclaimed with passion.

"No, it's way too dangerous for freshmen!" Principal Lane snapped.

Camilla sulked, then, to their right, they heard Tonuko's screams.

"Medics, we need medics, dammit! *Help*!" In Tonuko's hands was an unconscious Kate. Anya followed, carrying Hazel over her shoulder.

"W–Wait, where's Kyle?" Steven yelled.

Tonuko looked down and shook his head, then marched toward his mom.

"Mom, we need medics urgently! Kate is badly hurt!"

Mrs. Kuntai nervously looked at Kate, then nodded and called for the medics who had just arrived.

In the Pit, Moments Before:

I awoke coughing up water and gasped for air for a few seconds. Kate was kneeling next to me and pumping on my chest. She stopped C.P.R. when she saw I had awoken.

"Thank the Lord you woke up Kyle! We thought we lost you!" Kate cried as she hugged me tight. I hugged her back, then slowly stood. My adrenaline kicked in, alleviating most of the pain I'd felt.

The Creature grabbed the sword I had dropped, then lunged at me. I dodged it but it was clear I wasn't its intended target. The Creature stabbed Kate through her stomach and a loud crack echoed before the blade pierced through her back. Kate immediately fell to the ground. My eyes widened. The Creature cackled loudly and licked the blood off the sword's blade.

"Down goes one, down goes one, *down goes one!*" it repeated.

N–No, why did you stab her? Don't you want me, why would you hurt her? Take me instead, stop hurting my friends.

I yelled out angrily and tackled the Creature. It continued giggling as we rolled on the ground, but I kicked its stomach, knocking the wind out of it and finally shutting it up. The Creature soared into the air, then I leapt up at it and kicked it into a wall. The entire mountain side rumbled, then the Creature stretched its hands and launched them at me. The hands flew past my face, sticking into the wall behind me. The Creature pulled itself at me swiftly, and we collided. We both began falling to the ground, but the Creature used its arms to swing to safety. Meanwhile, I landed on a hard concrete pillar Tonuko had created to save me from falling to my death.

"Kyle, you gotta relax! We'll get her to safety! You are on the verge of death; you need to conserve your energy. Help is comin–" Tonuko said, trying to calm me.

*"I don't give a damn about the help coming! This bastard is killing my friends, so **I'll kill him!** He's not gonna hurt another person, I swear!"* I screeched furiously.

Tonuko was shocked as he began lowering me to the ground. Lokel leapt at me again, and we started fighting.

"Kyle doesn't sound like what he did just a day ago. He was yelling before about how he would beat the kidnappers and him this and he that, but now, he's

saying he's going to defend his friends. I see you Kyle, I see you!" Tonuko thought with a small smile.

I had successfully thrown Lokel into the wall, then landed in front of Tonuko and turned to face him. I put my hands on his shoulders and looked him dead in the eyes.

"Tonuko, take Anya, and Kate, and Hazel and get the fuck out of here!" I demanded.

"Are you crazy? I don't know what goes on inside that head, but I'm not leaving you here to die!"

I closed my eyes as I shouted in response, "Tonuko, my life is worth so much less than all of yours! I don't have a real reason to keep going, but you all do! Don't let me be the reason you die, get out of here with yours and everyone else's lives, dammit!"

Tonuko was completely stunned. He had no response. Tonuko stood looking at my frantic face for a few more seconds, then nodded his head.

"Alright, but when you make it out of here alive and a hero, we're gonna' talk about what you just said."

I nodded, not really hearing what he said, before turning back to the two kidnappers. Tonuko grabbed Anya's wrist and told her to get Hazel. The Creature was going to stop them, but Lokel grabbed his shoulder.

"Let them go, it's fine. We have the Kyle Straiter here and weakened. We'll get much greater compensation for having the son of Tyrant rather than a bunch of nobodies," Lokel explained quietly. The Creature stopped moving forward and smiled widely.

"A wise man you are, Lokel."

Lokel smiled, then looked at Anya and frowned.

"Goodbye, my sweet girl! I love you!" Lokel yelled to Anya.

Anya stopped in her tracks but didn't turn around. She instead continued walking away with Tonuko. Tonuko was carrying Kate, and Anya was carrying Hazel. Tonuko created a large pillar and sent the four up toward the surface. That left me alone with the two kidnappers.

"Come and get me," I snarled while standing defensively.

I didn't notice right away, but my arms and legs had grown slightly more muscular, and my hands up to my forearms had a darker tint to them . . .

Chapter 10

Two Equals Four

I stood in a face-off for a few moments with the kidnappers, then Lokel ran at me again. He released an onslaught of punches, but I dodged each one and caught his fist on the last punch.

"You miss your daughter, don't you Lokel?" I asked, trying to connect with him. Lokel became angry again and pulled his fist toward himself. He headbutted me, hurting both of us.

"You want to reconnect with your wife too, right?"

"Shut it, Straiter! You don't know me, so stop acting like it!" Lokel yelled. He dragged his hand on the ground, creating a glove around his fist, and punched at me. I threw my left arm up to block the punch, but his glove was so dense it broke my arm and sent me flying to my right. I crashed into the concrete wall, causing my head to bleed.

I was fed up with his denial, so I screamed, "Snap out of it, *you're her father!* You should be there for her, not hide away with this creep! Help me beat the Creature, then we can both go and face everyone, face our families!"

Lokel's eyes widened as the glove crumbled off his hand.

He's so similar to me. He can't face reality; he can't face the fact that he's not stuck in villainy. Lokel can get out of it though, he's not too far gone!

"Come on Lokel, work with me!" I shouted, pleading at this point.

Lokel looked at me and walked toward me. I could tell this made the Creature frantic.

"Lokel, you're with me! Don't listen to Tyrant's son. He's a manipulator just like his father!" the Creature screeched.

Lokel seemed to ignore the Creature and continued walking toward me.

Sadly, Lokel created two more swords and tossed one to me again. Our swords clashed, creating large sparks that flew out everywhere. We were sword fighting like before, but his movements were slower. Maybe I was moving faster, but I could predict what his moves were going to be before they occurred. After a few clashes, we each charged at the other. Lokel hopped off the back wall on the opposite side of me and super-jumped at my head. I slid underneath him and let my sword do all the work. The edges were burning because of my flaming hands, and the sword cut a deep, large gash from Lokel's forehead down to his waist. Lokel crashed into the wall behind me and fell onto his back. He was breathing heavily while staring up at the bright sky.

What did I do? Oh fuck, there's no way I just killed him. Please God, do not let him be dead!

"Lokel!" I cried while running toward his body.

The Creature was laughing in the background, but I ignored him and slid to Lokel's side. I held Lokel's head on my right forearm as my tears dripped onto my lap.

"Lokel, I'm so sorry. I didn't mean to—I just thought . . . Oh fuck, what did I do?"

Lokel reached his hand up and wiped my tears away.

"Kyle, you did nothing wrong. I purposefully acted recklessly so you would kill me. I can't face Anya. I just can't do it. Anya and Beth, they don't deserve the suffering I've put them through . . ."

"Don't give up on them, dammit! You can still go apologize; you have to! You owe it to her!" I screamed at him.

Lokel was now crying as well, and his smile was gone.

"K–Kyle man, I didn't want to go. I loved my family so damn much; they were my everything. That thing kidnapped me. H–He threatened to kill my family if I left. I–I had no choice! You have to believe me; *they have to believe me!*" Lokel sounded desperate now. Tears flooded his cheeks.

"They'll only believe you if you tell them! We can make it out. I can get you to a healer and—"

"I won't make it in time. You still have to defeat that thing, so no other family has to go through what mine did." Lokel could see the uncertainty in my face, so he continued, "You're a great kid Kyle. I'd be proud to be your father. Just, let Anya know that I loved her with all my heart."

"Don't you dare die on me. You *will* survive this," I shakily demanded.

Lokel weakly reached to the ground and pulled out a sword. He handed it to me with a smile.

"As long as I'm breathing, I'll help you beat that thing. You got it. I believe in you."

His words gave me courage. I stood and gripped the sword tight. My arms faded to a pitch black, and mist seeped out of my body. I shut the Creature's laughing up by leading with a knee to his face. The Creature crashed into the wall above its fish pool, then I led in with my sword, and stabbed through the Creature's stomach.

"I'll make you pay!" I screamed with all my might.

The Creature gasped when the sword pierced its body, and it kicked me off. Its leg stayed connected to me as his pushed me into the wall across the room. I raised my arm above my head, then sliced off the Creature's foot. It squealed like an animal, and the remainder of its leg shot back at the Creature's body like a tape measurer. The Creature was wobbly now, and blood was pouring out of its amputated foot. When I gripped the wall behind me, a large crater exploded out of it. I jumped at lightning speed at the Creature. It flung itself at me, screaming psychotically while it did so. I swung the sword at it, but the sword crumbled when it hit the Creature, doing no damage. I fell to the ground and tumbled a few feet, but I wasn't done. I turned around as the mist around me thickened and charged up for my final attack.

I combined my fire power, which for some reason was gray now, with as much super strength as I could muster. My right arm absorbed all the darkness on my body and grew to three times its original size. I leapt at the Creature and collided into it within the blink of an eye. I punched the Creature in the head, and as I swung down, I felt its skull cave in. When its head hit the ground, a large explosion occurred. I was thrown into the air, landing hard several dozen feet away. The explosion created a mini mushroom cloud along with a bright light. Lokel's body hit the wall again at a high speed, finishing him off.

Kyle Straiter, Strength One

I could barely keep my eyes open—one of them was bloodshot and the other was heavily swollen—but I still managed to crawl over to Lokel. I cried as I reached his body and yelled for him to keep fighting.

"Don't leave me, Lokel. Don't leave her! Fuck, I'm so sorry Anya! I'm so sorry!" I cried out. My crying was interrupted by a hand smashing my head into the ground.

"Quit your wailing for God's sake!" Daryll yelled while kneeling on my back. I continued to cry, so Daryll screamed, "Shut the hell up you annoying runt!" Daryll punched me in the back of my head with the barrel of his gun. All the adrenaline faded, making the pain of my injuries flood me all at once.

"Captain, please relax! Let's get him and these bodies to the surface!" a lady interrupted while looking down at Lokel.

"Shut yer' mouth! Kyle Straiter, did you murder these two?" Daryll screamed.

I nodded, then he took out handcuffs and cuffed me.

"Did you also murder the Nomeres? We found a brother and sister dead in a tunnel. Was that your doing?"

I thought for a moment because it wasn't. Tonuko and Anya killed the little girl, and they left Pete behind. However, I nodded, taking the blame for their murder.

"You've killed four people today, Kyle. *Four fucking people!* You're just like your daddy, a criminal scumbag!" Daryll grabbed the back collar of my shirt, picked me up, and slammed me into the ground again. "Hero in training my ass! You are a good-for-nothing waste of oxygen! You're lucky I don't kill you right now and say you died to one of these two *worthless assholes!*"

"*Shut up!*" I erupted while kicking Daryll across the room. I hopped to my feet, still handcuffed, and continued gasping for air as I yelled, "Lokel was forced into this because he was kidnapped! He loves his family so much, so keep his name out of your dirty mouth! How come on the first day here, my friends and I found the kidnappers while you and your squadron did *nothing!* **Fuck you!**"

Daryll stood and shot me twice. He shot my thigh and my shoulder, successfully taking me down.

"Let's go everyone, take that asshole and these other assholes to the surface!" Daryll marched across the room and stomped on my stomach. "Don't ever touch me again, you worthless runt."

The lady, who interrupted before, gingerly picked me up and harnessed me to herself, then began the climb back up the rope. That climb was the longest ten minutes of my life.

On the Surface:

David and Kane were at a standstill with Danielle and Principal Lane, along with Foul Odor, who had woken. Since Foul's stench was decreasing the Care-Giver's strengths, David and Kane couldn't land a solid hit. David vomited a puddle of blood for the fourth time before he yelled, "Kane, let's leave! I can't keep going, I'll die!"

Kane sighed and agreed.

A portal formed behind the two, and Kane waved as they passed through. Foul ran at the portal, trying to stop them, but it was gone as quickly as it formed. Some who were conscious cheered that the Care-Givers were gone, but many were worried about the injured. Heroes and police alike rescued the injured from the collapsed building. About the same time the hurt students and civilians were rescued, Daryll's squadron came back to the surface with me and the lifeless four.

"Mrs. Kuntai and Mr. Lane, your student is hereby under arrest for the murder of four legal citizens. He will be tried in front of the Seven Influential as an Angel Criminal," the woman officer informed Principal Lane and Vice Principal Kuntai.

"We understand," Principal Lane concisely stated.

"Anya, Anya, I'm so sorry!" I yelled to Anya, who was crying while looking at her deceased father. Tonuko hugged her tight, then looked over at me with soft, understanding eyes.

"Fuck, I'm so sorry! I didn't mean to, I swear! He loved you so much, he was forced into villainy! Please Anya, believe him! *He loved you!*" I was quickly cut off by Daryll.

"Didn't I say to shut your mouth?" Daryll hit me with the butt of his gun again, causing my blood to splatter. Tonuko was infuriated by this and had to be held back by Jon.

"What the hell do you think you're doing? That's a hero you're hitting!" Tonuko roared at Daryll. He walked away, chuckling to himself. Daryll escorted me to a police car and began filling out paperwork.

I'm a murderer, a complete failure. I'm sorry everyone. I failed . . .

My knees were weak, and my vision was shaky and hazy. After a minute, I collapsed onto the street, completely unconscious. I was carried to an ambulance and driven to the nearest hospital.

"If that jerk goes to jail, I swear I'll kick his ass!" Tonuko yelled furiously. He turned around and kicked a rock a dozen feet away, then looked over at the pit.

"I trusted you Kyle. You said you could handle it. What happened down there? Why is Anya's dad dead?" Tonuko was dying to ask me questions but knew he might never be able to.

Alex sat in the back of an ambulance while a nurse taped up his mangled wing. He took a deep breath, then an officer he recognized approached him.

"Officer Daniels?" Alex asked. One of Alex's eyes was swollen shut and blood covered his face.

"Alex, it's a shame to see you like this. We found your teacher down the street, but it turns out she's a fresh Care-Giver. Diana Palkun was an alias; her real name is Angelica Haslem, otherwise known as Lady Patch."

Alex's eye widened, then Officer Daniels handed him a paper.

"She's been taken into custody, but we found this on her. Please make sure to give this to your principal whenever you see him." Officer Daniels ruffled Alex's hair and gave him a big smile. "I hope I can have dinner with your family again soon so I can see you in a better condition. Rest up, big guy."

Officer Daniels left, and Alex opened the folded paper.

"Hey Alex, what's that?" Tonuko asked while walking over along with Anya, Camilla, Jon, and Devin.

"It's Kyle's field trip permission form . . . it says he lives at 10853 Western Sydney Drive. Isn't that the abandoned house in town?" Alex asked while looking up from the paper.

Tonuko snatched the paper from Alex's hand. He couldn't believe his eyes.

"That house has been abandoned for like six and a half years. You're telling me Kyle has lived there all his life? And who's Gem Straiter?" Tonuko asked rhetorically.

"Kyle and Tyrant have some kind of a connection. He has multiple strengths and Tyrant erases strengths. The introduction said Kyle's parents are unknown, but his mom is Gem Straiter here on a school form, and Kyle has lived in an abandoned house for almost seven years? Something's up," Tonuko angrily speculated.

"What are you doing reading a personal paper? Shame on all of you! Follow Vice Principal Kuntai back to the hotel immediately!" Principal Lane demanded after swiping the permission form out of Tonuko's hand. The uninjured students followed Vice Principal Kuntai down the street, and Principal Lane ran his hands through his flowing white hair.

"Mr. Lane, we need to send Alex Galeger to the emergency department for surgery on his wing immediately," a medic informed Principal Lane. He waved the medic off, signaling for the ambulance to take Alex.

"Mr. Lane, you're the principal of Kyle Straiter, correct?" a short, plump man in a black tuxedo asked while walking up to Principal Lane. His fat, red tie contrasted with the white undershirt, and his hair was black and greased back. "I am George Johnson from the Villain Investigation Association (V.I.A.). I'll need you to come with me for some questioning about relationships with Kyle Straiter."

"I'm sorry, but I'm only his principal. I do not know of his connections," Principal Lane lied.

"Wrong, you're lying. You can't get past me; my lie detector strength is unmatched. Please just come with me. We are on the same side for Kyle."

Principal Lane reluctantly obliged and followed George to a black V.I.A. van. They drove off to the nearest V.I.A. station.

On the Way to the Hotel:

"Mom, when can we visit our hurt friends?" Tonuko asked. Mrs. Kuntai sighed as she put her hair back into a high ponytail.

"I'd guess you can visit your friends freely tomorrow, assuming they're awake. However, as for Kyle, you will most likely not be able to visit him since he is an Angel Criminal," Mrs. Kuntai explained.

"What's an Angel Criminal anyway?" Steven asked, completely confused.

"You are such a nimrod. Kyle is technically a murderer by law, but he killed four villains. With that in mind, he did what a legal hero would do, but he's not a legal hero yet. Even though he killed two of the most-wanted kidnappers in recent history, he still killed legal citizens. Multiple heroes have had things like this happen with crimes, and they're classified as 'Angel Criminals.' He will have to go in front of the Seven Influential," Khloe explained, cutting off Mrs. Kuntai before she could speak. Steven still looked lost, so Khloe sighed, "You don't know the Seven Influential? They're the seven most-powerful heroes in our current society. They handle all Angel Criminal cases!"

"Oh, that makes way more sense. Thanks Khloe, you're the man!" Steven smiled as he softly punched her arm. Khloe rolled her eyes.

"If Kyle is found not guilty, he's free to continue training to be a hero. However, if he's guilty, well, that's the end of his hero career," Mrs. Kuntai informed the group solemnly.

Everyone went silent, then Devin stated, "He'll be not guilty." A couple people looked at Devin, confused on how he could be so certain.

"Yeah, that kid is pretty damn amazing. First off, they'll want him as a hero so he doesn't turn into a villain if he's jailed. On top of that, he just defeated the most elusive kidnappers of the century. That little man will be just fine," Jon chuckled while resting his hands behind his head. They reached the hotel as Jon finished, and Mrs. Kuntai turned to face the group.

"Very true, there's nothing to worry about. Now just try and get some sleep," Mrs. Kuntai concluded.

She'd begun walking back toward the fight scene when Tonuko blurted out, "Mom, do you know Gem Straiter?" Mrs. Kuntai stopped dead in her tracks and didn't give an answer. "It said in his introduction before our fight that Kyle's parents were unknown, but on a school official form, it listed his mom as Gem Straiter. What's that all about? You guys do know his mom?"

"Tonuko, I will not give you personal information about another student. How did you even get that form?" Mrs. Kuntai retorted.

"An officer gave it to Alex. He said he got it from our evil teacher. It had Gem's signature and everything," Tonuko added.

"Her signature? How's that possible, she's–" Mrs. Kuntai stopped herself from finishing the sentence.

"Mom, is she dead?" Tonuko asked bluntly.

Those words hovered in the air.

Nobody knew how to respond, except Mrs. Kuntai. "I am not in any position to talk about Kyle's family," she stated. Tonuko tensed his fist, and his eyes watered.

"We already know he hasn't been telling any of us the truth! We know he has more than two strengths. All these villains know his full name and keep talking about bringing him 'back' to some guy! Hell, I wouldn't be surprised at this point if Kyle wasn't even fourteen! Can't we just be told the truth for once? Can't you tell your own son something?"

Mrs. Kuntai looked wide-eyed at Tonuko. Tears brimmed from his eyes, then Anya hugged him and looked up at Mrs. Kuntai with her own watery eyes. "W–We're all scared. Please, just tell us something," Anya whimpered.

Mrs. Kuntai took off her glasses and wiped her eyes. She put them back on, then cleared her throat.

"Listen, I know how worried and frightened you are, but I can't spread private things about Kyle to his classmates. That's for him to decide when he's ready to tell you."

"That's the thing, he'll never be ready! He keeps his emotions all bottled up and only bursts in small spurts of anger and frustration!" Camilla shouted.

Mrs. Kuntai hesitated and bit her lip.

"Alright, alright fine. Gem and I were best friends throughout high school, but she got with a man I couldn't agree with her dating. However, she was madly in love. As much as I hated the guy, they were adorable, a dream couple. Then, the bad came. She and I drifted. I found out she had passed ten years after graduation and Kyle was alone. I had the option of taking Kyle in. It's what Gem wanted if anything bad happened, but they couldn't get him out of the house and gave up. I honestly didn't know if he was alive until Fallen took Kyle under his wing years later," Mrs. Kuntai explained to the group.

"So that night, when we chased after him, he was getting the permission form and forged his mom signature," Cindy thought aloud.

"I guess so, but that's all I'll tell you. I've already said too much . . . " Mrs. Kuntai bit her nail and looked around, lost in thought. She snapped out of it and looked at the group. "Get to bed, all of you! Don't you dare even *think* about wandering out of this hotel until morning!" She walked away, leaving the students confused.

"Something still isn't adding up. Where did his dad go?" Khloe asked rhetorically. Obviously, no one knew the answer—at least that's what they thought. In reality, Tonuko pieced it all together.

"*Everything's adding up. Kyle's mom died because bad things happened in her relationship with a man my mom didn't like. Every criminal is trying to bring Kyle back to a 'boss', Tyrant knew him . . .*" Tonuko thought with his hand on his chin. He knew the answer, and he was furious. Tonuko stomped off and went straight to his room. Everyone else shrugged it off and went to sleep.

Kyle's Mind:

I woke up in an abyss where I was floating. It felt as if I was in water, but I could breathe. However, when I tried to speak, nothing came out. I looked around, very confused, then saw a man float out of the darkness. The man was Tyrant.

"Kyle, what is this? Is this your doing?" Tyrant asked, genuinely confused. I shrugged. He rubbed his chin while thinking out loud, "This must be one of your ten strengths. Anyway, I heard you killed Lokel and the Creature. Well done, well done indeed."

Shut your face, I thought. Apparently, he could hear the thought because he laughed. *How do you already know I beat the kidnappers?*

"My boss was watching with BloodShot. Along with always having eyes on me, I have eyes everywhere."

My stomach dropped when he said this. My eyes opened so wide they hurt, and my head spun.

"Y–Your boss? You're the most powerful villain in history! Why do you have a boss? You never told me about a boss before!"

"You see, Kyle, my boss is nothing but a child, a teenager in fact. He's three years younger than you, eleven years old. He is so strong, though, that he was immediately placed above me when his strength was developed. A new, horrifying, deadly strength. Son, just because I'm the mob boss of villains doesn't mean I can't be–be scared."

I was speechless—to think, the man I've hated, one I thought had no emotions, was afraid . . . of a teenager.

How can he be so strong? What the hell is his strength?

"I believe it's called sickness, or illness, or something along those lines. His name is Plague, and he is being trained under BloodShot and me. With one move, he can end the world as we know it. I will not give you the exact details, because I can't trust you, but if he was as careless as the Creature, we'd all be dead right now."

I still couldn't believe my ears. Someone that strong is alive? A sudden pounding filled our ears, and my head felt as if it was about to explode.

"Don't you dare tell anyone a word about Plague, or I'll have BloodShot eliminate you! *I'm warning you Kyle!*"

I blinked a few times from the bright sunlight and opened my eyes. I could hear beeping from the heart monitor. I groaned in pain, but I was happy to be alive.

"Thank goodness you're awake," the doctor sitting at a desk next to me sighed. She was lanky, tan, and had big bags under her eyes. Her hair was long, brown, and curly.

"Wh–What day is it? What time is it?"

"It's Tuesday, September 2nd. It's about four days since you were brought in."

Shocked, I looked at her and yelled, "Four days?"

"Keep your voice down please, and don't talk too much. You need to conserve your energy. You lost a lot of blood. You were just running on adrenaline and hysterical strength in that battle. Also, you have a hero visitor from a nearby city whenever you're ready."

I nodded, and told the doctor to let the visitor in.

In walked a man wearing a red cloak and a plain, white mask with one eye-hole. I couldn't see any of his face. The doctor walked out.

"Kyle Straiter, my favorite cocky son of a bitch! You surprised me. The Creature and Lokel weren't an easy duo to take down." The man's voice was easily recognizable. My heart hurt, and I started hyperventilating. "Yes Kyle, it's me, BloodShot."

"I swear I haven't told anyone about Plague! I just woke up from a four-day coma!"

He nodded, seemingly happy with my response.

"I know, that's not why I'm here. I just wanted to pay a visit to my future partner in crime. I saw the dark force unleashed inside you when Lokel died. Something is living in you. It will take over your very soul when every single one of your friends die." I looked at him angrily and gripped the hospital bed sheets. "You will join me eventually. It's your destiny."

I felt a shooting pain in my left arm, leading to my chest. I grasped my chest, then the heart monitor began beeping very fast. BloodShot let out a muffled, evil chuckle as he slowly backed up. The doctor rushed back into the room and yelled for the nurses. BloodShot escaped easily, and I was given medicine that relaxed my heartbeat. A police officer walked in an hour later, took off his hat, and bowed.

"Kyle Straiter, you have a court date in front of the Seven Influential next Wednesday, September 10th. Your hero career will be decided on if you are not guilty and let free, or guilty and sent to jail."

I was terrified, more scared than any time I'd faced a villain. The reality was really setting in.

My hero career, over? It hasn't even started yet!

"I—I understand . . . sir." The police officer put his hat back on and sighed.

"I would also like to apologize for Daryll's behavior. I don't know what came over him, but it was unprofessional. Also, thank you for your service," the officer stated while giving me a smile. "Even if you are convicted as a murderer, you are a hero in the eyes of the families whose loved ones were returned to them. You are a hero, Kyle."

The man held out a photo of a boy whose black hair was in a bowl cut. I could vaguely recognize him as the malnourished boy I saw in the dark room. "My Logan is home because of you. Truly, from the bottom of my heart, thank you." The officer was tearing up, but he wiped his eyes and composed himself.

"No need to thank me. It's what a person should do. I'm so happy to hear Logan is home safe now."

The officer nodded with a smile, then left the room to go and talk with the front desk staff about the intruder.

I'm a hero . . .

Back at the Hotel:

"Mom, it's been four days! Can we please go visit our friends now?" Tonuko pleaded. Mrs. Kuntai sighed and shook her head.

"You heard the police: you aren't allowed to visit the hospital until Kyle is officially placed under arrest!" Mrs. Kuntai yelled. "I'm so tired of repeating myself Tonuko!"

"Actually, I managed to convince the police to let the kids in! You should be grateful Officer Daniels is such a good guy!" Principal Lane happily informed the group. Everyone was excited to see their friends, and Tonuko led the squad to the hospital. He reached the front desk at the same time as Principal Lane. The man at the desk immediately knew who they were.

"Down that hall are all your students, Mr. Lane. Your students are allowed to see everyone except Kyle Straiter. Only the principal and vice principal are allowed to see him."

The slightly disappointed group didn't let what they'd already known get them down. Jon immediately went to Kate's room. Devin found Hazel's room, and the rest went down the hall one room at a time. Alex's room was the first that they entered.

"Alex! I'm so happy you're okay!" Cindy squealed while running up to hug him. Alex hugged her back, then looked over at Tonuko. He gave Tonuko a smirk, holding out his fist.

"We did it," Alex said, sounding both relieved and proud. Tonuko grinned, then fist-bumped Alex.

"Hell yeah we did."

People questioned Alex; Tonuko stayed silent.

Tonuko's rage at me was growing by the minute, and not being able to talk to me—maybe ever again—to find out why I lied was pissing him off even more. Tonuko and his friends visited everyone else; they even checked on Kate and Hazel. When Tonuko entered Kate's room, the environment was completely different than earlier. Jon and Kate were embracing each other while crying, and Principal Lane and Mrs. Kuntai were sullen, teary-eyed. "Wh–What's the matter? Are you going to be okay Kate?" Tonuko asked, concern lingered heavily in his voice.

"*I'mnotgoingtobeahero,*" Kate admitted through her hyperventilating. Tonuko stared blankly and balled his fists. Though she babbled gibberish, he deciphered what she was saying.

"A section of Kate's spine was shattered. She will never walk again," Mrs. Kuntai explained, taking off her glasses.

"But Kate was a top prospect of her class, top twenty in the country. This can't be it!" Tonuko exclaimed. His mother hushed him and gave him a hug. Tonuko never cried, but he felt like something was lodged in his throat. After a few more minutes of comforting Kate, Principal Lane and Mrs. Kuntai left for my room.

"Why are you guys allowed in there, but we aren't?" Tonuko asked angrily. Mrs. Kuntai shushed him again, but more aggressively this time.

"Tonuko, we are in a hospital!" She whisper–yelled. Tonuko stayed silent, allowing her to explain. "Since we are his principal and vice principal, we are allowed inside briefly to talk to Kyle before he is sent to jail. Have a little respect for him. He is in a very dark place right now!"

Tonuko rolled his eyes, stuck his hands in his pockets, and walked away.

Mrs. Kuntai shook her head with a stressed expression, then turned to Principal Lane. He gave her a slight smile and shrugged. Mrs. Kuntai walked past him into my room.

"Oh, I didn't think anyone from school could visit me," I stated when the two walked in. Principal Lane gave me a handshake before he and Mrs. Kuntai sat in the chairs by my bed.

"How are you feeling, Kyle? You had some very serious injuries: a broken arm, two stab incisions, a broken nose, a popped blood vessel in your eye, trauma to your back and head, and a serious stress fracture near your heart. If that fracture was any closer, you would have been gone."

I looked down at my hands and tensed them.

"It doesn't matter. I'm a criminal now. I'm no better than my father." I looked over at the two with a distraught, terrified expression. My lip quivered, my eyebrows drooped, and my cheeks and eyes were red. "I killed Anya's dad, ruined her family. I'm a monster!"

The two comforted me for a few moments, then they stood once I was calm again.

"Kyle, I have a quick question: how long have you been forging your mother's signature?" Mrs. Kuntai asked with slight anger in her voice.

"Well, how else am I supposed to get things signed by my parents? How about I ask a question: why is stuff getting sent home when you both know about my situation?" Principal Lane sighed and looked out the window.

"That was Lady Patch's doing. She sent it to your house so you would be trapped into fighting Bobby the Care-Giver."

I nodded. I couldn't be angry anymore since it wasn't their fault. Principal Lane crossed his arms and glared at Mrs. Kuntai, then loudly asked, "Well, since we're asking so many questions, why did you blabber to students about Kyle's personal life, Danielle?"

"How did you find out about that?" Danielle questioned him while looking both shocked and guilty.

"Devin told me. Now, do you mind telling Kyle what you said to that group of students?" I looked confused and was slightly worried. Danielle bit her lip, then took a deep breath.

"W–Well, I caved in and told them how your mother passed," Danielle admitted. My mouth dropped. I was enraged.

Are you fucking joking!

I swung my arm to punch the bed post, but I hit my heart rate monitor instead and sent it flying into the wall. It made a loud bang, and when I looked up at the two, they looked worried. I took a breath and relaxed. "Sorry for losing my temper, b–but it's . . . now they're one step closer to finding out about Tyrant." They nodded. Suddenly, Daryll burst into the room.

"C'mon you criminal, time to go to the doghouse!" Daryll shouted as he marched up to me. The nurses had disconnected the wires and bandaged me up earlier, so I was ready to go. I was still very sore, but Daryll didn't care. He grabbed my broken wrist—which had been healed by a healer, yet was still painful to the touch—and ripped me out of the bed.

"Officer Daryll, take it easy on him! Christ, what is the matter with you?" Mrs. Kuntai exclaimed.

Daryll gave her a confused expression, then looked down at my body; I was crumpled on the floor, breathing heavily.

"You want me to take it easy on a genocider? Don't make me laugh, Danielle Kuntai. This boy is a villain in the making. It's obvious!"

Principal Lane cut him off by looming over him menacingly with his arms crossed. Principal Lane was a very tall, very muscular man, nearly seven feet tall and 280 pounds of pure muscle. Daryll's ego shrunk as he nodded, then gingerly handcuffed me. He led me out of the hospital. The worst part of it all was that I had to walk past my classmates.

They watched with what I could only assume was disgust and fear. I couldn't look any of them in the eye—I was too guilty and filled with shame. I was placed in a police car and driven to the nearest police station.

Lucky for me, I guess, our state's official courtroom for Angel Criminal trials was in the next town. I wouldn't need to travel for now. I'd stay in Veena until my trial date, when I'd be driven half an hour to the courtroom. I dreaded that day. I didn't want to know what kind of questions would be asked and what kind of adjudication I would receive.

I hope I'm never let out; I don't deserve to be a hero anymore. I blew my chance. I'm a fraud. I'm Tyrant's son, and my whole life is already planned out for me. It doesn't matter what I do. I'll never escape it. I don't deserve to be when I'm just a murderer . . .

Chapter 11

News

All the students except Kate and Hazel were released from the hospital that day. Principal Lane sent Vice Principal Kuntai with the students on the bus ride home, and he stayed in Veena until Hazel and Kate were released. The ride was sullen, very quiet. The energy died down when everyone saw me officially get arrested and sent away to prison.

Tonuko was still fuming. His anger was building by the minute. Unlike me, he was able to control his anger and keep it to himself. He didn't want to share the information he knew, and he wanted to be there for Anya since her father had just passed. Tonuko comforted Anya on the bus, but her reaction surprised him.

"I'll be okay. It was for the best. I missed my dad so much . . . He did so many bad things. I would take him back in a heartbeat, but he would have probably been p–put to death anyway by the Seven Influential." Tonuko was shocked by her acceptance. "I love him. He'll always be here no matter physical or not. I'll never be able to move on though if I worry about it all day."

"That is really mature of you, Anya. I don't think I could react like that if my parent passed a few days ago." Anya tried to force a smile and nodded, then looked out the window as tears dripped down her face. Tonuko embraced her as she cried for the next few minutes.

"So, Alex, are you excited to go back home? I bet all our parents really miss us," Steven asked while leaning on his knees, facing the center aisle. Alex nodded happily and picked at the bandage on his left forearm.

"Yeah, I really hope we can stay home for a few days. Our parents must be so worried. I mean, how could they not be? We were just involved in a massive villain fight with Care-Givers and the most infamous kidnappers ever. A student was arrested for murder. Our teacher was an undercover Care-Giver . . . the list goes on." Alex looked up, but instead of sadness or anger, he looked determined. "But that doesn't matter. We're all gonna be heroes, and when we are, we'll have big fights like this where nobody will die. I just know it!"

People in the surrounding seats smiled. It seemed Alex's mini-speech inspired some. Despite the students' feeling being lifted, most of the bus ride was silent. The trauma of the fight was too much to get over so soon.

A Few Days Later, a Couple of Cities Away:

BloodShot stepped out of the bus with a young boy at his side. Both wore the same type of mask, and the boy wore a black trench coat with a large collar and black cargo pants; his hair was pure white. Also, the tips of the boy's fingers were black all the way down to his second knuckles, but the cut off wasn't clean. Instead, the black spiked down farther and blended with his peach skin.

The two walked a few blocks, eventually making it to their destination: a small, one-story, faded yellow house with a gray roof. The roof had tiles falling off, and some of the windows in the house were shattered. BloodShot walked to the door as the boy hid behind him and knocked loudly. After a couple of seconds, they could hear shuffling in the house. The knob slowly turned, and the door creaked opened.

"Ah, Sir BloodShot, I'm glad you made it. Please, come in." The man who answered was gripping the white cross and "12" pendants dangling from his gray chain. The man's hair was long, white, and patchy. He stood with a hunch, shortening his already frail frame. BloodShot stepped in, readjusting his mask as he looked around.

"Where is King?" BloodShot sternly asked.

The man turned around and waved his hand, signaling for BloodShot to follow. They entered a doorway with a half-broken door and walked down the concrete stairs into the basement. When BloodShot turned the corner, he saw a man sitting on a large, burgundy wood chair with pink spurs of mist floating around his shoulders. One of the mist clumps flew out at BloodShot, making whispering noises as it did so. When it was closer, BloodShot could see that the mist had small, golden yellow dots for eyes. The mist flew around his head, then returned to the man.

"King, a pleasure to see you again."

"BloodShot, why are you here? Did you come to steal another from my posse? We're already missing Stafer. We've started up business again, got a grand for possessing a hero-in-training's father," the man, obviously King, ranted.

King was fairly muscular and tall. His appearance was quite abnormal: his irises and sclerae were all the same shade of purple and his pupils were tiny, golden yellow dots, the same as his mist creatures. Where his fingers should be were rich black claws, and his skin wasn't a normal human's color of skin, but instead gray with a hue of purple. BloodShot rolled his eyes, then leaned back on his right foot and put his hand behind the boy's head. The boy, who was about five-foot-eight (small in comparison to BloodShot, who was six-foot-seven), stepped from behind BloodShot but was still visibly timid.

"Who's this?"

"This boy is the future of villainy; his name is Plague. Plague has an extremely powerful strength, and when activated, he could very well kill anyone he touches. I know that you know many expert black-market crafters. I need a pair of strength-resistant gloves for Plague. You can take his measurements today," BloodShot explained in a condescending tone.

King snorted, then crossed his arms. "Oh, come to make demands, have you? You know I do nothing for free. Also, it seems the boy is touching you with no problems. If you had someone make you specialized clothing, why not have them make him specialized gloves?" King asked.

BloodShot crossed his arms to mimic King and glared into his eyes.

"You think I'm that stupid? Of course I would have had specialized gloves made for him, but my usual crafter was caught last week. You should know how seriously the idiotic heroes take the crafting of strength-enhancing and restricting items."

King nodded as he stood from his chair. "I know, I'm just pulling your leg. I'll have the gloves soon—"

"I'm not finished. On top of the needing gloves, I've come to hire you for a job."

King stopped moving to grab a cloth measuring tape and turned around to face BloodShot again. "As I've told you before, Tyrant has been struggling to find a healer to add to his Care-Givers for years. There is the famous Blavins' daughter in Tyrant's son's class. So, I need your group's help in kidnapping her. We might try to get Kyle as well."

"You expect me to risk my crew's life for Tyrant's personal needs? Get lost," King hissed.

BloodShot opened his cloak and put his hand on the handle of his blade.

"Unless you want to end up dead, I suggest you comply. The payment I was talking about isn't little by any means. Getting a healer for Tyrant pays a hefty sum of cash." BloodShot and King stared each other down and, unlike others who crumble in the bloodlust of BloodShot, King stood his ground.

"You can steal Stafer from me and make demands, but you will not threaten me in the presence of my kingdom."

BloodShot raised an eyebrow and let out a small chuckle.

"You call this dirty cellar in a garbage house a kingdom?" BloodShot asked in a biting tone.

King shook his head, then the yellow in his eyes lit up. He smirked and held his hands open and parallel to his sides.

"I wasn't talking about the cellar," King stated. The world around King, BloodShot, and Plague faded to pink. They were still standing on a concrete floor, but around them was a pink mist that stretched as far as the eye could see. Within the smoke, different vortexes opened and closed. Thousands upon thousands of the same smoke wisps were floating around. Plague gripped BloodShot's cloak tighter, then BloodShot took a deep breath and sighed.

"As much as I love to fight, that's not why I'm here today. I'm here to get an order for gloves for Plague and to inform you of the job opportunity and other recent news."

When BloodShot let go of his blade handle, King blinked. His blink forced BloodShot and Plague to blink as well. When they opened their eyes, they were back in the cellar.

"What other news do you speak of? I know you were in Veena, so is it about someone the Creature and Lokel managed to nab?"

BloodShot shook his head and grinned devilishly. "Better, they're *dead*." The cross man gasped and gripped his pendants tighter.

"Dead . . . by who?" the cross man asked frantically. BloodShot smiled, a teethy, maniacal smile. He put his hands up, as if he was proud or if he was the person who killed the kidnappers.

"Our very own Kyle Straiter. Tyrant's son is growing into his own person, but his roots are still caging him in. His evil instincts are coming out in spurts. Even better, his evil instincts seem to be giving him power. A dark presence is living inside that boy, and when he unleashed it on the Creature, he killed it within seconds!" BloodShot exclaimed.

From behind King's chair, a rattling and hissing echoed. A large woman—not fat or muscular, but overall, just bigger than a normal human—crawled out and leaned on the back of the chair. Crawled was an accurate description, as she didn't have human legs, but instead had eight large, cream–white, spider-like legs. Her skin was the same cream–white color and protruding from her cheeks were large, brown centipede fangs. They repeatedly twitched and hit each other, creating the rattling noise. Her eyes were entirely red, her hair was black, and she had horns the same color as her fangs. Her teeth were razor sharp, and she had normal human arms that were proportionate to her body. In total, she was around fifteen to twenty feet long; her head was two-hundred centimeters in circumference.

"I like the sssound of this boy. Kyle Sssstraiter . . . maybe I'll add him to my lissst," she hissed. She smiled widely. Her fangs glimmered in the dim light from a hanging lightbulb that she was practically hitting her head on.

"And who might this be?" BloodShot asked while straightening his jacket. BloodShot's mood quickly changed. He was more on edge.

"This is our reaper, the White Reaper to be exact. Her strength is devastating," King boasted.

White Reaper, Strength: HellFlame—she can create white flames and creatures out of thin air. After burning for a while, the flames spawn the creatures, which look like beetles with the same fangs as her. She also can turn her bones into long claws that pierce her skin and shoot out like more limbs. She can control them as if they are arms or legs, depending on where they come out of her body.

"Interesting, I wasn't aware of this addition. I assume she is called the reaper because of her kill count?" White Reaper tilted her head and smiled eerily.

"5. 8. 7." BloodShot tensed his fist and let out a small, quiet gasp.

"Five hundred and eighty-seven?" BloodShot asked, completely appalled. She slowly nodded. He cleared his throat.

"She's actually not a new addition. She is the pride of my squad, but we kept her hidden from you so you wouldn't steal her away from me. She's like the daughter I never had," King happily admitted while looking up at White Reaper.

"Oh, how gross. Anyway, Kyle will be going to court for his murders in less than a week, but I assume he will be set free as long as things go smoothly. If he is set free, we will begin planning the ambush on E.H., but not strike for weeks. There is rumor spreading of the connection between Kyle and us, so we want to forbid any attacks until the rumors die down. If the connection of Tyrant and Kyle is released to the public, that could ruin our entire plan with him."

King nodded. BloodShot spun around on his heels, causing his cloak to swoop in the air.

Plague's measurements were quickly taken, then the two Care-Givers walked out, leaving King to ready his request for the gloves. As they walked out of the house, they noticed the day had turned to night. King could manipulate time within his dimension and caused several hours to pass.

"BloodShot, why were you afraid of that girl?" Plague asked while looking up at him nervously. BloodShot looked around, then sighed.

"Her kill count is five hundred and eighty-seven. She appears younger than me by at least a couple of years but has more than five hundred kills more than I do. She's deadly but," his frown turned to a mischievous smile, "that just means when we ambush E.H., there will be at least a few deaths at her hands."

It was Friday, September 5th, only five days until my court trial.

Two Days Later: Madeline Jail, Cell 143:

I sat in silence against the wall in the back of my cell. Imagery of the dead bodies of police officers, the Nomeres, Lokel, and the Creature haunted my mind. Lokel's bloodied laceration and blank pupils, the Creature's caved-in face, my friends all hurt and partially dead while I could do nothing. It tortured me to think about it.

I don't deserve friends, I failed them. I'm in jail when I'm supposed to be training to be a hero. What the hell is wrong with me? Will I ever escape Tyrant's grasp?

I put my head in my hands and sat there, not crying, but with the painful feeling of failure and despair. The man in the cell across from me sighed, then stood, and walked to his cell bars.

"Kid, you got nothing to worry about. You had a reason to kill. It was villains in the process of hurting others. You'll be let outta here in no time."

I looked up at him and took a deep breath.

"I don't deserve to be let out. I went to jail in the first place. I'm just like him."

The prisoner raised an eyebrow and scratched his head.

"Just like who? Your daddy?" The prisoner asked in a mocking tone.

"He's not my dad. He's a lunatic, an animal. I hate him, I hate him with every ounce of my being. I'll never be like him, *never*."

The prisoner felt uneasy and nodded, then laid back on his cot. A few minutes later, Daryll approached my cell and banged on the bars with his baton.

"Straiter, you have a couple of visitors. C'mon kid, let's go."

I stood, confused, and followed Daryll. He led me to the usual room where prisoners communicated with their loved ones and told me which booth to go to. When I sat down and looked up, I saw Foul Odor through reinforced glass. He pointed at the phone to my left, so I picked it up and held it to my ear.

"Hey Kyle, I'm happy to see you've recovered well."

I didn't say anything, just looked down at the table. I was too full of shame to look him in the eyes.

"Well, I just wanted to say thank you for taking care of the kidnappers. Also, a couple of fighters and I have stepped down from fighting and agreed to help boost security at your school. I'll be working under Fox-Tails. Your principal said something about needing to beef up security until they can teach you students the proper mindset needed while a criminal is attacking. There's someone here to question you on personal relationships." Foul Odor looked at me one more time, then stood and handed the phone to another man who was wearing a black suit and a red tie. His slicked back, black hair shined in the light.

"Hello Kyle Straiter. It's a pleasure to meet you. I'm George Johnson of the Villain Investigation Association. I questioned your principal the day of the attack on your personal relationships, and I have to say, you do have an uncanny resemblance of your father."

I swiftly looked up wide-eyed at the man. My heart raced, and I could feel sweat form on my back.

"How the fuck do you know I look like Tyrant? Just what the hell do you want?"

George leaned back in the chair with a big, smug smirk.

"Actually, I didn't know. Your principal successfully avoided all questions about your family. But now I know! Now, there are a couple of questions I have for y–"

I cut George off by slamming the phone into the concrete desk. The phone smashed in half and bits of plastic flew everywhere. I glared menacingly at George as I was being handcuffed by Daryll. I continued to stare him down until I couldn't see him anymore.

George looked at the papers in his hand and sighed, "Too much?"

"Of course that was too much! You didn't have to trick him like that when he's in a vulnerable state like this!" Foul whisper–yelled with his fists tensed. George stopped smiling and looked at the broken phone in front of him.

"I am his lawyer. I need details about his family for the trial."

George stood from his seat and stopped next to Foul.

"Now that I know he's the–," he covered his mouth with the papers and very quietly whispered, "son of Tyrant," then, he continued normally, "I can figure out alibis and ways for Kyle to get around or avoid completely personal questions at the trial. However, I need to get in touch with him again. I think he'd be more cooperative if he let me finish explaining what my purpose here was."

Foul sighed and wiped his eyes, a common habit of stress, then reached into his short pocket. He pulled out his wallet, and from there, took out his Hero I.D. The two walked to the cells' entrance, and Foul held up his I.D. for the guard.

"Hello, Mr. Odor," the big guard smiled while opening the door.

The two walked in and saw Daryll locking me up again. As they walked toward the cells, they saw two tall, muscular, heavily armed men wearing ski masks and bullet-proof vests guarding my cell. Foul advanced to the cell bars and called out to me.

"Kyle, please listen, you got it all wrong!"

I turned around and stomped up to the bars while huffing angrily.

"Got what all wrong? This guy knows too much. He's gonna tell everyone! I'll never get out if everyone knows who my dad is!" I whispered loudly.

Foul shook his head, then George walked up to us.

"Kyle, I'm a part of the V.I.A., but I'm also a graduated lawyer. I am defending you in the case under the Seven Influential. I need to know your family relationships, family life, connections, all of that. I need to plan strategies to avoid it during the trial, so the information won't get leaked everywhere. Please, allow us to take you to the organization, and I promise you'll be more comfortable than here."

I hesitated and looked over at Foul.

"I'll be staying there until your trial. You won't be alone, I promise." I took a deep breath before nodding. George smirked, then turned to face the two guards.

"We have permission and access as the V.I.A. to transfer Kyle Straiter to our facility here in this city."

A dozen police officers made their way to my cage, and one of them pulled out a large carabiner with dozens of keys. All the keys lit up, then the one that unlocked my cell door floated in the air. The officer unlocked my cell. I was free to leave with George and Foul. They took me outside to a large, windowless black van that had the V.I.A. logo on the side. It was a gray circle with red details and "V.I.A." stretched across the middle. To my surprise, it was quite luxurious inside. We took off for the V.I.A. headquarters in Veena.

September 7th, the Day the Students Return to E.H.:

Alex walked to school without his usual smile plastered across his face. Students were relieved of living on campus until my trial, so everyone was able to see their families again. Alex's head hung low, and his hat covered his face. School didn't start for another thirty minutes, but he was meeting someone on campus. He walked through the bare halls and went to Iris's locker. Alex played on his phone, waiting until she finally arrived.

"Why did you wanna meet so early?" Iris yawned, out of breath and her hair a mess. She finally looked at him, "Alex, why are you wearing a hat? I've known you for ten years and not once have you worn a brimmed hat like that." Alex looked down, and she still couldn't see his eyes. Water droplets fell to the floor, and his legs shook. He fell to his knees, so Iris did the same. Alex ripped the hat off, revealing a huge black eye, cuts, and bruises covering his face.

"Please," he murmured, "just heal me." Iris immediately began healing him.

After a bit of hesitation, she finally asked, "What happened? We've been at home the past few days, so why are you so beat up?" He looked away, stopping her healing. Iris had to lean in more and continued.

"Don't worry about it. Just keep healing me," Alex muttered.

Iris did so, and when his bruises were gone, he shoved the hat into his bag and walked down the hall. Iris stood, worried, and made her way towards the stairwell.

"Wait, Iris!" Alex yelled from across the hallway. She turned around as he continued, "Don't tell anyone about this! This stays between me and you!"

"O–Okay!" Iris nodded.

He thanked her and turned the corner. Iris, still worried, walked down the stairs and out of the school. While making her way to the dorms, which were still open, so she could brush her hair and teeth, she ran into Tonuko, Devin, and Jon.

"Hey!" Jon waved while the three walked over to her.

"Why are you here so early?" Devin asked.

Iris rubbed her arm and looked at the floor, not knowing how to answer.

"I was just," Iris saw her hairbrush in her pocket, so she took it out and smiled, "grabbing my hairbrush from my locker. I forgot it here before we left for Veena."

The three obviously weren't buying it, but before any of them could ask anything, Alex walked up with his usual, big smile.

"It's true, I just saw her grabbing it!" He put his hands on Iris' shoulders and said hi to everyone. "We both got here a little early and talked by her locker!" Alex seemed overly happy today, making the trio even more suspicious. Tonuko looked down at Iris, whose face didn't match Alex's excitement by any means, then stuck his hands in his pockets.

"I get why Iris was here, but why were you, Alex?" Tonuko asked, trying to get Alex to break. Alex was smarter than that and had a quick-witted comeback.

"I had to get out of the house and clear my mind about the fight. It only happened nine days ago. I haven't really been able to relax yet."

Jon nodded and rubbed the back of his neck. "Yeah, it's been rough for everyone. Hazel and Kate still aren't back yet and Kyle's court trial is coming up in a couple of days. I think we'll all be able to start relaxing more now that we'll be together in school again," Jon ranted, trying to lift the mood.

"Yeah," Alex agreed. There was a silence among everyone, then Alex took his hands off Iris and said, "Well, I'm gonna take a walk around and grab a bite from the mall. See you two (Tonuko and Iris) in class, and you two (Jon and Devin) around." He walked away, and Iris' face faded into more worry.

Everyone could see the look, so Tonuko asked, "He's lying . . . isn't he?"

Iris looked up with puppy eyes and slowly nodded. Tonuko looked over at Jon and Devin, then ran his hand through his hair and took a deep breath. "We'll talk more about this later. He clearly wants to keep it a secret, and we should respect that right now and not spread around an assumption."

Tonuko watched Alex walk into the convenience store on campus, then turned and walked toward the school building. The others went their own separate ways, continuing on with their pre-school activities.

When the first bell rang, the freshman students, both advanced and honors' classes, were told to meet in the theatre. Tonuko walked to the auditorium, but when he opened the door, the atmosphere was completely different than usual. Instead of the joyful talking and laughing around the room, everyone was silent and solemn. One boy in particular was on the verge of tears. Daniel sat silently looking down at the ground, his hands plagued with a slight shake.

"You okay, Danny? Is it about Kyle?" Rose asked while rubbing his back. Daniel sniffled, then looked at her with agony lingering in his eyes.

"He's like a brother to me . . . I can't stand the thought of his dream we've talked about for years just being ripped out of his grasp. What if he gets a life sentence? He'll never be a hero!" Daniel sniffled again, squeezing his arm. "Maybe, if I had known what was going on, I would have been able to help. I wouldn't have let him fight alone and lose his temper like that! I know him, I know how to calm him down!"

"Danny, it's alright," Rose comforted, "You can't focus on the negativity and the past. You couldn't be there, and you can't change that fact. Now, all we can do is hope and pray he doesn't receive any kind of sentence. I'm sure there will be plenty of leniency for him in the court trial since he did take out the most dangerous kidnapping duo in the country!"

After she said that, a man stepped into the doorway. He had bright, pink hair in a ponytail and wore a mischievous grin. "Nah, I hope that little asshole never gets outta jail. Maybe spending some time in the doghouse will fix that horrid attitude of his!" the man mocked with a laugh.

Tonuko stood from where he was seated and tensed his fist.

"You better chill with that old man. I don't know who the hell you think you are, but you aren't going to strut into this school and start laughing about a tragedy."

The man stretched and cracked his back, then yawned.

"Well, I wouldn't say I'm old, nor did I 'strut' into this class. Also, it wasn't a tragedy for Kyle, so, three strikes, you're out!"

Tonuko grew angrier by the man's hysterical comments.

"Who even are you anyway?" Tonuko asked.

The man pulled his ponytail to make sure it was tight enough, then cleared his throat. "I am your new teacher, Fallen. The pleasure is all mine," Fallen smirked with a bow.

"Oh, fuck no, you can't be our teacher," Steven swore after also standing up. "You're barely even a hero, more like just an asshole that sometimes saves people."

Fallen laughed out loud and wiped a fake tear from his eye.

"Aww, man, that's too funny. If I save people, I'm a hero! Gosh, you kiddos really do need teaching! I'm gonna be replacing that evil hag as the freshman honors' teacher. My way of fighting may be a little out of the ordinary for a hero, but, meh', don't fix what ain't broke."

Fallen, Strength: Distraught—he can read anyone's mind and use their insecurities as a power source. The power Fallen creates forms into beams of pure energy that can vaporize any matter at will. Depending on how strong the victim's insecurities are felt will range the power of the energy. For example, someone with little insecurity will cause the energy to leave burn marks and scratches, but someone who is very insecure will cause the energy to completely vaporize any matter, living or not.

"I don't care if you think it isn't broken. Your strength may be strong, but that doesn't mean you can go around spewing insults to people about their insecurities!" Tonuko argued. He was getting very worked up and his face was turning red.

Fallen's eyes glowed as he stated, "I suggest you sit down boy, unless you want to end up like Kyle." The silence in the room was deafening. "You are the strongest freshman at this school now, that means you have a lot of power and influence over your peers. Based on how you're acting now, that power might go to your fuckin' head, and you'll end up rock bottom just like little criminal boy."

The last few words caused Daniel to snap.

"*Shut up!* Just because you're a pro-hero and an adult doesn't mean you're any better than us! Stop belittling everyone and stop insulting the kid who just risked his life to save all of us and all the wrestlers! Kyle defeated the two strongest kidnappers in the nation, something you, as a pro, couldn't do!" Daniel shouted after standing. He glared at Fallen, and Fallen held a stern look before chuckling.

"Ah, Daniel Onso. Of course you're getting worked up on Kyle's behalf. Listen kiddo, you might think of Kyle as this great, all-mighty hero, but heroes don't go to fuckin' jail . . . do they? It does not matter in the least how you view me, how you view Kyle, how you view the event that just happened. All that matters is how the Seven Influential view Kyle, no more, no less."

As much as it angered Daniel, he knew deep down Fallen was right. Tonuko did as well, but because of how angry he was his judgment was clouded. He swung his arm, creating a spike that shot out at Fallen.

"This is why we need the new class," Fallen sighed while putting his hand up. A small bit of orange energy spat out of his hand and covered the spike's sharp end. The sharp part of the spike evaporated, then the rest of the spike moved back into the spot it had been before Tonuko changed it.

"It's not worth it. Relax," Rake, who was sitting next to Tonuko, stated.

Fallen smiled at that, then put his arms behind his back and explained, "Now, as I was saying; I am replacing that villain's place as the freshman honors' teacher. I'll be adding in a new class, a very important class for you measles, in fact. Clearly after this fiasco, Kyle's troubles ending him in prison and countless other examples, we need a class to teach you youngins correct decision making—things like charging into a battle without knowing the enemy's strength, taking on an unnecessary two-on-one battle," then, a little louder, he listed, "forming a spike at your teacher's head, leaving a half-dead boy to fight full-power enemies, stabbing your teammate, allowing a teammate to nearly drown, the list goes on and on."

Tonuko became more uncomfortable and frustrated, and Alex blushed out of embarrassment.

"Alright, that's enough Fallen. Stop toying with the freshmen," Excalibur stated as he walked into the room. "This is a very serious class we need to teach." Both teachers walked down the aisle and stepped onto the stage in front of them. Excalibur elaborated, "I am the freshman advanced teacher: Excalibur. Fallen and I decided this class is a necessity because of the countless bad decisions we've seen lately. We urgently need to teach you how to act in real combat situations because, sad enough to say, with Kyle around, we'll be fighting many more villains, and more dangerous villains than ever expected."

"Again, some of these bad decisions include not utilizing your strengths to help others. Sorry to call you out, but I'm not sorry because you could have prevented so many injuries if you would have used your strength, Mr. Call," Fallen spoke while giving Jaxon a side eye. Jaxon looked down, disappointed in himself. "Another example is saving that pathetic boy Kyle without even considering using your strength, something an idiotic sophomore did."

"You shut your fucking mouth!" Hunter erupted as he practically jumped out of his seat. Daniel was furious with this statement as well.

He leapt and screamed, "What gives you the right to say Kyle deserved to die? He saved the day by getting rid of the villainous scum! What the fuck did you do? Huh?" Though she knew it was true, Anya was saddened to hear her father called villainous scum.

"Silence, all of you! Fallen, knock it off with the patronizing! This is a very serious class, so let's all act like it!" Excalibur yelled after stomping his foot to get everyone's attention. Fallen couldn't help but chuckle.

"Alrighty, there are three students worthy of recognition because they made fantastic decisions in the previous encounter with villains. Iris Blavins, Zach Taling, and Steven Mallnen!"

The three stood and their body languages were completely different. Zach was indifferent. Iris was embarrassed, and Steven was basking in glory.

"Iris utilized her strength to heal the injured. Zach stopped multiple people from being carelessly injured and almost successfully saved everyone from a collapsing building. Finally, Steven used his strength to rescue classmates and civilians from the rubble of the collapsed building instead of charging into battle like a lunatic." Fallen glanced at Daniel, then the three sat down.

"Now, let's get started. Say a villain with an unknown strength broke in, and Fallen and I weren't here. What would you do . . . Zayden?"

Zayden thought for a couple of seconds, then smiled and flexed.

"I'd make my way to him underground and pop up behind him to get a clean hit and a chance at knocking him out!"

Excalibur and Fallen looked at each other. Fallen snorted.

"Uh, no. You should dig your way to a different classroom to get help for your classmates and have someone call the authorities depending on how dangerous the man is. Example, if it's David of the Care-Givers, call for immediate backup and have someone call the authorities. However, if it's just some random crook, no need for the authorities, we have enough heroes here to easily stop the scum."

Zayden felt embarrassed and silently swore to himself, then Excalibur asked someone else.

"How about you Khloe? What would be the smart thing for you to do?"

"I should seek immediate cover, since my strength doesn't give me any kind of protection or way to escape to get help, and wait for one of my classmates to get help." Fallen clapped slowly and loudly with a big smile stretched across his face.

"You are now my favorite student. Well done, Carrie."

Khloe looked confused and offended at the same time.

"Uh, you mean Khloe?"

"Yeah, yeah, whatever. How about uh, you Mr. Tough Guy? What should you do?" Fallen asked while pointing at Tonuko.

Tonuko thought for a moment with his hand on his chin.

"My instincts tell me to fight him, since I can get him from a far distance, but—" Fallen made a loud buzzer noise.

"Wrong!" he shouted. "You should duck for cover and use your manipulation strength to try and trap him in a cement box with no windows!" Tonuko balled his fist and glared at Fallen, who in return gave him a big smirk.

"If you didn't cut me off, I was gonna say—"

"Hmm, don't care. How about you Danny-boy since you wanna' always add your opinion. What should you do if David the Care-Giver walked in right now?" Danny wiped his eyes and glared at Fallen.

"I should go invisible and take his gun from him," he muttered. Excalibur smiled and clapped for Daniel.

"Well done, Daniel, that's why you're the sharpest kid in advanced. You and Zach are the academic top advanced kids, so how about you Zach: what should you do?"

Zach's expression didn't change, and he leaned back in his chair with his feet up on the seat in front of him.

"I should either create a box around the villain and make the lasers as close and as many as possible to minimize the bullets that can escape or make two large laser walls blocking his way to us and his way out so that 'Zayden' will have more time to fetch help." Zach blinked one eye at a time and ran his hand through his flowing hair.

"Excellent job, Zach, but look a little happier maybe?" Excalibur asked while crossing his arms and smiling.

"I'll try my best teach'." Fallen looked around the room for the last example of this scenario. He put his finger to his goatee and tapped it while scanning.

"What about you? What's your name?" Fallen asked while pointing at Jessica.

"My name is Jessica Alter, and I would hide and wait for help to arrive!" she answered.

Fallen looked at her weirdly, then questioned, "You wouldn't fight at all, or make an attempt to secure the criminal?"

Jessica shrugged and thought for a second.

"Well, I could create flowers all around him to try and trap him and keep creating more if he tried to escape."

Fallen smiled and clapped loudly again. He tapped his goatee again and looked out at the room.

"It seems the honors' class girls are smart, but surely not the boys! I need a smart boy to answer this next one!"

The room was silent, then Cindy sighed.

"Kyle was the smartest boy in our class," she solemnly stated. The room was still silent. Fallen stood still and clenched his jaw.

"Kyle this, Kyle that, is that all you kids talk about? Kyle is just this amazing, flawless student, right?" Everyone was shocked at the outburst, and Fallen continued, "Newsflash, no, he sure as hell isn't! Kyle was a loner, worthless, no friends, no scholarships, no will, nothing! I would know because I mentored him this summer!"

"Will?" Alex asked. Fallen gave him a weird smile, his eyes wide, and nodded.

"Yes, sir, no will to live boy! Kyle wanted to give up, but Mr. Hated-Ol'-Me saved his ass! I helped him learn to love himself! Now that he decided to get arrested, who the hell knows if that will is there or not! The kid could tell the judges, 'Mister and Misses Judges, just put me in jail! I don't want to be no hero' or he could up and tell em' 'Mister and Misses Judges, please just let me go!' So, from now on, until he returns or doesn't, no more Kyle talk while in the classroom! Ya'll need to learn to focus on yourselves!"

Zach raised his hand, then Fallen asked, "What the hell do you want boy?"

"Why did your accent change from like, uptight, to more like a southern accent?" Fallen moved his body to face Zach.

"I don' know, kid, it's just how weird I am!"

Zach shrugged, and the class continued.

"Now, miss Kyle lover over there, answer this for me! If Kyle became a villain and came to kill alla' us, what would you do?"

Fallen was yelling to Cindy, but an advanced-class girl snarkily chimed, "I thought there was no more Kyle talk?" Fallen swatted at her as if she was a fly and continued looking at Cindy.

"I—uh, well, I would—um, I would . . . I don't know."

Fallen smiled and raised his hands while changing his expression from anger to a smile.

"That there is my very point! Hate me all you want kids, but I'm here to help! Any single one of you can become a villain, and the others would have no clue how to react! You need to be able to think on the spot about these things! Don't beat yourself up about them, but don't just think they're impossible. Everything is possible, but not everything is worth your time!"

Tonuko stood and looked Fallen in the eyes. He began clapping. A couple of others joined, and eventually everyone was clapping. Fallen bowed and basked in the glory, then shouted, "Alright, that's all for today! I got your minds movin', and that's all I need. Time for the fun part of the day, trainin'!" The class cheered as Excalibur and Fallen walked down the aisle to lead the students to the Dome.

Chapter 12

Broken Boys

When the classes arrived at the Dome, the inside was changed. There were shooting ranges with dummies, combat rings, and different simulations of various environments. Before the classes separated, Fallen grabbed Jaxon's shoulder and whispered, "Activate your strength on the classes right now."

Jaxon raised an eyebrow.

"You mean control everyone?"

"Exactly, now go," Fallen swiftly responded.

Jaxon shrugged, then breathed in and out. He breathed out pink smoke that flooded the air. People breathed in the smoke, causing their eyes to fade to red. When the students and Excalibur were fully under Jaxon's control, Fallen smiled and crossed his arms.

"If you get smarter, stronger, just think a little more, you can be extremely powerful. You aren't just a destined sidekick, Jaxon Call. Show me what you can do."

"Walk," Jaxon stated. The group walked, synchronized, then Jaxon commanded, "Stop." They stopped and Fallen clapped.

"With a little more confidence, you can do this in the field with a higher success rate! Call 'em off!"

Jaxon slammed the door to the Dome behind him, nullifying his strength. Excalibur fixed his sleeve while glaring at Fallen.

"Just fixing up a student," Fallen smirked.

Excalibur shook his head. The teachers commanded everyone to go to a station. The students were assigned specific stations to work on what they needed. Fallen and Excalibur walked around, giving advice to the students. Excalibur complimented students and gave recommendations. Fallen, on the contrary, gave strict criticism and ridicule.

Tonuko was pitted against a robot with big, heavy boxing gloves. He was supposed to take beatings from the robot, ranging from blocking to flat out being punched, to increase his strength and endurance. Iris was with him and would heal him after each beating. This would help increase her endurance with her healing.

"Tonuko, look over at Alex," Iris said softly while nudging her head to her right. Tonuko looked over and saw Alex put a bag down off to the side of the arena. Tonuko raised an eyebrow while panting, then Iris explained, "He has a hat hidden in that bag that he used to cover up his injuries. Maybe you could ask him about it?" Tonuko, who had been resting on his knees, stood up straight and put his hands on his hips while he thought.

Alex, who was waiting for a simulation in the dark, looked around nervously. Tonuko came up with a plan and executed it accordingly. He walked over to the bag Alex had placed on the floor, which caused Alex to scurry over and attempt to snag the bag. Tonuko grabbed it just as Alex did, and they started fighting over it.

"Hey, this is mine! What are you doing Tonuko?" Alex yelled while gripping the bag with two hands. Alex pushed Tonuko, causing him to lose his handle on the bag, then Tonuko tackled Alex. Students gathered around and the teachers attempted to step in. Tonuko gave the bag one more huge tug, causing the zipper to rip open. The contents of the bag spilled out, including a plain, white, curved-brim hat with a few blood stains on the brim. Cindy bent down and picked up the hat before Alex could get it, then looked at him with concern.

"Why is there blood on this?" Alex looked at her, but the innocent, happy sparkle was gone from his eyes. His cheeks and nose were red, and tears brimmed his eyelids. Alex was shattered. For the first time ever, his classmates saw tears fall from his eyes.

The Angel of the freshmen was broken.

Alex got to his knees and wiped tears from his cheeks. Cindy then knelt in front of him and gave him a tight hug. Others who Alex had known for a while joined in the hug. Tonuko stood and dusted himself off. He wasn't pleased to have fought Alex for this. No one was happy seeing this scene.

"Everyone, leave the Dome, but stay outside the doors! None of you better leave campus. It is too dangerous on the streets for a bunch of tired students to be wandering!" Fallen commanded while pointing behind the large group of students at the door.

The classes left, allowing Fallen and Excalibur to talk privately with Alex. Fallen had Alex stand and walked him to one of the benches. Alex didn't look up the entire time as he continued to silently cry. This made everyone more worried. Fallen sat next to Alex and leaned forward to look at his face.

"Alex, what's the matter? What happened?" Fallen asked. Although he hadn't known Alex for long, he knew something serious was wrong.

"M—My home has just been, not good l—lately," Alex stuttered through his tears. Excalibur and Fallen looked at each other.

"From what I've heard, you met with Iris this morning and had several injuries. What caused those injuries?" Alex stayed silent and wiped his eyes. "Alex, it's okay to tell us what happened. We're not going to get you in trouble or anything," Excalibur assured him.

Alex remained quiet, leaving the teachers unsure of what to do next.

Outside:

The classmates stood around outside of the building. Some peered into the Dome through a glass slit in the door to see what was happening. Cindy saw that Alex wasn't talking, then she wiped a tear from her eye. Jessica, an old classmate of Cindy's and Alex's, was fanning her eyes while attempting not to cry.

"Aww, Jess, c'mon, you're gonna make me cry," Cindy sniffled before hugging her.

Jessica sniffled as well, then cried out, "He's the Angel of our grade, and Angels aren't supposed to cry!" Her last words became incomprehensible through her tears.

Tonuko, who stood nearby, tensed his fist.

"We need to figure out what the hell made him break down like that. Who gave him those injuries?" Everyone was silent, so Tonuko stated, "It's clearly something going on at his house."

"We should go pay a visit to see what's going on there. He lives a couple miles away. If we run, we can make it there in under half an hour," Donte thought aloud; he was another of Alex's old classmates. The freshman honors' class had five Edith graduates: Alex, Cindy, Jessica, Donte, and Iris.

"Are you crazy?" Steven asked loudly. "If we get caught leaving campus during the school day, we'll get in huge trouble! We shouldn't be snooping in Alex's house either!" Tonuko turned to Steven with his fist bawled.

"Yeah, well, Alex came to school today with cuts and bruises! He's crying in there because someone is hurting him! If you don't wanna get caught, fine by me, but I'm going!" Tonuko exclaimed in response.

Steven backed down.

"Ever since Veena, you've been a real jerk to us," Steven quietly retorted. Tonuko ignored the remark, then looked at the rest of the group.

"Who's with me?" he shouted.

All but a select few were quiet and hesitant. Donte, Camilla, Jessica, Iris, Rake, and Cindy agreed to go; the others stayed silent.

"His parents work from home, so they should be there," Cindy informed the group. They agreed on the fastest route, then set off. Just as the seven students reached the gate and the last one passed through it, the teachers walked out of the Dome. Fallen saw Iris turn the corner and sighed.

"Call Fox-Tails. We need him to round up those kids. Can't have them wandering around unsupervised, especially with Kyle being gone. The target on our students' backs right now is too big for comfort," Fallen said to Excalibur.

Excalibur nodded, then pulled out his phone and quick-dialed Fox-Tails' number. The remaining students were told to go to the theatre and wait. Alex was still inside the Dome.

Donte led the group to Alex's house, slowing down a few times so others could catch up. It was a standard two-story house and looked peaceful. A blue mini-van was in the driveway, as well as a grey S.U.V.

"Let's ask these bastards what they're doing to their son," Tonuko muttered through his teeth. He stomped up to the door, but before he could knock, Fox-Tails leapt from a couple dozen feet away and tackled him. He flipped Tonuko over and knelt on his hands. The rest of the guards caught up and restrained the six other students.

"We're got the runaways secured. We'll be bringing them back to campus now," Fox-Tails informed someone through an earpiece he was wearing.

"What the hell do you think you're doing?" Rake shouted, trying to squirm free from the E.H. guard's grasp.

"You all should not be leaving campus during school hours," Fox-Tails said after helping Tonuko stand.

The guards forced the seven to start walking toward school but were interrupted by Tonuko shouting, "We're trying to figure out what's going on with our classmate! He could be getting abused. We should be going into that house and questioning Alex's parents!" He attempted to rip his hands out of Fox-Tails' grasp, but Fox-Tails' hands didn't budge.

"That's noble of you but leave it to us adults. Trust me, we aren't happy to see one of our students hurt, but we cannot investigate without a permit. Not only is that illegal, but you attempting to solve a crime is going to lead to your arrest," Fox-Tails sighed.

Tonuko didn't argue back, instead he quietly grumbled to himself the entire walk back to campus. When they arrived, the students were brought straight to Principal Lane's office where he, Mrs. Kuntai, Fallen, and Excalibur were waiting.

"Well look at what we have here," Fallen angrily stated while pacing back and forth in front of the seven, who were still being restrained by E.H. security guards. Fallen held his hands behind his back, then stopped in front of Tonuko and gave him a side-eye.

"Maybe I'm just a little forgetful, but I thought I told my class to stay inside the campus because the streets around here are dangerous right now!"

"Why glare at just me? Six other kids left too, and I wasn't even the one to suggest it," Tonuko sneered. He angrily glanced at the guard holding him, who let go. Tonuko rubbed his wrist, then looked back at Fallen, and crossed his arms.

"Well Mr. Tough Guy, you are currently the leader of your class since Kyle-boy is, y'know, in jail and all. Anything you do, others will follow. You need to be setting a good example and be more responsible so your classmates do the same!" Fallen reprimanded after crossing his arms to mock Tonuko.

"Oh, my bad. I didn't know I had to do your damn job for you! You're the teacher. You're supposed to set the example and lead the class to success! I'm just a student who needs guidance too!"

It was clear Tonuko was getting very flustered and, since it wasn't Fallen's intent, he backed off with his biting tone.

"We at E.H. are teaching you to be self-sufficient future leaders. Everyone knows you will for certain be the leader of a future organization with many sidekicks and future generations looking up to you. Being able to do the same for your classmates is phenomenal practice. You should be thankful you have this opportunity," Fallen explained. He took a few steps back and stood next to Mrs. Kuntai, expecting Tonuko to relax and stop arguing. However, he was wrong.

"Well you know what, Kyle was supposed to be our leader, mine too! Look at what happened to him! I looked up to him and tried following in his footsteps because at Veena with the kidnappers, Kyle put all of us first and nobody died! But when I put my trust in him and left him to fight like he said he could, he killed four people and got arrested! Now look at us! Our reputation has plummeted, and I have to be this big responsible adult with no problems or worries of my own!"

"Tonuko, that's not–" Fallen was swiftly cut off by Tonuko, who finished with an angry mutter.

"No, I understand perfectly what you're expecting. I won't disappoint again." With that, Tonuko stormed out of the room.

"Tonuko, don't just leave! Get back here!" Mrs. Kuntai shouted while taking a step forward.

Tonuko was already gone. The other six were reprimanded by the teachers and principals, then sent home along with the other freshman students. Alex was sent home as well and told to call the school if anything happened. He was reassured that someone would answer if he ever called. He was escorted home, and just like that, the first day back to school was over for the freshmen.

V.I.A. Headquarters, Veena:

I awoke in the bed George provided me and yawned. I thought I was having trouble sleeping because I was in the cold prison, but it wasn't any better here. I still had nightmares.

I sat up and stretched for a minute, then stood and walked into the bathroom connected to my room. I saw myself for the first time in a week . . . and I looked horrible. My bright, blonde hair stuck up all over the place, bags upon bags were built up under my eyes, and my sky-blue eyes seemed dull. I scratched my head with another yawn, brushed my teeth, then showered. I changed into the clothes Foul had bought from a nearby thrift store. The shirt was too big and the shorts a little too short for my liking, but clothes were the last worry on my mind. I walked downstairs and sat on an uncomfortable leather couch. It was very stiff, fitting for an association's headquarters. Foul came in a few minutes later and grabbed a mug, then filled it with coffee.

"Do you want some?" he asked.

I shook my head while turning on the news. My bloody, disoriented face being arrested was plastered on the screen. I was the main story.

"The headstrong Eccentric High student Kyle Straiter has been arrested for the murder of four. Although the four that were killed were criminals, Kyle Straiter is only fourteen years old and is not a legal hero. The crazy boy supposedly killed a man begging for his life, then caused a massive explosion while killing the other kidnappers, our eye-witnesses say."

Foul quickly grabbed the remote and changed the channel, but the damage had been done.

Is this how everyone views me, even my classmates? I guess they have reasons to. If I wasn't here, those at E.H. wouldn't live in fear wondering when they'd be attacked again. They have to rely on me to fix the problems I could never fix for myself. Why couldn't Tyrant have killed me instead of my mom?

"I thought I was a hero. I thought I saved people. Why are they making me sound like the villain?" I asked, staring blankly at the television. I looked down at my hands and two black dots spiral onto my palms. It felt like a liquid was dripping down my face, but I didn't think I was crying. I put my hand to my face and felt my cheek, then pulled my fingers away. A thick, blood-like black liquid was oozing out of my eyes and mouth, but when I looked at Foul, he seemed to not see it.

"Listen Kyle, people make up stories to stir up controversy within the crowds. When you are deemed not guilty by the Seven Influential, this will all be forgotten, and you'll be seen as a hero!" Foul explained trying to lighten my mood.

I weakly nodded as George walked down the stairs.

"Morning gentlemen," George said loudly while smiling big. He poured himself a cup of coffee, then added a few sugar packets. He walked over beside the couch, picked up the remote, and shut off the T.V.

"It's too early for that."

"George," I asked, "do you think I'll be let free?"

"I am one-hundred percent certain you will be found not guilty and sent home. It's not that I think you will be let free. It's a fact that you will."

I nodded without looking at him. As George and Foul talked, I went back to my room. I laid on the bed, facing the ceiling, and analyzed the black dots on my hands. They were the same hue as my arm had been when I punched the Creature to kill it. They weren't holes like I thought when I first saw them.

What . . . are these?

I put my hand on my head, hearing a deep, sharp whisper in my ears.

"Kyle."

I looked around, but no one was in the room. I rubbed my head, then my stomach made gargling noises, and an immense pain exploded within me. I hunched over while hugging my stomach, then fell to my back and laid in fetal position. I laid like this for half an hour, unable to speak or move, then I heard a knock at my door.

"Kyle, it's time to discuss your family. George said we should start planning so we can muster up as much information as possible to maximize what we can avoid," Foul said while walking into the room.

I didn't move or respond, so he walked over to my bedside.

"You alright?"

When he touched my shoulder, the pain vanished. I turned around and nodded, acting like I had just woken up. I followed Foul to a room in the back of the building. There was a long, wooden table. I sat across from George, and Foul sat next to him.

"Alright, Kyle," George started while neatly stacking his papers, "tell me about your home life as a kid. Was it fun and kind, or–?"

"It was horrible. I was forced into learning about the villain business by Tyrant, and," I stopped while staring down at the table. It still hurt my heart every time I had to say what happened out loud. I finished, "and I had to watch my mother die in my arms after she was stabbed by him." I bawled my fists and clenched my jaw. "I hate him. He killed her. He took her away from me."

"I'm sorry to hear that, Kyle; that's an awful tragedy to go through." George was writing vigorously, then clicked his pen and scanned the top sheet on the stack in front of him. "So, Kyle, who is this Daniel Onso I'm seeing? Is he a close friend, a cousin? What is he to you?"

"Daniel is the closest person to a sibling I've ever had. He was always there for me when I'd run away crying because Tyrant beat me up again, and he was the one who helped me train my new strengths whenever I manifested them," I weakly responded.

George nodded, then Foul looked over at the sheet of questions.

"What did Tyrant think of Daniel?"

I swiftly responded, "Hated him. His parents were well-known heroes on the rise when we were children, so Tyrant typically shunned me for spending time with a 'hero's kid.' My mom always let me play with Daniel though."

George continued writing while he asked, "Here's a big question: How do you feel about Tyrant now? Also, how do you feel about villains in general?"

I looked down at the palms of my hands again while thinking.

How do I feel about villains? That should be an obvious question . . . do they still not trust me?

"I hate Tyrant with every ounce of my being. He's the reason I'm here, and *I'll be the reason he goes.* I *have to* avenge my mom and kill Tyrant, I have to." I squeezed my fist tight, causing veins in my forearms to pulsate. "And I will *never* be a villain. They are corrupt people who want to hurt others. I could never do the things villains do."

"Thank the Lord. Considering you are the strongest teenager this society has ever seen, it's nice to have the reassurance that you will always be on our side!" Foul smiled as he leaned back in his chair.

I'm not the strongest . . . Plague . . . if Tyrant is afraid of him, just how strong is he?

"Yeah, thankfully I'll stay a hero." I felt the ooze pour from my eyes again, and it felt as though something was ripping through my stomach. I stayed still, not daring to moving an inch.

"Good to hear, good to hear," George murmured while flipping the page on his notepad. I gripped my shirt and hunched over.

"Kyle, are you okay?" Foul asked. He looked at me, confused, then George glanced over as well. I put my head down and projectile vomited a black and red substance before running off. I bumped into the wall as I left the room, making my way straight into my bedroom. I closed and locked the door behind me.

What's happening to me, what is this?

I laid in my bed, curled into the fetal position again, hoping, praying the pain would go away.

George knelt down and poked his pen into the odd substance I had thrown up. Foul could hear a sizzling. When he rounded the table, he saw George's pen was melted in half. George looked up at Foul with both confusion and concern.

Kyle Straiter, Strength One

Chapter 13

Two-Faced

I groaned in agony on my bed. Even after a day, the pain wouldn't go away. The court case was tomorrow, but I could barely think or walk.

BANG! BANG! BANG!

"Kyle, we need answers! If you lose this court case, your entire future is gone! Please, open up! Are you in pain, are you alright? Please, answer me!" Foul shouted while banging his fist on my door. I ignored him and slipped out of consciousness. I could hear Tyrant calling my name. I awoke after someone slapped me across the face.

"Kyle, wake up, dammit!" Tyrant shouted while shaking me. I blinked a few times and saw Tyrant in front of me. We were floating in the void again, but this time I heard a loud thumping that pained my stomach every time it occurred.

"You called me here yesterday. Why haven't you said anything?"

I looked around in a daze and flinched after every noise.

"Kyle?"

The thumping . . . do you hear it?

"What thumping? What are you talking about?" I groaned and held my head. Tyrant looked concerned, but before he could say anything, a presence loomed over me.

"***Tyrant.***" It was the same voice as the whisper from before, but this time it was an inhumanely deep, heart-quaking rumble of a voice. I swiftly looked up and around, but nothing was there. Tyrant's face was paler than usual as he tensed his fists.

"Kyle, what the hell was that?" I didn't answer, just kept looking around in circles. The pounding continued and grew louder. "*What was that!*"

I don't know how I'm calling you here, but next time I do, don't respond

He rolled his eyes. A loud noise resembling someone scratching their nails on a chalkboard filled our ears. A light beamed above me, then I jolted awake in my room and was thrown into the ceiling. I dropped back onto my bed, rolled over, and fell onto the ground. The loud noises caused Foul and George to run to my room. Eventually they broke in. I was laying on the ground, not unconscious but breathing heavily. My arms were pitch black, and eyes were glowing a bright white.

"Kyle, what the hell? Are you alright?" Foul asked, clearly worried.

I blinked and the light vanished. The darkness was sucked from my arms back into the black dots on my palms. I got up onto my knees and elbows. Foul knelt beside me and tried to get me to talk. I was too weak to speak and simply continued panting.

After a few minutes, George pulled out his phone and said, "I'm calling an ambulance. Something is clearly wrong with him."

Out of my palm, a black tentacle-like object flew at George and hit the phone out of his hand. The tentacle retracted back into the dot.

"No, don't, I'm fine."

George nodded, bent down, and picked up his phone and then slowly walked out of the room. Foul was as shocked as George. He left the room as well and closed the door behind him. I fell over to my side, and laid lifeless . . .

Kyle Straiter, Strength One

That Same Morning, at E.H.:

Alex ran to school, but he couldn't run straight due to a slight limp. His right eye was swollen shut. He had bruises on his arms and legs, and a shallow gash across his chest. He finally made it to campus, running straight to the Dome. He burst through the doors but collapsed immediately after.

"Holy shit, is that Alex?" Jon shouted while running over along with his teacher, Mrs. Davidson.

Mrs. Davidson commanded for one of the sophomore girls to go get the freshman teachers, then she checked Alex's pulse. Thankfully it was still there, and his breathing had steadied slightly.

"Alex, what happened?" Jon asked.

"D—Demon, he's a demon!" Alex cried through his gasps for air.

Mrs. Davidson and Jon looked at each other, both very confused.

The sophomore girl threw open the theatre doors and shouted, "Mr. Fallen, Mr. Excalibur, it's that Alex kid! He's collapsed at the Dome doors!"

Fallen nodded and ran out of the theatre with the girl. Excalibur and the classes followed closely behind. When they arrived at the Dome, Alex was still on the ground, breathing heavily.

"I have to go control my class, but he was saying something about a man being a demon," Mrs. Davidson frantically informed Fallen.

He nodded and knelt beside Alex, as did Excalibur. Iris joined them and began healing Alex. Some of the first years covered their mouths, others couldn't even look.

"Can we confront his parents now?" Tonuko asked Fallen loudly.

Fallen looked down at Alex's body, then squeezed the ground. His fingers dug into the concrete, and when he pulled them out, he muttered, "Let's go."

It was the most serious they'd heard Fallen, and it scared them. Excalibur and Iris stayed with Alex, as did most of the freshmen. The group of six who'd left school the previous day went with Fallen and Fox-Tails. Donte led the group to Alex's house. Fallen was silent the entire time. His strength had activated during the walk. His hair was floating, fists were glowing a bright pink, and orange streaks ran up his arms. Fox-Tails' claws were out and sharp, and his limbs were visibly more muscularly defined than usual. His fangs were so long that they hung out his mouth and one fang pierced his bottom lip.

When they arrived at the house, everyone stopped, looking at the heroes.

"What are you going to say?" Rake asked.

"I'm gonna do a lot more than talk," Fallen sinisterly stated as he marched to the front door. He banged loudly on the door, causing Cindy to jump.

"He almost broke it down," she whispered to Rake.

The students were now afraid of Fallen. As the door slowly opened, an unfamiliar man peered out. Donte took a step forward, but Tonuko grabbed his arm. Donte looked back and saw the terror in Tonuko's eyes.

"Who the hell are you? Where are Alex's parents?" Camilla shouted while tensing her fists.

"Camilla, I am Mr. Galeger. Shouldn't you know?" the man eerily responded.

Jessica cringed and said, "No you aren't."

The man reached out his purple hand, but Fallen swiftly raised his own and gripped the man's wrist. The wind from Fallen lifting his hand shattered a window, and a very loud crack was heard all the way at the end of the driveway where Fox-Tails and the students stood.

"You clearly aren't Alex Galeger's father, so who are you?" Fallen snarled. "What are you doing to him?" Fallen let go of the man's wrist, allowing the man to rub his broken bone.

"Why, yes I am. I always have been his dad. I thought I told that goody-two-shoes . . ." A purple flame spiraled in his hands as he continued, "to keep his damn mouth shut!"

Mr. Galeger blasted a large burst of flames, completely covering Fallen's body. Smoke floated into the sky and when the flames died down, Fallen was holding his hands out at opposite shoulders. He was not burned. Scaly wings ripped from Mr. Galeger's shirt. He tackled Fallen into the air, then threw him onto the grass. Tonuko used the opportunity of the fight to run toward the house to try and find Mrs. Galeger. As he was running, Mr. Galeger pounced at him, but Fox-Tails intercepted his attack, spearing him out of the air. Tonuko swiftly scurried past the two, then made it through the front door.

"Mrs. Galeger, where are you? I'm Tonuko Kuntai. I'm here to help you!"

He heard a commotion in a door to his right. He hesitated before opening it. Mrs. Galeger was tied up at her hands, ankles, and mouth. As Tonuko tried to untie her, he was blinded by a pink and orange light.

Outside, Fallen had his hands raised in the air, palms to the sky. He clenched his fist and a pink laser shot out of a cloud, piercing and melting one of Mr. Galeger's wings. Mr. Galeger spun in the air, then crashed in the middle of the street. Fox-Tails moved quickly, using rope he had brought to restrain Mr. Galeger.

Fallen floated into the air and opened his hands, which were still raised above his head. A beam of pink shot from the sky onto Mr. Galeger. The beam was translucent and inside the circle of pink, Mr. Galeger's demon features were sucked out of his body. The beam floated into the sky, exploding like a firework. Fallen fell, landed in a crouched position, then looked up at Mr. Galeger. He looked completely different and was unconscious in Fox-Tails' hands.

Fallen, Real Strength: Transformation—he can conform anything caught within his pink and orange essence into whatever he pleases. Although he is powered by insecurity, he can control the power of the conformation. As well as this, he can store the power he's gained from an individual's insecurity, but he will slowly start to feel insecure about the same thing the person was if he contains it for too long.

Outside, the students were in awe; inside, Tonuko swiftly snapped out of it and untied Mrs. Galeger. Cindy ran into the house to help Tonuko then asked, "Mrs. Galeger, what happened?" Mrs. Galeger was breathing heavily and struggling to stay conscious.

"Th–There was a man, a d–demon. He posses–sed Alex's f–father," Mrs. Galeger stuttered. Before they could ask anything else, she passed out. Twenty or so E.H. security guards ran to the scene while half aided Fox-Tails, the others aided Fallen.

"Fallen, are you alright?" A woman with long, purple hair asked.

Fallen nodded while panting, then looked down.

"I–I'll be fine. Un-possessing someone takes a crap ton of energy, and the thoughts the demons give . . . they're horrifying."

The woman nodded, helping him stand.

Tonuko ran out of the house carrying Mrs. Galeger and pushed her into one of the guard's hands.

"Bring her and Mr. Galeger to Nurse Blavins A.S.A.P.!" Tonuko commanded.

The guard was shocked and turned to Fox-Tails. Fox-Tails smirked and nodded to the guard. Two guards ran off with the Galegers, then Fallen walked over to the students.

"Tonuko," Fallen started weakly.

Tonuko thought he would be scolded so he looked down.

"Thank you! You took charge and found Mrs. Galeger, then immediately got her medical attention. Heroic choice, Tonuko, heroic choice."

Tonuko smiled and nodded proudly.

"Thanks, and good job taking down Alex's dad without killing him. Can't say Kyle would've done the same."

Everyone was shocked by the insensitive statement, but Tonuko wasn't laughing as if it was a joke. His face turned stern, then he walked away in the direction of the school. Fallen looked over at Fox-Tails, who just shrugged with a completely lost expression on his face. The rest of the group followed distantly behind Tonuko.

In the Nurse's Office:

Alex looked over at his mom and un-possessed dad, then smiled. His dad was finally back. He could be the Angel again.

After the dangerous fiasco, Principal Lane issued for all students to immediately return to living in the dorms. It was sudden, so students were sent home early to pack, then return. The last of the freshmen returned at 9:30 p.m. Some students sat around in the lobby, including Tonuko, Jessica, Khloe, and Zayden.

"So, Kyle's trial is tomorrow, huh?" Zayden asked while leaning on the counter.

Everyone nodded, then Jessica sighed dramatically.

"The older kids seem certain he'll come back, so we have nothing to worry about. I wonder if it will be broadcasted . . . maybe we'll be allowed to watch it during class."

Tonuko, whose arms were crossed, squeezed his biceps.

He stood and loudly muttered, "He could go rot in prison for all I care." The others were confused but assumed Tonuko was talking out of his ass because he was shaken about what happened earlier.

The Next Day, 9:00 a.m.:

I woke up on the floor in the pitch-black room. I rubbed my eyes and tried to stand. It took me a second to build the strength to get up. When I did, I had a massive headrush. My head hurt and felt staticky. I reached for the light switch, but my knees felt wobbly, and I fell into the wall. I used the wall to stay standing, then the static grew more aggressive. It sounded as though someone was speaking . . . yelling . . . to me. When I flicked the light on, it was gone.

I slowly walked down the stairs and saw George sitting on the couch. He was bouncing his leg anxiously. When he heard a stair creak, he looked over with a big frown.

"There're clean clothes on the counter over there. Put them on so you look less dead. We're leaving in ten minutes. It's a thirty-minute drive and the trial is at ten," George informed me.

I nodded, grabbed the clothes, and went back upstairs. I changed and brushed my teeth, then walked downstairs, and joined Foul and George in loading into the car.

"To no one's surprise, your trial is going to be broadcast nationally. This means your friends, school, family, and dad can all view it. Also meaning that if they ask any questions about your relationships that we cannot avoid, we must plead the fifth," George explained to me and Foul.

"How much can I plead the fifth?" I asked quietly.

George scratched his arm while driving and looked at me through the rear-view mirror.

"We don't need to avoid any questions about the actual criminal case, we know we can win that, but if there are any questions about your family that you cannot vaguely answer and satisfy the Seven Influential, then you must use it. *Everyone* is going see this, Kyle. If it gets out that you are related to Tyrant, it's over."

I gulped and nodded, then looked out the window.

I could never be a hero. My career should end because of these murders. Maybe I should just join Tyrant, maybe it is my unavoidable destiny. Everyone has a destiny, right? Even if it's to be a villain, or to die. Everyone dies. There's no real purpose in saving others who will just die at some other point, right? No . . . that's not true. The happiness I felt when that cop told me I saved his son's life, that was worth every second I suffered in that fight. I can't lose, I can't let people know my relations. I have to save myself. I can dig myself out of this grave. It's what Mom would've wanted . . .

Angel Criminal court cases worked much differently than a usual trial. The defense could present their evidence to the Seven Influential in the form of a paper copy, but only the Seven Influential could question the suspect. They knew best the difference between a criminal and a hero. In addition to this, there was no jury. The Seven Influential would vote whether the suspect would be released or not . . . essentially my career was in the hands of the seven strongest heroes.

When we arrived at the courthouse, it was a luxurious marble building with stone pillars and statues. There were paparazzi everywhere. Their camera flashes blinded me as I walked into the courthouse. When we entered, I saw a long pathway with hundreds of seats on either side. In the back of the building were the seven massive seats where the Seven Influential sat. They had a long desk in front of them, and beside them was one lone seat, the spot I would sit for questioning. Additionally, there were two seats with desks in front of the Seven Influential. Those were the lawyers' seats. I gulped as I sat in the lone seat. My stomach dropped watching the massive number of people pour into the building. Cameras were set up all around, all aimed directly at me.

I wonder what my classmates are doing right now.

At E.H.:

All of the freshmen sat in the theatre after Fallen and Excalibur announced they would be watching the court trial. They deemed it would be a good learning experience for the students. Fallen wheeled in a large T.V., then turned it on. I was visible, sitting in my seat. There was no sound and at the bottom of the screen a message looped:

KYLE STRAITER, ANGEL CRIMINAL COURT TRIAL IN FRONT OF THE SEVEN INFLUENTIAL. POSSIBLY STRONGEST CHILD IN THE WORLD BEING TRIED FOR MURDER.

Those last words stuck with Daniel. "Being tried for murder, I still can't believe it was him," he said while biting his nail. Rose rubbed his back as she looked at the screen.

"It's not as serious as it sounds. Heroes have to kill all the time, especially when the villains don't care enough about their lives to quit. Kyle must have had to do it. None of us know but him," she sighed.

Anya, who was sitting in the front row with Tonuko and Rake, looked down while twiddling her fingers.

He took the blame for the person I killed, and if my dad wasn't a villain, Kyle might have not been tried at all. Why did he take the blame? she thought to herself.

Out of the corner of his eye, Tonuko glanced over at Anya. He put his arm around her, and whispered, "Don't worry, Anya. We'll find out why he did it." Anya nodded, then looked up.

"Kyle apparently aced his entrance exam. He's super smart. It doesn't make sense why he would just randomly lose it and kill someone," Anya quietly said while squeezing her hands together.

Court Room, 10:00 a.m., Start of the Trial:

I looked up at George, who gave me a small smile and nodded. I could tell he was trying to reassure me, but my nerves wouldn't go away. I was terrified. Suddenly, a horn blasted, and someone walked into the room from a dark doorway behind the Seven Influential. The man was short and very muscular with thick arms. He wore a cloak with short sleeves. Lining the cloak's hood down to his feet was a tube full of a green and yellow liquid.

C.J. Dane, #7 Hero, Strength: Leak—he can leak acid from all parts of his body and uses a special cloak to prevent it from spilling. When he takes off the cloak, his entire body is surrounded by acid and gives him superhuman abilities such as the ability to skate on the ground and the ability to latch a string of acid onto any surface and swing on it. Also, he can form solid structures and items out of his acid.

He sat at the seat farthest from me, then a girl with pink, straight hair, lime-green skin, and a very bright, colorful jumpsuit walked in and sat next to him.

Aubrey Tato, #6 Hero, Strength: Color Bomb—she can shoot out bombs of multi-colored molten fluids. The more colors the hotter the fluid. She has two types of bombs, ones that shoot out her left hand and ones that shoot out her right. The left-hand bombs are more pastel colors and rapidly cool at any temperature outside her body. She uses these to capture villains or seal holes. Her right-hand bombs are rainbow colored and heat up over time. This liquid can heat up to 500 degrees Fahrenheit.

The next girl to walk in sat next to Aubrey. She looked holographic, completely see-through, paper thin, and a light blue, almost gray color.

Eleanor Dainey, #5 Hero, Strength: Hologram—she is a holographic person that can make clones of herself. The clones cannot be hurt by most physical attacks. They carry the weapons Eleanor carries and have the same martial skills as her. The most clones she can make without overworking herself is ten.

It was clear by now that the strongest heroes would sit next to me, making my nerves skyrocket. The next man to walk in was fit—not super muscular or scrawny—and wearing a long, black cape, goggles on the top of his head, and overly large metallic blue gloves.

Maverick Case, #4 Hero, Strength: Lightning Bug—harnessing the power of electricity that he can create out of his hands or feet, he can unleash powerful bolts of lightning or bursts of electricity that are like waves of power. Through training, he's mastered his electricity control to such an extreme that his lightning has turned from yellow to black and the electricity potency is particularly destructive and powerful.

I was shocked at the pure power sitting near me. All four heroes were lightyears ahead of me in strength. Why don't the Care-Givers focus on them instead of me? They've stopped so many villains and saved so many people.

"Everyone, please rise for the three strongest heroes in our country," a guard standing in front of me stated. We all stood and in walked the third hero. He had a light dangling from his head, fangs, and fins sticking out of his cheeks. He looked like an Angler Fish.

Dame Qualin, #3 Hero, Strength: Angler Fish—he has a light dangling from his head that can shine as bright as the sun, can breathe underwater, and swim inhumanely fast. This strength gives the user a thirst for blood, but Dame counters this by drinking animals' blood daily and building up a resistance over time.

"This is always so overdramatic! Please, we're just people too, nothing special!" Dame yelled to the guard before sitting.

Next, the hero I feared most walked in. The person's gender was unknown, but they were the second-strongest hero. They wore a walnut wood mask with native symbols painted in black. The symbols were worn down but still recognizable. I could see their eyes stare me down as they sat.

Kaliska, #2 Hero, Strength: Native—they can use dead cells from the ground to summon zombified animals that are much larger and stronger than the animal was before it passed. Kaliska can also use the power of a Native Bible to unleash beams of pure power, eradicating anything within twenty feet of the book.

Kaliska said nothing and sat next to Dame. They were known as the coolest hero, and Kaliska was barely the second-most powerful hero.

In walked the strongest hero in the nation. His aura shook the room. He was a very skinny, lanky, extremely tall man. He wore a long trench coat with a popped collar, steel-toed boots, and a fedora. He bowed after entering the room. Something compelled me to bow back.

Zane Kinder (Puppeteer), #1 Hero, Strength: Puppet—he can turn his soul into a transparent puppet that is controlled through his fingers by a very, very slim black rope. The puppet's mouth is always open and can mimic the strength of multiple people within a mile each direction. The puppet cannot be harmed by physical attacks, but any attack that lands on Zane or damages the puppet's strings affects both Zane and his puppet.

As Zane sat down, he stared into my soul. I was completely terrified, so terrified in fact, that I couldn't return his gaze.

"Bring forth the evidence," Zane stated while holding his hand out in front of the desk, not breaking his eye contact with my head. The defense lawyer walked over and handed Zane a thin paper packet, then walked back to George and sat down.

"Not much evidence, huh?" George whispered to the defending lawyer.

"The ones I'm defending have been missing for years. I have no evidence to use," the lawyer whispered back.

Zane looked at the two. They quickly shut up. Zane flipped through the packet, then handed it to Kaliska, and leaned on his desk while looking at me.

"Kyle Straiter, why don't you tell us how you feel about the event that occurred," Zane suggested, although it felt more like a command. I gulped, then tried to speak. The mic screeched loudly, so I apologized before beginning.

"Well, I was fighting to protect my friends a—and the kidnapped people. We fought the Nomeres and Spike in a tunnel underneath the wrestling complex, then—"

"Who's this Spike you speak of? Is he alive?" Kaliska asked, swiftly cutting me off.

My eyes slightly widened. I looked down while shaking my head. George sweated and couldn't help but slightly facepalm.

"Who killed Spike?"

"I–I did. Spike was attacking me while I was trying to get past him to retrieve my two kidnapped friends, so I needed to get him out of the way. I didn't try to kill him. I just threw him into the wall and–"

"Didn't try to kill him? Kyle, is this a joke to you?" Kaliska asked, cutting me off again.

I felt sick when they asked that and shook my head again. Kaliska rolled their eyes and waved their hand at me. "Someone else ask him a question. We'll never get anywhere hearing him try and describe the events."

I've barely been able to describe them because you keep cutting me off.

"I'll take a question. What led to you murdering the two kidnappers?" Eleanor asked. Her tone was much nicer than Kaliska's.

"W–Well, I tried to reason with Lokel, since he is the father of one of my classmates. I kept telling him to join me and take down the Creature so he could go home and see his daughter." I squeezed the ends of my shorts. "He loved his daughter . . . he loved his family. It was the Creature's fault he was involved in any of this." Everyone was silent, so I cleared my throat and continued. "After Lokel was bleeding out on the ground, I told him I would bring him to the surface to get medical attention. The Creature was going to attack again, though, so Lokel gave me a sword and told me to fight for him. That's what I did. I attacked the Creature and that led to his death. That was the end of the fight."

A couple of pictures were taken, then Eleanor asked, "You just attacked the Creature and fully caved in his skull? There was a stab wound in his abdominal area, but where did this other injury come from?"

I opened my mouth to answer, but I saw George shaking his head out of the corner of my eye. I stayed silent.

"*Well?*" asked Eleanor.

"I plead the fifth."

"Very well," Eleanor sighed, clearly annoyed. Dame took the next question and flipped through the packet in front of him.

"So, Kyle, what about the deaths of the Nomeres and Spike? How did those occur?" Dame asked with a more laid-back tone than the rest.

"Spike was the first to go. As I said before, I hit him into the wall. My intention was to knock him out, but a giant mound of dirt fell from the ceiling and crushed him. After that, the girl expanded with her rubber strength and blocked my flames, so I punched her, but I guess I punched her a bit too hard. Finally–"

Kaliska slammed their fist down and stood.

"Punched her a bit too hard? There was a gaping hole in her stomach along with her blood spilled all over the place! That seems like just a little too hard to you?"

I gulped.

"Her strength made her body like rubber, and when I punched her, my fist stretched in her stomach and pierced through. This caused her to spew blood through the hole as the excess air escaped the hole. I thought she would simply deflate, but I should have thought harder about how strengths are just an extended part of our bodies."

Kaliska took a deep breath then sat down.

At E.H.:

Anya looked up at the screen and her eyes watered.

He really covered for us . . . she thought.

In the Courtroom:

"What else happened during this long fight that pushed you into violence?" C.J. asked.

I thought for a moment and had flashbacks of all the horrid things that happened.

"W–Well, I had to fight my own classmates because the Creature took over their minds, and Anya Lokel was hurting because of her dad. They took a junior who I look up to, Hazel Sparks, and intended to use her like they do their other kidnapped children. But the worst part was when I was being

drowned . . . and Kate saved me . . . then, the Creature . . . he stabbed her."
I couldn't contain myself, and I cried out, 'And now, she'll never be a hero!'"

E.H.:

Hunter looked at the screen, shocked. "He really–, cares about my sister?"

Zach nudged his arm.

"Duh, of course he does. I heard he started going ballistic only after she got hurt."

Hunter looked over at Zach, then back to me on the screen.

Courtroom:

"I am very sorry for the trauma this experience has brought you," C.J. stated while holding his hand near his heart.

I nodded, quickly wiping my eyes.

"How about we talk about you, since you're here and all," Aubrey smiled while leaning back in her chair.

"Objection, that is irrelevant to the case!" George shouted while standing up.

Zane waved him off while glaring down at me again.

"Overruled. Aubrey, continue."

My stomach dropped. I felt like I could throw up. George repeatedly tapped his pen, then wiped sweat from his forehead. This part of the trial would decide everything . . .

"How does your mother feel about this trial? Speaking of her, can we get any information on her?"

I looked over at George, who shook his head again.

"I plead the fifth." Aubrey looked at the papers in front of her while mumbling, then Maverick spoke up.

"Well, how about your life as a child? Any reoccurring problems there that would have caused you to lose control during this fight?"

George nodded his head, so I knew what to do.

"I–I had an aggressive family, so it made me a bit aggressive I guess."

Although unsatisfied, Maverick nodded.

The judges were looking at their papers, then Zane asked, "How many strengths do you have? The world now knows of your three, since you were hiding one, but are there more that you are hiding? Seems pretty odd that the number went up, no?"

"U–Uh, yes. It is pretty odd," I started while glancing at George. He obviously was shaking his head, so I stated once again, "I plead the fifth." My leg began bouncing, and I was starting to sweat. Foul was extremely nervous as well, and he was seated closest to George.

"George, they're getting angry! He can't keep this up!" Foul whispered frantically. George leaned back in his chair and moved his head toward Foul without taking his eyes off me.

"It is Kyle's Constitutional Right to plead the fifth. There's nothing they can say about it," George confirmed.

"Very well," Dame angrily said. "How about your father? That is someone we have no information on. Care to elaborate on who he is and what kind of influence he's had on–"

"I hate him," I stated, cutting Dame off. There was a loud gasp throughout the building. I could tell my angry response greatly angered the heroes.

E.H.:

"Wait, so Kyle does have a dad? I thought his parents were unknown," Steven asked.

Many others joined in his confusion, but Tonuko was just furious. He squeezed his chair's armrest, and his eyes were locked on me.

You fucking lied to me, you scumbag.

Courtroom:

"Firstly, you will not cut off a member of the Seven Influential while he is speaking. Second, we were told you have not only never met your father, but nobody knew who the father was when you were born. Lastly, if you don't straighten up your attitude, I will personally teach you a lesson!" Kaliska erupted while rising. Kaliska jumped over the desk, landed on the ground, then stomped in front of my stand. Kaliska pulled me off the chair and asked loudly, "Who the hell are your mother and father?" Kaliska held me by my collar. I could hear their breathing through their mask.

"Kyle Straiter, we do not have all day. Answer. The. Question," Zane stated a minute later.

I closed my eyes tight and tensed my fist. Flashbacks of all my beatings, my mother on the floor after Tyrant stabbed her, the Care-Givers attacking me and my classmates, it all rushed back to me at once.

"You cannot deny his right to deny any information he does not want to answer! You cannot deny his rights!"

"I'll deny whatever the hell I please!" Kaliska roared, shutting George up.

I grabbed Kaliska's hands, then erupted, "SAMUEL STRAITER, I AM THE SON OF SAMUEL STRAITER, BETTER KNOWN AS TYRANT! MY MOTHER IS GEM STRAITER, AND SHE WAS MURDERED BY HIM AND DIED IN MY HANDS SIX-AND-A-HALF YEARS AGO!"

Chapter 14

The Vows I Take,
The Promises I Make

Kaliska set me down and took a step back. Tears streamed down my cheeks, my jaw was clenched, and my face was red. Zane stepped down from the podium in front of the Seven Influential and stood in front of me. I was filled with rage before, but when he loomed over me, I was just scared. I knew it was over. I messed up. I broke and gave out the one bit of information about me that I was never supposed to. I was filled with surprise when Zane hugged me. I felt overwhelmed with emotion.

Everyone knows now, everyone. I'm Kyle Straiter, the son of Samuel Straiter, the man on top of the crime world.

E.H.:

Nobody knew what to say, and Fallen shook his head.

"He . . . lied to all of us," Cindy weakly said while looking at the screen.

"H–His father is the world's most infamous . . . most powerful villain," Camilla stuttered, her voice shaking.

"So what?" Daniel shouted as he stood. "He's still Kyle Straiter, and clearly he's trying to become a hero even if his family wanted otherwise!"

"Daniel, *did you know?*" Tonuko screamed while standing and slowly turning around. His face was filled with fury. Daniel was frightened and didn't respond, but his silence was enough of an answer.

"Daniel and I were there for Kyle when he was younger. He had it rough. His dad was crazy and would beat him every damn day! You think he'd follow in the footsteps of a monster like that?" Jaxon argued. He stared right at Tonuko. "C'mon, man, you've been getting close with him. You must have heard his declarations of killing that bastard. It's all the kid lives for!"

"I mean, we were there for Alex when his dad got possessed. Now that I think about it, during all the times Kyle had an emotional outburst, everyone just shunned him and ridiculed him. Why shouldn't we be there for him like we were for Alex, because Alex had some visible wounds while Kyle's are inside?" Zach added, laying back in his seat.

"Did any of us make an effort to help him when he was hurting, or did we think he was so strong and cocky he didn't need our help?" Anya asked while standing next to Tonuko.

Tonuko looked down at her with a mixture of confusion and anger.

"He murdered your dad a little over a week ago and now you're defending him?" Tonuko shouted to Anya.

"He did it to save us, Tonuko! We left him in that pit to die, and he came out on top! How can we blame him for risking his life to save ours?" Anya argued, standing her ground as usual.

Tonuko was speechless, completely dumbfounded. He tensed his fist, then stormed out of the theatre.

"Where the hell is he going? Listen, all of you supporting Kyle, from the bottom of my heart, thank you. I worked with him all summer, listened to his silent cries and pleas, and helped him overcome what his father did! He needs our help just as much as we need his, so those who are opposing him, grow the hell up!" Fallen yelled. He ran to the door, looked back at Excalibur, nodded, then chased after Tonuko. Excalibur snapped out of his shock and nodded back.

"Yes, his past does not define his future. Nothing his father has done has anything to do with him. We cannot hate him for something he can't control!"

Camilla looked down, and softly apologized.

"Sorry, it's just shocking that part of the reason we've been attacked so many times is because Tyrant is going after his son."

"Part of the reason? It's all his fault we've been attacked so much and been hurt! We wouldn't be dealing with Care-Givers if Kyle didn't exist!" Zayden yelled at her.

"Don't talk about him like that! He may be the reason we were attacked in the first place, but our bad decision making got us hurt! Kyle can't control what we do, only what he does. You know what he's done? Risked his life and nearly got killed protecting us!" Alex retorted. The class started arguing, destroying the progress they'd made building friendships.

Courtroom:

Zane, Kaliska, and I all returned to our seats. The black tears oozed out of my eyes, but I ignored them and looked at Zane.

"Mr. Straiter," Kaliska started. I flinched, assuming I was about to either be arrested or yelled at. Instead, Kaliska continued, "Thank you for being honest with us and revealing your trauma. The fact that you saved all those kidnapped people, even if it meant murdering five criminals, and that you acted like a hero instead of your scum of a father, is inspiring."

I smiled at Kaliska and nodded my head.

"Thank you. I'll never end up like him," I softly responded. Kaliska nodded and gave me a thumbs up.

"It is not what you are given, or the road others pave for you, that dictates your future. It is you, the work and dedication you put in, and your accomplishments that make you succeed," Maverick profoundly spoke.

Foul stood and clapped, then another person joined, and another, and eventually the entire crowd was cheering for me, for Maverick, for heroes.

"Kyle, I am willing to drop any charges of murder on one, and only one, condition," Zane smiled while standing from his seat. I nodded, then Zane said, "As long as you promise to live up to the ceiling that you are given, prove the world wrong, and make it a better place in your later years, then I will be confident in my decision."

I looked up at Zane, my eyes twinkling, and I nodded.

"Yes, I promise!"

The Seven Influential all stood and swiftly looked around at each other. With a nod, the answer was obvious as to what my sentencing would be.

"And one more thing, Kyle," Zane said while reaching his hand out to me. "Promise me that one day you will compete with my son to take my spot. You will fight to be the best hero in history."

With that final promise, I shook Zane's hand and was filled with glee. My black tears were gone, as well as the pain in my stomach. It was as if nobody even remembered I was Tyrant's son.

"Very well, then, you are dismissed and free to return to your studies. Be a good student, and an even better hero," Zane smiled, waving me off.

"I will, and I hope to see you again, but for a good reason next time!" They laughed, then the Seven Influential returned to the back room.

George, Foul, and I walked out of the courthouse first, being applauded as we did so. There were nearly twice as many paparazzi as before. When we reached the van and got in, Foul turned around and poked at me while wearing a massive smile.

"Look at that Kyle. I told you we'd be fine!" Foul shouted before giving me a high-five.

"You did well up there kid, really well. I'm sorry the information had to get leaked, but it seems as though it was for the better. Everyone knows whose side you're on!" George said as he left the parking lot.

There was a moment of silence, then Foul sighed.

"As happy as we are, the world does officially know who your father is. It's best we get you back to Eccentric High as quickly as possible."

I nodded, and George sped toward the highway. I was delivered home around 7:00 p.m. When I stepped out of the car, Foul joined me, since he also would be living at E.H. I took a deep breath, then stretched my back, and smiled widely.

"The number-one hero said I would be the best hero in history! How freaking awesome is that?" I exclaimed, making Foul chuckle. I pranced down the walkway and made my way to the freshman dorms. I'd been so happy the past couple of hours, I'd forgotten that the trial was nationally broadcast. My nerves caught up to me when I reached the front of the dorms, but I took a deep breath and opened the door.

It's my first time seeing my classmates in over a week. I wonder what's happened . . .

The building was dead quiet, not a soul was in the main area. It was peculiar. Usually at least a few people would be down here eating or watching T.V.

I guess it is a school night. Maybe the new teacher is stricter on bedtimes and crap. There's no way everyone follows the rules though.

I walked to the couch and jumped over the back of it. I laid there, sinking into the cushions while smiling to myself. I was home. I heard someone walking down the stairs and saw Khloe turn the corner. After seeing me lay there, she crossed her arms and rolled her eyes.

"I'm gonna guess you guys watched the trial?" I asked nervously.

Khloe leaned back on her right foot and nodded. I gulped but didn't know what to say.

"I can't believe you didn't tell any of us. I mean, seriously?" Khloe snapped before turning.

"It's a sensitive topic, I didn't know how to bring it up!" I yelled at her as she walked away. There was no response. I rested my head. Knowing people were mad worried me. I heard the front door open followed by several footsteps walking into the room. I lifted my head and saw Alex, Tonuko, and Anya. I smiled.

"Hey guys, been a hot minute, eh?"

Alex gave me the same energy, a big smile and wave. When Tonuko began walking over, I held up my hand for a high-five. However, I noticed his fists were tensed. He took another step toward me, then groaned, and looked up.

"Fuck, you're not worth it." Tonuko didn't give me a second glance before stomping away and up the stairs. My hand was just hanging in the air, and my confused smile was still smeared across my face. I slowly put down my hand as my smile faded and looked over at the other two.

"He's uh—not taking the news well. He keeps calling you a liar," Anya sighed before sitting down across the couch.

"How are you holding up though? I mean, getting that off your chest must have been a relief, but it had to have been scary!" Alex asked as he sat next to me.

I sat up straight and ran my hand through my hair while looking down.

"I'm fine. It was just a huge relief to finally not have to hide it anymore. It's been . . . haunting me my entire life." Alex looked startled, so I asked, "You alright?" The black liquid poured out of my eyes and mouth, but I didn't know why.

"Yeah, yeah, I'm good. It was just a big shock to hear about how the Tyrant is your dad."

I nodded and leaned back.

"I understand. It is a big shocker. That's why I kept it a secret, but Kaliska shook it right out of me. Kaliska was just too scary, I had to say it," I slightly chuckled, reminiscing about how much they yelled at me.

"Some people can't seem to understand that. They think you were lying because you are still connected with your dad or something—not that you were lying because, you know, it's a pretty big deal!" Anya sighed.

"We were arguing a lot after you came clean. I mean, class had to be canceled because there was so much fighting going on. People couldn't accept you for you," Alex added while glancing over at me. The liquid oozed again, and Alex looked startled like before. "And you're sure you're okay, right? You don't need to talk about anything?"

I was confused now by his worry.

"Yeah, I already said I'm fine."

He nodded, then they told me about what happened with Alex's father. It made me mad knowing that a villain would do something like that to a family as nice as Alex's. "I'm so sorry to hear that. Is your dad okay now?"

"Yeah, he's doing much better. My mom is recovering swiftly too, all thanks to Nurse Blavins!"

I nodded, relieved to hear the news. We all were silent again, but my snickers interrupted us.

"Sorry, I just can't believe Fallen is our teacher. I mean, what a character he is!" We laughed while thinking about our Fallen interactions.

"Yeah, Fallen started out a complete ass! He was poking fun at the kidnappers fight and how you went to jail, but now I just see him as a total badass!" Alex smiled.

After a few seconds, I stood and cracked my back.

"I'm gonna go make sure all my stuff is in my room and try to talk with some of the others. I guess, wish me luck?"

Alex gave me a thumbs up, but Anya shook her head.

"You're gonna need it. I mean, I think your entire floor is P.O.'d."

I let out an overexaggerated dreadful groan, making the two giggle, then I started up the stairs. When I reached my floor, it was dead quiet. All the doors were closed, except one. I walked over and saw Cindy doing her homework. I knocked twice on the door. When she looked over, her smile faded.

"What are you doing here, liar?" Cindy asked before standing.

Shit, she's mad at me too. I was kinda hoping she and Alex would be on the same side.

"I was just uh . . . wondering how you were. I haven't seen any of you guys since the fight, and even then, we couldn't necessarily talk." There was a painful silence. She suddenly stood and walked towards me. She was wearing a blue tank top, fuzzy pajama pants, and slippers.

"What were you doing over there?"

"Homework," she swiftly responded as she put her hand on her door. I gave her a confused look and scratched my head.

"Homework? Academic school ended in middle school. What homework are you doing?"

"Oh, right, you've been gone. Our teachers started a new class about decision making and stuff on the battlefield. Y'know, since some of us don't know how to act when we're under attack."

Unnecessary attack, lowkey hurt . . .

"Can I see what this homework looks like?" I asked while taking a step forward. Cindy put her hand on my stomach, stopping me from approaching.

"I think it's best you leave. You're probably the last person whose help I want when it comes to decision making. I'll be sure to let you know if we have an assignment about horrible battlefield decisions though!"

She just keeps them coming, huh?

"Don't forget who was the one who saved everyone from the kidnappers. I didn't make bad decisions, I was in a bad situation and had to act to make sure we didn't lose anyone," I defended myself calmly, raising my voice would only make people angrier.

"You weren't the only one fighting to save people, so don't act like it! Fighting isn't the only way of being a hero! Tonuko escorted everyone from the pit. Zach tried to save countless people by holding up an entire building. The police and heroes fought off Care-Givers . . . don't sit there and act like you were the only person doing something!" Cindy shouted. Her cheeks were turning red as she gave me a death-stare.

"How am I supposed to beat the kidnappers, escort people, and fight off the Care-Givers? There's only one of me," I responded, now a little annoyed by her ignorance.

Cindy huffed and muttered as she turned around, "Of course, what else should I expect?"

I was going to walk away as well, but I stopped when I heard that. "Excuse me?" I asked, looking back at her. She swiveled on her heels and crossed her arms while still glaring at me.

"What else should I expect from the son of Tyrant other than selfish cockiness?"

I was stunned.

"W–Wow, so after everything that's all you think of me?" With hurt in my voice, I continued, "After I busted my ass to make sure you would be okay, after I risked my life protecting your friends, after I took all the blame of everything, this is what I get in return? One confession just ruins everything, right?"

She looked away and stared at her desk. I couldn't tell if she was still mad, sad, or felt guilty, so I walked out and quietly shut the door behind me.

So, that's all that I'm viewed as now? Even after the Seven Influential forgave me, after I was recognized for saving lives and being a hero, I'm treated like garbage. I'm just Tyrant's son now . . . aren't I?

With that heartbreaking conversation, I went straight to bed, although I didn't sleep a lot. Throughout the night, the static returned in waves . . .

I awoke and turned off my alarm, then laid there for couple minutes. I took a deep breath before sitting up and held my head.

Nasty headrush, probably because I can't remember the last time I ate a full meal.

I stood out of my bed, showered, dressed, and brushed my teeth. I couldn't even look at myself in the mirror. I had to brush my teeth in the shower. After I finished my morning routine, I threw on a plain, black sweatshirt and headed downstairs.

Ever since the confession, it seems as if people aren't very social. I get that it's early in the morning, but usually people are out and about. Tonuko is mad at me, like fuming, but he was still talking with Alex and Anya even though they supported me. Why isn't anyone else like that?

Instead of going on my usual morning run, something I hadn't done in over a week, I decided to get something to eat at the little strip mall (mentioned in the invitation letter sent out) on campus.

I've never been to the strip mall. I wonder what kind of stuff it has.

There were four stores next to each other, each a little bigger than a classroom. Two of the stores sold clothes, one for warm weather and the other for the cold. All the clothes were branded with E.H.'s logo. The other two stores were for food. One was a convenience shop with pre-packaged food as well as fresh foods. The other was a food truck with two chefs who made whatever dishes were on the menu for the day—one breakfast item, one lunch item, and one dinner item. I considered getting a cooked meal but decided instead to just grab a packaged muffin from the convenience store. I continued down the path while opening the wrapper, then noticed there were swimsuits in the warm-weather shop.

Is there a pool here? Come to think of it, I've never actually been on the other side of the school. What's over there?

I made my way down the path, past the school, then saw a huge, fenced in pool. I was pretty surprised I'd never noticed it considering its size. Half the pool had separators for lanes of swimming, and the other was open water.

Maybe we could all go swimming together one day. Well, I guess that's if all the sour emotions go away . . .

I continued touring around campus and walked past the sophomore and junior dorms. They looked the same as ours. The senior dorms were very bare and dark. I continued walking and eventually reached the front gate.

Before I walked in front of it, I heard a ton of yelling, talking, and general commotion.

What the hell? Who's here so early?

I walked past the wall and looked through the metal gate. My stomach dropped. There were countless guards trying to contain the hundreds of newscasters, cameramen, people in general. After I made my presence known, the commotion halted for a quick second, then everyone erupted with questions and yelling. The cameras were now on me as people reached their microphones past the guards.

"Kyle Straiter, how is life back at school with everyone knowing you are the infamous Tyrant's son?"

"Are you being accepted by your peers, or have you lost all your friends?"

"Are you the reason for all the attacks on your class by Care-Givers?"

"Will there be another attack in the close future?"

I walked to the trash can next to the gate, threw out my muffin wrapper, then walked away. I could hear the screaming getting louder and the barrage of questions continued, but I ignored it and headed for the school's front doors. Fallen always drilled into me to not give the media the time of day. Speaking of Fallen, I wanted to pay him a visit before class started. I went up the stairs and strolled down the hall until I reached my classroom. When I looked in through the door, I saw Fallen sitting at his desk correcting papers. I knocked before turning the knob. Fallen looked up then grinned.

"There's the criminal! How've you been, Kyle?"

I couldn't help but smile. When we walked toward each other, we grabbed the other's hand and pulled in for a one-arm hug.

"I mean, you can probably guess I've been better," I responded after pulling off the hug. He took a step back, then sighed.

"Yeah, yeah. I can only imagine the kinda stress you've had on you this past week and a half. It must be tough knowing your class relied on you and trusted you, but now half the country hates you after only a day."

I sat at the first desk by the door, and he leaned on his podium at the front of the room.

"Since I was so happy about not being found guilty, I barely thought about the fact that my class probably saw the trial. So far, it seems like almost everyone here hates me now."

He shook his head, frustrated.

"I don't know what others told you, but it was an ugly scene in that theatre. Everyone was pointing, shouting, swearing, insulting, just being total a-holes to each other. Unnecessary info was being spewed; it was just . . . horrible. People were flat-out upset that Tyrant's son, son of a villain who's hurt so many people they know, is at this school. On top of that, knowing that you've not only been lying about how many strengths you have, but also the fact that it's probably because of you that we've been targeted by the Care-Givers . . . it just ignited more flames."

I rested my arms on my desk and slouched in the chair while nodding my head.

"I think some of them were just jealous of my two strengths at first, but during the kidnapper fight, I had no choice but to use more to beat my mind-controlled teammates and the kidnappers. Kidnappings, torture, abuse—they were . . . no; the Creature was just pleasuring his insanities."

Fallen stood and grabbed a piece of chalk, then walked over to the chalk board, and started to write. The school didn't have the funding for white boards, so every class had chalkboards. Fallen wrote in big letters:

Honesty
Bravery
Trustworthy
Respectful
Caring
Understanding

"These are the six qualities society expects heroes to retain. At first, HotSauce was known as the perfect hero. He had everything people wanted to see in someone who saves lives. He took the bare minimum a hero could make, worked overtime, traveled to help every city he could. He was amazing. However, since his death," Fallen raised his hand, then drew a large, thick "X" over the words, "the faith and trust in heroes has plummeted. The most selfless man alive died because he acted selfishly and tried to gain more power.

That fact broke all heroes' images. Knowing that someone you respected and trusted died because of their selfish desires, whether they were good or bad, breaks people. It makes them hate that person and the concept of what they fought for."

My eyes widened, and I tensed my body.

"Th–The faith in heroes, is–going down? But we fight to protect everyone! If they don't trust us, who will they trust?"

On top of that, what Fallen just said kind of sounds like my situation. I lost their trust and respect.

Fallen nodded and sighed before elaborating, "Look, we're not supposed to tell any students, for fear of creating panic, but it has to be said. Riots are starting all over the country demanding rights for civilians and banning heroes from cities. Society everywhere does not trust heroes to take care of them and believes they are only looking out for themselves and their money. The riots exploded in our state after your confession . . . "

"Don't they realize we're fighting for them? Heroes surfaced to protect people from criminals!"

Fallen shook his head and waved his finger.

"No, heroes surfaced to protect people from villains. Criminals have always been a thing and that's what cops were for, but villains, they're 'super criminals.' They abuse their powers, to—well, to put it plainly, to kill. Criminals either looked for money, or just weren't very strong and could be contained by police. However, villains were too powerful for the police to handle, and that's when people stood and fought back against these power-hungry villains. Heroes were cherished and loved by the people at first, but now, people are arguing that we cause more damage and put more lives at risk than we save. It's a hard and weird subject to understand if you aren't in their shoes."

I looked down at the desk and thought back to the destroyed building, the innocent people scattered around crying, the hole in the street caused by David's grenades, then looked back up.

"Yeah, that makes sense. We do destroy a lot of property during battles. Who even paid for the damages at Veena?"

Fallen put down his chalk and erased the board.

"I have no idea; they were paid for before I was hired as a teacher. Anyway, you should get going to the theatre. Excalibur and I will be talking to your class about something very important."

Fallen was extremely serious after he said that, so I figured it was best not to mention that I had no clue where the hell the theatre was. I scooted out of the classroom and walked to my locker, then looked down at both ends of the hall. I saw many bare classrooms. Some that were previously off limits were now open since construction was finished.

I wonder why there are so many classrooms here. What other classes besides homeroom, training, and I guess decision making are possible at a hero school?

I made my way back down the stairs, and saw Alex walk in through the front door.

"Alex, thank God you're here!" I shouted, running up to him.

He looked confused, then asked, "What, is something wrong?"

I shook my head and rubbed my neck, a little embarrassed.

"Well, not really. It's just . . . where in the world is the theatre?"

He chuckled and closed his umbrella—I could now see it had started to rain.

"Just follow me."

We went to his locker first so he could put his umbrella away, then he showed me where the theatre was. In the far back of the building, on the first floor, there was a huge room with multiple rows of comfy-enough looking chairs. Excalibur was seated on the stage, not responding to anyone who talked to him, and a couple of other students were seated already.

"Are there assigned seats in here or–?"

"No, you can sit wherever," Alex quickly responded.

He sat next to Jessica and Scarlett, so I followed. I assumed those two weren't mad at me since they were friendly with Alex when he said hi to them. However, when I sat next to Alex, Jessica scoffed, stood, and walked toward the other side of the aisle.

"Jess, come on!" Scarlett begged, but to no avail.

"Sorry Kyle, she isn't taking the news very well. I don't understand why people are so mad about it."

I shrugged, but Alex leaned on his knees and looked at Jessica.

"Her cousin was killed in a building explosion caused by Tyrant a year ago. I have a feeling seeing Tyrant's son isn't making her feel any better."

I looked down, full of guilt. Even though I had nothing to do with her cousin's death, I felt fully responsible.

"That's horrible," I sighed.

"Yeah, it is! Maybe we'll be next since the Care-Givers are attacking us because of you!" Jessica angrily screamed. I knew it would be best to stay quiet. When she reached the end of the aisle, she sat next to Donte. Our classmates started piling in, and everyone who opposed me sat away from me, while the people who accepted me sat near me. Out of the thirty-two students, only twelve sat near me.

Wow, so this really has ruined friendships. Donte and Steven, Jessica and Scarlett, Alex and Cindy, Tonuko and Anya, Zayden and Rake, these people who were all good friends are now glaring and seething at each other. What do I do?

While everyone yelled and argued, Excalibur stayed quiet. Suddenly, Fallen kicked open the doors. The loud bang made everyone shut up. He walked in with his hands in his pockets, scanned the room, then clenched his jaw.

"Look at all of you, letting these petty emotions get in the way of your growth as a grade. This is absolutely fucking ridiculous!" Fallen ridiculed while making his way down the aisle. Excalibur hopped to his feet and punched his hand against the wooden stage.

"All you've been doing is bickering about something that shouldn't matter! This is immature and wrong, and you should be punished! Yesterday was absolutely *unacceptable!*" Excalibur shouted. I could see guilt grow on my classmates' faces.

Woah, how bad was yesterday?

"Since more than half of you have decided you cannot accept the student who you praised not too long ago—merely because he spoke up and got something off his chest—Excalibur and I have decided to issue a lockdown on all freshmen!" Fallen revealed while holding his hands up and grinning evilly.

"We aren't supposed to leave campus either way, so what will a lockdown do?" Tonuko asked, obviously being a smartass. Fallen shook his head and pointed behind him.

"The campus? More like your dorm building," Fallen retorted. Chaos ensued.

"Isn't this a little extreme? We have a lot of training to do, and the shadowing is coming up soon!" Steven argued after standing.

"Sit down boy!" Fallen snapped. Steven complied. "You all have the shadowing in a little over a month, and you will be missing out on training during this lockdown. That's why you shouldn't be yelling at us but instead be utterly disappointed in yourselves! We could be working on power-ups and all that crap; however, since you are being childish and immature, we have no choice but to amend your trust in each other." Fallen paced back and forth in front of Excalibur. "Trust is the most important part of being a hero because you must work with sidekicks, as well as other heroes, and trust that they will have your back. If you can't even trust yourselves, the future heroes, then how can we have trust that you will be able to go out and shadow hero organizations?" Fallen explained.

"Shadowing is one of the most important events of freshman year! If we can't train and get stronger, then how are we supposed to be able to train under a pro-hero and be ready?" Cindy asked.

Fallen shrugged, looking as though he was trying to hold back laughter.

"That's a great question Cindy, but I do not have the answer. This lockdown isn't just because of the hatred that's developed since the trial. We've noticed the freshman class is relying heavily on the chefs, and they aren't doing many activities as a grade or even as classes! Every other class has gone shopping, used the pool, or at least trained on their own damn time with each other! The laziness and social distancing in this grade are sickening considering you should be working as hard as you can to become the best heroes you can be! You will not be allowed to buy food, considering you won't be leaving the dorm. We will provide groceries once a day. You will have enough food for breakfast, lunch, and dinner."

Everyone mumbled and grumbled to each other. Excalibur marched up the aisle and opened the doors. He kicked the doorstep down, then smugly grinned and made big swoops with his arms before pointing his hands out the door.

"Go on, get back to your dorms. You may want to open some windows. It can get stuffy in there," Excalibur snickered. Fallen couldn't help but chuckle, and the teachers followed us as we trudged to our dorms. I was the last to enter the building, but before I made it through the door, Fallen put his hand on my shoulder.

"Fix up your relationships, and don't forget what I taught you: friendships save lives," he whispered. I didn't turn around, just watched as Tonuko turned the corner and went up the stairs.

"Don't worry. I'm gonna fix this," I gave him a thumbs up as I turned around and smiled. "It's what I owe to the people who respected me."

He smirked. After I had entered, he closed and locked the doors. Jon walked by with Devin and the two burst out laughing.

Jon was holding his stomach as he wheezed, "Wow, the freshies are getting put in lockdown? That is priceless! They need to just get along already!" Fallen and Excalibur joined in the laughter.

"That's what we're saying! Now that they are stuck in the building with each other, with a shared common space, they'll have to finally start damn socializing with each other!" Fallen snickered.

Chapter 15

Tension

A little more than half of the students immediately went to their rooms. The others stayed in the common area and made an effort to talk to each other.

"Well, I guess this is our life for a while," Rose sighed while sitting at a barstool and resting her head in her arms on the counter.

Daniel chuckled and responded, "I mean, it could be worse. We could be out fighting more villains or something!"

They all agreed, but I didn't respond.

Iris walked up to the counter and looked afraid to talk. "U- Um, does anyone actually know how to cook?" she blurted out.

We looked at each other, but no one answered.

After a few seconds, Scarlett grabbed Jess and wrapped her arm around Jess's shoulder. "We can do it! We took cooking lessons when we were younger!" Scarlett announced gleefully.

"Really?" Alex asked. "I've known Jessica for like eight years, and I've never known she knew how to cook and never knew she's known you."

"Yeah, we're neighbors and my aunt used to give us cooking lessons on the weekends. It's been a while, but I think we can do it," Jessica clarified quietly.

We heard a knock at the door, so I walked over and answered it. To our surprise, Hazel walked in along with Jon and Devin, and they were carrying bags of food.

"We got your food haul, freshies!" Hazel laughed while putting down the food.

She and I hugged, then I exclaimed, "I didn't know you were back already! You're okay, right?" Hazel nodded, then wiped a tear from her eye. She pulled me back in and hugged me again.

"Kyle, just so you know, I will always accept you. Nothing about your past will change how I view you now," she reassured me.

Once we stopped, Jon leaned on my shoulder and waved his hand in front of his nose. "You freshmen sure are stinky; want me to pick up some air fresheners?" I rolled my eyes, while shaking my head. Jon snickered, then reached his other hand into one of the plastic bags and pulled out a carton of eggs. "Two bags are breakfast, two are lunch, and two are dinner. There're recipe sheets, written by yours truly, in each bag for the meals today, but you're only getting them today!"

"Thanks guys. We're definitely gonna follow these recipes to the letter," Scarlett said while rifling through the first two bags. Devin backed up and peered out the door, seeing his and Hazel's class leaving the school.

"Well, we're gonna get going. Get over this social hump fast so you can get back to training. Also, Fallen and Excalibur made a rule that you aren't allowed to close your doors before 10:00 p.m. It'll force you to be more social during the day," Devin informed us before walking out.

Hazel and Jon said bye to us, then left. We groaned about the new rule and gathered around the counter.

"Let's go to our own floors and tell everyone about the door rule. Jessica and Scarlett, you can stay down here and start unpacking the groceries if you want," Khloe directed.

I hesitated, then took a deep breath and exhaled quietly.

"Alex and Khloe, you stay and help Jessica and Scarlett. Iris and I will tell Tonuko and Cindy."

I turned and looked at the stairs, but Khloe and Alex were confused. Alex just stood and shrugged.

"Alright, it's good to not leave all the work with Jessica and Scarlett anyway," Alex smiled while picking up the gallon of milk from one of the bags. Khloe was a little more hesitant.

"Are you sure it's smart for you to go near Tonuko right now? He's pretty mad," Khloe asked.

I shrugged and shook my head. "We're never gonna' get out of here if we can't get along. Tonuko and I were going to have to talk it out eventually."

With that, Iris and I left for our floor. When we made it up the stairs, Iris scurried into Cindy's room.

When I walked past Cindy's open door, Iris poked her head out and asked, "Are you sure this is a good idea?"

I thought for a moment, then yawned and blinked a few times. I put my hands on my head and nodded. "Tonuko can't stay mad forever. If he does, then he's just a little baby," I snickered while walking away.

I made it to Tonuko's door and stood in front of it for a few moments. I took a very deep breath, in through my nose, out through my mouth. I found myself more nervous than when I'd confronted Cindy, but after all that had happened my nerves were incomparable. I knocked on the door, then stated, "Tonuko, it's Kyle. We need to talk."

"Get the hell away from my room, lying-ass criminal," Tonuko hatefully remarked.

I put my hand on the knob, then opened the door. In the room to my right, Iris and Cindy were hiding, yet listening. In his room, Tonuko was seated on his bed, the only light coming from the window that he was looking out.

He turned to look at me as I argued, "I'm not a criminal, you know that! When someone I'm related to, but not close to, turns out to be evil, that makes me the same? What kind of stupid logic is that?"

Tonuko stood and marched over to me, then poked me in the chest, hard. "You lied to me; you hid your connection with Tyrant. You think this is all just a big game, *huh?* You can't just lie straight to my face, act all heroic and mighty, then when everything you've said turns out wrong, act like nothing ever happened! You've got that villain blood surging through your veins. It's going to rise up and takeover eventually and when it does, I'll be there to *take you down!*" He shoved me back and I stumbled into the hall. He walked out into the hallway, then I stepped forward and grabbed his shirt collar.

"Just because my dirtbag father is a criminal doesn't mean I'm one! I just beat down two powerful villains with direct connections with my dad!"

Tonuko's icy stare didn't ease up; he glared into my eyes and clenched his jaw.

"That event proved more that you're just a villain hiding with us. You're in denial, but you can't control your animalistic instincts! *You killed five people! You weren't any kind of damn hero!*" he snapped at me.

"You and I both know I killed three people, not five. We know who killed the Nomeres. I took the blame for you and Anya so you wouldn't have to deal with the backlash of being good people with wrong actions," I responded immediately in a quiet seethe.

Tonuko grabbed the collar of my shirt. "Stop being so cocky! You didn't have to do anything! Don't act like we owe you, or like you saved our asses!" he erupted.

I heard footsteps on the stairs. People were gathering at the end of the hall.

Why the hell is everyone saying I'm being selfish and cocky? I saved them from the villains! Is this what heroes get for saving the day: being shunned and yelled at?

"Don't you understand? I almost died trying to stop the kidnappers from getting anyone else! They tortured Hazel, paralyzed Kate, possessed you. I risked my life to make sure you got to safety! Don't you dare forget what the hell I told you during the fight!"

Tonuko's eyes slightly widened as he remembered.

"*Tonuko, my life is worth so much less than all of yours! I don't have a real reason to keep going, but you all do! Don't let me be the reason you die, get out of here with yours and everyone else's lives, dammit!*"

"Stop trying to make me feel guilty!" Tonuko screamed, shaking me back and forth, then throwing me down the hall. I got up and tackled him onto the ground.

"You've never cared about anyone; all you've been is violent and put us in danger! You have no self-control!"

He punched me in the face, so I retaliated with a punch of my own.

"I haven't cared because I don't know how to care about people! Why are you so closed-minded that you can't understand that I've never in my life had anyone care for me? Everyone is acting as if there's a reason to protect each other . . . it makes no sense!"

He tackled me and put me in a headlock, then a girl ran at us and speared me out of his grasp. She and I rolled on the ground for a couple of feet. She sat up and held my arms behind my back.

"Would you two knock it off? It's been like fifteen minutes, and you're already fighting!" the girl shouted after rolling her eyes.

Tonuko charged at me again, but I kicked him in the stomach before he could reach me. I heated my arms so the girl holding me would let go and dove at Tonuko. After a few more seconds of us fighting, Rake managed to contain Tonuko, and the girl got a hold of me again.

"Chill out man. Why are you so against him?" Rake asked frantically.

Tonuko wiped blood from his nose, then sighed instead of answering the question.

"Everyone, just go downstairs. Steven and I will help. Having more people who aren't biased will aid in settling this," Cora commanded.

The students reluctantly followed, then Cora and Steven walked over between Tonuko and me.

"C'mon Tonuko, fighting him won't solve anything. I don't wanna make you madder or anything, but he's kinda like beaten you twice and you two have caused massive damage both times. We can't destroy these dorms, it's the place we sleep and eat!" Steven shouted.

Cora crossed her arms while looking down at me, then asked, "What gave you the idea that it was smart to confront him only a day after your announcement?"

I shrugged. The girl behind me shook her head while sighing.

"I can't believe you two babies are the top students in our grade! Come on and make up already!" the girl complained, gripping my arms tighter.

"Who even are you?" Tonuko patronized.

Her tough attitude fell as she whined, "Aww man, you don't know my name? That's so embarrassing! I'm Skye Harlem, the queen of the advanced class!"

I finally calmed down enough to get a good look at her. Skye had big, red horns, red hair in a braided ponytail, large wings folded on her back, and her skin was a bright orange.

Skye Harlem, Strength: Demon—contrary to Alex, she can create a substance made of pure darkness that is freezing to the touch. She grew demonic-looking wings when she developed her strength. On top of that, Skye can grow her nails out at will and she has four fangs.

Finally, Skye let go of me, and Rake did the same for Tonuko.

"Could you guys, like, maybe just talk it out instead of fighting?" Rake asked as he wiped sweat from his forehead.

"I guess so, but you guys get out of here," Tonuko grumbled, still glaring at me.

Cora, Steven, and Rake cautiously left, but Skye didn't budge.

"I'm gonna help you guys through this! You can't fight over something as silly as Kyle's family! If he's here, you have to realize it's for a reason, right?" Skye walked over, then sat, forming a triangle between us.

"I know he's here for a reason, but what the hell is it? You've told me before how much you want to kill Tyrant, but when I offer peace and common ground, you get all angry and argue that you have to do it on your own! What are you, why are you so set on killing him? Everything I hear you talk about with villains is how you hate Tyrant and how you want to kill Tyrant . . . How am I supposed to believe you will be a consistent teammate on my side, not an outlier on your own side?" Tonuko ranted while running his hand through his hair.

"I didn't lie about what I said to you after the training tournament. I'm here to train, to get strong, to be a hero, and to kill Tyrant. Plain and simple," I stated sternly.

"But then what? That's the thing, what are you going to do after that?" Tonuko shouted as he stood.

I simply continued staring at him. Tonuko looked down at me in disbelief, then tensed his fist. He stomped over to me and grabbed the collar of my shirt again.

"That's going to be it, right? You want to kill Tyrant, then kill yourself! That's why you told me your life isn't worth the same as ours. You don't think of your life as worth anything! You were born to be the end of Tyrant and his bloodline!"

Skye quickly stood and grabbed Tonuko's arm, but she couldn't move it. "Tonuko, please! There's no need to get violent!" she pleaded while pulling his arm.

Tonuko stared me dead in the eyes and clenched his jaw.

"Kyle," he seethed, "promise me you aren't going to die at your own hands." Tonuko's statement stunned me. I was at a loss for words and could only stutter. "You have to promise me, dammit!" He slightly shook me as he yelled.

Why? Why does he care whether I die or not? We were just arguing, not even ten minutes ago, about how I should die because I'm a lying criminal. Is he lying now, or was he lying before?

"Uh–I–"

"Kyle, you have to promise me!" Tonuko's eyes shimmered in the light. I couldn't tell at this point if he was angry, sad, or something else.

Why are you so adamant on this Tonuko? What's going on in your mind? Why do you care if I'm alive or not? I don't understand.

"Why do you care if I promise you?" I asked bluntly. I wasn't used to all these emotions.

"I care because you're my friend, you dumbass!" Tonuko shouted while shaking me back and forth another time. I stared up at him, utterly befuddled. "People here care about you! We aren't just classmates to go to school with. We're your friends that you will spend at least the next four years with. Stop talking about your life having no worth and saying Tyrant this and Tyrant that! I don't care about how horrible and dark your murkiest secrets are. I'll still be your friend and your ally! Forget the fact that you're Tyrant's son. When you lie to me about important things that you need help with, you make me feel like you can't trust me! On top of that, when you always imply you don't care about your life, it makes me feel sick! You're going to stick around for a while Kyle, promise me you will!"

I didn't know what to say, I was so . . . happy that someone cared whether I was here or not.

All my life, I've just been Tyrant's son, a curse on the world. I thought everyone would think that too if they ever found out, so I convinced myself it was the truth. Maybe . . . it's not . . . Maybe I do deserve happiness . . .

"I–I promise," I stated.

Tonuko didn't smile, nor did I; he simply dropped me and turned to walk away. He stopped after a couple of steps but didn't look back at me.

He looked straight ahead as he said, "You and I have a lot of pressure from other people. We're two very strong freshmen, and the future of heroes as we know it. So, until we're both at the top, and I'm ahead of you, you're not allowed to leave." With that, Tonuko walked down the stairs to talk with those gathered on the first floor.

I stood dumbfounded, staring at the stairs. Skye put her hand on my shoulder and gave me a smile.

"Well, that was pretty intense! But hey, I'd say you two are a-okay!"

I slowly nodded.

"Y–Yeah, I guess we are." I didn't look at her. I continued staring wide-eyed straight ahead. We stood there for a few more seconds before I declared, "I think I'm going to go downstairs and talk to some people. You, uh, have fun doing whatever you do." I stood and walked toward the stairs, and Skye followed me. I didn't care though, maybe we would be friends.

Caraline City, Thursday Morning; 3:33 a.m.:

The mist thickened as hail mixed with sleet rained down harder. A whooping gust of cold blew over the countless, scattered corpses. Thunder boomed in the sky. A man walked through the streets while wailing. His navy-blue cloak was stained red at the bottoms as it dragged on the ground, and his loud steps made by thick boots echoed throughout the dead streets. His honey-colored eyes practically glowed and his brown hair was messy and long, bangs hanging in his face. Trash was littered everywhere, drenched from the weather, and blood soaked the streets, washed around by the rain. The man's cries were almost loud enough to overtake the noise of the rain.

Lightning struck the ground and exploded a part of the street in front of him as he yelled, "Why must society follow these *disgusting* habits of battle? Hero and villain. It's just segregating and separating–" Another bolt struck, and strong winds took down a building, causing a massive crash. *"Our beautiful lives!"* he concluded.

A dead woman's face was stuck in a shocked expression. Barely held in her hand was a large sign attached to a wooden pole that read:

CIVILIAN LIVES MATTER
YOU'RE HARMING US NOT HELPING
STOP SOCIETY CRUELTY

The crying man was the hero of the protest. He defeated those objecting to the large, record-breaking protest that stemmed from other states. In the process, he killed every last protester. Was this man truly a hero of the people, or a villain hidden in plain sight?

In King's Cellar:

"You can't just switch the plan on us! We had prepared to make an attack next week!" King roared furiously at BloodShot. "We have specifically laid low and lost out on thousands of dollars to not build suspicions about our attack on Eccentric High!"

BloodShot put his mask on, scoffing, "Shut your mouth, would you? I'll do whatever the hell I want, whenever I want, and however I want it done! I'm the leader of this operation, so I control when it happens. Kyle snitched about Tyrant. We can't get into the city without being caught. Heroes, citizens, news reporters, they're all pouring into Camby to see the school with Tyrant's son and the top-ranked student of the freshman class, Tonuko Kuntai!"

The man with the white cross walked down the stairs and kept his distance from BloodShot.

"When can we attack?" the cross man asked.

BloodShot sighed and looked at his watch.

"I'll let you know when I know! You're all just so useless! I have to go, but I'll return soon to collect Plague's gloves from you, King!" BloodShot waved behind him as he walked off, swatting at them as if they were measly bugs.

"You're going to let that mutt boss us around?" White Reaper seethed after she heard the door close. One of her beetles crawled out of her mouth and into her robe, then white flames spiraled into existence on one of her legs. King swerved around, letting his cape flow in the air, then walked away. "I could kill him if I wanted. He shouldn't be able to tell us what we can and can't do!"

King stopped and looked at White Reaper over his shoulder.

"I know, but he's right. The city's population is going to skyrocket, and their school is going to be the center of attention for television across the world. Considering the rumor of the education system changing drastically, people are also going to be moving closer to public schools they can afford. With more people comes more crime, which equates to more pros, and that means a higher chance of us all being arrested and put to death. We don't want that, do we?" King's pupils glowed with that last sentence, then he walked into the back room of his cellar.

After Plague and BloodShot left, they walked toward the train station. Plague looked down and fiddled with his fingers, then glanced up at BloodShot.

"Why do we have to wait so long to bring Kyle to Tyrant? I wanna' see this high school!" Plague suddenly blurted out.

BloodShot looked at Plague out of the corner of his eye. He sighed, "Time will tell; don't forget that, young one," He looked both ways before crossing the street. Plague held on to BloodShot's cloak as they crossed.

"What about with Mr. Tyrant?" Plague asked. "What will happen with him and the others if time will tell? Haven't they been doing this kind of stuff for a long time?"

"There's no need to worry about him. Tyrant was the most powerful villain and made an even stronger son. Throughout his time at the top, Tyrant broke down people's faith in heroes. He's had the biggest impact anyone has ever had on society since strengths first surfaced back in the early 2000s. Sure, it's only been a couple of hundred years, but strengths have had a stronger impact than the first types of technology."

Plague took this all in while staring at the ground trying to think of more questions.

"Why are strengths such a big deal if they've only been around a couple hundred years?"

BloodShot led Plague over to a bench outside a luscious park. The two sat down.

"Before strengths surfaced, technology was human's biggest focus. However, since strengths—then known as powers—started appearing in children, the focus immediately shifted. There have only been four generations older than 20: mine, Tyrants, and the two before his. Tyrant is a third-generation strength user, and I am a part of the fourth generation. You are a part of the fourth generation, as are Kyle and other children of two third-generation parents. Around sixty percent of people in the world have strengths, and thirty percent are heroes or villains/criminals. Therefore, strengths are advanced, but not very understood. You need certain DNA to be able to control or hold a strength, and those who don't have it live normal lives like people of the past. Those who can control their strengths either use their powers to their advantage or to stop others they feel abuse their powers." Plague swung his legs back and forth and rested his hands on the bench underneath his thighs.

"Will others be able to hold more than one power like Kyle can?" BloodShot looked around at the people walking. A large grin was painted on his face.

"Certainly someone will try, and that someone will succeed. It's clearly very possible, but it might just be a very rare mutation, like a disease." Plague nodded his head, then looked at his fingertips. He wiggled his fingers, and his eyes slightly sparkled.

"A disease, like mine." BloodShot smirked as he stood from the bench.

"We'll master that strength, my child, then you will truly shine."

E.H. Freshman Dormitory, 9:30 a.m.:

After I made it down the stairs, I looked around at some of the unknown faces. I wasn't sure who to talk to because I didn't want to get into another big argument with someone who was mad at me. I looked around, feeling pretty anxious, then Skye leaned on my shoulder while standing on the last stair and pointed across the room.

"Those two over there are my best friends here. Go say hi to them, they're really nice!" Skye suggested with a big smile. She pointed at two girls who were talking. One of them had dark green skin; shiny, light blue goggles on her head; a big, green turtle shell on her back; and a few scales on her cheeks. The other was just as showy: blue hair with small, red streaks and her face was pale with the same color red patches all around her body and face. I nodded while taking a deep breath, then, after some hesitation, made my way over to the two advanced students.

"Uh, hi," I said, slightly interrupting their conversation, "I'm Kyle from honors. What are your names?"

They looked over at me, then the girl with blue hair smiled and introduced herself and her friend.

"Trust me, we know who you are Kyle! I'm Emma, and this is my friend Violet!"

I smiled because of her enthusiasm and shook her hand, then held my hand out to Violet.

"Nice to meet you both. I see you have an animalistic strength; that's pretty awesome," I stated trying to be kind. I figured I should try to sway conversations away from me and my life at this point.

"Oh, yes, my strength is quite fantastic!" Violet shouted while aggressively shaking my hand. Her goggles shined in the light as she grinned widely.

Violet Dedge, Strength: Turtle—because she developed an animalistic strength from spending so much time with her pet turtle, she has a large shell that attaches to her back and can be pulled off by only her hand. It is impenetrable by most attacks, having the ability to nullify fire, water, winds, etc. She also can swim abnormally fast and breathe underwater.

"I bet you'd be great in the pool behind the school!" I thought aloud.

Her ocean-blue eyes lit up with glee, and her smile seemed to grow bigger.

"I know, right?" Violet agreed. "I was hoping we would all be able to go sometime, have a little advanced and honors competition in the pool!

I'm happy about this lockdown because it means we'll get close enough to all go together!"

I nodded. *She's so positive. Honestly, it's a nice change of pace.*

Suddenly, I felt someone's arm around my shoulder. When I glanced over, I saw Zayden standing next to me with a big smirk across his face.

"Did I hear there's another person with an animalistic strength? I'm Zayden Attack from Honors, and you are?" Zayden held his other hand out to Violet, who in return shook it just as violently as she shook mine.

"You heard correctly Zayden. I'm a turtle! I'm Violet Dedge, and this is my friend Emma Lance! Pleasure to meet you shark boy!" Zayden and I both chuckled, then Zayden let go of her hand and stopped leaning on me.

"Wow, you sure are energetic! It's a nice contrast from all the anger that's been going around." The two agreed, then Zayden turned to me and put his hands on my shoulders. I was confused, especially since he was looking straight down.

"Kyle, I just gotta say . . . I'm sorry. I was one of the people against you when you first confessed, and I argued it was all your fault that villains attacked us. I shouldn't have said that. It's not—"

"Listen, if you really think about it, I am the reason the Care-Givers have been obsessed with us. That's why I fought so hard to try and make sure no one around me would get hurt. Next time, I promise I'll fight my own fight without killing anyone," I declared to not only Zayden, but also to the two advanced girls.

Zayden looked up with a smile, then pulled me in for a quick hug.

"I bet you will," he stated while pulling off.

The other two smiled, and Violet said, "You don't need to fight alone though." My eyes widened as I looked at her. "Us advanced kids, other than Daniel and Zach, haven't done much. Next time a villain attacks, you can at least count on Emma and me to fight right alongside you! No fight is just your own, we're all here to support you! That's what heroes do, right?"

I don't understand . . . first Tonuko, and now these three . . . why is everyone so adamant about helping me? I'm Tyrant's son. I deserve pain, suffering, and torment for all my life. I thought everyone hated me because of my family, so why are they being—so nice? It's . . . so comforting . . .

"W–Wow, I don't know what to say. Th–Thank you," I stuttered as my eyes slightly watered.

"No problem, we're all gonna be heroes, so we'll all be working together for decades to come!" Emma smiled.

"So, does this mean . . . we're allies?" Violet and Emma looked at each other, then chuckled.

Why are they laughing? Am I wrong, are they faking, do they not actually care? Is that how Tonuko felt too, did he not actually—

"No, Kyle, it means we're friends!" Violet clarified. My smile grew wider, and I beamed with joy.

"O–Oh, right, that's what I meant!"

They giggled and said goodbye, then walked toward the stairs. Zayden also left, so I made my way over to the counter and leaned on it. Scarlett finished cleaning up the table, then walked over, and stood next to me while facing the rest of the room. There were students scattered around talking, but I noticed it was mostly honors' kids talking with honors' kids, advanced kids talking with advanced kids, or students who went to the same middle school.

"Do you think we'll be let out sooner rather than later? I mean, there are already a lot of people socializing," Scarlett asked before crossing her arms.

I turned around and shook my head.

"You're not wrong that there are quite a few people talking, but don't you notice how anti-social the talking is? People are only talking to those they already know, so it's not much progress. No offense, but honestly, how many advanced kids do you even know?"

She thought, then threw the small towel in her hand on the counter and sighed. "Yeah, you're right. I don't really know any I guess."

Daniel and I made eye contact, then he headed toward me, along with Rose and Skye.

"I hear you don't know any advanced kids . . . well I guess it's time to meet some!" Daniel smiled while reaching his hand out to Scarlett.

Daniel and Rose started talking to Scarlett, but Skye just stood wide-eyed next to me.

"O.M.G., is that Iris?" Skye blurted out while pointing at Iris. Iris turned around, and her face lit up with glee. Skye jumped over the counter, surprising me by her sudden outburst of athleticism, and hugged Iris tightly. "I haven't seen you in, like, a year! How have you been?"

"Hey Skye, I've been pretty good. How about you?" Iris softly responded while returning Skye's hug.

"I've been good, good, great! Sorry, I just missed you so much!" They stopped hugging, and everyone either stood or sat around the counter.

"Aren't you the queen of the advanced? I feel like I remember hearing that earlier," Scarlett asked Skye.

"Oh yeah, I am the Queen! Second ranked in our class, in fact!" Skye boldly announced loud enough for everyone in the room to hear. Daniel and Rose looked at each other, then snickered.

"What's so funny?" Skye interjected.

"Sorry about how cocky she is everyone. Skye just loves attention!" Daniel laughed.

Skye scrunched her nose and crossed her arms while retorting, "I am not cocky! I am the most humble, gorgeous, outstanding student in our grade! How dare you say otherwise!"

There was a short silence, then the three burst out laughing. I looked over at Scarlett. We made eye contact, and both shrugged.

"So, what are you two ranked in your class?" I asked, looking at Daniel and Rose.

"Well, I'm the tenth-ranked student, and Daniel over here is the big, bad fifth!" Rose answered, nudging Daniel with her elbow.

I smirked while looking at Daniel, and he looked back with a mixture of confusion and annoyance.

"Wow, only fifth? Man, I thought you were stronger!" I teased.

He rolled his eyes, then let out a chuckle.

"Aww, shut up hot shot, fifth is pretty good I'd say!"

I nodded with a small smile.

"Yeah, I know, I was just joking. With how much you complain about your strength, I thought you would be lower!" Daniel cracked his shoulder and walked toward me, then fake punched me.

Everyone else laughed. I'd been downstairs long enough, so I went to sit in my room. I laid on my bed, pulled a blanket over me, and closed my eyes.

Maybe I just really need a nap.

I drifted off, then a couple of minutes later Alex walked by my room. Fear filled his eyes as he saw me lying in bed with an enormous pitch-black arm reaching out from my chest. He stood there, utterly horrified.

"Wh—What the hell is that?" he whispered to himself. The hand wound up, then slammed my bed. A large, disgusting creature crawled out of my body. Alex hid behind the wall, breathing heavily and sweating.

"It's the same color as those tears from yesterday . . . what is that?"

After a couple of seconds, Alex heard footsteps marching toward my door.

They stopped when Cindy asked, "Alex, what are you doing?"

Alex turned to Cindy with terror in his eyes and he said nothing. Cindy walked from her room to mine and looked in. She saw me sleeping, then chuckled, "C'mon, let him sleep! Let's go downstairs!"

Alex saw the creature looming over Cindy.

It was as tall as the ceiling, had tentacles sticking out all over the place, and was inhumanely muscular. The creature's face had almost no identifiable features, except a large mouth with razor-sharp teeth. Cindy grabbed Alex's hand, then led him to the stairs. He looked back one last time and saw it stare into what felt like his soul. They walked down the stairs, leaving the creature standing outside my door, seemingly guarding my sleeping body.

Flashback:

"We've only just started. Why the hell are you crying already? Get up boy!" Tyrant shouted with his fists balled. I wiped the tears and blood from my face and weakly stood while coughing.

"Papa, it hurts! I wanna go inside, please!"

Tyrant stomped toward me and scoffed.

"Shut up, you cannot go in yet! We need to train you so you're ready!"

I closed my eyes and tensed my fists, then went into another coughing fit.

"Ready for what? I just want to play with Daniel!"

Tyrant tensed his body, then sped at me and kicked my side so fast that I couldn't react. I flew through a window and landed a few feet away from my mom. I stood, coughing even more, and ran to her.

"Momma, he keeps hitting me again!"

Mom hugged and shushed me gently. "It's okay, sweetheart, you know he loses his temper sometimes. He just wants to see you succeed! Don't worry, we'll power through this, together," she said.

Tyrant threw open the sliding glass door and stomped inside to where we were.

"Kyle, go on and go play with that disgusting hero's kid. Your mother and I need to talk."

I nodded as I fearfully ran through the house and out the front door. Before I fully closed it, I could hear my parents arguing loudly. I looked back and saw Tyrant and my mom screaming at each other. I closed the door and ran through the streets. I made my way into cat alley, running as fast as I could while crying profusely.

He is not my dad.

I made it to a busy street, then turned and sprinted into the big park (where E.H. is now built) that separated Daniel's house from mine.

He is not a real man.

Once I was across the park, my tears slowed. My jaw was clenched, fists were tensed, and eyebrows were furrowed. I could barely focus my eyes because I was so furious.

He's just a strength-stealing demon.

Chapter 16

Class Competition

I woke abruptly to the sound of someone knocking on my door; it was Camilla. She leaned on my doorway as I yawned, then informed me, "Sorry to wake you, but dinner's ready. I'd assume you're pretty hungry since you slept through breakfast and lunch." I blinked a few times, then glanced at my alarm clock. It was 6:00 p.m., which honestly surprised me. I sniffed and smelled meat cooking. My stomach growled loudly.

"Yeah, seems I'm right."

"It smells so good," I said before standing from my bed. Camilla looked around my room, then flicked the light switch on and turned.

"You should really clean up in here and turn on a light for once!"

I rolled my eyes as she left, then walked to my desk and grabbed a pack of mints from the drawer. I popped two in my mouth while rubbing my eyes, trying to adjust to the light.

Nap breath is nasty, and did she really have to turn the light on?

I yawned again as I walked downstairs and saw everyone else sitting at the table. Scarlett and Jessica were bringing the food to the table, and out of the corner of my eye, I saw Daniel waving me over. When I sat down, Daniel was on my right, Skye was on my left, and Alex, Khloe, and Tonuko were across from me. Everyone dug into the large trays of boneless barbeque chicken wings and French fries.

Once everyone had a plate of food, Steven asked, "How did you guys manage to make this?"

Jessica smacked him on the head as she walked by and rolled her eyes. "Ow, that was a compliment!"

We all laughed and began eating.

"So, I've been thinking about it all day: when is the angel versus demon fight going to happen?" Tonuko asked.

I smirked and nudged Skye on the arm.

"Yeah, who would win?" I asked, trying to instigate the two.

Alex and Skye chuckled, then Skye puffed out her chest and flipped a bang of her hair.

"I don't wanna crush the poor little angel too hard, so it'll probably never happen!" she cockily boasted.

Alex looked up with a confused expression and pointed at her, then at himself.

"Wait a minute, Advanced versus Honors?" Alex and Tonuko snickered, but Skye just rolled her eyes and crossed her arms.

"Oh whatever, that doesn't even matter!" she argued.

"I mean, it kinda means everything about strength!" Donte chimed in with barbeque sauce all over his hands.

"Okay dead last, I could probably take your spot in Honors if they gave me the chance!" Skye mocked while playfully glaring at him.

"Hey, I got put up against the Queen of Honors in the first round!"

Across the table, Rake shouted through his chuckles, "Yeah, and your strategy to defeat a wind user was to create wind, you dumbass!"

Donte shook his fist.

"I'll kick your ass Rake!" he retorted. There was a quick silence, then countless people burst out laughing.

"Sure Donte, maybe if you beat him, you'll be fifteenth instead of sixteenth!" Cora taunted.

"Cora, you aren't in single digits either!" Anya giggled, nudging her.

Tonuko and I stayed quiet during the argument. Alex and Camilla didn't say anything either. Hunter leaned back in his chair and grinned.

"Notice how all the lower numbers are the ones arguing? Meanwhile, all the top people don't care about their rank!" Zach snickered at him as he put down his glass of water.

"Hunter, Skye was the first to say something about rankings," Zach nonchalantly said.

"Also, are you even in honors, buddy?" Steven asked in between shoveling fries into his mouth.

Hunter's cheeks turned red as he stuttered, "W–Well, I'm the best–I mean the top of–"

"Exactly," Steven interrupted. He went back to stuffing his face, then a few eyes turned to Tonuko and me.

"How are the two cockiest kids in our grade not saying anything?" Cindy asked.

Tonuko and I simultaneously looked up and around to see everyone staring at us.

"Hey, we–I am not the cockiest kid in our grade!" Tonuko yelled in response.

"Woah, woah, woah, what the hell does that mean?" I asked, putting down the half-eaten wing in my hand.

Tonuko grinned and put down the food in his hand as well.

"I mean, you know what I'm saying."

"Aren't you the one who came here so you would be top of the class with no competition?" I asked before laughing.

"Whatever!" he angrily shouted, "I mean, it kinda worked!"

We all said "Mehhh" at the same time, signaling it clearly didn't. After that, we continued talking while we finished our food, then cleaned our dishes, and loaded the dishwasher.

While some waited to clean their plates, Violet leapt onto the countertop, clearly against Emma's pleas.

"Everyone, I have a fantastic idea!" Violet excitedly squealed. We all looked at her. She suggested, "Why don't we ask tomorrow if we can go to the pool? We'll still be together, and doing a class activity like they suggested, so I'll bet Mr. Excalibur and Mr. Fallen would let us!"

Tonuko put his plate in the sink and shrugged. "I mean, that's not a bad idea at all," he thought aloud.

"Yeah, I agree. We can ask them tomorrow when they deliver the groceries, or if it's Hazel, Jon, and Devin again, we can ask them to get our teachers," Alex added from the couch.

"I knew you would eventually say something about it," I said to Violet as she got down from the counter. I yawned for a few seconds, then rubbed the top of my head and looked over at the stairs.

Gosh, I've been sleeping all day, but I'm still so exhausted . . . maybe I really need to catch up on sleep since I had such a tough time getting any last week.

"I think I'm gonna head to bed," I told Tonuko, Violet, and Emma, who stood near me.

Tonuko raised an eyebrow and looked at me weirdly.

"You've been strangely tired the past two days. I mean, you just took a nap for almost ten hours," he observed.

I shrugged while rubbing my eye.

"I didn't sleep a whole lot last week, so I think my sleep schedule is heavily off," I said. I wished them a good night and, as I walked by the couch, Alex waved to me.

"I'll close your door for you since you're not allowed to for another couple hours," Alex smiled. I nodded and waved to him, then trudged up to my room and passed out as soon as my head hit the pillow.

A few hours later, Alex turned the corner on the stairs and looked up at my door. It was a half hour past ten, so Alex decided he would close my door and go to bed himself. When he reached my room, he saw the monster walking around again. Alex covered his mouth, thought for a moment, then ran back toward the stairs and made his way up to Daniel's floor. He knocked frantically on Daniel's door.

Daniel answered a few seconds later. "Oh, hey Alex." Daniel saw the worry on Alex's face, so he asked, "Something wrong?"

"Just, come with me," Alex commanded while grabbing Daniel's forearm. The two went back down the stairs, and Alex cautiously approached my door, confusing Daniel even more. Alex took a deep breath, then peered into my room. The creature was standing over me—back to the door—just watching me.

"You see that thing?" Alex whispered.

Daniel looked around the room with a raised eyebrow and shook his head.

"Uh, what thing am I supposed to be looking for?"

The creature walked to the door and bent over, sticking its horrifying face only a few inches from Alex's. A tentacle raised from its chest and pressed on Alex's lips, then the creature shushed him. The tentacle retracted and the creature slowly marched back to me and continued his watch. Alex looked absolutely horrified. His hands trembled.

"What's wrong? Is there something I'm missing?"

Alex shook his head while wiping his lips, then turned to Daniel.

"No, no never mind. I think I'm just hallucinating; I didn't sleep well last night," Alex sighed.

Daniel put his hands on Alex's shoulders, then turned him around.

"Then you should probably go to bed now. I don't think anyone is gonna be hanging around downstairs tonight; we're all already getting sick of each other!" Daniel joked trying to lighten up Alex's mood.

Alex couldn't help but smile and nod.

"Alright, well, I'll see you tomorrow. Hopefully we can go swimming."

Daniel nodded and said bye to Alex, then looked into my room one more time. Nothing was there, so he shrugged, closed my door, and went back to his room.

Maroline City, 10 Miles from the State Capital: Takorain; Thursday Night, 8:35 p.m.:

The crowd of protesters roared with anger, and a few news helicopters gathered in the sky.

"These heroes are destroying our cities!"

"Why do we have to fight?"

"Strengths are not weapons!"

The famous protester chuckled and smirked as he stepped out from the crowd. His honey eyes were glowing, and the hood of his cloak rested on his head.

"Yes, why must we settle our differences through petty, destructive violence? Shouldn't strengths be used to better the future? To protect our children?"

The police moved forward in a line with their riot shields braced in front of them.

"Why do you have heavy artillery, officers? Why do you feel so threatened by us? Are you . . . afraid?" The protester held out his hands, palms facing the sky, and stood boldly.

"Back up, all of you! You have opinions and the right to express them, but you cannot use them to attack us!" an officer shouted, pushing the protester with his shield. The man stumbled over but caught himself with his right foot. He clenched his fist and looked up at the officer with ferocious eyes that struck a life-threatening fear through the officer's body.

"Do not ignore me, and *do not* touch me!" The protester swung his arm across the line of officers. Rain poured down and lightning shot from the sky, creating a massive explosion. Mist seeped from what seemed like nothing, while winds picked up speed. "I am The Upriser and *I will be heard!*"

Officers moved forward, standing in a line behind the crater formed from the explosion. They unloaded their rifles at him, but with a swoop of his hand, a tornado spiraled into existence and sucked up all the bullets. It crawled toward the officers, ripping up the streets as it moved. A brave man from the crowd of protesters ran and grabbed The Upriser's shoulder.

"What are you doing? We are peacefully protesting, not rioting! What's your problem man!" the man shouted.

The Upriser grabbed the man by the neck, then ripped his hand off of himself. The Upriser turned around as he lifted his fist to the sky. A bolt of lightning shot down and was absorbed by a large ring on The Upriser's right ring finger. The Upriser then moved his arm and pressed the ring onto the man's forehead. The man freaked out and frantically kicked his feet.

"I'm sorry, sir, but sacrifices must be made to birth a new, perfect world," The Upriser spoke. His deep, booming voice shook the crowd to the bone.

The man began screaming, and as quickly as his screaming had started, he stopped moving. Electricity poured out of his openings, then he exploded in The Upriser's hand. All that was left when the smoke cleared was a thick puddle of blood. The crowd of protesters screamed and ran, leaving some of them in tears.

"Where are you going, why are you running? I'm with you, I'm helping you make your cause heard!"

"You're a monster, a villain!" a civilian lady shouted from the fearful crowd.

The Upriser's eyebrows furrowed, and he clenched his fists.

"Villains are a part of the *disgusting* thing we are fighting against!" His screams brought more powerful winds, and he swiveled on his heels and walked away. Behind him, a thick building had been sliced in half by the powerful winds and fell onto the sprinting crowd, crushing those in its path.

"You all do not understand, *you are the villains!* I will cleanse the world of you, you *pathetic sheep!* Tyrant, Puppeteer, BloodShot, Kaliska . . . you will all be *purged!* I will create the *perfect, peaceful world!*"

A giant lightning bolt struck the debris of the fallen building, creating an enormous explosion and gruesomely killing any who had escaped its collapse. All helicopters had been taken out of the sky and all police force and heroes who were at the scene were dead. Blood ran the streets under The Upriser's feet again as he marched while crying. He made his way toward the train station, eager to find the next city of protesters.

E.H., Friday Morning, 9:30 a.m.:

After finishing my morning run, I showered, then dressed and fixed my hair. I hung up the towel I'd used, walked out of the bathroom, grabbed my phone, and made my way downstairs. I nabbed an apple from the wooden bowl on the countertop, then jumped over the back of the couch, and sat down. I looked around, found the remote, and turned on the news.

"There are still no leads as to who the bloodthirsty rioter, who has been wreaking havoc on protests, is. This is the fifth protest he has attended; all have been left with no survivors. He has killed twenty-five heroes, along with hundreds of police officers and protesters. No one knows whose side he is on, but the Seven Influential have declared him as a national threat to civilization. The man, who calls himself 'The Upriser,' is still on the loose, so be cautious of any protests you had planned to attend if you are in this circle," the news castor explained. The screen changed to a map showing a large circle in our state. Camby and Takorain, the capitol, were included.

"Jeez, that doesn't sound good," Camilla said while on the last step of the stairs. She walked over while watching the T.V. and sat next to me.

"I know, this guy is weird. I've seen a little coverage on him before. In the video I saw, he gave a speech about creating a new world or something before he commits the homicide," I explained with my eyes fixated on the T.V. A video was played, and it was a person showing a street in the first city The Upriser had attacked. There were bodies and debris from collapsed buildings scattered all over the street. The Upriser was seen strolling down the street while crying.

"Why must we fight when I'm on your side? I want to free you from the shackles heroes and villains put on us! We can rise up together and create a purified, perfect world!" The Upriser wailed.

I listened, and Camilla flinched at the visible corpses on the streets.

"This guy," I started, leaning forward and watching as lightning struck the street and exploded, "he's not trying to take down heroes or villains by himself . . . he's trying to band the people against us, against heroes and villains. He's going to collect followers."

We looked at each other, both wide-eyed.

"If he collects enough people toward his cause, there might be a new kind of social group—not a hero or a villain but an uprise of people wanting change," Camilla concluded.

I leaned back in my chair and sighed.

"I mean, it probably won't ever happen. What kind of people want to work together with a leader who kills people on his side?" I asked rhetorically.

I wish I was right, and in that moment, I thought nobody would ever support the cause of The Upriser. Little did I realize he wasn't the only psychopath in the world.

We sat in silence for a moment, then heard commotion coming from the stairs. Suddenly, Violet flew and landed in front of the stairs. She used the stairs' railing to swerve around the corner.

"Are the teachers here? Did they come yet?" Violet screamed.

Camilla raised an eyebrow, confused because she hadn't been downstairs when Violet made the announcement the previous night.

"Violet has been going on and on about asking the teachers if our grade could go to the pool. She's been talking Emma's ear off apparently. You're a little excited, I assume?" I asked with a chortle.

"A little? I'm so ecstatic I couldn't even sleep last night! I can't wait to get back in the water!" Violet shouted with pure joy.

Camilla and I couldn't help but chuckle, then there was a knock at the door. We heard keys jingle, so Violet bolted toward the door, then excitedly hopped as the door slowly opened.

"Heyo'!" Fallen announced while stepping into the dorm.

"Teacher, I have a question!" Violet shouted practically in his face.

Hazel walked in behind Fallen, who had flinched from the loud Violet. I stood and walked to them, then put my hand on Violet's shoulder, and pulled her back a few steps.

"I'll ask for you, Violet; you're a little too excited right now," I chuckled quietly.

Excalibur walked in carrying some of the groceries and smiled when he heard what I said.

"Nice to hear you two know each other's names. I assume there has been some talking going on in here then?"

I grinned and nodded. "Yeah, yesterday was surprisingly social. I think the pressure of the shadowing has opened all of our eyes." The teachers were happy with that response, then Violet elbowed me hard in the side, signifying for me to ask the question. "Oh yeah, we've decided on an activity that would help us get even closer!"

"I'm listening," Fallen said in a monotone voice.

"Well, you would have to let us leave the dorm . . . but we were wondering if everyone could go to the pool?"

Fallen looked back at Excalibur, who shrugged.

"Alright, we'll let you go, but on two conditions." Fallen held up two fingers as he explained, "First, everyone in the dorm has to go, no exceptions. Second, you have to figure out a sport, activity, training workout, or something of the matter to do together. You cannot just relax there; you must be doing something. Also, I'm pretty sure the sophomore honors' class is using the pool to train later today, so you might get kicked out earlier than you want."

We thanked him as they left.

I sighed out of relief, then turned and announced happily, "I guess we're all going swimming today!" Violet exploded with excitement and sprinted upstairs to tell Emma. Camilla and I looked at each other, then laughed. "Should we wake up Jessica and Scarlett for breakfast first? The four of us could probably crank out a meal for everyone within the hour."

"I think Violet might actually explode if we make her wait any longer," Camilla giggled while shaking her head, "We can just have an extra-big lunch today."

I agreed. We went to all the floors to tell everyone about the pool situation. We decided to leave at 10:15 a.m., a half hour after everyone knew we were going. I went back to my room to try and find my swimsuit.

"I know it's in here somewhere. I just . . . don't know where." I searched my entire room, practically flipping it upside–down, but for the life of me I could not find that swimsuit anywhere. Tonuko and Alex walked past then laughed as they peered into my room.

"Kyle, what in the world happened here? Was there a tornado?" Alex asked.

I frantically looked around, then sighed.

"I uh, can't find my suit anywhere."

I looked at the two and noticed their summer-festive outfits. Alex was wearing a loose, white-collared shirt with a black bucket hat and black-and-white polka-dot swim trunks. Tonuko was wearing a collared shirt with watermelons scattered all over it; his swim trunks had a large watermelon with a slice taken out of it on the side.

"Just go buy one at the store," Tonuko suggested and pointed out my window. I looked behind me at the clothing store, then picked up my wallet.

"I can spot you some money if you're running low," Alex added with a heartwarming smile. I shook my head.

"You might be late, so you better start running!" Tonuko snickered.

I rolled my eyes with a grin, then ran past them and made my way down the stairs and out the door as fast as I could.

I'll be damned if I'm late.

I grabbed the first pair of swim trunks I saw, put them on the counter, and took out my wallet. The elderly lady scanned the tag on the shorts, then gave me a smile as she looked up.

"That will be twenty-five dollars," she said. I opened my wallet but saw only a ten-dollar bill and two singles. I gulped, then looked back at the dorm.

I saw some students leaving for the pool already, so I asked, "Do you have any cheaper ones?" I asked while pulling out the three bills.

The lady looked at the money in my hand, then looked back up at me, and shook her head. I sighed, knowing I would disappoint my class if I was the reason we were kicked out of the pool.

I'm sure Fallen and Excalibur wouldn't be happy if I wasn't in the pool with everyone. Maybe I can just use shorts or–

"It's on me, Kyle Straiter," the lady smiled with a wink. My eyes twinkled, and I smiled brightly.

"W–Wow, thank you so much!" I glanced back and saw people leaving the dorm, so I hurriedly put my money back into my wallet, grabbed the trunks, then sprinted out of the store.

I passed Violet, who angrily yelled, "You better not be late Kyle! Pool time is important!"

"I know, I'm going as fast as I can!" I spun around to shout, then spun back around, and ran faster to get into the dorms. I made it inside and up to my room, then finally changed into the trunks and walked down the stairs.

Honestly, there's no point in running. Pool time might be very important to Violet, a literal turtle, but I can wait. I'll only be late by a minute or two.

I walked out the door and was on my way to a fun day in the sun.

I stepped through the front doors of the school and navigated the bare halls trying to find the pool entrance. I had my towel draped over my shoulder, goggles on my head, and I was wearing a white tank top. I reached the back of the school and heard splashing on the other side of large, wooden doors I had just passed. I backtracked, then turned and opened the doors. The sunlight blinded me as I stepped outside onto the hot cement.

"Kyle!" Violet shouted, marching up to me. She was in her suit, and her shell was glimmering in the sunlight. She grabbed it and smacked me on the top of the head. "You're so late! Come on and get in the pool!"

"Jeez Violet, calm down a little! Unwind and have some fun!" Anya shouted from across the pool. She was about to jump in the water, but Tonuko ran up behind her and full on tackled her into the pool.

"Damn," I whispered, chuckling a bit as well.

Violet gave me a side-eye, then she grumbled, "That'll be you next if you don't hurry up and get in!"

"Alright, I've just gotta put my stuff down and throw on some sunscreen!" I told her, then walked over to one of the tables and placed my towel on it. I realized something very important: I don't even own sunscreen.

"Kyle!" Alex yelled from the pool, "You can use my sunscreen! It's the spray bottle on your right!" I thanked him before grabbing the bottle and spraying my body. I put down the sunscreen, then took a step toward the pool. A pit formed in my stomach.

Shit, I thought I got over this!

"Kyle, what's wrong?" Anya questioned me, swimming over to Alex.

I took a few more steps toward the edge, then stretched my arm.

"Oh, psh, it's nothing. I'm just feeling, uh, tight right now."

I still can't get over my fear . . . not since Caden . . .

Daniel got out of the pool and shuffled over to me. Since he'd known me for so long, he could tell I was stretching because it was my nervous habit.

"Wait a minute, don't tell me–!" I quickly shushed Daniel, then turned him around so we were both facing away from the pool.

"Yes, I'm still afraid of water! It's just–ever since–just no!" I heard a snicker behind me. I looked back and saw Tonuko laughing.

"What the hell are you gigglin' at Moody Earth?"

"I said don't call me that!" he shouted while leaning on the pool's edge. Anya jumped up and pushed his head underwater, then gave me a taunting smirk.

"What's wrong Kyle? You afraid of the 'scawy' water'?" she mocked.

"What the hell? Of course I'm not afraid of some dumb water!" I argued.

"Alright, then jump in," Alex suggested, joining in the mockery.

I stopped stretching and puffed out my chest.

"Alright, maybe I will!" I walked over and dipped my toe in the water. A shiver went up my spine and I backed up. Everyone started laughing at me, and I blushed out of embarrassment, then took a deep breath.

Come on, Kyle . . . if you can beat two powerful villains, you can jump in a damn pool! It's just water, nothing more!

"Quit stalling you loser!" Tonuko yelled, acting bored.

I gave him a sneering expression in response, then quietly hyped myself up and ran toward the edge. I skidded to a stop and didn't jump though, causing everyone to continue laughing.

"Oh come on Kyle, it's just some water! Violet practically lives in it!" Emma shouted.

Tonuko and Alex looked behind me, then grinned at each other. Alex got out of the pool and ran over to Violet, who was standing behind me with a mischievous grin.

"What are you two doing?" I asked anxiously while backing up. I felt Tonuko grab my legs, then gulped. Violet and Alex ran at me, then speared me into the pool. I fell back first into the water, then opened my eyes, and looked at the surface. I had flashbacks of Caden trapping my head in his bubbles, practically trying to drown me, then of Lokel nearly drowning me. After I closed my eyes, I felt someone grab my hand. I opened my eyes slowly and saw Violet smiling at me while pulling me to the surface. I took a deep breath and looked around. Everyone was laughing and having fun, splashing one another, and doing tricks as they jumped in.

Maybe this isn't so bad . . .

Violet jumped on me while giggling.

"See, it's just water! It's not gonna hurt you!" she shouted.

"Yeah, I guess you're right!" I admitted with a smile.

After a couple of minutes everyone was in the water, but we couldn't agree on an activity.

"What about that? Isn't that water polo?" Zach asked while pointing at two goals and a ball in a corner of the fence. He got out of the pool and grabbed the supplies, then threw them into the pool. Violet caught the ball, then grinned.

"I *love* water polo! How about a little class competition, ay'? Advanced verses honors?" Violet suggested.

"Bring it on fishy!" Steven mocked as the classes separated.

We lined up at our respective goals and assigned goalies. We chose Rake, and they chose a boy I'd never seen. He was very tan, a little lighter than Alex, and had frosted tips on his black, curly hair. After getting things sorted, we counted down, then swam at the ball in the middle of the pool. Donte activated his super speed and bolted toward the ball. He grabbed it, creating a huge wave in the process. The wave swept most of the advanced kids off their feet, including the goalie, so Donte had an easy throw in to make the score 1-0.

"Looks like you'll have to try a little harder than that, Violet!" I boasted.

She grabbed the ball and started swimming the length of the pool. She dodged honors' kids left and right then, instead of going straight for the goal, she grabbed her shell and threw it at Rake. It smacked him in the head, then spun around and flew right back to her. Violet whipped the ball into our goal, tying the score at 1-1.

"Looks like you'll have to try a little harder, Kyle Straiter!" Violet smirked. After a few more points, commotion, and yelling, we heard someone shout from the fence closest to the school.

"Wow, you freshmen sure are competitive!" We stopped playing and looked over. Foul was patrolling, wearing his wrestling outfit as he did so.

"Woah, Foul? What are you doing here?" Daniel asked, astonished.

"A few wrestlers and I were asked to patrol the school. I couldn't say no, thinking about your grade, so we started yesterday after you were put on lockdown!" Foul clarified with a chuckle.

"Wait, so does that mean you aren't a wrestler anymore?" Alex questioned, sounding a bit disappointed.

Considering Foul Odor was the rising star wrestler of the nation, knowing he had to quit because of us would make everyone feel guilty.

"No, I'm still a wrestler; we all are. We're just taking a break for this school year until the villain activity calms down. As much as I love wrestling, your safety is a priority for the other patrollers and me. We're gonna be working under Fox-Tails for the time being," Foul explained.

Catastrophe turned the corner with a raised eyebrow just as Foul finished his explanation.

"Hey kiddos, I thought you were on lockdown. What happened?" Catastrophe asked, walking up to Foul.

"We were allowed to go to the pool together!" Violet gleefully screamed. Catastrophe acted like his ear was hurting from her screaming and rubbed it.

"Golly girl, I'm right here!"

"Sorry, I'm just super excited to be in the water!" Violet apologized.

"Her strength is Turtle," Emma explained, "so she gets very excited when it comes to swimming and water."

"Unlike baby boy Kyle over here! This tough guy is scared of water!" Tonuko snickered while nudging me. I pushed him, then heard Foul laughing.

"Scared of water? Kyle, c'mon man!" Foul and Catastrophe continued laughing as they walked away, but I angrily blushed. We continued playing for another hour, then spent a half hour doing other competitions. The honors' class swept the advanced, winning all battles. After the last one, Jon burst through the door with a towel on his head and his shirt off.

"Time to beat it, freshies! We've got training to do!" Jon cackled while standing with his legs spread wide and fists pressed on his hips. There was disappointment all around, and everyone got out of the water. After we'd dried off, we made our way to the front of the school.

"Man, why can't we be in the pool for just a little longer?" Skye complained, crossing her arms and pouting. It was a group of Skye, Alex, Tonuko, and me, and Emma and Violet were a couple of feet ahead of us.

"I'm surprised you're so upset about this. I mean, not as upset as her though. Violet might be depressed now," Tonuko snickered, pointing at Violet. She trudged forward with her head held low, then she shook her fist behind her at us.

"You just shut your mouth," she muttered.

"It was so much fun competing with you guys. I guess I can't say that advanced doesn't get enough credit, because neither class is really getting any credit at all," Skye sighed. I looked at her, confused.

Alex thought aloud, "Oh yeah, when you think about it, we fought two infamous kidnappers and two super-powerful Care-Givers, but we've had almost no news coverage. There've been crowds of news people here, but they were for Kyle's trial." We stopped walking and stood in a half-circle.

"There definitely should be more hype about this school, all things considered. Who knows, maybe there actually is, and we just don't watch the news enough. When was the last time anyone checked the national rankings?" Tonuko asked.

"All I know is Kyle is gonna come to light and go from unranked to top ten, and Alex is top one-hundred, although maybe a bunch of B.E.G. (Bade's Exceptionally Gifted) kids moved up in the rankings. Who knows," Skye pondered.

Tonuko scoffed when Skye mentioned B.E.G. and crossed his arms.

"Ugh, B.E.G.; I hate that school. They gave me a full ride, but I didn't accept. I've heard from heroes connected with my mom and dad that it's a bunch of strict, stuck-up teachers."

My mouth gaped and I clenched my fists.

He had a full ride to the top school in the nation . . . and declined? Are you fucking joking?

"You dumbass, why in the world would you decline an offer like that? You know how many people dream of going to B.E.G.? Who cares if a few teachers are stuck-up, it's a dream school!" I yelled in disbelief. I expected an argument, but instead just heard giggles and chuckles. "What's so funny?"

"Wow, Kyle, just wow! How do you know how many people dream of going to B.E.G.? It's obvious you're talking about yourself!" Alex laughed while patting my shoulder.

I quickly calmed down and couldn't help but join in the laughter.

"Who cares anymore, I mean, I'm happy I went here instead. I've met some pretty cool people," Tonuko smiled and looked toward the dorm.

"I can't believe how smart and calm you honors' kids actually are!" Skye blurted out through her giggles. We looked at her, confused. "Well, not to be mean, but us advanced students always thought you all were dumb and loud. I mean, that robot kid is always the first to talk, so can you blame us?" Skye asked.

We agreed and sighed, thinking about loudmouth Steven.

"Y'know, after seeing Fallen save Alex's dad, I realized something . . ." Tonuko spoke. "None of us act like real heroes." Those words silenced the group. "And don't even try to argue it Ky–"

"No," I interrupted, "you're right. Just because I beat villains, doesn't mean I acted like a hero. A great hero recently taught me that heroes should portray these traits: honesty, bravery, and trustworthiness. They also need to be respectable, caring, and understanding. However, most importantly, a hero is someone who people can look at and feel safe with," I explained to the group.

"Yeah," Alex agreed, "honestly, all we've done is fight so far. That's it, just fought villains. We haven't saved anybody, or made others feel safe, just attacked anyone who's against us."

Tonuko beamed with joy, then took a step forward and stuck his hand out between us.

"Let's all promise, as some of the strongest in our classes, to be real heroes in the next villain attack. Who knows when that'll be, but we have to change our ways, and change them quickly," Tonuko suggested with a smirk.

"Since when were you so mature?" I mocked.

Tonuko rolled his eyes.

"Just agree, dammit!" he yelled. We all put our hands in and agreed, then finished the walk back to the dorm. I took another shower, and as I dried off, I wrapped the towel around my waist and looked around at my dark, dirty room.

Y'know, for how annoying Tonuko gets . . . he's right. We're at a hero school, so it doesn't matter what villains want to attack us or why. We just need to protect those around us. That's why we train, to be strong enough to make others feel safe when we're around.

"Kyle, Scarlett and Jess said lunch will be ready soon!" Alex informed me, walking by my room and waving.

I nodded and looked at the pile of clothes at my feet.

Maybe I should clean up.

Even though the smell of the food downstairs was amazing, I decided to take Camilla's ridicule and clean my room. After a couple of minutes, all the clothes were picked up off my floor, and I was changed and ready for lunch. After turning the corner of the stairs, I saw everyone patiently waiting for me. The table was loaded with burgers, potato chips, watermelon, apples, and even a bowl of pudding. I licked my lips as I walked to the table and grabbed a chip off my plate.

Fallen and Excalibur stepped into the dorm before I could sit down. They looked impressed by everyone sitting together and the delicious-looking food.

"See," Excalibur nudged Fallen, "I told you the long table was the right choice."

Fallen snickered, then took a step forward.

"Everyone, we've decided to end the lockdown tomorrow because, although your socializing is very important, this shadowing event will most definitely be the biggest one in Eccentric High history!" Fallen announced, making us very happy.

"So, um, how will this shadowing work?" Skye asked with her hand raised.

"You all have been getting requests to go and visit a Hero Organization from countless heroes over the past day and a half. For example, Kyle, you have gotten more than one hundred requests," Excalibur pronounced.

"Over a hundred, *in one day!*" Steven angrily shouted, almost pouting.

"And Tonuko," Excalibur started with a big smile, "you have amazingly gotten nearly two hundred!"

The room went silent. Even though I'd beaten Tonuko twice, even though I basically single-handedly defeated the infamous kidnappers, even though the Seven Influential put their trust in me, Tonuko . . . had more than me?

Chapter 17

The Almighty Sons

"I mean, I guess he is ranked number one in the nation for freshmen, so it's not too surprising," Alex said while picking at his food. Fallen nudged his head forward, telling Excalibur to put the packet he was holding on the table.

"This packet shows all the people who've gotten offers and what offers they received. The top three are Tonuko, Kyle, and Iris," Fallen explained.

Iris looked shocked and pointed at herself with wide eyes.

"M–Me? Why am I higher than the others?" Iris exclaimed.

"Well, it's quite simple Iris. You have one of the strongest healing strengths in the world, meaning heroes will want you at their organizations to have a powerful healing sidekick," Excalibur explained.

Alex walked over and flipped through the packet, looking for his name.

"Aww man, only one offer? That's so embarrassing!" he nervously chuckled while rubbing the back of his head.

Fallen put his hand on Alex's shoulder and gave him a reassuring smile.

"Also," Fallen announced, "when you decide who you want to shadow, you will call their organization. After that, they will state if they want just you, or if they want you to bring a couple of classmates. Some heroes will choose the top students of their classes simply to have them bring their top prospect buddies as well. Also, Kyle and Tonuko, we have fantastic news about who's requested you!"

We looked curious and listened intently.

"It will not be hard for you two to choose, I imagine, as almost all of the Seven Influential have requested you! Kyle, you got requests from all but Kaliska; Tonuko, you got requests from all but Puppeteer," Excalibur informed us.

The room went silent again.

"K–Kyle got a request from the number-one hero, but I didn't?" Tonuko asked in a scarily monotone voice.

"T–Tonuko, c'mon man! You got twice as many offers as me, so does it even matter?" I stuttered while holding up my hands. A nervous drop of sweat rolled down the side of my head as Tonuko turned toward me.

"I'm supposed to be the number one in the nation, right? If that's the case, how come he keeps getting more credit than me? He's not even ranked!" Tonuko shouted while pointing at me and looking at Fallen.

Fallen crossed his arms, then shook his head.

"Listen kid, the rankings honestly don't matter until the Hero Olympics. We'll be informed about the official rankings of the freshman class a month before the Hero Olympics, and they could have changed drastically, no one knows. Until then, get off your high horse!" Fallen ridiculed.

"Yeah, it's alright Tonu! Even though Kyle got an offer from Puppeteer, you got one from the coolest hero, Kaliska!" Anya said, trying to encourage Tonuko.

He took a deep breath and apologized, then the teachers walked out. Tonuko didn't talk to me for the rest of lunch. After I was finished and my plate was cleaned, I called Puppeteer's Organization.

"Kyle, are you calling Puppeteer right now?" Daniel asked excitedly. He sat next to me at the counter as I nodded.

"Here we go," I sighed while looking at the number I had found online. I hesitated, then clicked the number, and put the phone to my ear. As it rang, a bunch of people gathered around to listen in. After a few more seconds of ringing, someone answered.

"Hello, this is Puppeteer's Organization. You are speaking to his assistant, Lady Antress. What is the problem in your area?"

I gulped, then took a deep breath.

"I'm not calling for a problem, actually. This is Kyle Straiter, from Eccentric High, and I was calling to accept the offer to shadow at Puppeteer's Organization."

Lady Antress sounded surprised, then she profusely apologized.

"My apologies for not recognizing it's you! So sorry to be rude, I'll get Puppeteer! He just came back from a meeting with Kaliska, so he may not be the happiest," Lady Antress warned me.

I was put on hold, then moved the phone away from my mouth and smiled anxiously.

"She's getting him now!" I softly told everyone. Daniel looked as if he was about to explode with excitement.

Rake asked, "Which of his sidekicks was on the phone?" Before I could respond, I heard Puppeteer on the other end of the line. I put a finger up to Rake, and focused.

"Hello, am I speaking to Kyle?" Puppeteer asked.

I took another deep breath, then sat up in my seat.

"Yes, this is him. I'm calling to tell you that I accept your offer and will be shadowing at your organization."

I heard him chuckle, then it sounded as though he was flipping through papers.

"Ah yes, I'm glad you accepted. Just to go over a few minor details: I will not need you to bring any of your friends, just you, and I'll provide housing for you in my organization," Puppeteer explained.

Daniel could hear him through the phone and looked disappointed when Puppeteer said I will go alone.

Damn, I was hoping I could bring at least one other person. That would've taken away a lot of my nerves . . .

"That's not an issue, is it?" he asked, sounding suspicious.

"Oh no, that's perfectly fine! It might be a letdown to some of my friends, but that doesn't matter too much. Heroes can't always work with others; they'll work alone most of the time anyway!" I answered quickly. There was a long pause, which worried me.

Did I say something wrong? I didn't sound passive–aggressive, did I?

"Right . . . we work alone sometimes. You won't be alone, though, because my son, Xavier, and hopefully one of our family friends, will also be shadowing here. Only seems right he does!" Puppeteer chuckled again. I joined with a nervous laugh. "Anyway, I'll let you go, but I look forward to seeing you again."

"Bye," I nervously stated, slightly elongating the word. When I heard the beeping of the call ending, I put my phone on the table and stared straight ahead, wide-eyed. The others were confused.

I anxiously told them, "H–His son, Xavier from B.E.G., is going to be there, along with one of their family friends. It's just going to be me, the number-one hero, the number-one hero's son, and their close friend."

Everyone erupted with excitement and happiness.

"Woah!" Alex exclaimed as his eyes lit up.

"That's so cool Kyle! Gosh, you're so lucky!" Skye screamed, obviously jealous.

"Too bad you can't bring anyone else," Rake sighed, "I was kinda secretly hoping you could and would bring me. I don't wanna have to research for some animalistic hero!"

"You'll be fine, Rake. Maybe you'd learn more if you went to an animalistic hero's agency anyway!" I laughed.

We all agreed, yet there was one student who hadn't joined in the excitement. Tonuko was standing by the staircase, glaring at the group.

He took out his phone and searched "Kaliska's Organization." He stared at the screen for a few moments, then dialed the phone number, and put the phone to his ear. Anya stood close by, intrigued. She held his hand as Kaliska answered.

"Greetings, Kaliska from Kaliska's Organization here. How may I be of assistance?" Tonuko took a deep breath, just as I had.

"Hello Kaliska, it is Tonuko Kuntai calling. I wanted to call to tell you that I accept your offer to shadow at your organization," Tonuko stated. He bit his lip as the phone went silent, then Kaliska answered surprisingly gleefully.

"Oh, Tonuko! I'm happy you decided on my organization! There's not too much to talk about right now, other than the fact that housing will be provided, you will be joined by a student from Bade's Exceptionally Gifted, and I am allowing you to bring two classmates! Don't be shy though, bring a student from both your honors class and advanced! I want to see for myself if there is a difference between skill level in those classes!"

Tonuko smiled and breathed out, obviously relieved.

"Well, alright! I'll be sure to bring one of each! Do you have a preference of what ranking they should be in our classes?" Tonuko asked while looking at Anya.

"No, not at all. Unlike some other pitiful heroes, I couldn't give a damn about rankings or whatever. I've heard about how heroic you've acted since a young age, and that's the reason I requested you! Bring others who you feel embody what being a hero truly means. Thanks for calling, but I'm getting another call and it might be urgent. No need to call back about who you've chosen. I know you'll choose wisely!"

With that, Kaliska hung up.

"Kaliska wants me to bring two others that embody what a hero is. They also said they want me to bring one advanced student and one honors student."

Anya smiled and rubbed the back of his hand with her finger.

"That's great! Congrats!" she complimented.

Tonuko looked around the room, clearly thinking.

"I wonder what advanced kid I should take. I mean, I already know the honors' one I'm bringing is you—"

"No," Anya quickly interrupted, "don't choose me just because we're close. Even though I'd love to shadow Kaliska's Organization and learn from them . . ." Anya looked down, and softly muttered, "I know I don't embody a hero yet. Ever since I killed that girl, I've been realizing how far behind I am from you and the others."

Tonuko looked shocked and hugged her tightly.

"Are you sure? This could be a once-in-a-lifetime opportunity! Kaliska would probably adore you!" He was clearly attempting to convince her to change her mind; however her decision was made.

"That doesn't matter Tonuko!" She raised her voice, then calmed down quickly. "Think about everything that has happened so far. Fallen and you even noticed it: we aren't really acting like heroes. I saw on the news that two B.E.G. students fought off two Care-Givers recently with zero casualties. Puppeteer's son, Xavier Kinder, and a girl named Rachel took the Care-Givers down almost effortlessly and saved all the civilians around them! That's what heroes do Tonuko!" she quietly explained.

Tonuko thought about arguing, but he knew she was right.

"I guess you're right. Even though the school just opened, our class is probably one of the strongest around. We have, most likely, two kids in the top ten in the nation, and apparently at least one other in the top one-hundred. Yet, when we fought those kidnappers, all we did was focus on fighting, and we caused countless avoidable casualties. I was talking to my mom about the experience, and the damage was in the hundreds of thousands of dollars. I mean, an entire building collapsed."

Tonuko agreed while running his hand through his hair.

"We all need a reality check. This isn't a comic book where heroes fight villains with no consequence, and if the hero wins, the day is saved. This is real life with consequences for our actions! We all need to smarten up and act more like how HotSauce was!" Anya finished for him.

Tonuko squeezed his phone while looking down at it, then nodded.

"I will show this grade what it means to be a real hero, I promise! The next time a villain strikes, I'll take into consideration all that we've learned and act accordingly. I'll prevent the casualties of my friends and the nearby civilians and show the media who we are! I could have gone to B.E.G. and been in that fight, but I'm here. We technically have more experience than those B.E.G. kids, so I'll start acting like it!"

Anya smiled and hugged him again.

"I'm sure you'll do great whenever another battle happens. Either way, I've had a couple of other heroes in mind that I wanna shadow. I saw some heroes on my list that suit me well!" She pulled away and walked up the stairs. He watched as she turned the corner, looked down at his phone again, then up at me.

I'll make sure you don't die, Kyle. No more deaths will happen on my watch, he thought.

Tonuko walked to the couch and sat next to Alex. Alex looked over and smiled as he asked, "How did your call go?" Tonuko nodded while looking at his turned-off phone.

"It went pretty well. I get to bring a kid from honors and one from advanced." Tonuko looked directly into Alex's eyes. "With that being said, would you care to join me in shadowing Kaliska?"

Skye listened in as Alex gleefully accepted the offer.

"Of course I'll go! Thank you so much, this means the world to me! The only offer I had was from a family friend!" Alex shouted as his eyes sparkled. Tonuko chuckled, then leaned back on the couch.

"Kaliska said I need to bring people who embody what a hero is. In all honesty, Kaliska was hyping me up as some natural-born hero, but I'm not. I may have a few of the qualities Kyle talked about, but you have the real important ones," Tonuko admitted with a sigh.

"What do you mean?" Alex asked.

"Well, it doesn't matter how many people or villains I beat. What matters is being someone who lightens the mood of the traumatized victims and can save them while bringing a smile to their faces. You're someone who everyone looks up to for joy; that's why when we found out you were being hurt, everyone got super angry and heartbroken. You have what I need to work on: being the sunshine people need in their life."

Alex grasped his shirt where his heart was and his eyes watered. "Wow, you'll never know how much that means to me Tonuko! Th–Thank you!"

Tonuko smiled and looked up.

"Well, when you're the angel of our grade, people can forget that you need some reassurance too!"

Slowly, a pair of horns and red hair crawled into Tonuko's view. He raised an eyebrow as Skye's beaming face appeared.

"So, Tonuko, I hear you need a heroic advanced student?" Skye asked mischievously. Tonuko rolled his eyes and crossed his arms.

"How are you heroic?" Tonuko questioned.

Skye scooted over and rested her arms on Alex's head.

"Well, I did run into yours and Kyle's fight without hesitation to break you two up! Also, I stayed with you and helped you get over your argument!"

Skye pondered as she tapped her cheek. Tonuko thought as well before nodding.

"Yeah, that's true. We aren't here to play games though. Do you truly think that you can represent our advanced class well?"

She swiftly shouted, "Don't worry earthy-boy! I won't let you or my class down!"

He smirked, confident with his decisions.

"Alright, I'll let you come. However, you better work your ass off while training this month, you too Alex! I don't want Kaliska thinking we're all slackers who are only there because we're in the top of our classes!" Tonuko sat up and glared at the two, mostly at Skye.

"You've got nothing to worry about," she reassured him. "Even if I seem like a bubble-head, I do work hard! I'm the queen of my class for a reason!" They continued talking, and I couldn't help but eavesdrop, considering they were talking so loudly.

"Man, Tonuko sounds so mature when he's talking about that stuff. I just sat there dumbfounded when talking to the number-one hero," I sighed to Daniel.

"Hey, Kyle!" Tonuko yelled, startling me.

"Y–Yeah? What do you want Moody Earth?" I asked, looking back at him. He smirked, quite annoyed, but tried to ignore my nickname.

"You're shadowing the number-one hero with the number-one student from B.E.G.'s freshman class . . . don't let us down, alright? Be mature, respectful, smart, and a hero," Tonuko seethed.

I waved him off as I spun around in the swivel barstool.

"Duh, no need to tell me twice! We're here to be the strongest heroes we can be, so of course I'll be a hero when I'm at Puppeteer's Organization!" I mocked, clearly annoying Tonuko.

"Yeah, whatever! Just think about what we've all been saying recently after taking our decision-making class!"

I raised my eyebrow but didn't respond.

The hell is that supposed to mean. Is he saying I don't know how to act like a real hero? And did he really have to add smart into that, as if I'm not always smart?

"What does he mean by that?" Daniel asked while shaking his head. I shrugged and rested my head on my hand. Camilla took a deep breath.

"Something's changing with him. He's been talking really mature lately," she observed while looking over at the couch. After a few seconds, she looked back at Daniel with a smile. "So, did you get any offers Daniel?"

He picked up the packet and scanned it for his name. When Daniel found his name, there were three hero organizations under it.

"Ugh, my parents requested me." He rolled his eyes and tossed the packet onto the counter in front of him.

"Hey, that's good for the long run. You'll be able to learn from them on how they use their strength in the battlefield," I said while patting his shoulder.

Daniel Onso, Strength: Hidden—he can become invisible at will, but while he is invisible, he can only see people by their skeletons, similar vision to an x-ray machine. An advantage to his x-ray vision is he can see through walls on command. As well as this, he becomes two times stronger in this invisible state.

"I guess, but while doing that, they'll just get upset about how I don't have a good grasp on my strength," Daniel sighed.

"You'll only get better at it by training with people who have the same strength!" Violet shouted while slapping Daniel on the back.

Scarlett, who was washing plates, began scrubbing more aggressively. Suddenly, she swiveled around and huffed.

"I just don't understand how Fallen and Excalibur expect us to learn power-ups in one month! That's absolutely ludicrous!" Scarlett complained.

Camilla walked over and took the plate out of her hand while wearing a comforting smile.

"Don't hold the plates when you're all flustered. I'm sure the teachers will help us figure it out!" Camilla reassured her. Scarlett grabbed a towel and wiped her hands after putting down the sponge.

"Yeah, you're probably right. It's just all so stressful, y'know?"

We agreed, then everyone discussed power-ups. Most of my day was spent hanging around the lobby area or in my room. During dinner, people were excited to talk about what heroes they were thinking of shadowing. All the others were dreaming of the different heroes that would request them. Tonuko, Alex, Skye, and I were going to be living our dreams . . . or so we thought . . .

Parane, a Suburb Just Outside Takorain; Friday Evening:

Drenched from the rain outside, The Upriser walked into a broken-down motel and put his I.D. on the front desk. A suspicious-looking man in a blue button down and beat-up grey dress pants looked at it and grinned, then gave The Upriser a room key.

"Take all the time you need here, Lawrence," he said.

The Upriser nodded, took the key, and found his room. He opened the door and locked it behind him as he took off his navy-blue bowler hat, placing it on the small desk. He walked over to the window and peered out of it.

"There will be very large protests soon. The annual freshman shadowing is happening in a month and the people will want to fight back. Takorain is home to Kaliska and Puppeteer . . . " The Upriser looked down at the busy street as the clouds cleared, and hissed, *"Perfect."* He closed the drapes and spun around. "I'll show those strong heroes-in-training the corrupt world they're trying to succeed in."

E.H. Dorms, 9:00 a.m.:

I slowly opened my eyes and blinked a couple of times. I yawned as I looked at my clock, then my stomach dropped.

Fuck! Since it's Saturday, I forgot to set my alarm!

I swiftly showered, brushed my teeth, dressed, then ran out my door and down the stairs. To my surprise, Tonuko was sitting at the counter casually talking with Skye. They looked over at me, both confused.

"Why the hell are you running around like a crazy person?" Tonuko asked.

I looked around, confused as well, then pointed at the door.

"We're late for school . . . right?"

Skye and Tonuko looked at each other before laughing. Now, I was even more confused.

"It's Saturday! The information packet said any weekend classes will start an hour later!" Tonuko chuckled.

I sighed out of relief as I made my way over to them.

"So class doesn't start for another thirty minutes?"

They nodded, so I sat at the counter with Tonuko. He was staring down at his cup of water, hesitating.

"Listen, Kyle, about what I told you yesterday," he started. I looked over at him as he continued, "I wasn't trying to be an ass, but I was being serious. Have you seen the story all over the news right now?"

I shook my head. I couldn't think of any kind of connection between The Upriser and me representing our school while shadowing at Puppeteer's Organization.

"Two B.E.G. students, Xavier Kinder and Rachel Carson, fought off two Care-Givers. However, unlike us, they fought the Care-Givers off without any casualties to civilians. The fight also caused very minimal damage to the city," Skye explained for Tonuko.

I get that it sounds super heroic and stuff, but why are they telling me this?

"Don't you understand!" Tonuko suddenly shouted while squeezing his cup. It felt like he could read my mind. "We've fought many villains, and somebody has gotten seriously hurt every single time! The one big battle that we had a chance to prove ourselves in resulted with five enemy deaths and countless casualties. That's not even mentioning the hundreds of thousands of dollars of damage we caused!"

I was going to say something, but nothing would come out of my mouth, so I looked down at the counter instead.

We beat the villains . . . but at what cost?

"Kyle, when Tonuko said that to you yesterday, he just meant that we need to represent ourselves and our school better. It's obvious E.H. students have strength, but during our villain interactions, we failed and B.E.G.'s students passed. We have more experience with the Care-Givers, but we were completely humiliated by B.E.G.'s top students!" Skye sighed. I nodded in agreement, then stood and put my hand between the two.

"Let's all promise to be better in the next villain fight then! Sure, it's E.H.'s first year being open, but we can skyrocket its reputation! What do ya' say?" They looked at each other, then nodded and put their hands on top of mine.

After agreeing on the promise, we walked out the door towards the school. Through the front gate, we could see there were more newscasters than before. They were yelling at us, asking countless questions.

"How do you feel about other schools also dealing with the Care-Givers?"

"Do you feel you could have handled your battle with the kidnappers better?"

"Kyle Straiter, do you think you are the reason students your age are being preyed upon by criminals?"

"Do you think going to shadow hero organizations is a good idea considering the activity of the Care-Givers and the appearance of The Upriser?"

Like usual, we ignored them and continued walking until we made it to the school. We strolled into the theatre, where Fallen and Excalibur were talking. We were the first students to arrive, so we sat together. We discussed power-ups while waiting for the others to arrive.

Takorain, Capitol City Where B.E.G. is Located; Thursday (Two Days Ago) Afternoon:

Xavier Kinder led his class out of the infamous B.E.G. training grounds, known as Junction One, and into the city. Their teacher stayed back to download the video of their hostage rescue simulation and told the students to go back to their classroom. Xavier laughed with a girl who had short, greasy black hair and huge eye bags as the class walked down the main street. Cars zoomed past, and there were people scattered on the sidewalks, walking in and out of stores and restaurants.

"That fake hostage-thingy was easy-peasy! No need to thank me for carrying by the way!" said a girl with long, white hair sprinkled with light blue snowflakes.

Xavier laughed out loud as he stretched his arms above his head.

"You really believe you carried? I guess I'll let you have your fun!" He rested his hands on top of his head and continued leading the group toward their school. Seconds later, screams filled the air, and people ran from the end of the block the B.E.G. students were walking down. Xavier grabbed the arm of a woman who was running away, then asked in a serious, comforting tone, "What's wrong, what happened?"

"Th–There's Care-Givers . . . down the street!" she screamed through her gasps. Xavier looked down the street as he let go of the woman and squinted. At the end of the block was a large blue and purple portal.

He looked back at his class, and commanded, "Rachel, come on! Everyone else, protect the civilians and split into groups to cover more ground. Make sure everyone is safe!"

The group agreed, then Xavier and Rachel bolted down the street toward the portal as the rest of the class split into a few groups. When Rachel and Xavier were about fifteen feet away from the portal, a man stepped out. He wore a fuzzy black headband under his white hair and spun a diamond-encrusted stopwatch around his fingers. He tossed it into the air, catching it with the same hand. Another man also floated out of the portal. He was sitting in the air with his legs crossed. The coat-tails of his jacket dragged on the ground. He had very long, purple hair up in a spiky ponytail, and all over his hair were small, yellow outlines of stars. He floated about two feet above the ground and kept his eyes closed. Xavier tensed his fists and stood in a defensive stance.

In contrast, Rachel slouched, looking very tired. "Who are you again?" Rachel yawned. The white-haired man smirked and held up his hands.

"That should be pretty obvious! We are followers of Tyrant, two of his Care-Givers!" The man opened the stopwatch, then suddenly Xavier's head smashed into the ground. "I am Kaci Clockwork, the master of time!"

Xavier's Point of View, Slowed-Down Time:

I couldn't move and saw the man, who I knew was Kaci Clockwork, slowly walk toward me. He stood next to me and leaned over to my ear as he put his palm on my forehead.

"I can see that you can see," Kaci whispered.

After that, he pushed my head toward the ground and kicked my feet out from underneath me. As much as I tried, I couldn't move any part of my body except my eyes. Kaci stood straight up after positioning me and closed his watch. My head smashed into the ground, and he said, "I am Kaci Clockwork, the master of time!"

Normal Point of View:

Kaci stepped onto Xavier's cheek and snickered as he applied more weight.

"You two must be from that gifted school. Pity . . . such bright futures are going to be taken away at my hands. Oh well, we need to make a statement, don't we, Favian?"

Favian nodded slightly, but did not open his eyes nor move a muscle.

"We must follow orders, that is our job," Favian said.

The portal behind him sucked in on itself, allowing him to finally open his eyes. Rachel got lost in them—there was no pupil or anything, just pure galaxy inside his eye sockets. After Favian blinked, his eyes changed to normal white with red pupils. Rachel's eyelids sagged, giving her eyes the appearance of being barely open, and she yawned again.

"What kind of a name is Favian?" Rachel mocked nonchalantly.

All of a sudden, instead of being calm, Favian looked irked as he clenched his fists.

"What kind of name is Rachel? It's not nice to make fun of others!" Favian argued while glaring at her.

A white silhouette of Xavier jumped out of his body, then Xavier wiggled his fingers. The silhouette swung and punched Kaci in the face, causing him to step off Xavier and stumble back. A stream of black liquid, which appeared to be blood in its veins, flowed through the ghost. It swiftly grabbed and lifted Kaci. It hugged him and squeezed tightly. Xavier stared at Kaci, slowly moving his fingers closer to each other. As his fingers moved, the ghost squeezed tighter.

Xavier Kinder, Strength: Puppet—like his father, he can turn his soul into a transparent puppet that is controlled through his fingers by a very, very slim black rope. The puppet's

mouth is always open and can mimic the strengths of people within a two-mile radius. The puppet cannot be harmed by physical attacks, but any attack that lands on Xavier or damages the strings affects both Xavier and his puppet.

"Favian," Kaci gasped, "portal!"

Favian pointed at Kaci, then one of the same purple and blue portals sucked Kaci out of the ghost's grip. A new portal was created in the same spot as before behind Favian. Kaci stepped out again and straightened his jacket.

"Seems as though we are in a brawl against the number-one hero's son. How enticing," Favian stated while looking at Xavier.

Xavier didn't respond, but instead swung his ghost, via the rope, at Kaci. The ghost clotheslined Kaci, causing him to fall back toward the portal. Before he fell, Kaci stopped time again.

Xavier's Point of View:

Kaci threw his hand back—stopping himself from fully falling—and grimaced at me.

What a nuisance. I can barely move again. As long as my ghost is out though, I can win.

"How purely pitiful; heroes-in-training, eh? Why train to be someone who fights outcasts and leaves others to rot at the bottom?" Kaci questioned while walking toward me. He wound up a punch, but before he could make contact, my spirit turned around and socked him in the back of the head. Kaci fell onto me. When his stopwatch brushed against my forearm, I could move again. I swung my hands behind me, pulling my spirit toward us. It wrapped its arms around his waist and tackled Kaci to the ground. I jumped back when the two landed and looked around. No one was moving, birds were still in the sky, my classmates, who were helping others, were frozen . . . time had simply stopped.

"What the hell is this strength? Turn it off!" I yelled at Kaci, who was standing. He cracked his jaw, then looked up at me with furious eyes.

"You are strong, but naïve. You're the perfect weakness to my strength, so it's not smart for me to stay," Kaci thought aloud. He closed his stopwatch, causing time to resume. He side-eyed Favian. "Let's go."

"Already? How horrid to think we were bested by two teenagers. Oh well, just an unlucky matchup," Favian sighed, creating a portal behind them.

Kaci swiftly walked through it before Favian could float through, Rachel ran extremely fast, jumped into the air, spun in a circle, and kicked Favian in the side of the head. He flew into the wall of the building they were in front of. Rachel landed gracefully.

"We can't let them get away Xavier!" Rachel shouted sleepily. By the time she finished her sentence, Favian had already created a new portal under where he landed. The two Care-Givers were gone.

Normal Point of View:

The snow-flake hair girl turned the corner, skating on ice that was radiating from her feet.

"Hey, are you two alright? The area has been evacuated!" Xavier's spirit walked into him, then the two melded together and he put his hands in his pockets.

"We're fine, but they escaped. For being two Care-Givers, it wasn't much of a challenge, right Rachel?"

No response. Xavier looked over, confused, but he wasn't shocked to find her sleeping on the ground. He scooped her up in his arms like a baby, then the three caught up with their classmates at the front of the school.

"Woah, you fought them off with barely any scratches?" a boy with light brown and blonde hair shouted at Xavier. Xavier wiggled his finger around in his ear, pretending to muffle the noise.

"No need to holler, I'm right here. It was a bad match up for those guys; anyone without a spirit strength would have most likely been killed by Kaci Clockwork," Xavier stated.

A breeze blew through his hair as he looked back at the now-peaceful city. He sighed while shaking his head.

"Turn the lights off," Rachel muttered as she slowly opened her eyes. She stood out of Xavier's arms and rubbed her eyes. "Who cares if somebody else wouldn't have survived. We fought them, not someone else, and we survived."

Xavier smiled and nodded. They heard running and panting behind them, so Xavier turned and saw his teacher gasping for air.

"A–Are you kids okay? I he–heard what happened from the p–police!" the teacher nervously stuttered.

"We're alright; Rachel and I took those villains down like they were nothing!" Xavier boasted with a big smirk across his face.

"B–But what if you got hurt? Gosh, I–I should have been there with you; I'm the pro!" the teacher yelled while rubbing his bald head. The snowflake girl wrapped her arm around the teacher's shoulder and gave him a big smile.

"Man, you are such a nervous wreck. Your hero name fits you perfectly!" she exclaimed.

Nervous Hero: Gladiator/Gerald Hatkins, Strength: Warrior— he can immediately sharpen any item he holds in his right hand and any shield he holds in his left cancels out all strengths that attack it. Though he's a nervous wreck, he has unbelievable swordsmanship and martial arts skills.

"A–Anyway, Xavier, your father contacted the school about you going to h–his organization to shadow!" Gladiator informed Xavier.

"Alright, I'll give him a call when we get inside."

The class headed back to their classroom and took their seats. Xavier took out his phone and called his dad. The phone rang only once before Puppeteer answered.

"Hey buddy, shouldn't you be in class right now?" Puppeteer asked.

Xavier chuckled as he heard Puppeteer flipping a few papers. "I am in class. Gladiator just told me about the shadowing. I heard I'm going to your organization."

"Well, of course you are. Where else would you be going?" Xavier smirked and leaned back in his seat.

"I can't think of any better place! Is it going to be just you and me for the week?" Xavier questioned, sounding slightly hopeful.

"Well," Puppeteer responded, "I did invite this other kid from another school. Before I tell you about that, I want to let you know I just talked with Ashlyn's mom—such a nice woman—and I was thinking you could bring Ashlyn with you if she doesn't already have a place in mind!"

Xavier looked over at Ashlyn, the snowflake-haired girl, then shrugged.

"Yo, Ash, you wanna come with me to shadow my dad's organization?"

Ashlyn's eyes lit up as she sped over to his desk. She leaned on it while looking at Xavier with gleaming eyes.

"Of course I do!" She stood straight up, twirled a piece of her hair then asked, "Is anyone from another school going?"

Xavier nodded, then put the phone back to his ear.

"So, who's that other kid you said was going? What school do they go to?"

The phone went silent, Puppeteer was hesitating and was clearly anxious to tell Xavier.

"W–Well, he's from Eccentric High . . ." Xavier's face turned from intrigue to disgust.

"Why the hell did you invite a kid from that problem school? Who is it: Tonuko Kuntai, Alex Galeger? You said he! Wait . . . don't tell me . . . "

"It's that strong fella', Kyle Straiter!" Puppeteer admitted, trying to sound happy and hoping to lift Xavier's mood. It didn't work.

"You invited a damn criminal to your organization?" Xavier seethed angrily.

"He's not a criminal Xavier! If he was, he'd be in jail by my decision! I pardoned him, so I know if he's a hero or not! You know what, he might be stronger than you!" Puppeteer retorted.

Xavier hung up, then rested his chin on his hand and sighed. Ashlyn was confused but interested.

"A criminal? Who did he invite?" Ashlyn asked, leaning on Xavier's desk again.

"That killer, Kyle Straiter, from E.H." Xavier grunted.

Ashlyn, on the contrary, was bursting with excitement.

"Oh my gosh, no way! Kyle is such a hottie!" she squealed and blushed. "Just imagine if he and I hit it off! Maybe by the end of the shadowing, we'll be super close!"

A girl with long, green curly hair looked over at Ashlyn and giggled.

"Look at you fan-girling, Ashy! What's up with you liking Kyle Straiter so much?" the girl teased.

Ashlyn spun around and flung little snowflakes throughout the room.

"He's just so dreamy!" she sang, giggling and blushing even more. Xavier rolled his eyes and looked out the window.

"You're unbearable, just like that kid," he grumbled. "At least he isn't weak."

E.H.:

Approximately twenty-five minutes after we arrived, everyone was finally in the theatre. Fallen shushed our talking, then stood on the stage with his hands behind his back.

"I know it's only been a day since we told you all about the shadowing, but has anyone chosen where they will be going?" Fallen asked while looking directly at Tonuko and me.

We raised our hands, along with a few others including Alex, Skye, Scarlett, Camilla, and Jessica.

"No surprise for some of you. Tonuko, is anyone in a group with you?" Tonuko nodded, then pointed at Alex then Skye.

"Yep, Kaliska told me to bring one honors and one advanced student." Fallen nodded his head, not surprised by Kaliska's request.

"As expected of Kaliska. How about you Kyle? Safe to assume your choice wasn't very hard," Fallen smirked.

I chuckled as I leaned back in my chair.

"Yeah, it was pretty easy to choose. Too bad I can't bring anyone though."

Fallen and Excalibur were again not surprised.

"That's Zane for ya'. I'm sure he's having his son go, though," Fallen stated, expecting a response from me.

I nodded.

Excalibur stood from the stage and announced, "Today, the classes will be separated. Teaching power-ups takes longer than our typical training, so we're going to have the honors class go to the Dome first and the advanced students will stay in decision-making class. Afterwards, we'll switch. That's how classes will go all month."

There was a wave of disappointment among all the freshmen. As he stood, Tonuko looked at Skye and gave her a stern glare.

"I'm trusting that you'll work hard all month."

She shrugged and nodded.

"You don't gotta worry about me, I always work hard! You better not let me outwork you!" Skye mocked.

Tonuko chuckled while shaking his head, then all of us honors kids left for the Dome.

Upon arrival, Rake questioned, "Shouldn't we go to a more open area if we're all doing power-ups? They can get pretty crazy."

Fallen smirked and flicked a switch by the door. The roof above us retracted and moved down the sides of the walls. "Now, let's begin, shall we?" Fallen asked with his grin still plastered on his face. "Who here has already practiced with power-ups? If you have, step forward."

Tonuko, Anya, Rake, Steven, and I all took a step.

"Rake, since when have you had experience with power-ups?" Jessica asked while petting a sunflower in her hand.

"Rake and I went to the same school, and at the end of the year, we had basic training with power-ups," Steven answered for Rake.

Jessica rolled her eyes and looked away, leaving Steven confused for a moment.

"I'm impressed with how many of you have had experience with power-ups! Now, Kyle, how about you demonstrate yours first since I know the level you're at!"

I walked toward the middle of the stage and heard a scoff from Tonuko behind me. I grinned a little, then took a deep breath to focus. I threw my hand into the air and held it high above my head. A sword made entirely of flames spiraled into existence from my palm.

"Ember …" I started. The flame sword's blade expanded, growing higher and wider until it was shaped like a lion, "Roar!" I swung the blade down. The lion roared as it pounced and bit down into the ground. When it made contact, a mini explosion went off, sliding me back a couple feet due to the air pressure. The explosion blinded everyone and when the smoke cleared, a very small mushroom cloud was left, similar to the one left after my attack on the Creature. People clapped, so I bowed before brushing the dust off my shirt.

"Lame!" Tonuko mocked while walking toward me. I chuckled and gave him a slight push, then he got settled and cracked his knuckles. "My turn!" He walked to the center of the stage, the same place I stood before, and stretched out his arms. He crouched low as he swung his hands onto the ground. A large wave glided through the ground; at the same time, a cement ball rose from the ground a dozen feet away from him. "Wave of …" he started loudly. The ball was thrown into the air when the wave reached it, then a hand rose from the ground and soared at it. "Demise!" The hand, being controlled by Tonuko, smacked down upon the ball. The ball flew at high speeds into the ground and was demolished. All the creation crumpled down as Tonuko cracked his right shoulder.

"Wow, that was spectacular! I expected nothing less than flashy from the number-one freshman in the nation!" Fallen complimented while softly clapping.

"Boring!" I teased while fake-yawning.

Tonuko rolled his eyes and slightly smiled as he walked back to the group. Steven was eager to go next and ran to the front of the class.

"Mine's more of a classic power-up! Y'know, maxing out my strength!" Steven shouted.

He looked at the ground and closed his eyes, focusing hard. His body morphed to metal, and red and blue wires sprouted out the sides of his arms and legs. Steven super-jumped into the air and landed in a crouched, heroic position. "Robotic Takeover!" he yelled with a smile. The class began clapping, then he turned back to human while panting. "I can't stay in that form for long 'cause it drains a lot of stamina, and I can't make my organs robotic just yet," Steven explained.

"That exceeded my expectations! I'm surprised you're so advanced with maxing out your strength; well done!" Fallen commended.

Steven strutted back to the line, then patted Rake on the back. Rake was clearly more nervous than the rest of us. He didn't say anything as he walked out onto the stage. He flung his hands out, throwing all his fingers off his knuckles and onto the ground. They morphed into one massive snake that was about two dozen feet in length and had large wings. He jumped onto the snake's back, then the two soared into the air. Rake crouched, flipped off of the snake, and swung a punch in the air.

"Airstrike Defeat!" he screeched as the snake flew by him and bit the air. Honestly, it was pretty awkward.

"It, uh, would've been a lot cooler if someone was . . . y'know . . . there," Rake sighed.

Fallen shrugged and clapped.

"We all get the idea, and it's pretty neat! It could use some touching up though, but well done nonetheless!"

Rake trudged back to the line. All that was left was Anya. She smirked as she trotted out to the stage, then she stomped her foot.

"Armor of," she blurted while rocks crawled up her body. When she took a step forward, the rocks already on her body smoothed out. "Destruction!" she exclaimed as she threw up her hands. Two sharp rocks—the same kind she'd used in the weapon in her fight with Tonuko during the training tournament—formed out of her palms and shot out, hitting the far wall at high speeds. They exploded into rubble upon impact. Her rock armor crumbled back onto the ground as she flipped her hair.

"Very impressive!" Fallen shouted while clapping. We rejoined the rest of our class then Fallen said, "I'm very impressed with those of you who've had experience. Now, time for the rest of ya' to get started!"

We all split into groups of four and spread out on the stage, which was now larger than it had been during our training tournament. My group included Camilla, Alex, Cindy, and me.

"I think I've got an idea. I've tried out this kinda stuff before, and this move might be the one!" Alex smiled before taking a step forward away from the other groups. We watched as a ball of light lit up in Alex's hand. "Light," he punched his hand into the ground, creating a hole, and sent a stream of light underground. It ripped through the surface of the cement as it traveled about two dozen feet. "Oracle!" he shouted. The light grew extremely bright, and the explosion echoed throughout the Dome. When the light faded, there was a hole in the ground, and Alex panted while looking at the destruction.

"Nice one, Alex!" I complimented, clapping loudly. He gave me a thumbs up with a big smile, then, Camilla grabbed my left arm.

"Hey, Kyle, can we talk?" she asked, looking almost embarrassed. I was confused and nodded cautiously. She hesitated, then took a deep breath, "Look, I just think you're super cute, and cool, and smart, and . . . I don't know I really like you," Camilla explained, shocking us all. I stared at her blankly for a few seconds.

That was . . . so random. What the hell?

"Uh . . . alright. Thanks," I responded, still dumbfounded.

Why would she randomly say all that? I mean . . . who doesn't really like me? So weird . . .

I turned back to Alex and Cindy, assuming that was it. Camilla's cheeks grew redder as she stared at the back of my head. She glanced around the room, seeing people's muffled expressions and giggles. Her expression changed from happy to very angry and displeased. She swiveled around, then held her arms in an "X" formation in front of her face.

"Wind Breaker!" she roared as she swung her arms down. Two wind blades flew at the Dome's front door and obliterated it. Camilla stomped away and out of the building, leaving Cindy, Alex, me, and everyone else completely shell shocked.

"Not the damn door! Do you kids know how expensive this kinda stuff is?" Fallen cried while running at the debris.

I blinked a few times, standing with my mouth gaping, then heard a holler of laughter across the Dome.

"Nice one Kyle! You sure are good with the ladies, huh?" Tonuko shouted through his wheezes.

I turned around and saw him practically on his knees from laughing so hard. I rolled my eyes, then walked back toward Cindy and Alex.

"I guess I said something wrong?" I sighed. Alex and Cindy nodded, both looking disappointed in me. After a couple seconds of silence, we all chuckled and helped Cindy think of a power-up for her strength.

I can't believe she had that big of a reaction about me. I'm sorry Camilla, but I just don't understand. Why would you want to get so close to someone when in the end you'll lose them?

Chapter 18

Final Peace

I awoke to my alarm, then punched the off button hard, causing the digital clock to fall off my nightstand. I opened my droopy eyes and turned onto my back to face the ceiling. It was Thursday, October 3rd, just two days before the shadowing.

How the hell am I supposed to go shadow Puppeteer in two days? I can barely move my body because of damn Hell Month!

Flashback:

"Come on you lazy bums! Move it!" Fallen screeched, watching us run at the border of the school walls. "Only five more laps, let's go!"

"Why," Alex wheezed, "do we have to run so much?"

Donte zoomed in front of the group, then slowed to our pace and laughed.

"Come on guys! This ain't even that bad!" he mocked while back peddling.

"Easy for you to say!" Zayden gasped as the group slowed even more.

This campus is fucking huge, how are we supposed to do ten laps? This is ridiculous Fallen! I know you're over there giggling to yourself!

I looked over and saw Fallen giggling.

Called it.

When we finally finished our laps, we lined up in front of Fallen in the same formation as we did in our classroom seats. Everyone, except Donte, collapsed onto the ground while trying to control their breathing.

"Not done yet! First off, *one hundred pushups!*" Fallen commanded.

Everyone groaned and swore.

"Why do we have to do so many Fallen?" Cora yelled, laying on her back.

"Because," Fallen explained, "if your bodies are strong, your strengths will be strong! Strengths are a part of the body, children, so if you work at a strong, healthy body, you will have a strong, healthy strength!"

After a minute, we got into pushup stance and Fallen yelled "Down!" every couple of seconds.

Present:

I held my lower back and groaned as I sat up.

"Everything hurts!" I yelled, slowly standing. I waddled over to my wardrobe and grabbed a change of clothes. I took a brief shower, brushed my teeth, put on my clothes, then left my room. I trudged down the stairs and saw a few people laying on the couch. Camilla was sitting at the counter with Jessica. They left as soon as they saw me. I shrugged and walked over to the couch to see who didn't make it up the stairs today.

"So this time it was Rake, Donte, Rose, Logan and Mary! Yesterday wasn't even a leg day. How could you not make it up the stairs?" I mocked with a laugh, leaning against the back of the couch near Donte.

"My legs are really strong," Donte started, grabbing his thighs, "but not my twiggy arms!" He shook his arms, then groaned in agony and let them drop onto his chest and head.

I chuckled and smacked his bicep, then yelled, "Come on Donte, we're done for the month! Fallen said today he's just gonna explain some things then it's a free day, and tomorrow we're gonna be packing and prepping for the big leave day!"

Donte yelped when I slapped him and acted like he was going to get up and hit me. When he moved to stand, he cried out and instead stayed seated.

"Kyle," Donte sighed, putting his hand on his forehead. "You're an asshole."

I laughed and walked over to Rake, who was still sound asleep and snoring. I decided to give him a nice wake up call.

Don't want him to be late to class, y'know?

"Time for school, Rakey-Poo!" I screamed in his ear.

He jumped and stood defensively next to me, then cramped and fell to the ground.

"Fuck off, Kyle! I'm too sore for your shit today!" he seethed while holding his left arm.

I laughed again, then waddled over to the counter.

"You guys are such sissies! I made it up the stairs every day of Hell Month!" I bragged as I slowly sat.

I saw Tonuko turn the corner. He was walking with a big smirk on his face and his chest puffed out. "Psh, that's nothing! I'm not even sore today!" I rolled my eyes as he sat next to me. I heard muffled chuckling to my right, so I looked over and Tonuko started, "Hey Kyle."

"What do you want Moody Earth?" I asked, already knowing he was going to make fun of me.

"Your relationship with Camilla really . . . *burned up* . . . didn't it?" His voice got higher as he finished, "It's like these *burning* emotions just took over!" Tonuko burst out laughing and smacked me on the back.

I pushed him with my right hand, causing him to fall off the barstool.

He yelped, "Ow, my fucking back!" when he landed.

"I thought Mr. Tough Guy wasn't sore today?" I countered.

Tonuko rolled his eye while still chuckling, then I offered my hand to help him stand. We talked for another twenty minutes about transportation to Takorain, then trudged along with a few others to class. We said bye to the advanced kids, walked into class, and painfully sat. Camilla was already seated and refused to bat an eye at me.

"She's still really mad at me," I whispered to Cindy.

She giggled and gave me a shrug. Everyone arrived within the next few minutes. Fallen stood from his desk and leaned on the podium in the front of the classroom.

"Mornin' class! How did everyone sleep?"

We responded with a dull moan, causing him to chuckle. "As expected. I'm sure you're very happy that today and tomorrow are off days before the shadowing!" We cheered, yet without energy. "Now is your last chance to ask me questions about the shadowing. Any questions at all?"

Scarlett raised her hand, so he pointed at her. "If some people are going to organizations near each other, are we supposed to travel together?" she asked.

"Yes," Fallen answered, "For example, Tonuko, Alex, Kyle, and Skye from advanced will travel together since Kaliska's and Puppeteer's Organizations are in the same city. Also, don't forget to pack all your necessities! You will sleep at your respective organization for a week—assuming you're not going to a family or family friend's organization, where you can sleep at their house. You'll be there from this Saturday to the next, so be sure you have clean clothes and stuff like that for all seven days! You will leave bright and early on the 5th and will be expected to return by 10:30 a.m. on the 12th."

Tonuko raised his hand, then asked before Fallen called on him, "What happens if we encounter villains? What is expected of us?"

Fallen rubbed his chin, looking as though he was hesitating.

"As your teacher, I must tell you to not engage alone. If you, for example, are with Kaliska, proceed with caution. If you do proceed, do not fight to injure but instead to protect. That is the best advice I can give you. Legally, you are not allowed to severely injure villains; you are only allowed to use self-defense to capture them. Say Alex hits a villain and knocks him unconscious, but that's it; that is perfectly okay and encouraged. However, if he attacks a villain, makes him bleed, breaks his bones, then knocks him out, that is not okay. That is what I mean when I say fight to protect, not injure."

Everyone nodded. His explanation made perfect sense.

Fallen waved us off, saying, "The Juniors set up some ice baths in the Dome—a tradition of Hell Month in hero schools—so go and ice yourselves. You don't have to, but I strongly recommend it. You're free for the rest of the day!"

Most of us made our way to the Dome. Inside, there were over a dozen black tubs filled to the brim with water and ice.

"Freshies, how was your Hell Month?" Hazel asked with a mocking grin.

"You knew about this month and didn't warn us?" I sinisterly muttered while pointing at her. She smacked my finger away, then threw her arm around my shoulder, and walked me toward a tub.

"You guys did great! Sure, the soreness of this month is brutal, but it's so worth how much stronger you get! Hop in a tub, it's refreshing!"

I shrugged and took off my shirt and socks, then dipped a toe into the bath. A shiver went down my spine. When I took my foot out and took a step back, Jon ran up and shoved me from behind, causing me to fall face first into the frigid water. I stood, crossing my arms while shivering.

"Jon, you asshole!" I screamed.

Jon was bent over wheezing because he was laughing so hard. A few feet behind him Kate was laughing as well. My teeth chattered as I stuttered, "Th–This shit is freezing!"

"Come on ya baby, it's not that bad!" Tonuko yelled, walking to the tub next to mine.

"Shut your mouth Moody Earth!" I retorted. "How about you get in one if it's not so bad?"

"I am, you impatient pig!" Tonuko scoffed while taking his shirt off. *Wow, a pig? You dick.*

He was slowly getting into the bath when Jon gave him the freshman treatment, pushing him in like he did to me. Tonuko jumped, already shaking and chattering, then splashed some water at Jon.

"Ay, watch it!" Jon chuckled, hopping backward.

We all laughed. Tonuko and I continued our ice baths while talking to the sophomores and juniors about their shadowing experiences.

The next day was frantic.

"Dude, I'm freaking out! What if I make a bad impression and the whole world finds out?" Alex asked while gripping my shoulders and staring into my eyes.

"I'm sure you'll be fine. Don't worry too much or you might actually mess up," I reassured, taking his hands off of me.

He started biting his nails, so Tonuko put his hand on Alex's shoulder.

"You'll do great! There's a reason I chose you!" Tonuko said with a smile. Skye walked over and gave Alex a smack on the back of the head.

"Yeah, relax Angel Boy! I'm in advanced, but I'm less worried about my abilities than you!" Alex rubbed the back of his head and pouted.

"Kaliska is just such a cold-faced hero. You don't know what's going on under that mask. Did you see how much they yelled during Kyle's court trial?" Alex muttered.

Tonuko shrugged before crossing his arms, then blew a dangling piece of hair out of his eye.

"She seemed pretty chill over the phone, so maybe that anger during the trial was just a front to intimidate Kyle," Tonuko pondered. Everyone looked at him, with no verbal response, confusing him. "What?"

"She? Did you not hear his voice? Kaliska is obviously a boy!" I argued.

Tonuko raised his eyebrow and crossed his arms.

"No way everyone knows Kaliska is definitely a girl! The mask probably has a voice modifier attached!" Tonuko retorted.

Alex scratched his head, then sighed, "Honestly, it could go both ways. Let's just do whatever they tell us to and not make a bad impression."

We agreed.

"Everyone, the delivery for our outfits came!" Khloe shouted from downstairs. We swiftly made our way to the lobby, eager to finally see our hero outfits.

Rake opened his box, but his face turned to disappointment.

"Aww, man, really?" Rake complained while reading a piece of paper that was stuck in his box. I opened mine and saw the same note.

"Damn, so they didn't have enough materials for our outfits. We really have to wear these out?" I asked, looking at the dark khaki-colored tank top and black shorts. The tank top had the cursive E.H. school logo in black across the chest, and the shorts had the logo in the same dark khaki color on the bottom of the right pantleg. I sighed, then took the box upstairs. I finished packing my suitcase, wheeled it outside, and left it next to my door. I decided to relax downstairs with everyone else, since it would be a week before I'd see most of them again. I sat on the couch along with Cindy, Khloe, Donte, and Steven.

"There is no way I am wearing that outfit in public. I have my own short shorts that are identical to the ones I requested for my costume that I could just bring!" Donte complained, rolling his eyes and crossing his arms.

"Short shorts?" Steven asked, attempting to hold back his laughter.

"I'm paying homage to the running sports of the past that were popular before strengths! They wore short shorts, so I wear short shorts!" Donte grumbled, glaring at Steven.

We all chuckled, then Cindy turned to face me.

"So, Kyle, are ya nervous?" she asked.

"Yeah," Khloe added, "shadowing the number-one hero is a huge deal. Isn't it stressful to think about?"

I thought for a few seconds, then confidently stated, "Nah, I'll be fine."

Cindy moved her hair behind her ear and looked down wide-eyed. "Watch out, your cockiness is showing!" she whispered loudly.

I smiled and rolled my eyes, then put my hands behind my head and took a deep breath.

"Oh no, me being cocky? That's ridiculous!" I acted distraught, which made them laugh.

"Don't let Xavier Kinder see you being all cocky like usual! I heard he's super mature and stuff; doesn't deal with nonsense, y'know?" Khloe giggled.

"Whatever! If he's got a problem, then he's got a problem! What's he gonna do, cry about it to his daddy?" I dragged my finger down my cheek, mimicking a tear while sticking out my bottom lip, then laughed.

"Lunch is ready!" Scarlett sang, practically dancing the large bowl of noodles to the table.

"Seems like you're excited Scarlett!" Steven analyzed. He sat in his usual spot at the head of the table.

"I can't wait to go and shadow my auntie! Jess and Camilla are going with me; it's going to be so much fun!" Scarlett explained.

I took a scoop of the noodles in a meaty red sauce and plopped it on my plate.

"That's exciting! Daniel's gonna be shadowing family too!" I commented.

Daniel sighed as he sat next to me.

"Yeah, in the next city over actually. I live on the border between two suburbs, but my parents stick to patrolling in Parane."

Scarlett gasped and pointed at herself.

"No way, we're going to Parane too! Wanna walk over there with us?"

Daniel nodded and smiled, then I patted him on the back.

"You guys are lucky your places are within walking distance. We gotta take a train for half an hour!" I complained and looked over at Tonuko.

He raised an eyebrow, looking surprised.

"Takorain is only a half-hour train ride? I could have sworn it was longer. You know what that means?" Tonuko asked. I shook my head, so he answered himself, "We're not even that far from B.E.G. honestly. If the kids are cool and we hit it off, we could definitely hang out with them during breaks or something."

"You turned down your offer to B.E.G. because they're all stuck-up and cocky, so why do you want to hang out with them all of a sudden?" Skye asked in a mocking tone.

"*You turned down an offer to B.E.G.?*" those who didn't already know shouted. Tonuko nodded with a shrug.

"Yep, I didn't wanna go to some stuck-up school. Notice I said the school was stuck-up, not the kids. Most of them are pretty chill from what I've heard."

We continued talking and finished lunch. Most of the nervousness diminished after everyone got their worries off their chest and received some support. Others finished packing, got some much-needed rest after Hell Month, and overall, we took it easy today. Tomorrow would be one of the biggest days of our lives.

Meanwhile, at B.E.G.:

Xavier rustled in his closet, attempting to get his suitcase down from the top shelf in his walk-in closet.

"Dammit, how is it this stuck? I got it up there, didn't I?" he grumbled to himself as he continued tugging on it.

Ashlyn sang loudly, "Xavier, are you almost done packing?"

Xavier jumped and lost his footing, falling backwards onto his butt. He glared up at her. The suitcase slowly moved forward, then fell off the shelf, and smacked him on the top of the head.

"Oh man, that had to hurt."

"What do you want?" Xavier seethed, rubbing his head and standing. He grabbed the handle of his suitcase and threw it on his bed as Ashlyn walked into the room.

"I'm just so excited to see my love!" she sang.

Xavier continued rubbing his head as he looked through his drawers and rolled his eyes when he heard her comment.

"He isn't your love, Ash. We don't even know him; what if he's an asshole and hates us?" Xavier asked bluntly. Her face went from joyful to anguished, and tears brimmed from her eyes.

"Wh–Why would you say that?" Ashlyn stuttered, sounding as though she was about to cry. Xavier rolled his eyes again.

"I meant he'll love you." Ashlyn smiled and skipped out of the room while humming.

Xavier had finally started to pack when Rachel walked into his room and laid on his bed.

"Rachel, wrong room," Xavier said, not even batting an eye as he continued packing. He heard a snore, so he shouted, "Rachel!"

She opened her eyes, then yawned.

"Oh, sorry. I came to tell you that teach' said Ashlyn, you, and I have to walk together to the organizations. He said something about it being required even if the organizations are intercity," Rachel explained.

"I assumed, now get out," Xavier hissed. He looked down at his bag, heard another snore and clenched his jaw. He grabbed his blanket off the floor, threw it on Rachel, and moved her to the center of the bed. Xavier closed his suitcase and stared out his window. A static of anger was building in his mind as the days passed.

"Kyle Straiter, son of Tyrant." Xavier grabbed his blinds and pulled them closed. "What the hell does my dad see in criminal trash like you?"

Puppeteer's Organization, 9:00 p.m.:

Puppeteer sat with his fists covering his mouth, watching his computer screen. In an email sent from Kaliska was a link to a video titled, "Protest." He hesitated before moving his mouse onto the link and clicking it. The video began, showing the viewpoint of a bystander in the massive Maroline City protest. People were holding up signs and shouting, all marching forward down the street. Police and heroes alike were patrolling the protest, not interfering but keeping a close eye on the crowds. Suddenly, a circular object flew past and collided with a hero's head, knocking him unconscious. Chaos ensued. A mob of people charged at the police and heroes, completely stampeding over them. A line of officers slammed down their riot shields, temporarily halting the crowds. After some back-and-forth shouting, the infamous Upriser stepped out from the crowds. Suddenly, all of those who were once screaming at the police were backing away, scared. The phone shook slightly.

After being pushed, the Upriser sent down a lightning strike that killed all the officers and heroes, then he absorbed another lightning bolt and killed a man who attempted to stop him. The woman holding her phone dropped it while screaming. Countless cries and yells sounded in the distance before a booming crash occurred—the building falling on the crowds. Rain poured harder on the streets before the phone camera glitched and shut off.

Puppeteer stared at the black screen, not moving a muscle.

"Just what the hell is your goal," he muttered quietly, rewinding the video a few times. He stopped it a second after the Upriser killed the brave man. Although tears streamed down his cheeks, the Upriser's lips were curled up in a spine-tingling grin.

"What is your strength?" He glared at the Upriser for a few more seconds before closing the tab and swiftly turning around. He looked out his window. From his office, he could see B.E.G.'s campus. A pit grew in his stomach as he stared at the school building.

"When will you show your face again?" Underneath his keyboard, slightly folded, was a newspaper.

The headline read, *"Potentially Biggest Protest in History Being Held in Takorain."*

About the Author

Shane Kavanaugh is a debuting author born in Oak Lawn, Illinois whose first book, *The Angel Criminal*, describes the life of a mentally troubled boy attempting to learn how to survive in a superhuman world. At first, he wrote this book to put all of his frustrations and emotional anguish onto paper, but he evolved his desire to write into wanting the book to be a beacon of hope for all struggling with their mental health and obstacles in their lives. He is a twenty-year-old student at Marquette University in Milwaukee, Wisconsin where he writes countless fictional novels while studying business.

You can connect with Shane Kavanaugh on Instagram @shane.kav16 or email shanekavanaugh7@gmail.com